ADVENTURE TIME™

THE OOORIENT EXPRESS

ADVENTURE TIME: THE OOORIENT EXPRESS, JULY 2017. Published by KaBOOM!, a division of Boom Entertainment, Inc.

BOOM! Studios, 5670 Wilshire Boulevard, Suite 450, Los Angeles, CA 90036-5679. Printed in China. First Printing.

ISBN: 978-1-60886-995-4, eISBN: 978-1-61398-666-0

kaboom!™ CARTOON NETWORK FREDERATOR

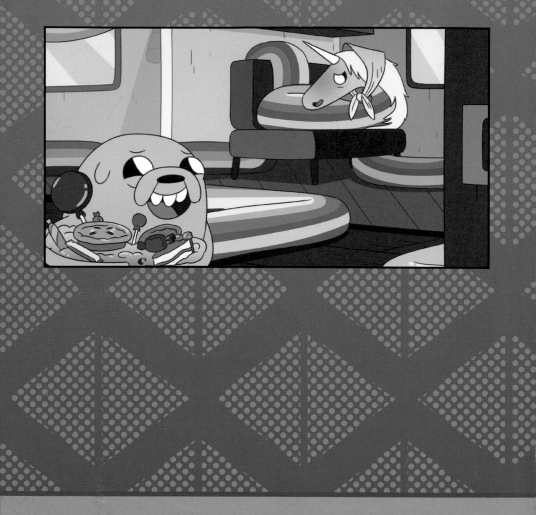

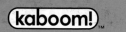

Created by Pendleton Ward

Written by **Jeremy Sorese**

Illustrated by **Zachary Sterling**

Colors by **Laura Langston**

Letters by **Warren Montgomery**

Cover by **Britt Wilson**

Designer **Grace Park**

Associate Editor **Chris Rosa**

Editor **Whitney Leopard**

With Special Thanks to Marisa Marionakis, Janet No, Nicole Rivera, Conrad Montgomery, Meghan Bradley, Curtis Lelash, Kelly Crews and the wonderful folks at Cartoon Network.

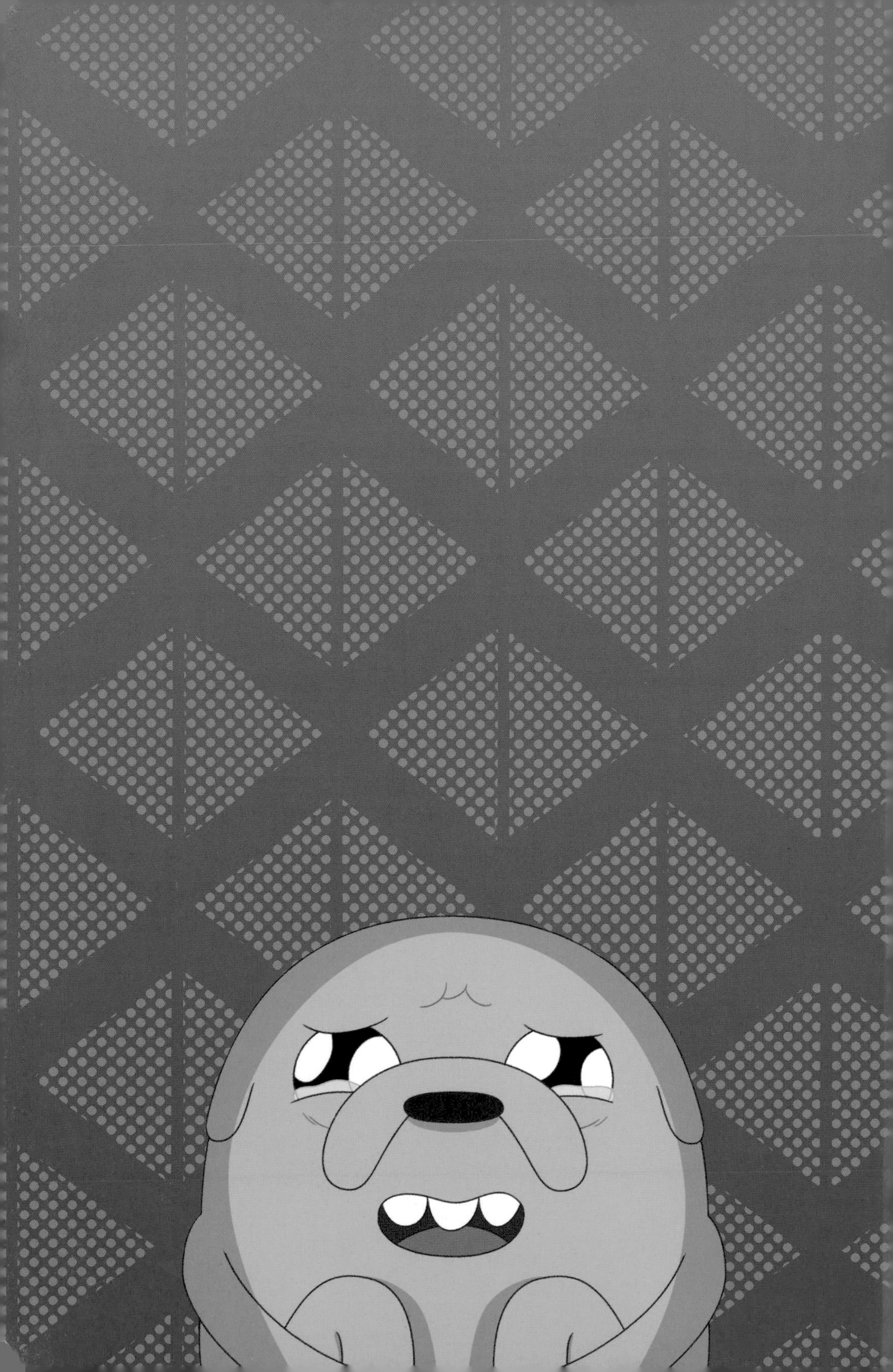

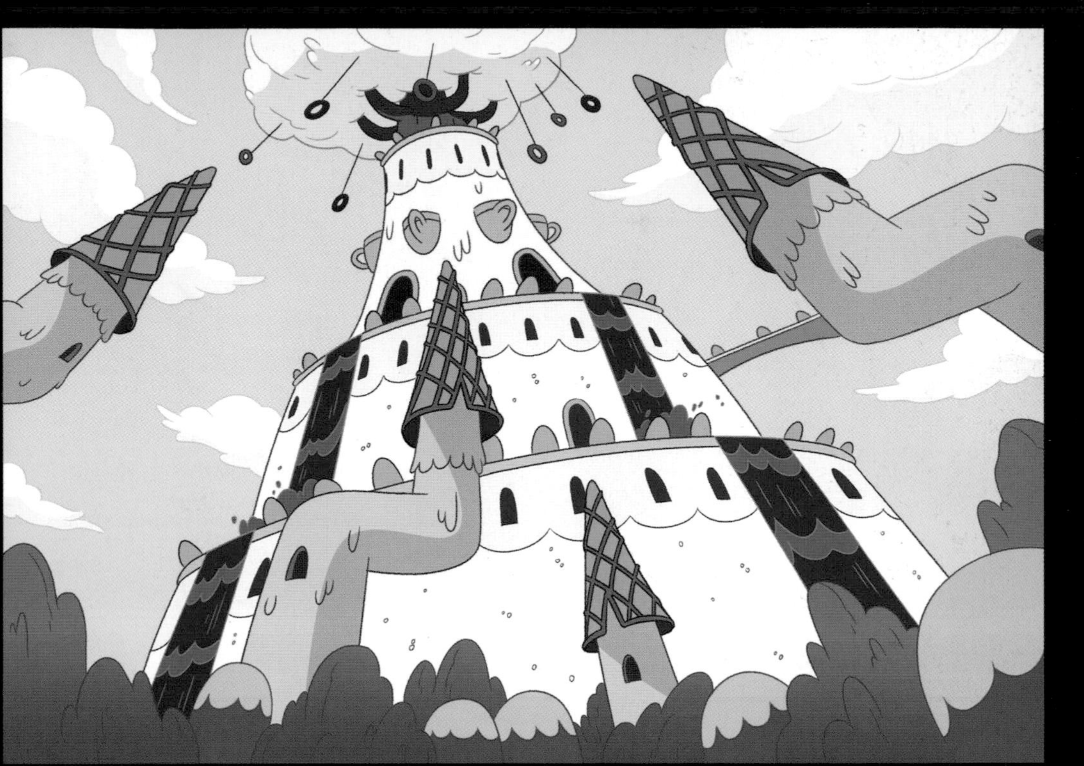

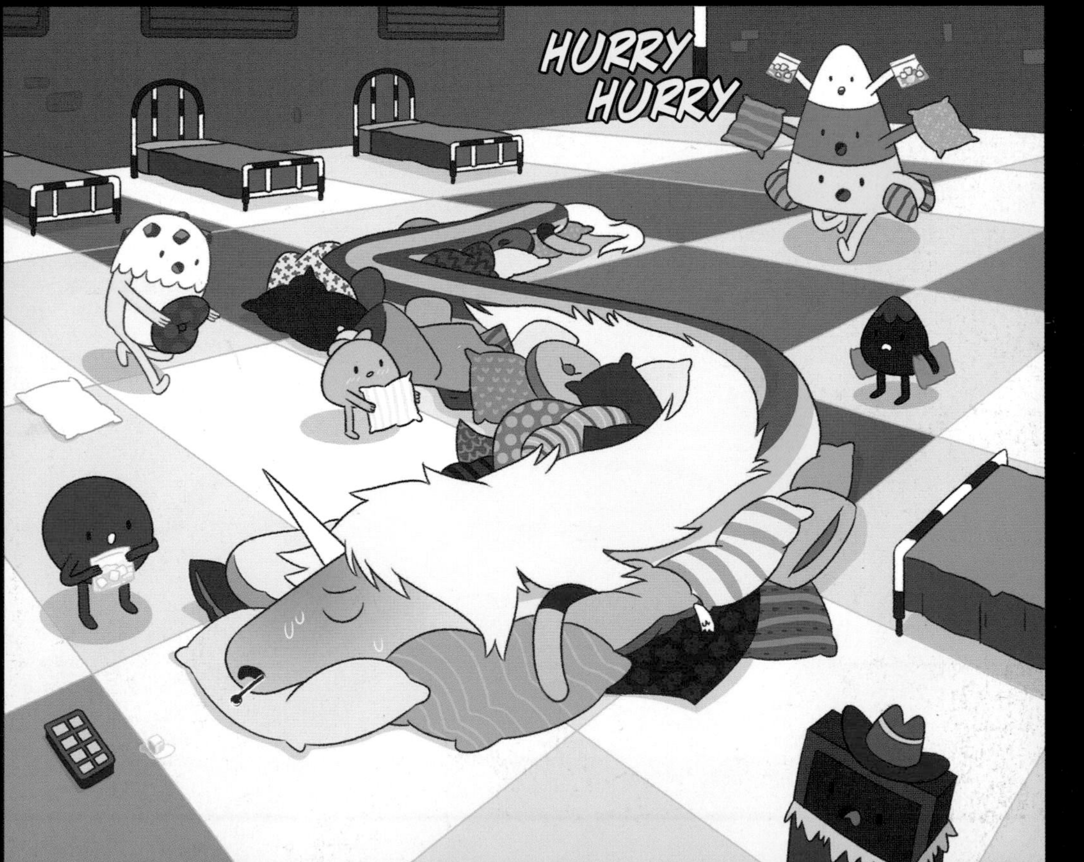
HURRY
HURRY

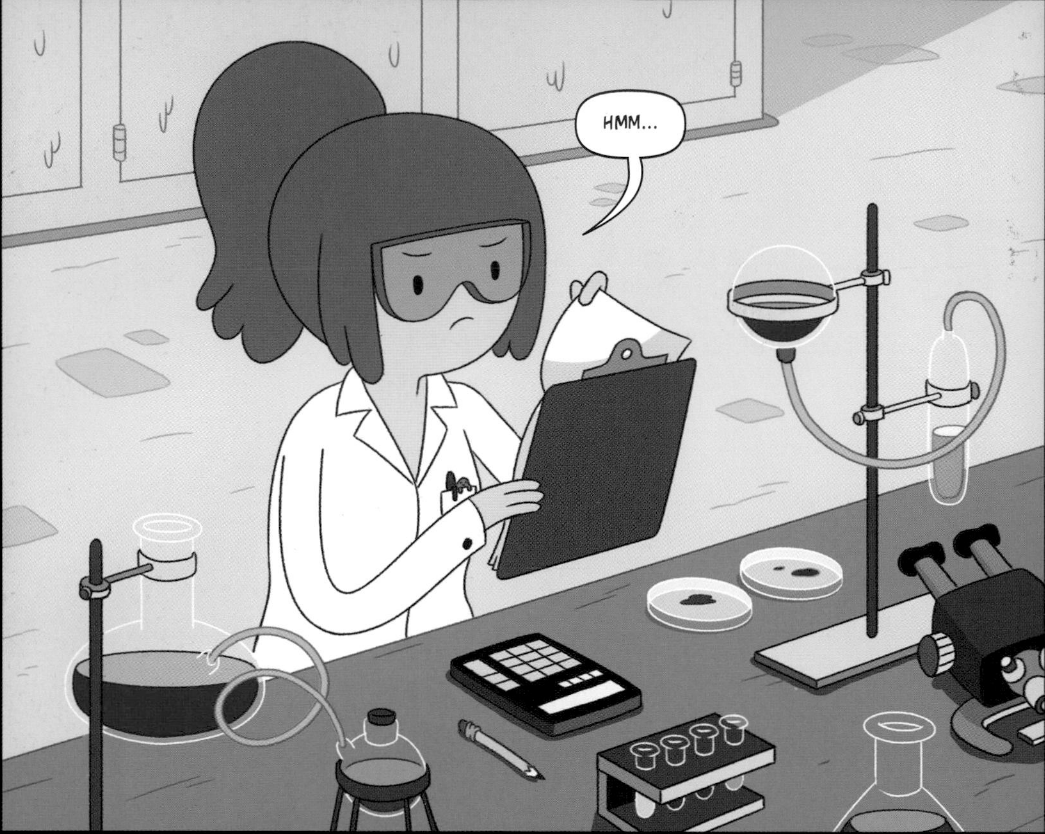
HMM...

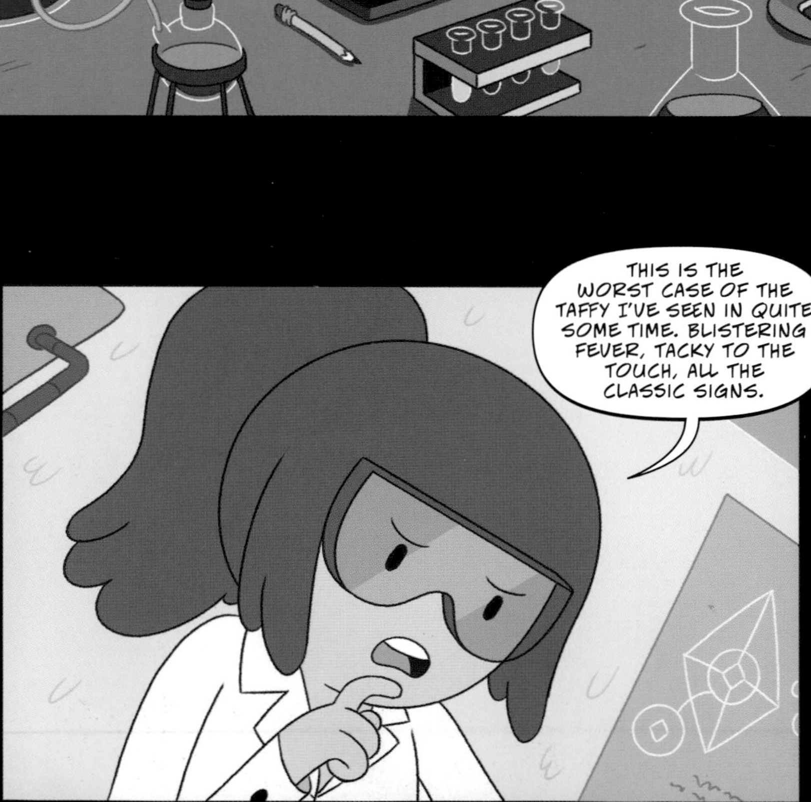
THIS IS THE WORST CASE OF THE TAFFY I'VE SEEN IN QUITE SOME TIME. BLISTERING FEVER, TACKY TO THE TOUCH, ALL THE CLASSIC SIGNS.

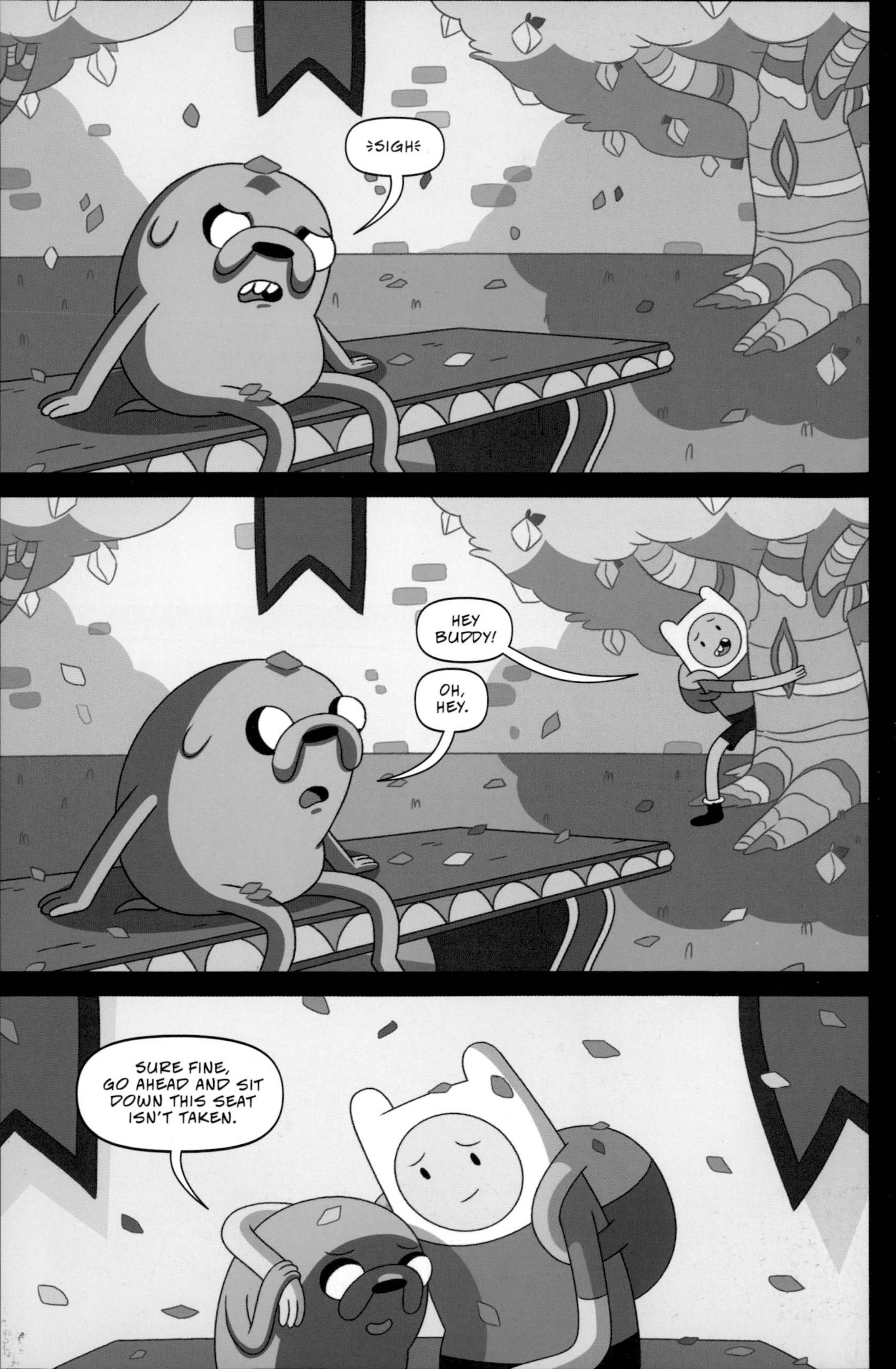

SIGH
HEY BUDDY!
OH, HEY.
SURE FINE, GO AHEAD AND SIT DOWN THIS SEAT ISN'T TAKEN.

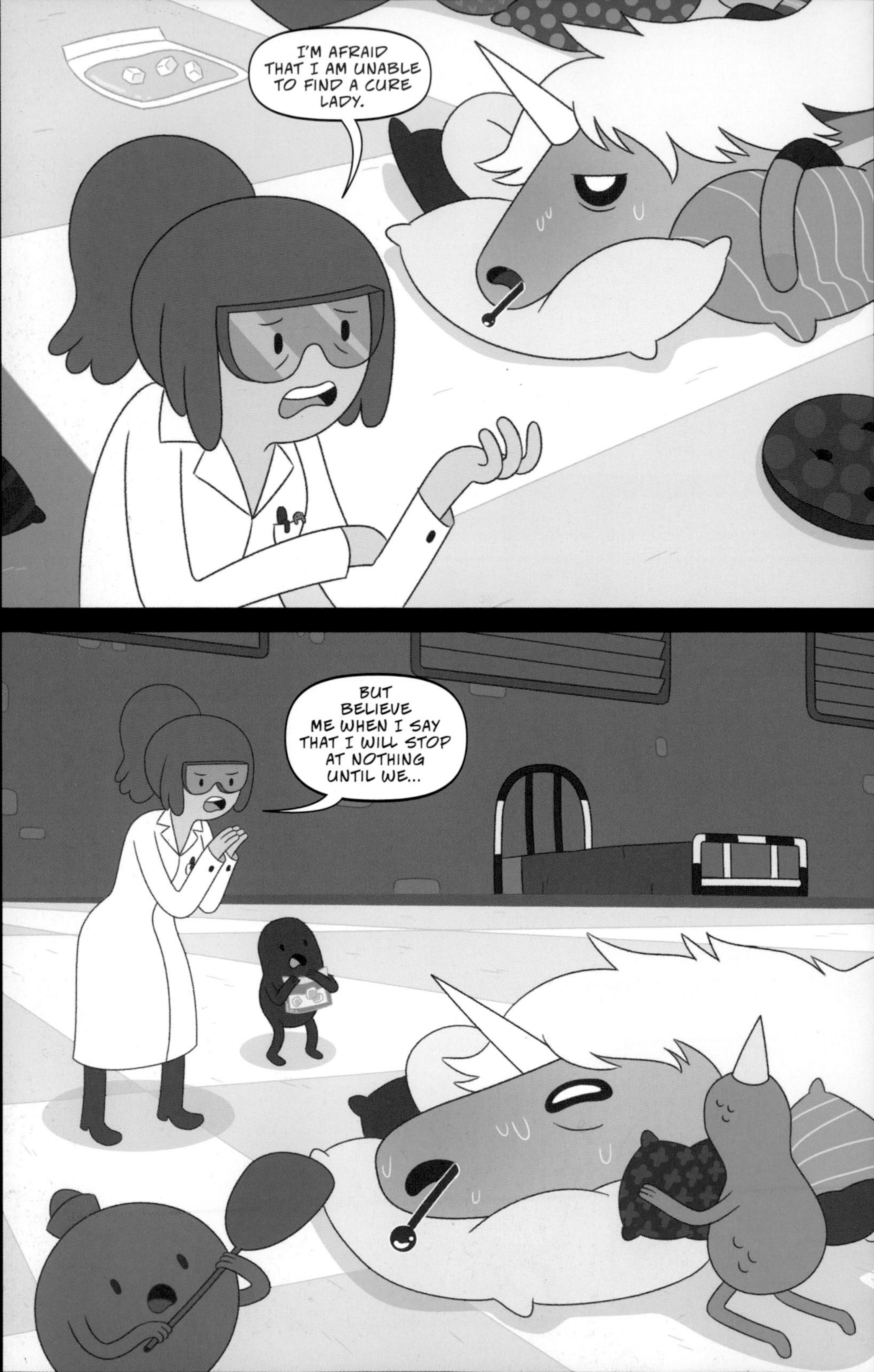
I'M AFRAID THAT I AM UNABLE TO FIND A CURE LADY.
BUT BELIEVE ME WHEN I SAY THAT I WILL STOP AT NOTHING UNTIL WE...

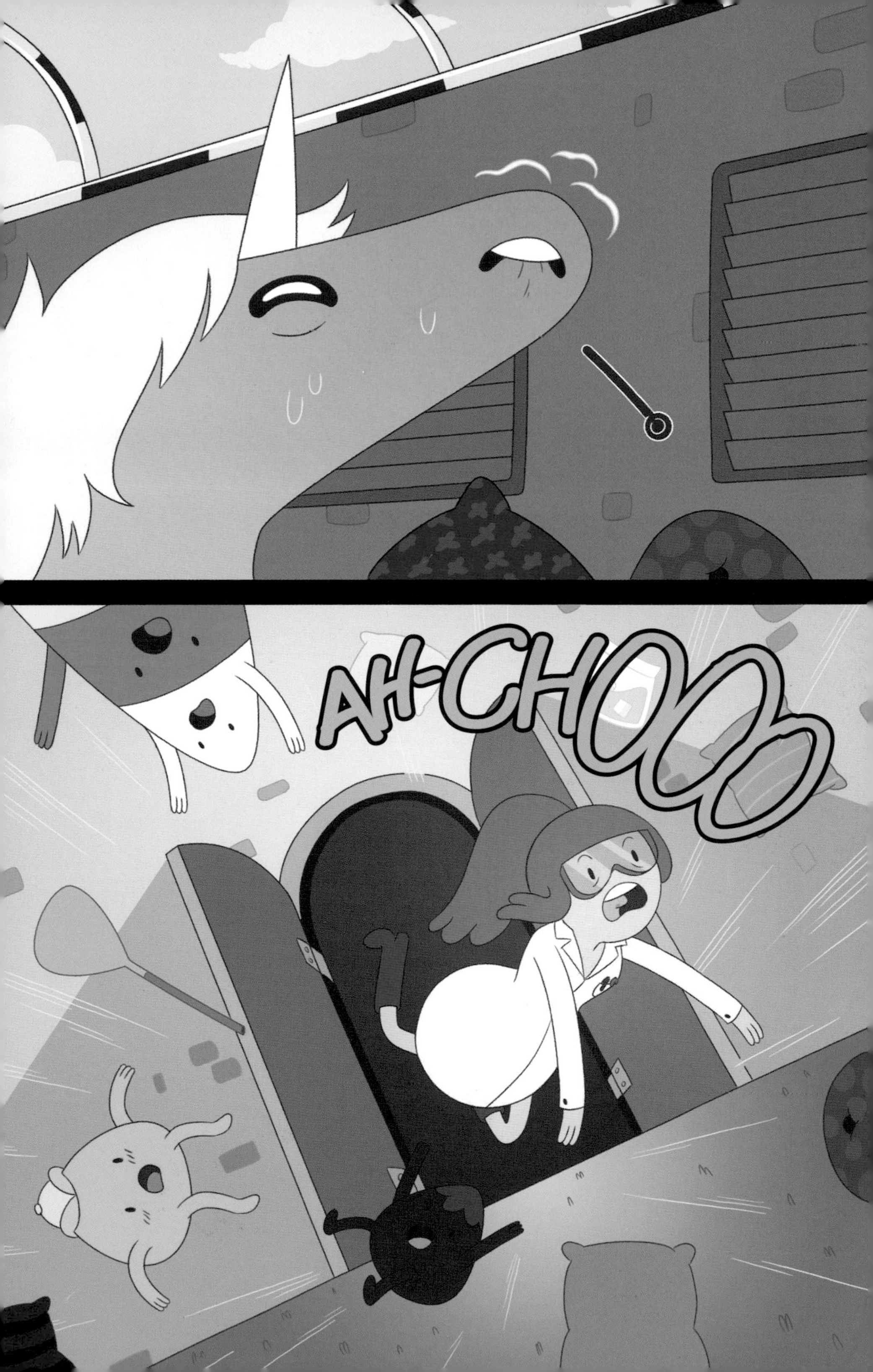
AH-CHOOO

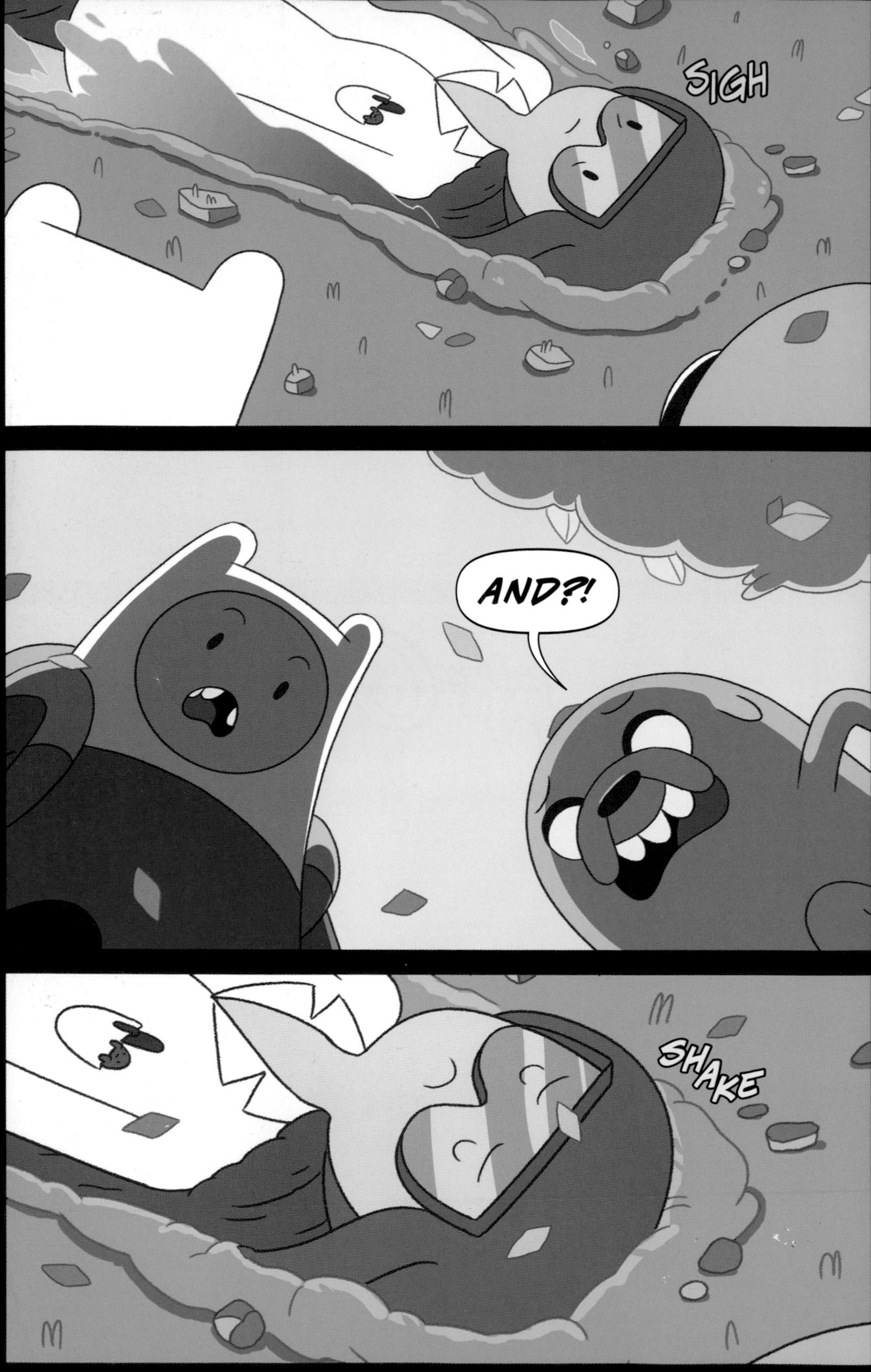
SIGH
AND?!
SHAKE

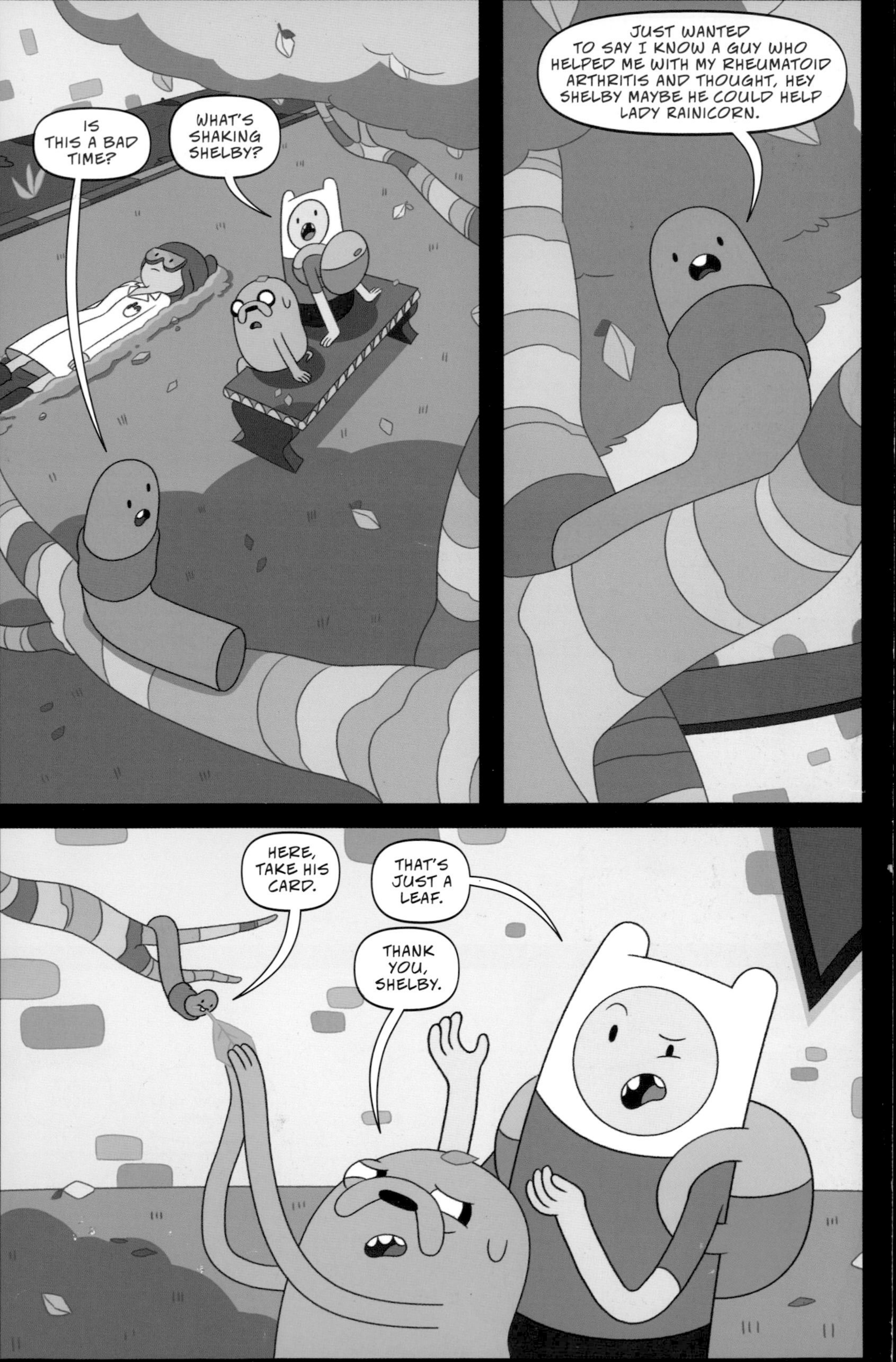
IS THIS A BAD TIME?
WHAT'S SHAKING SHELBY?
JUST WANTED TO SAY I KNOW A GUY WHO HELPED ME WITH MY RHEUMATOID ARTHRITIS AND THOUGHT, HEY SHELBY MAYBE HE COULD HELP LADY RAINICORN.
HERE, TAKE HIS CARD.
THAT'S JUST A LEAF.
THANK YOU, SHELBY.

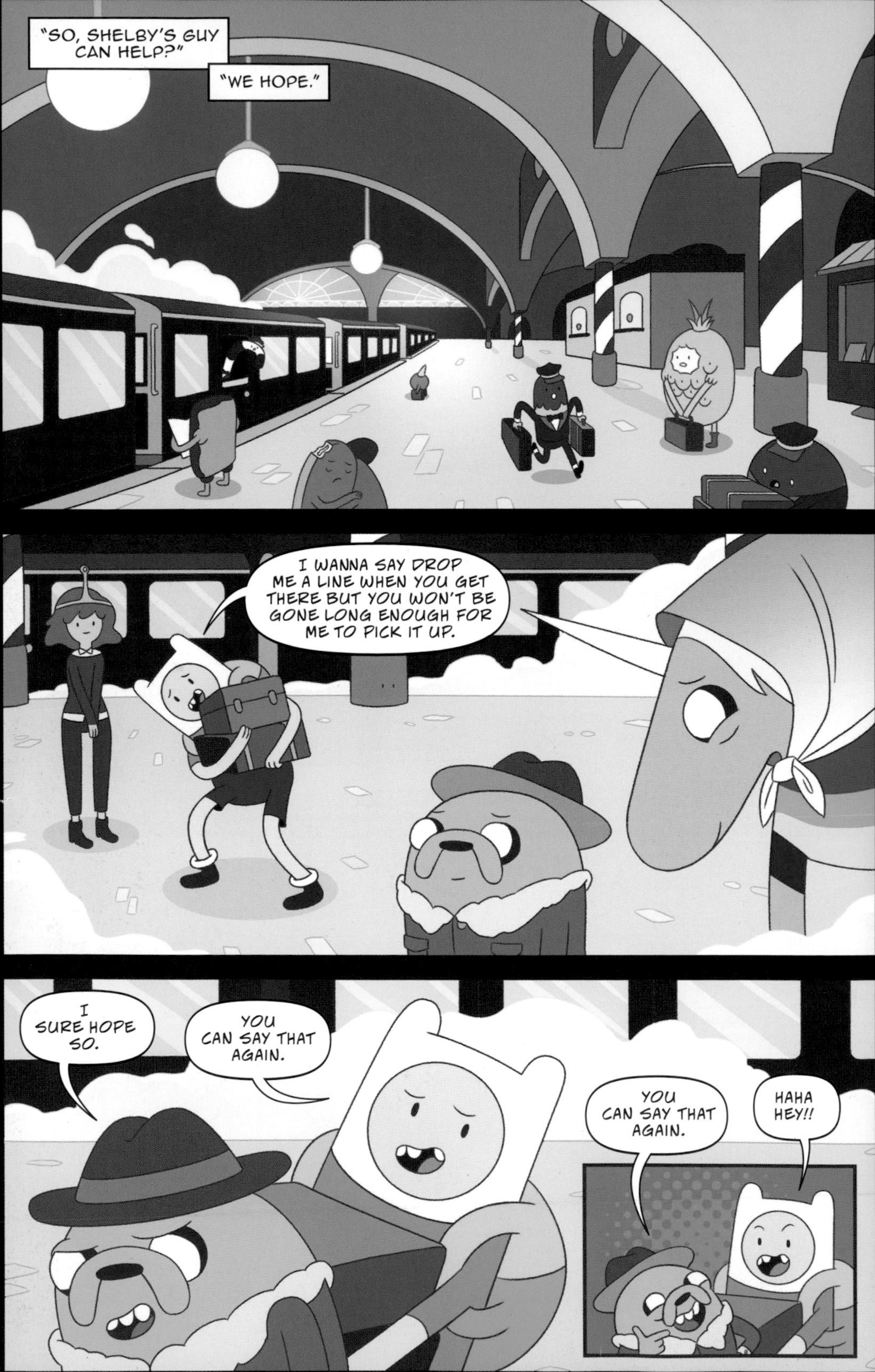
"SO, SHELBY'S GUY CAN HELP?"
"WE HOPE."
I WANNA SAY DROP ME A LINE WHEN YOU GET THERE BUT YOU WON'T BE GONE LONG ENOUGH FOR ME TO PICK IT UP.
I SURE HOPE SO.
YOU CAN SAY THAT AGAIN.
YOU CAN SAY THAT AGAIN.
HAHA HEY!!

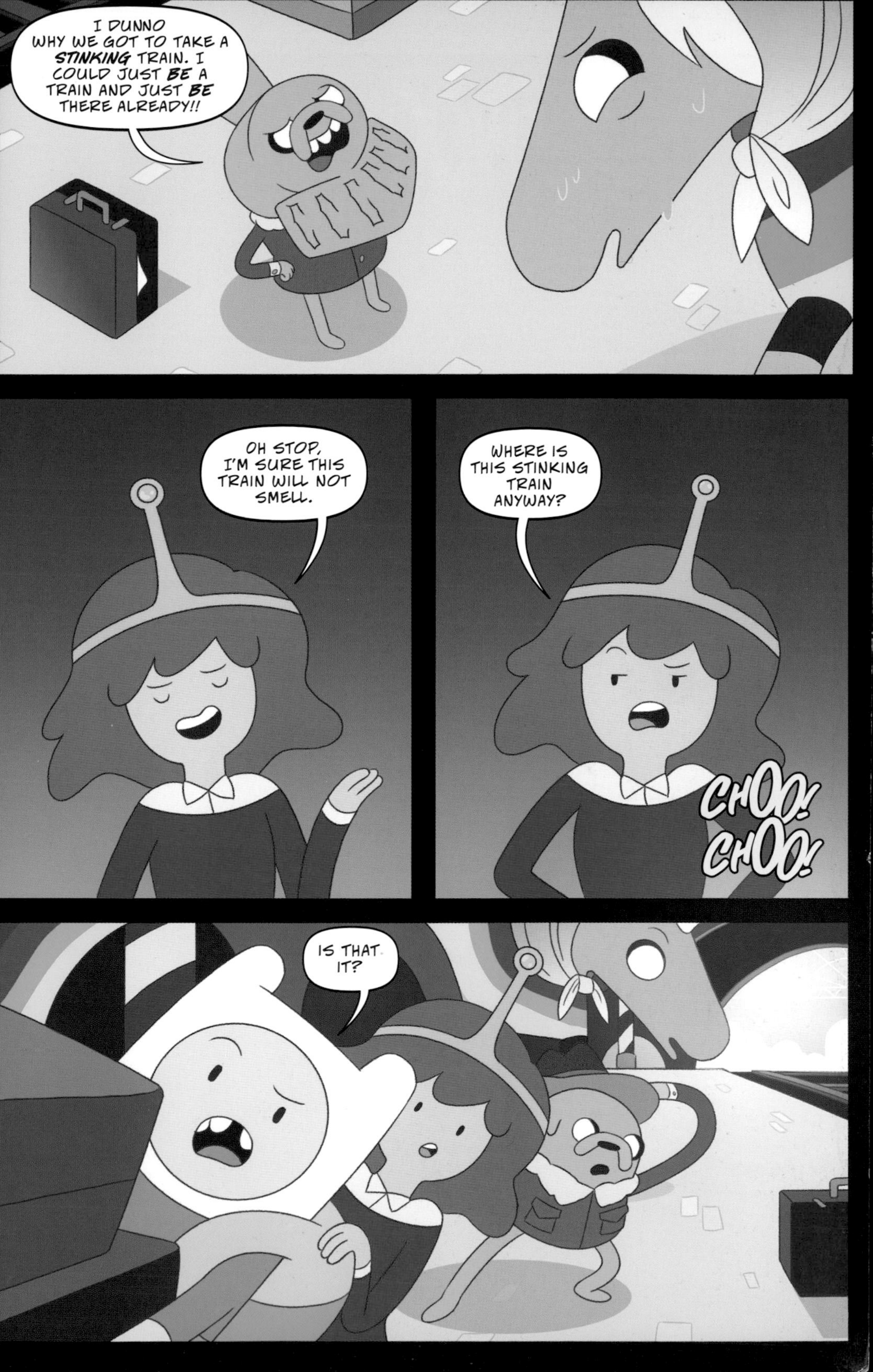
I DUNNO WHY WE GOT TO TAKE A STINKING TRAIN. I COULD JUST BE A TRAIN AND JUST BE THERE ALREADY!!
OH STOP, I'M SURE THIS TRAIN WILL NOT SMELL.
WHERE IS THIS STINKING TRAIN ANYWAY?
CHOO! CHOO!
IS THAT IT?

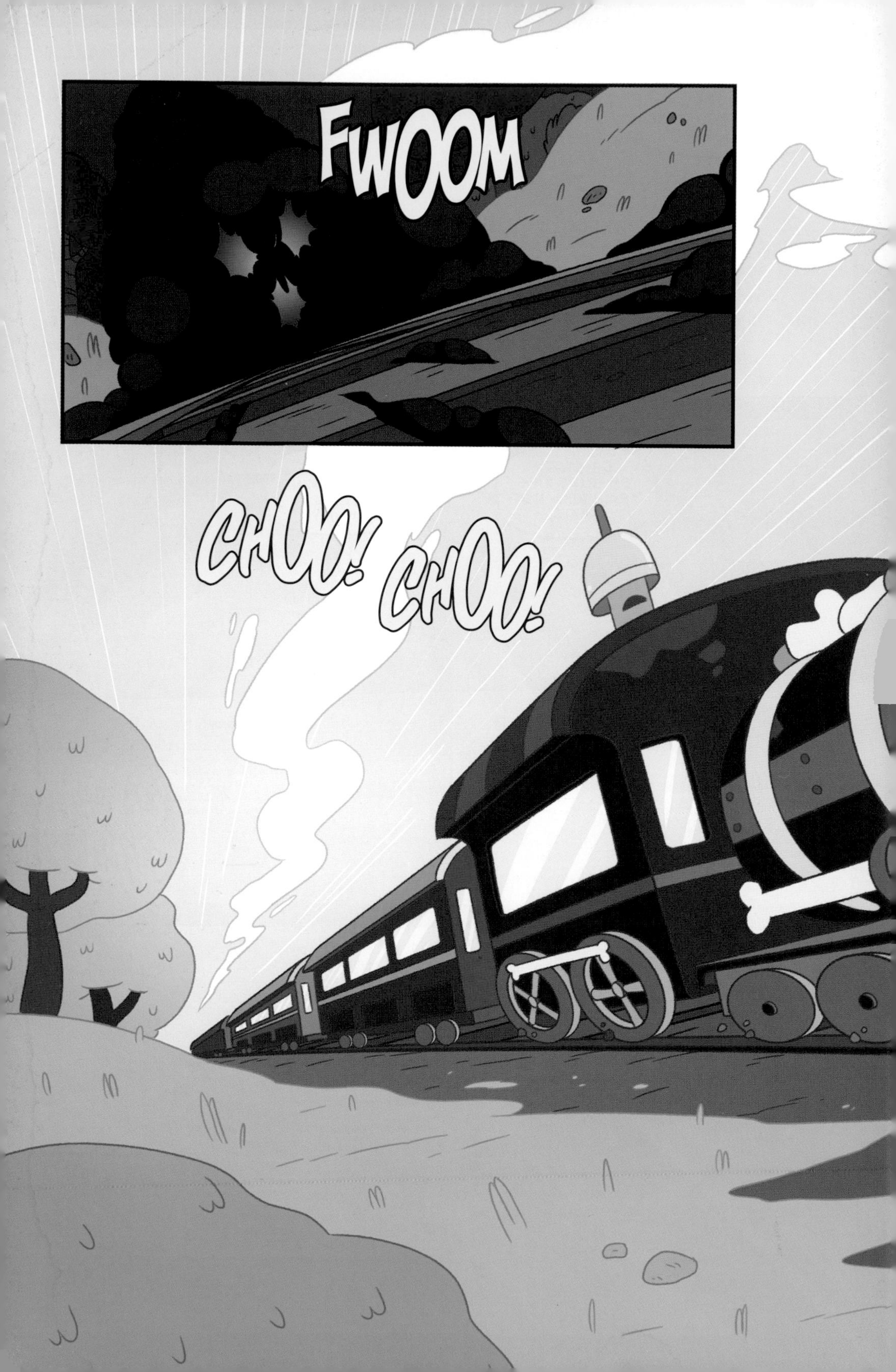
FWOOM
CHOO! CHOO!

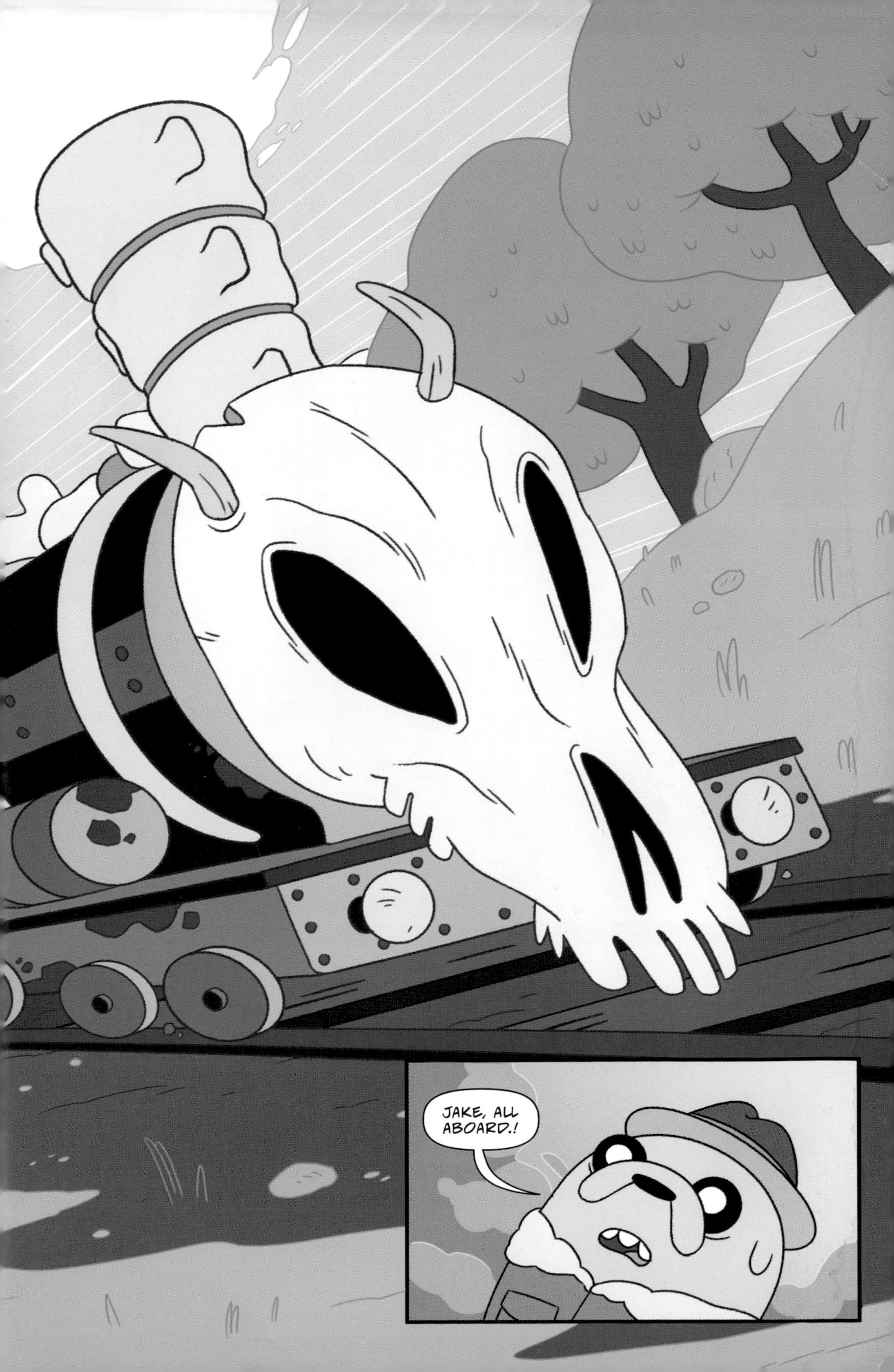
JAKE, ALL ABOARD.!

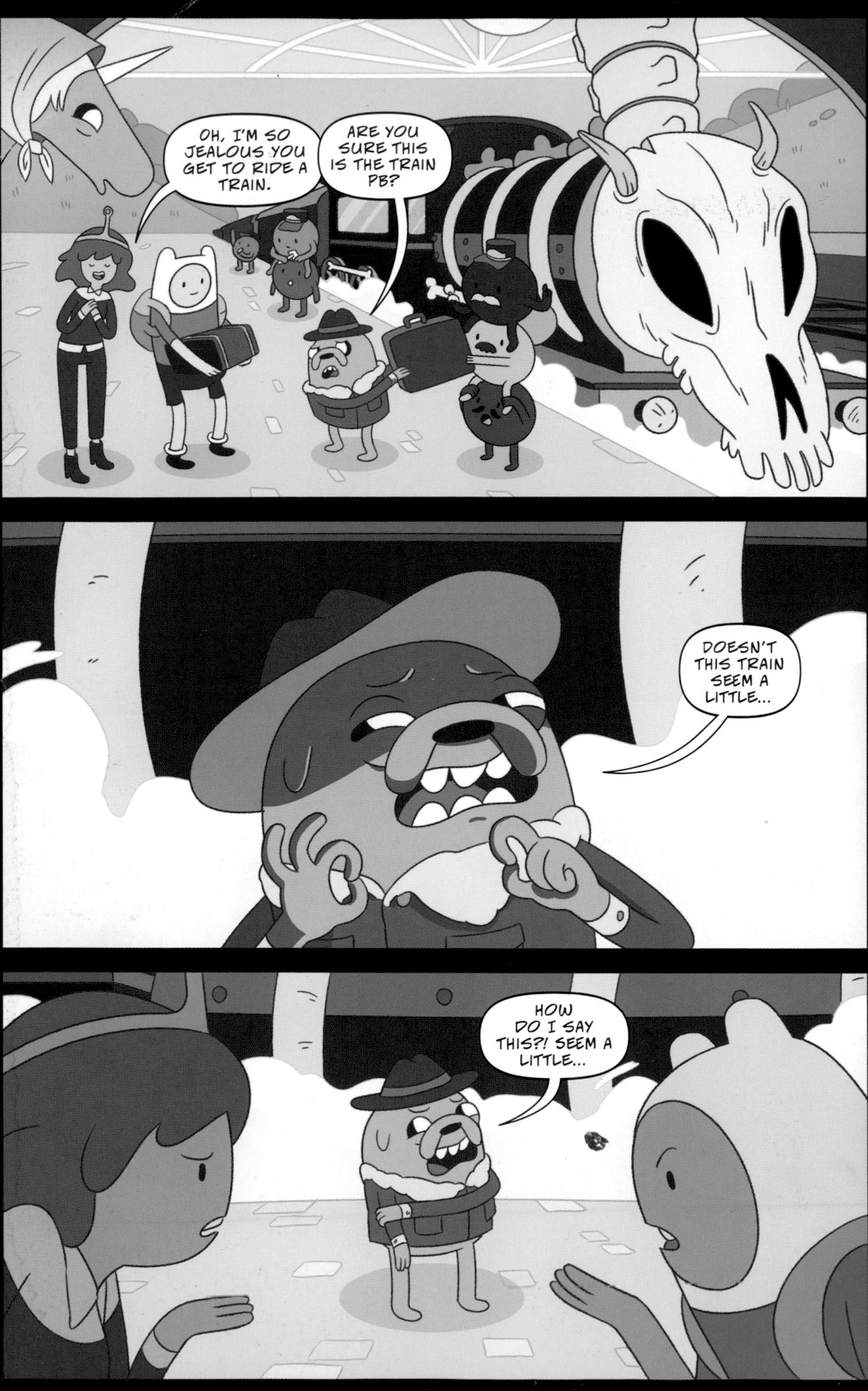
OH, I'M SO JEALOUS YOU GET TO RIDE A TRAIN.
ARE YOU SURE THIS IS THE TRAIN PB?
DOESN'T THIS TRAIN SEEM A LITTLE...
HOW DO I SAY THIS?! SEEM A LITTLE...

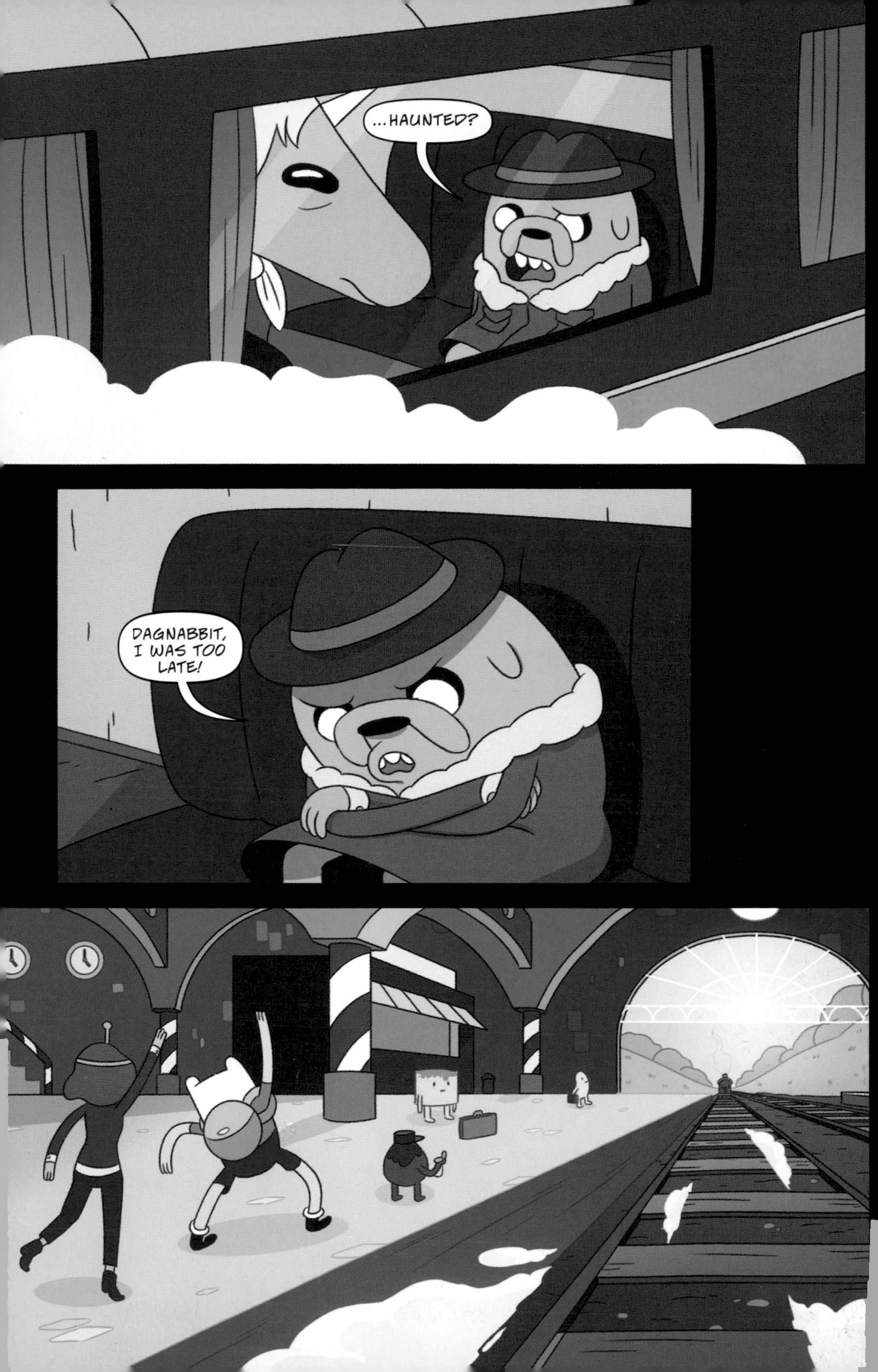
...HAUNTED?
DAGNABBIT, I WAS TOO LATE!

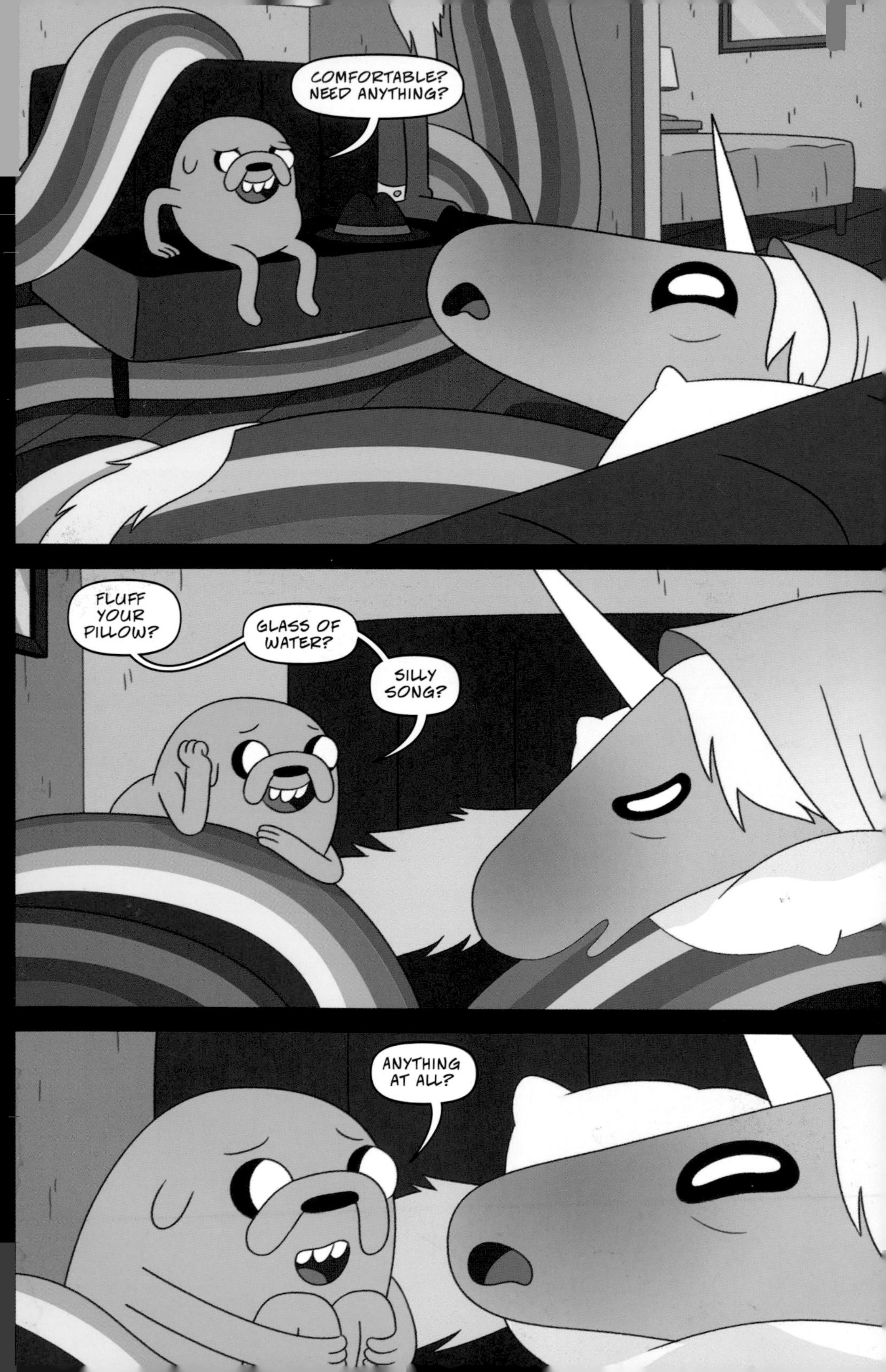
COMFORTABLE? NEED ANYTHING?
FLUFF YOUR PILLOW?
GLASS OF WATER?
SILLY SONG?
ANYTHING AT ALL?

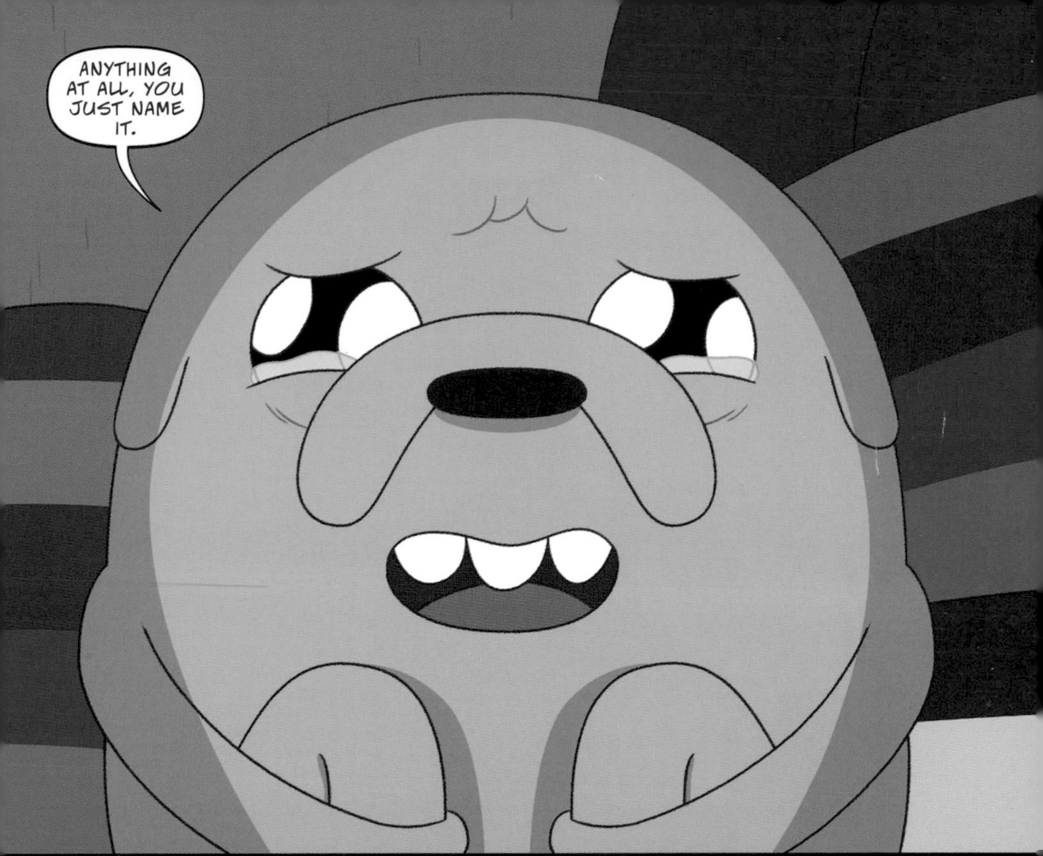
ANYTHING AT ALL, YOU JUST NAME IT.

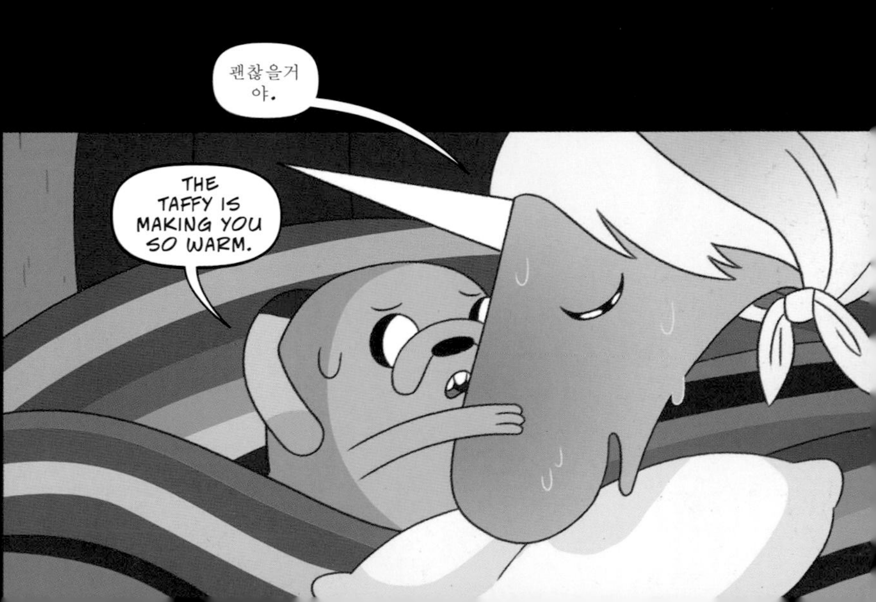
괜찮을거 야.
THE TAFFY IS MAKING YOU SO WARM.

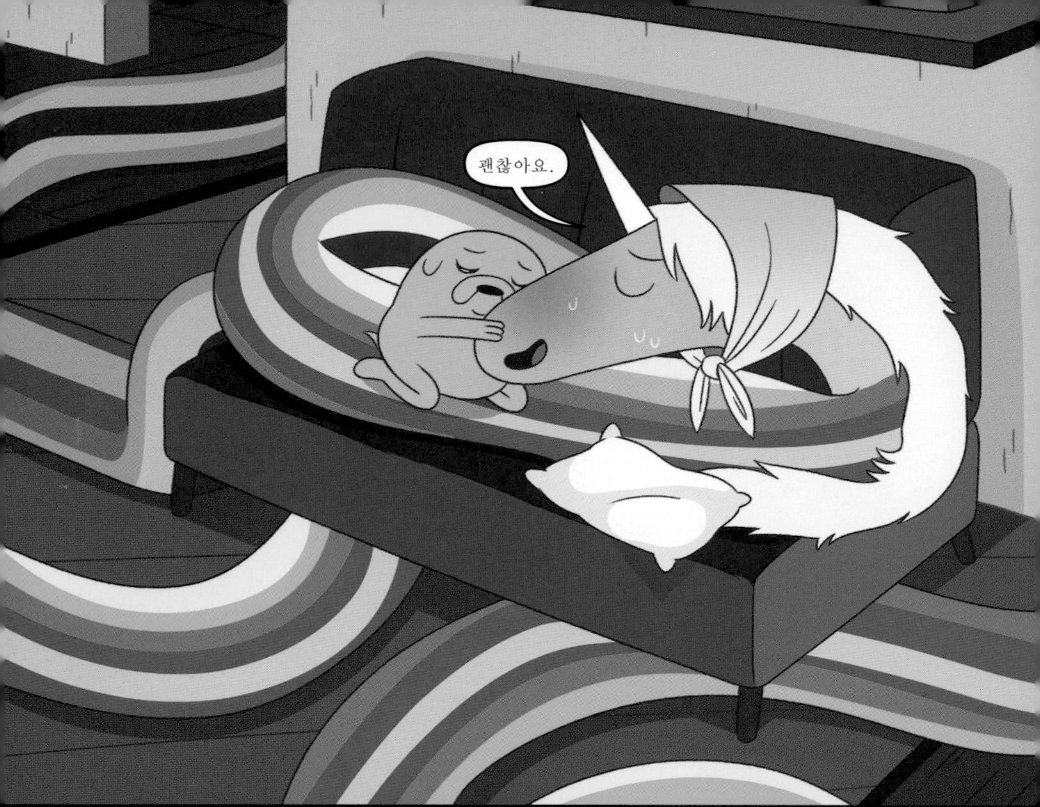
괜찮아요.

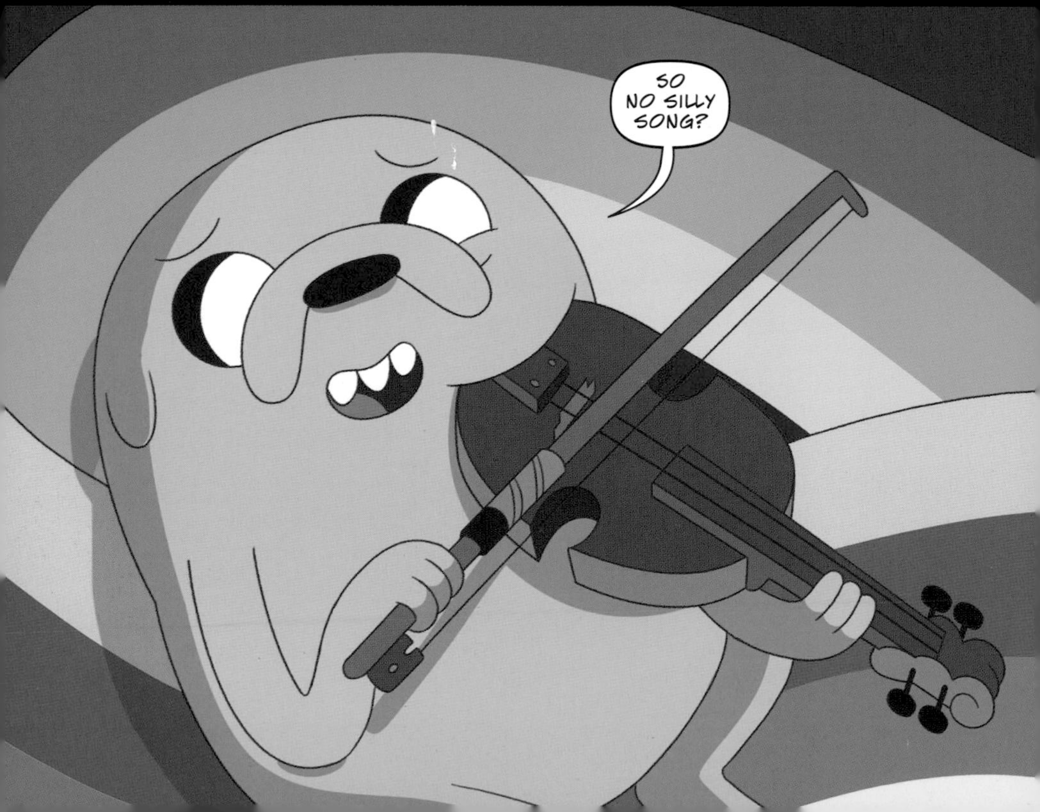
SO NO SILLY SONG?

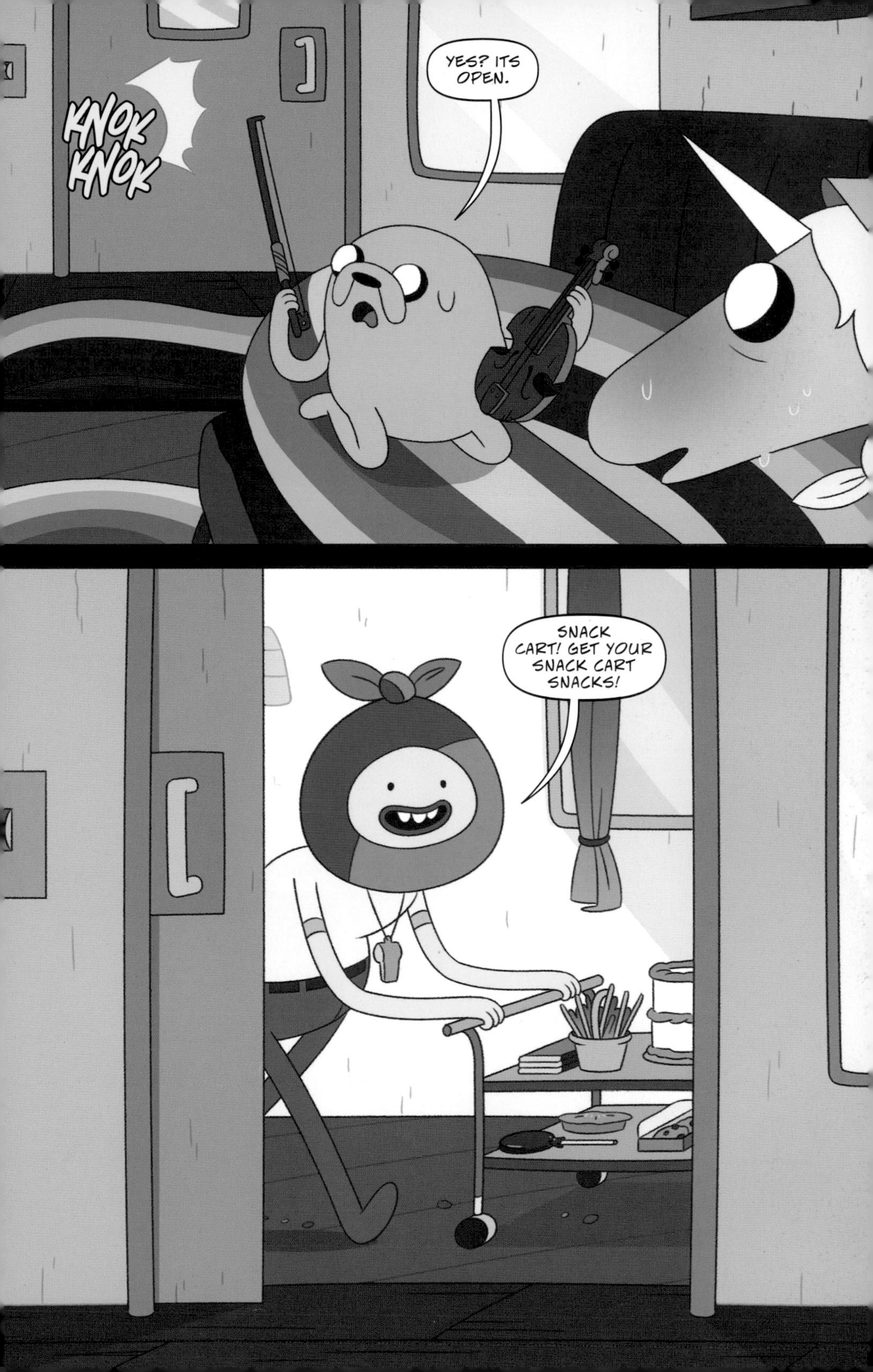
KNOK KNOK
YES? ITS OPEN.
SNACK CART! GET YOUR SNACK CART SNACKS!

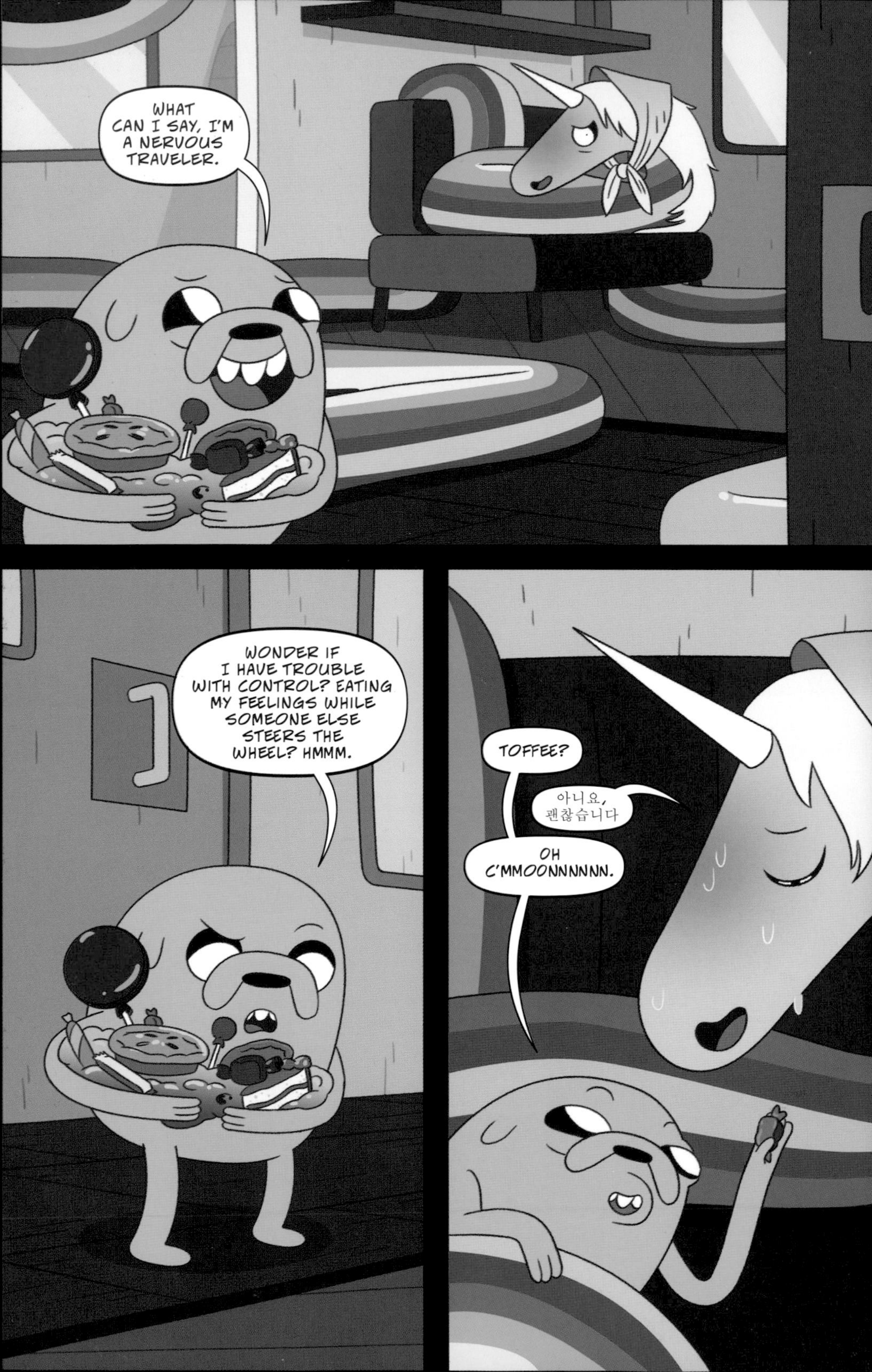
WHAT CAN I SAY, I'M A NERVOUS TRAVELER.
WONDER IF I HAVE TROUBLE WITH CONTROL? EATING MY FEELINGS WHILE SOMEONE ELSE STEERS THE WHEEL? HMMM.
TOFFEE?
아니요, 괜찮습니다
OH C'MMOONNNNNN.

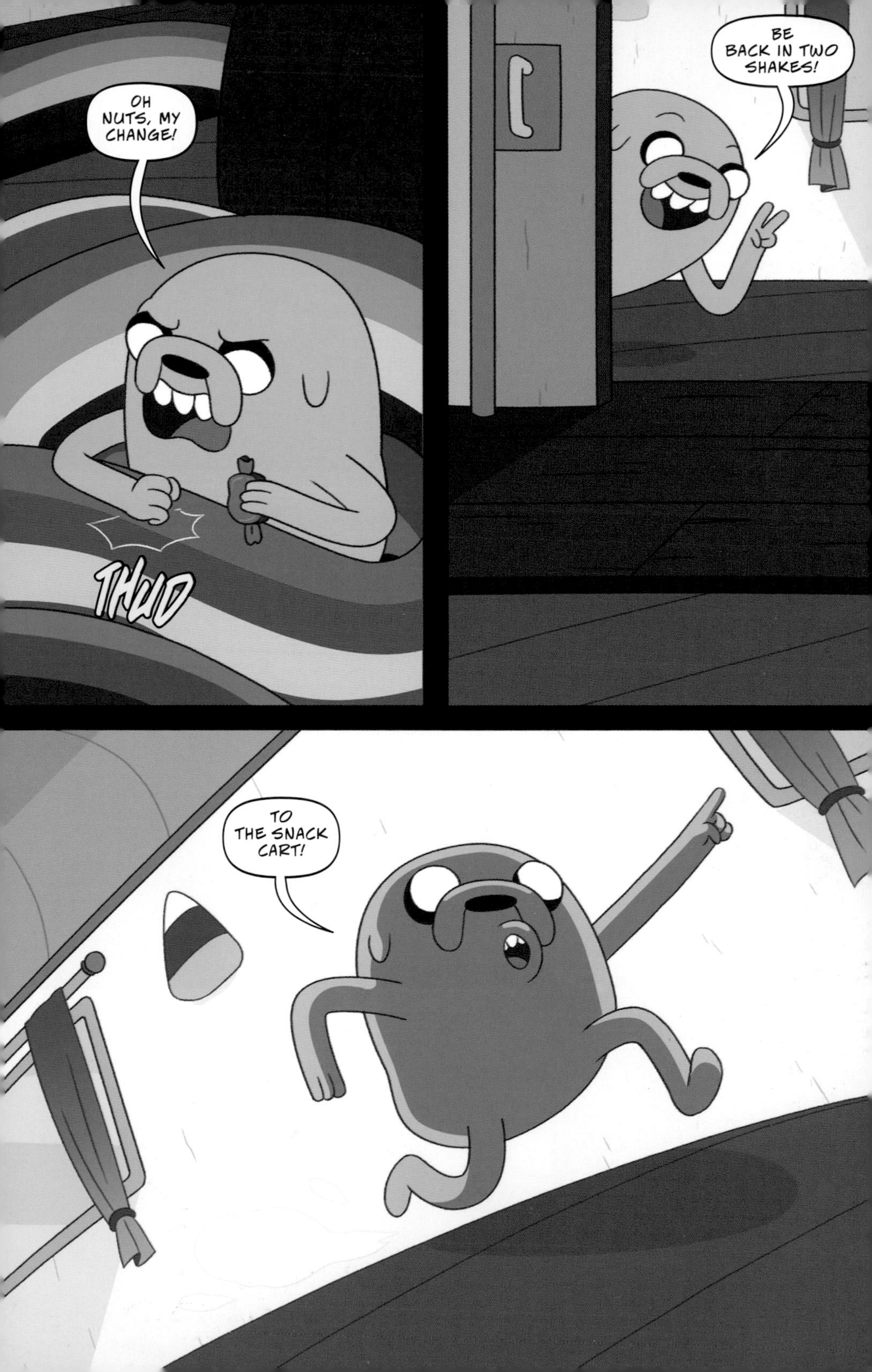
OH NUTS, MY CHANGE!
THUD
BE BACK IN TWO SHAKES!
TO THE SNACK CART!

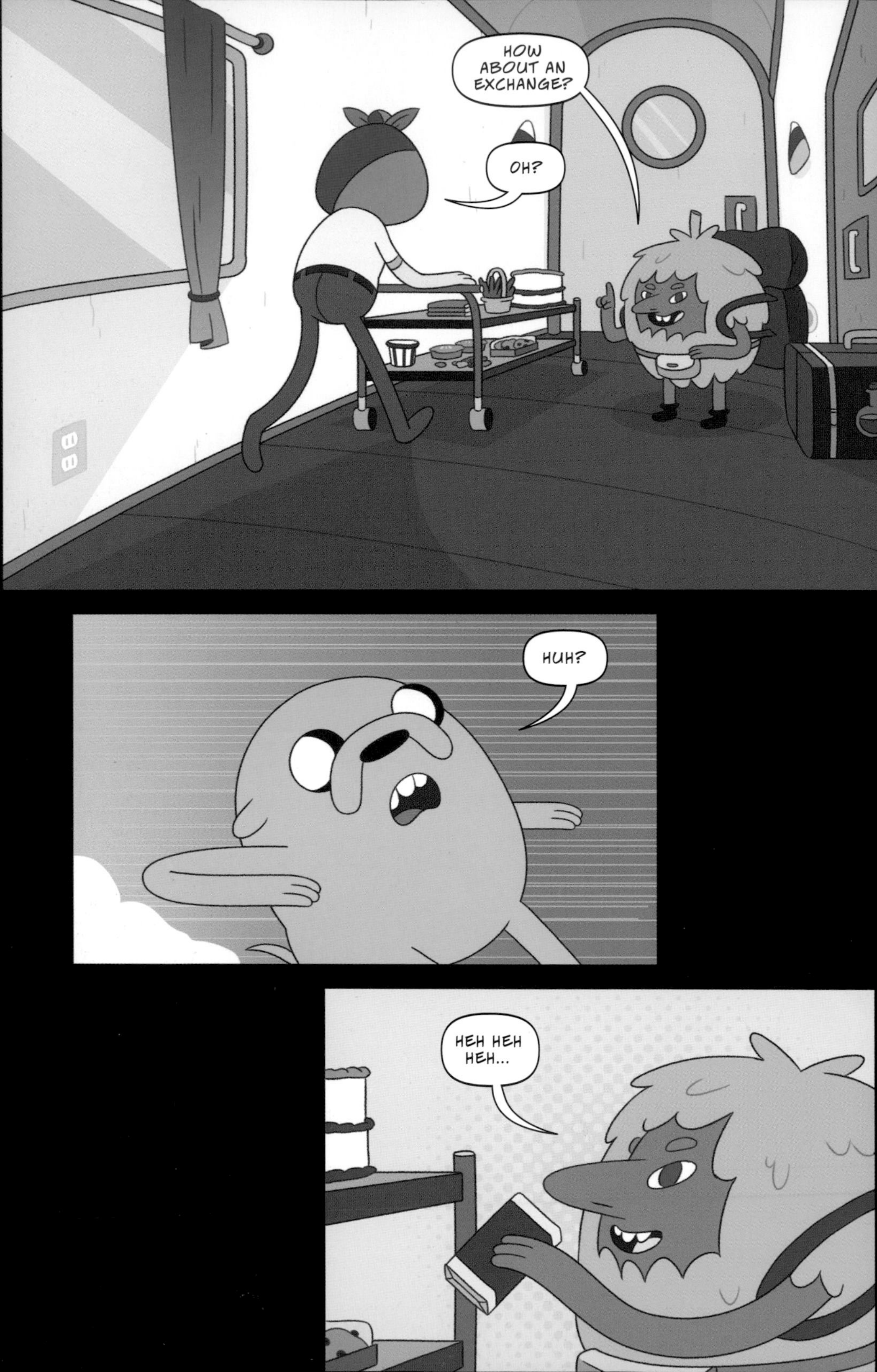
HOW ABOUT AN EXCHANGE?
OH?
HUH?
HEH HEH HEH...

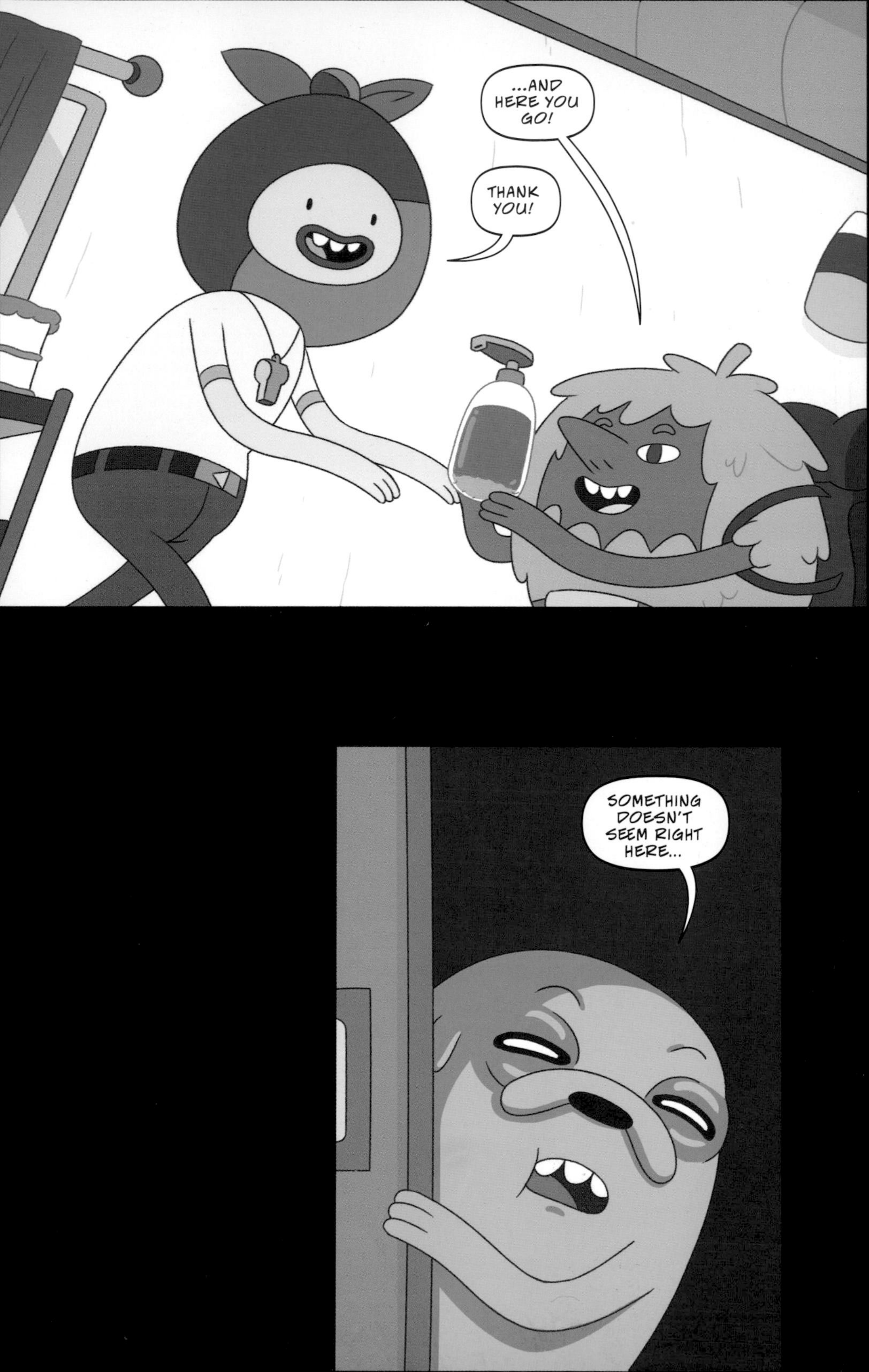
...AND HERE YOU GO!
THANK YOU!
SOMETHING DOESN'T SEEM RIGHT HERE...

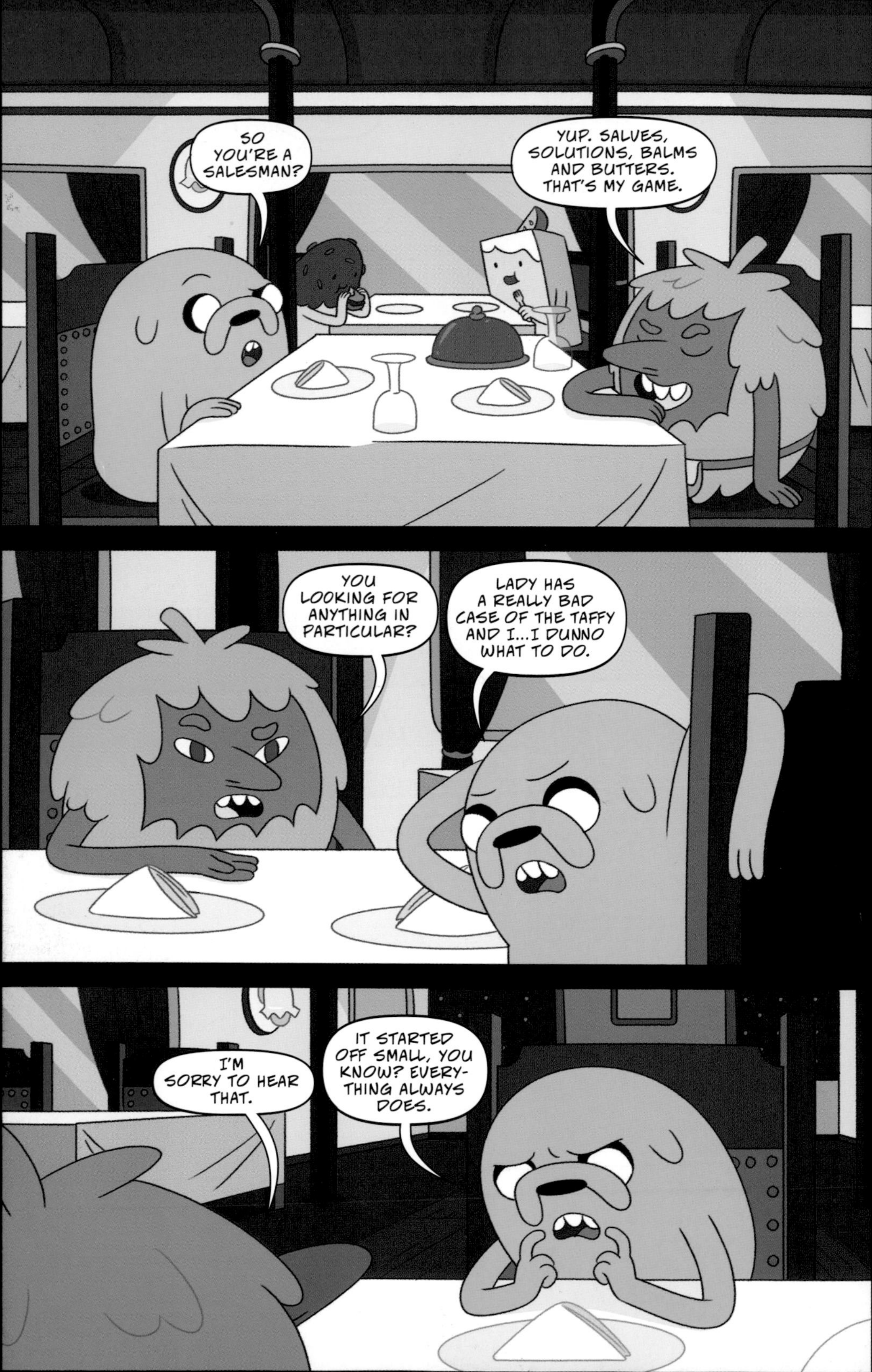
SO YOU'RE A SALESMAN?
YUP. SALVES, SOLUTIONS, BALMS AND BUTTERS. THAT'S MY GAME.
YOU LOOKING FOR ANYTHING IN PARTICULAR?
LADY HAS A REALLY BAD CASE OF THE TAFFY AND I...I DUNNO WHAT TO DO.
I'M SORRY TO HEAR THAT.
IT STARTED OFF SMALL, YOU KNOW? EVERY-THING ALWAYS DOES.

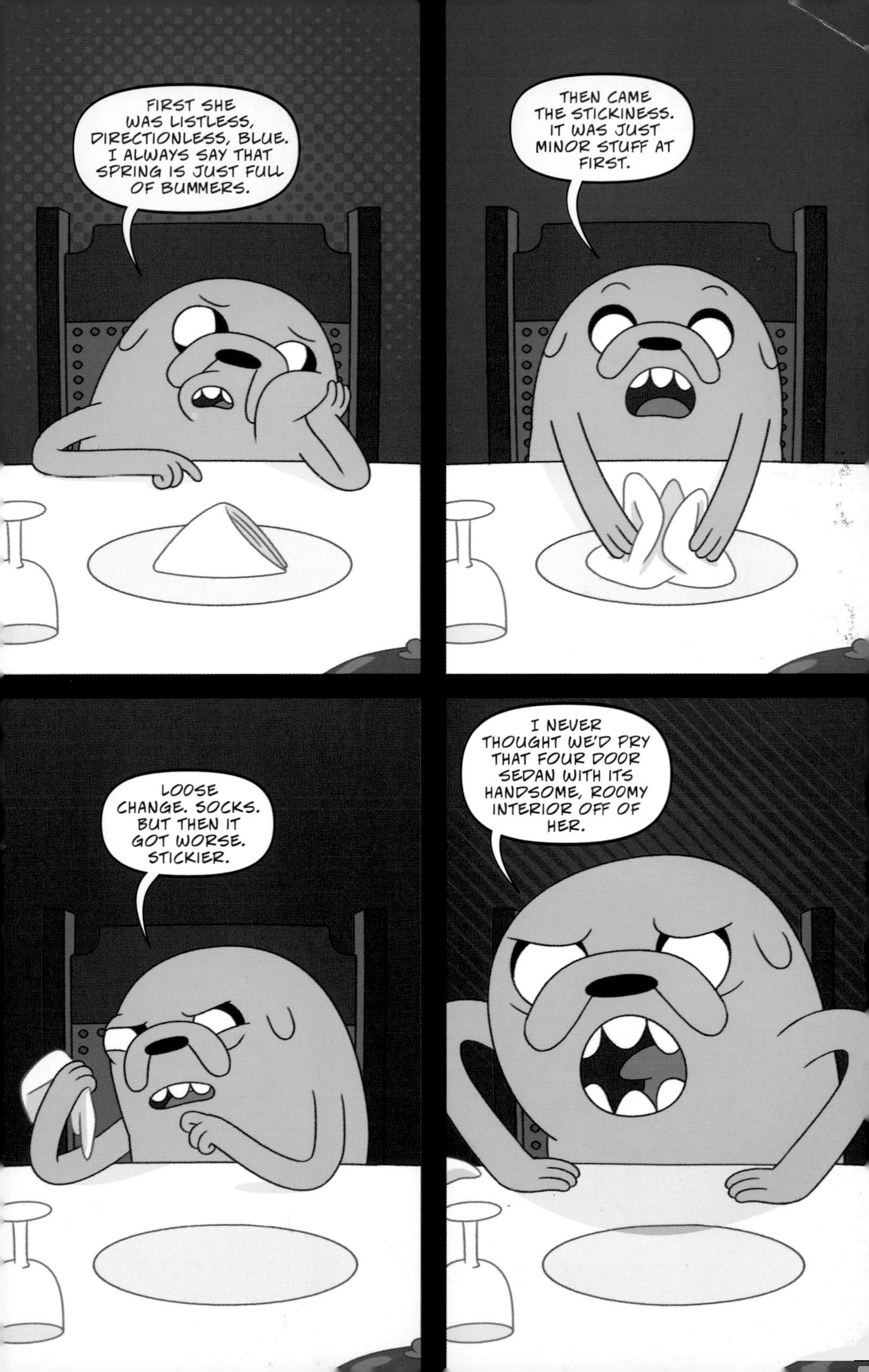
FIRST SHE WAS LISTLESS, DIRECTIONLESS, BLUE. I ALWAYS SAY THAT SPRING IS JUST FULL OF BUMMERS.
THEN CAME THE STICKINESS. IT WAS JUST MINOR STUFF AT FIRST.
LOOSE CHANGE. SOCKS. BUT THEN IT GOT WORSE. STICKIER.
I NEVER THOUGHT WE'D PRY THAT FOUR DOOR SEDAN WITH ITS HANDSOME, ROOMY INTERIOR OFF OF HER.

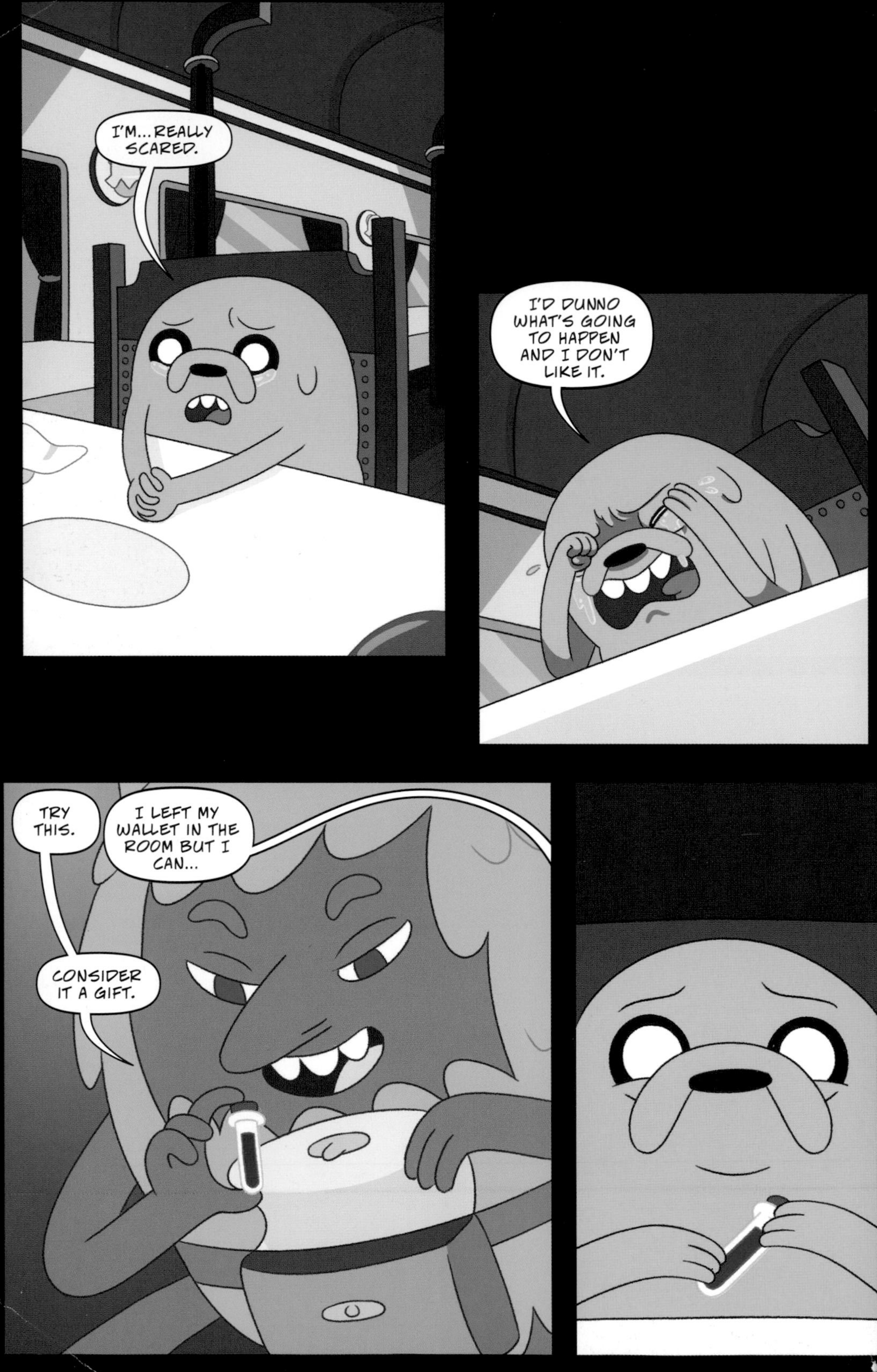
I'M...REALLY SCARED.
I'D DUNNO WHAT'S GOING TO HAPPEN AND I DON'T LIKE IT.
TRY THIS.
I LEFT MY WALLET IN THE ROOM BUT I CAN...
CONSIDER IT A GIFT.

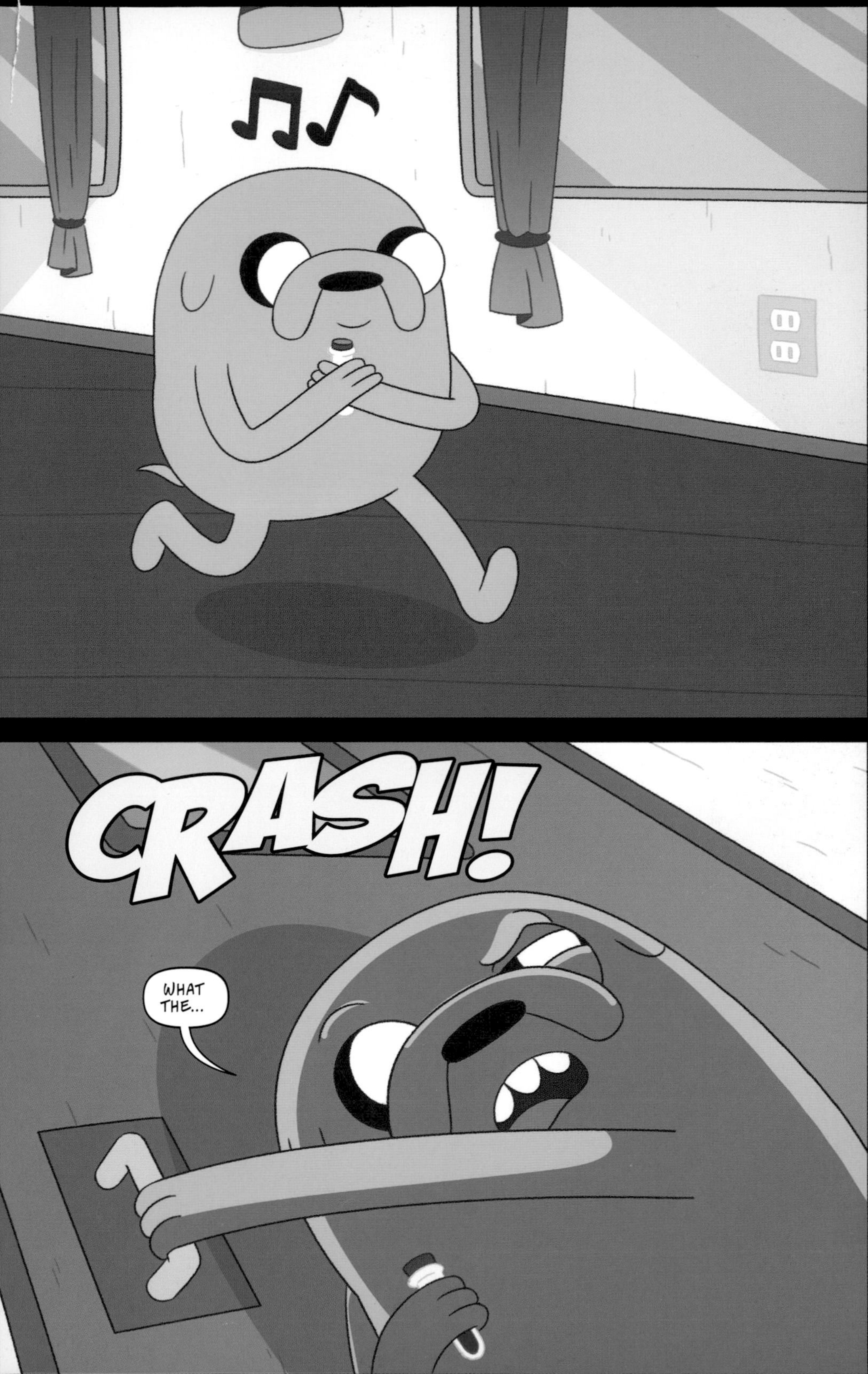
CRASH!
WHAT THE...

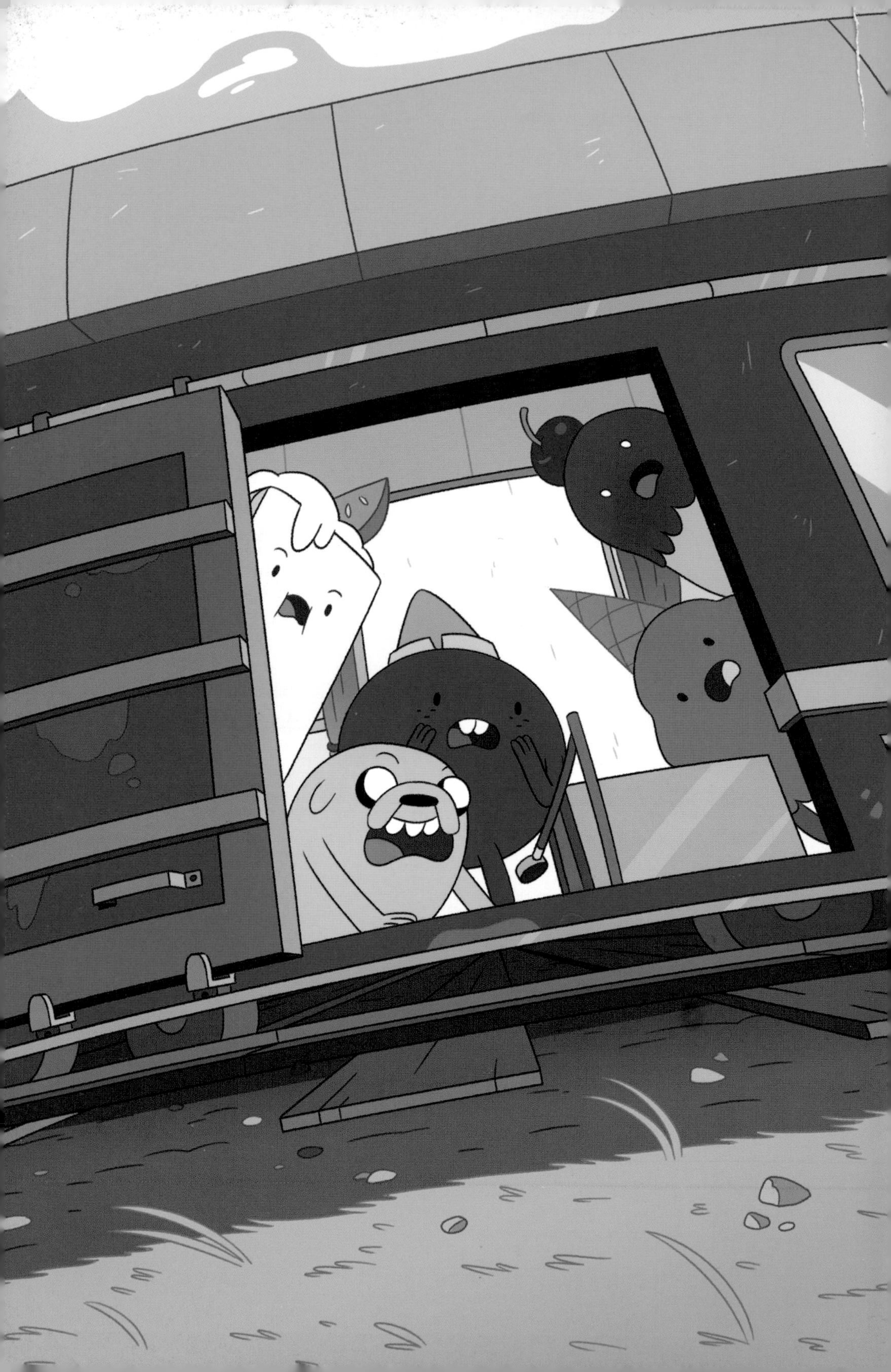

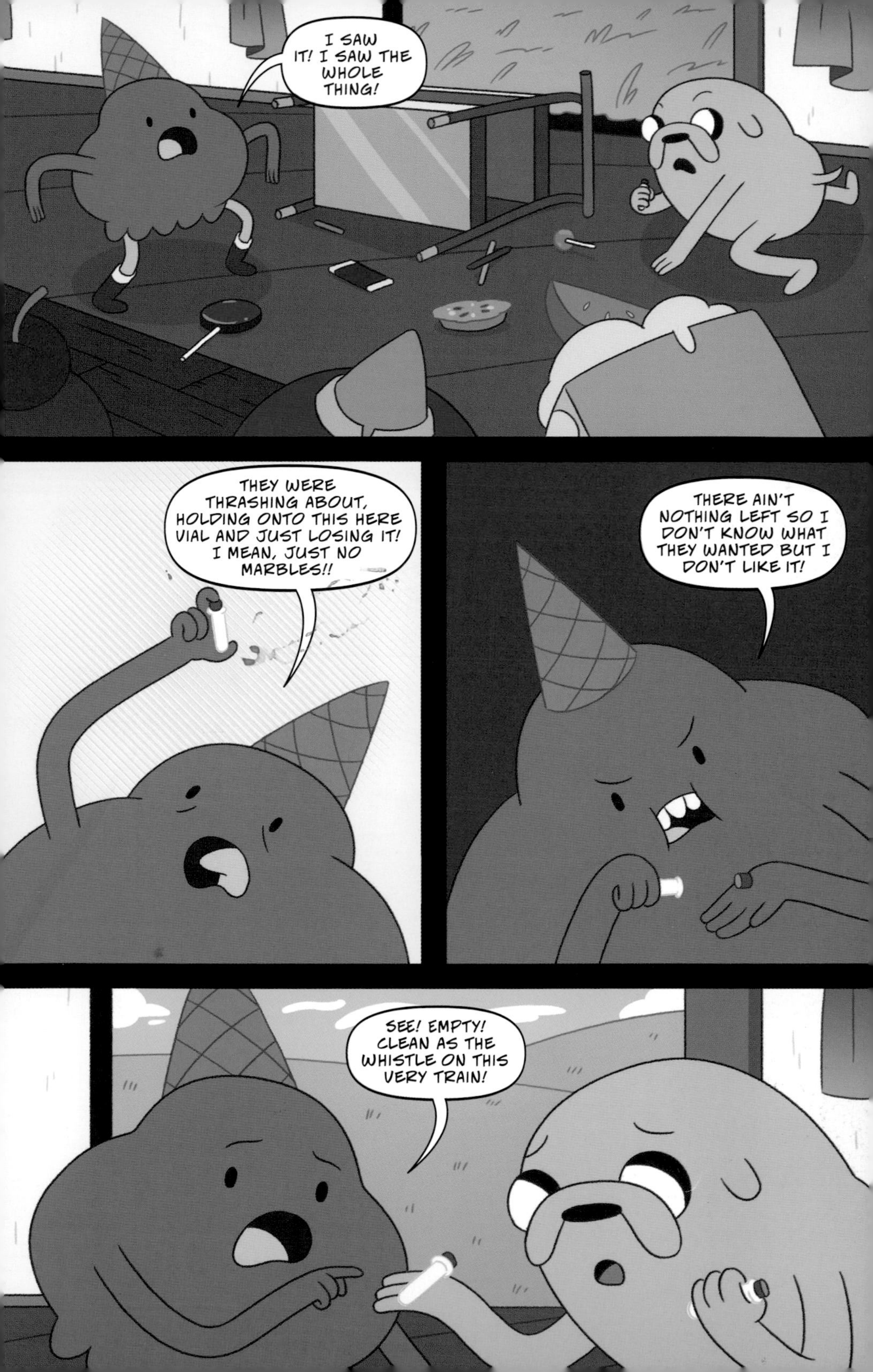
I SAW IT! I SAW THE WHOLE THING!
THEY WERE THRASHING ABOUT, HOLDING ONTO THIS HERE VIAL AND JUST LOSING IT! I MEAN, JUST NO MARBLES!!
THERE AIN'T NOTHING LEFT SO I DON'T KNOW WHAT THEY WANTED BUT I DON'T LIKE IT!
SEE! EMPTY! CLEAN AS THE WHISTLE ON THIS VERY TRAIN!

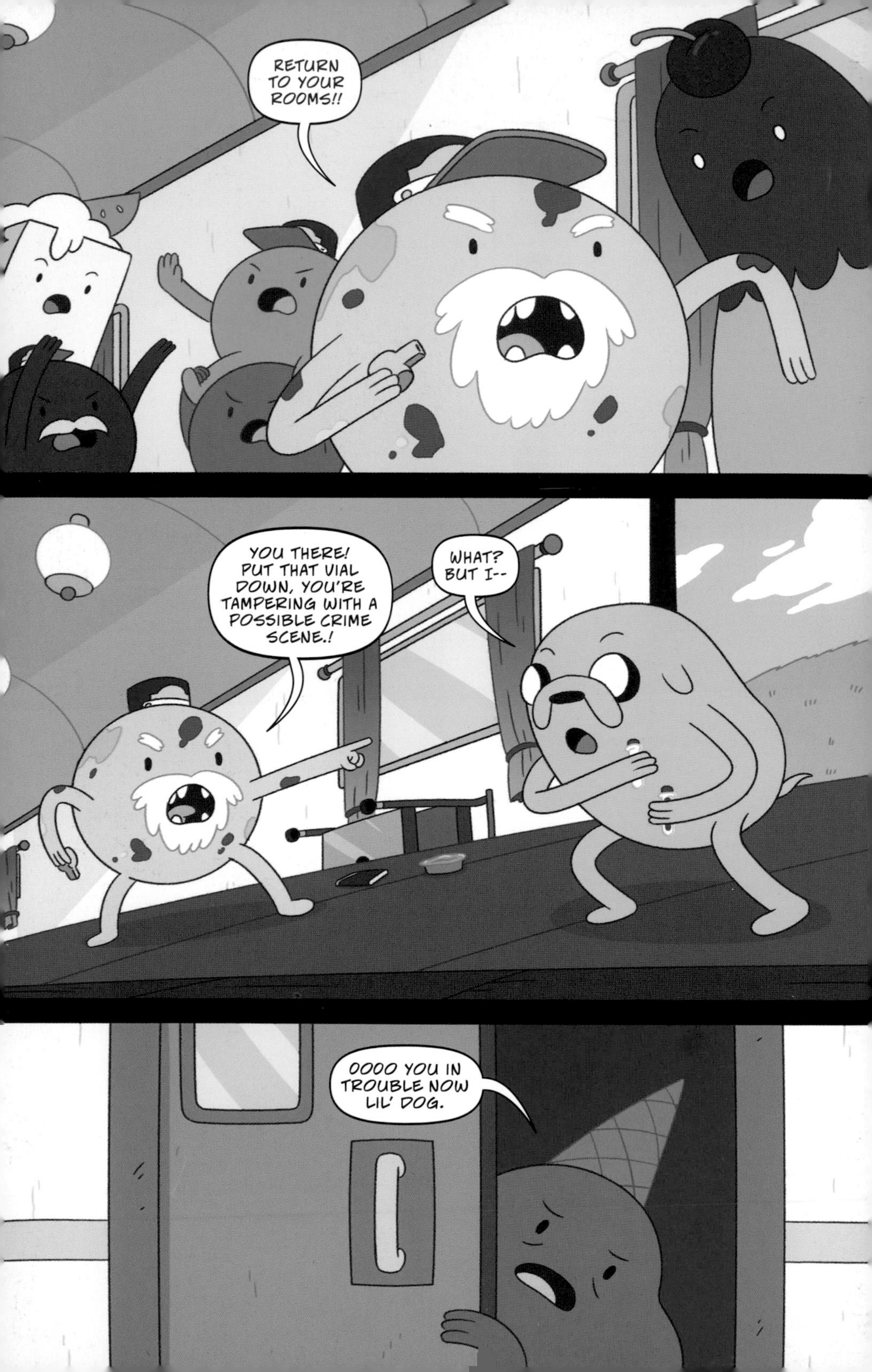
RETURN TO YOUR ROOMS!!
YOU THERE! PUT THAT VIAL DOWN, YOU'RE TAMPERING WITH A POSSIBLE CRIME SCENE.!
WHAT? BUT I--
OOOO YOU IN TROUBLE NOW LIL' DOG.

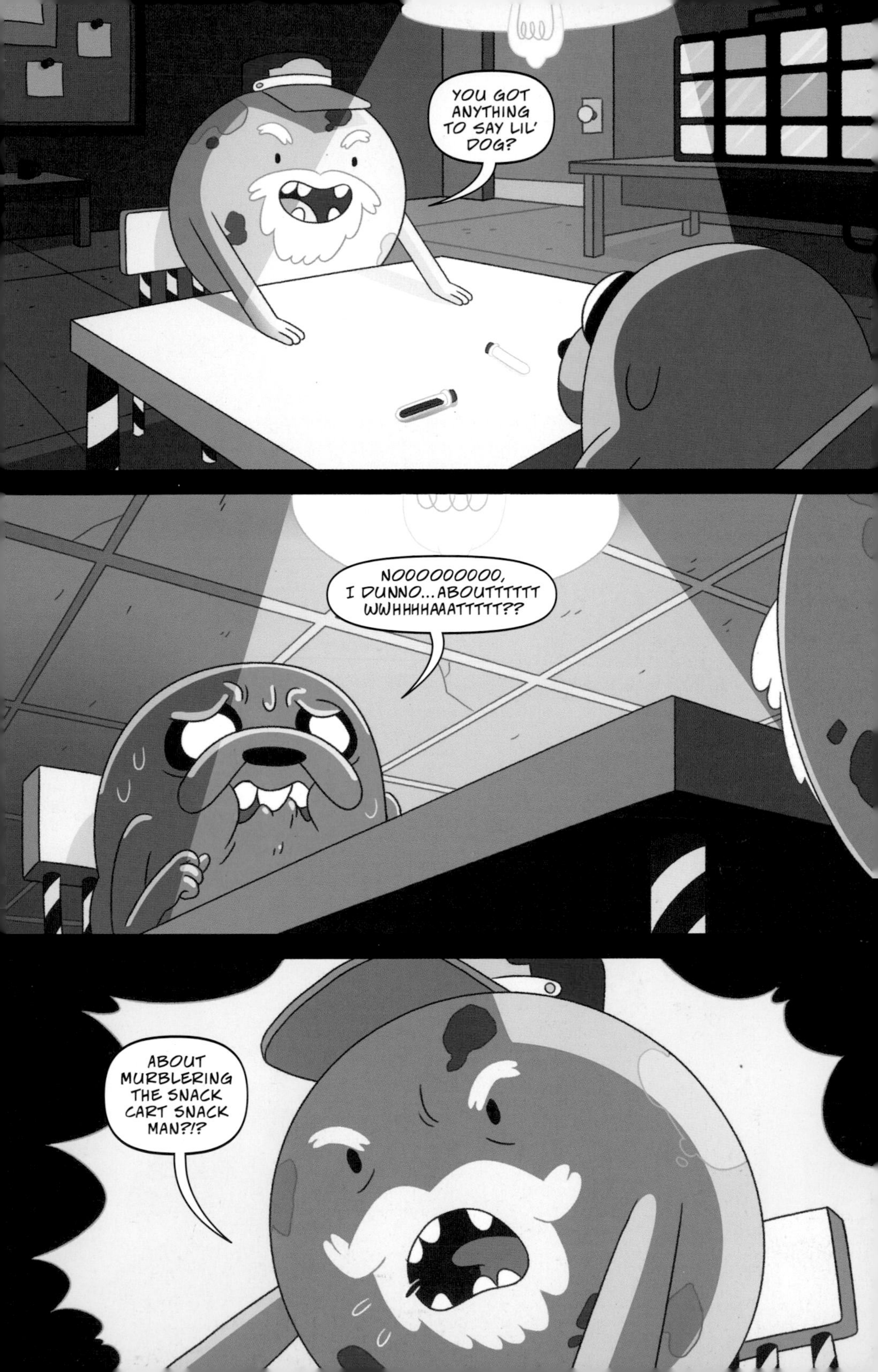
YOU GOT ANYTHING TO SAY LIL' DOG?
NOOOOOOOOO, I DUNNO...ABOUTTTTTT WWHHHHAAATTTTT??
ABOUT MURBLERING THE SNACK CART SNACK MAN?!?

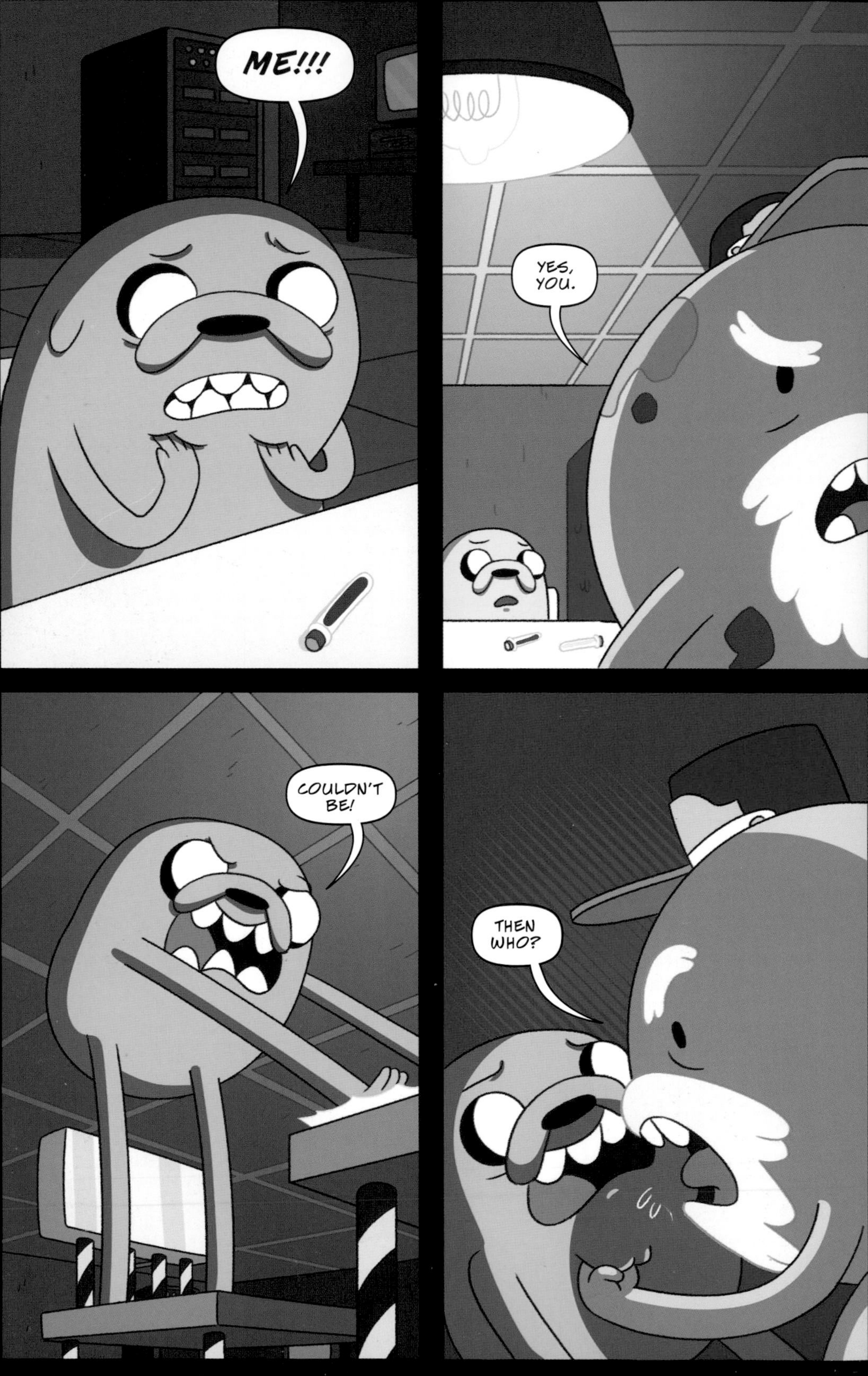
ME!!!
YES, YOU.
COULDN'T BE!
THEN WHO?

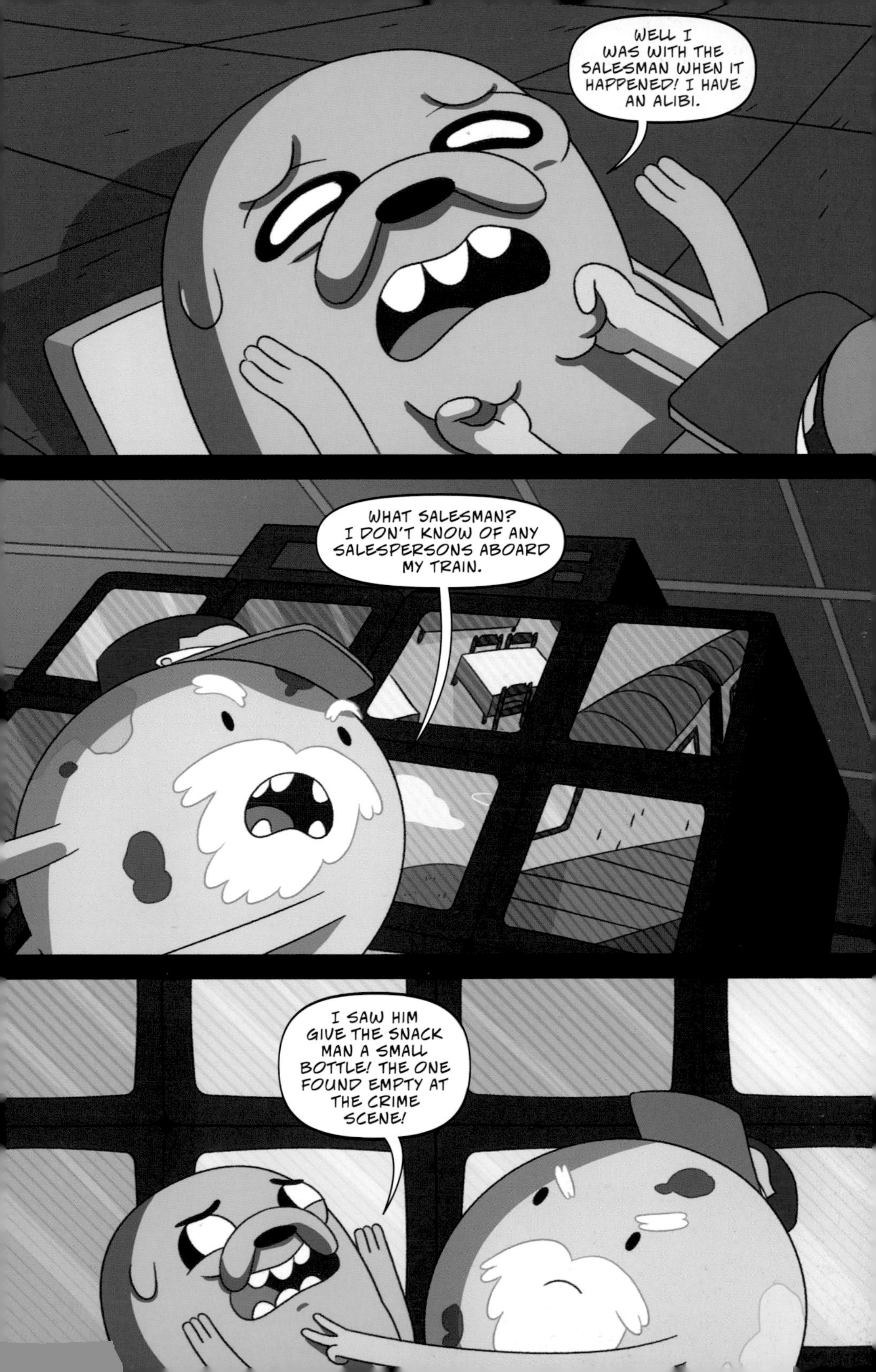
WELL I WAS WITH THE SALESMAN WHEN IT HAPPENED! I HAVE AN ALIBI.
WHAT SALESMAN? I DON'T KNOW OF ANY SALESPERSONS ABOARD MY TRAIN.
I SAW HIM GIVE THE SNACK MAN A SMALL BOTTLE! THE ONE FOUND EMPTY AT THE CRIME SCENE!

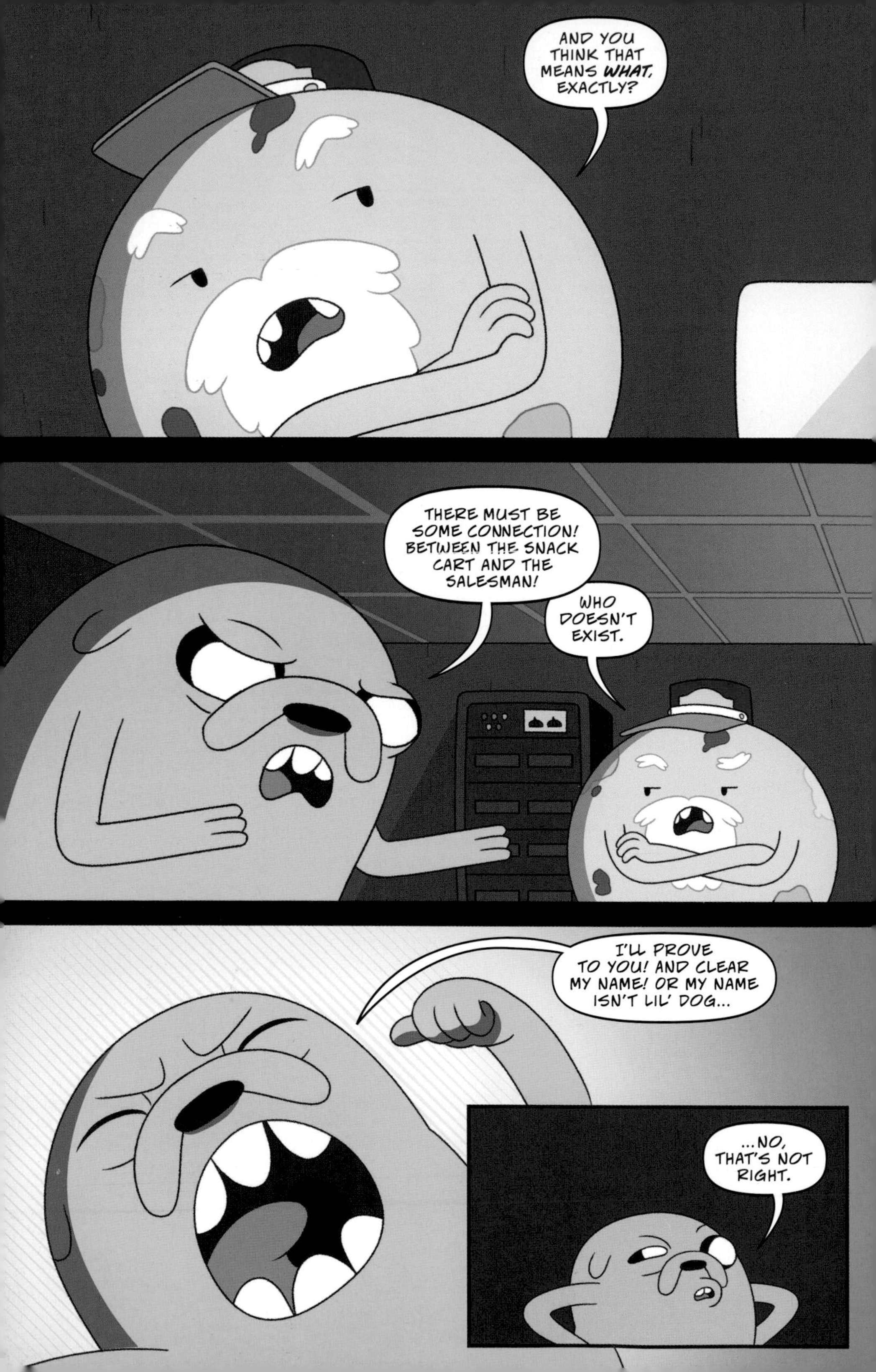
AND YOU THINK THAT MEANS **WHAT**, EXACTLY?
THERE MUST BE SOME CONNECTION! BETWEEN THE SNACK CART AND THE SALESMAN!
WHO DOESN'T EXIST.
I'LL PROVE TO YOU! AND CLEAR MY NAME! OR MY NAME ISN'T LIL' DOG...
...NO, THAT'S NOT RIGHT.

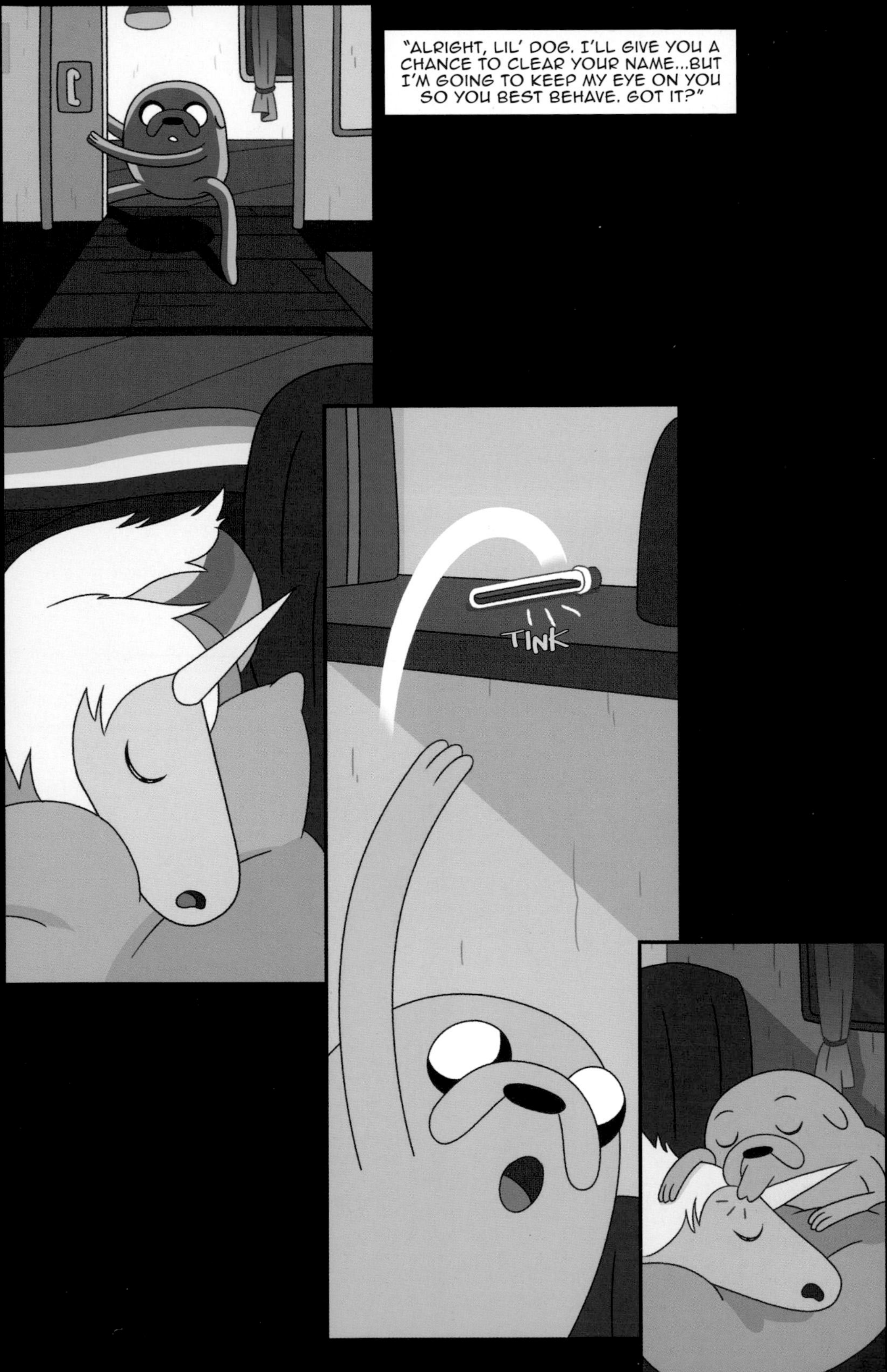
"ALRIGHT, LIL' DOG. I'LL GIVE YOU A CHANCE TO CLEAR YOUR NAME...BUT I'M GOING TO KEEP MY EYE ON YOU SO YOU BEST BEHAVE. GOT IT?"
TINK

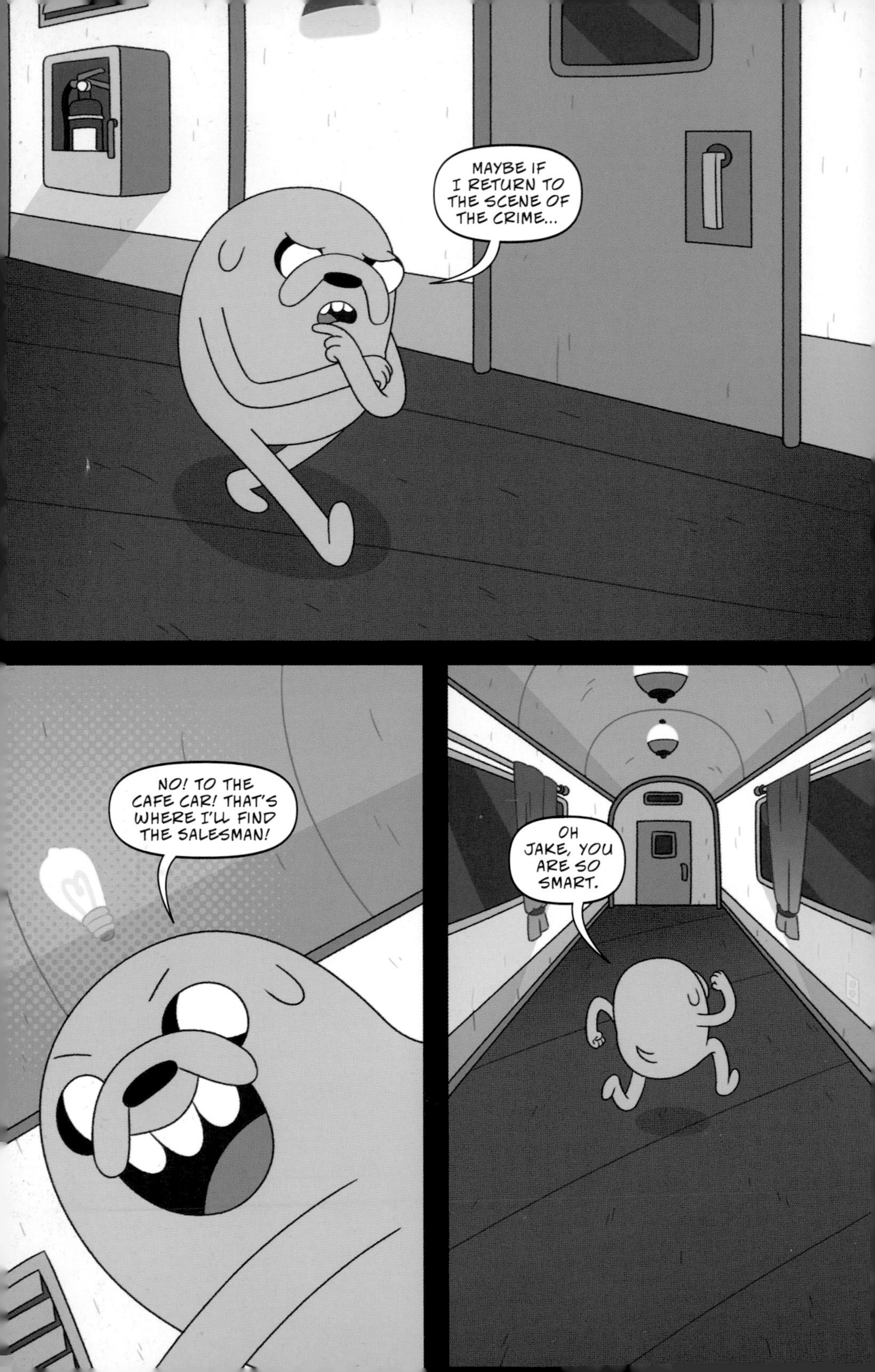
MAYBE IF I RETURN TO THE SCENE OF THE CRIME...
NO! TO THE CAFE CAR! THAT'S WHERE I'LL FIND THE SALESMAN!
OH JAKE, YOU ARE SO SMART.

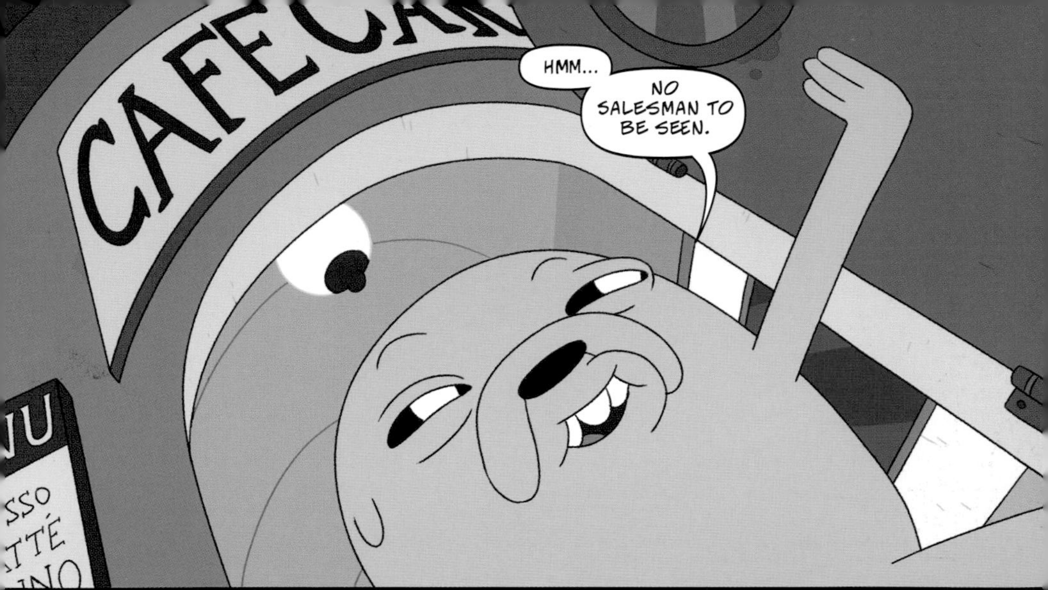
HMM...
NO SALESMAN TO BE SEEN.

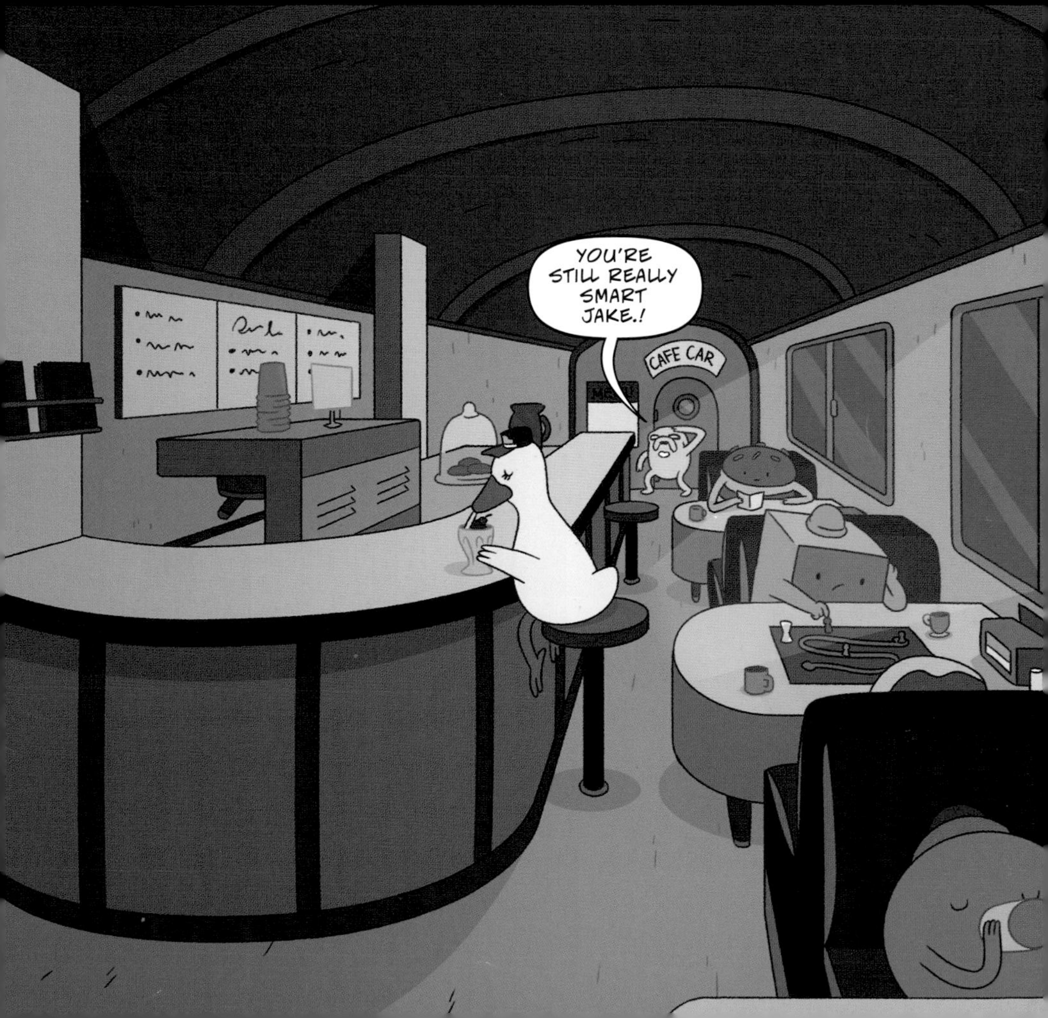
YOU'RE STILL REALLY SMART JAKE.!
CAFE CAR

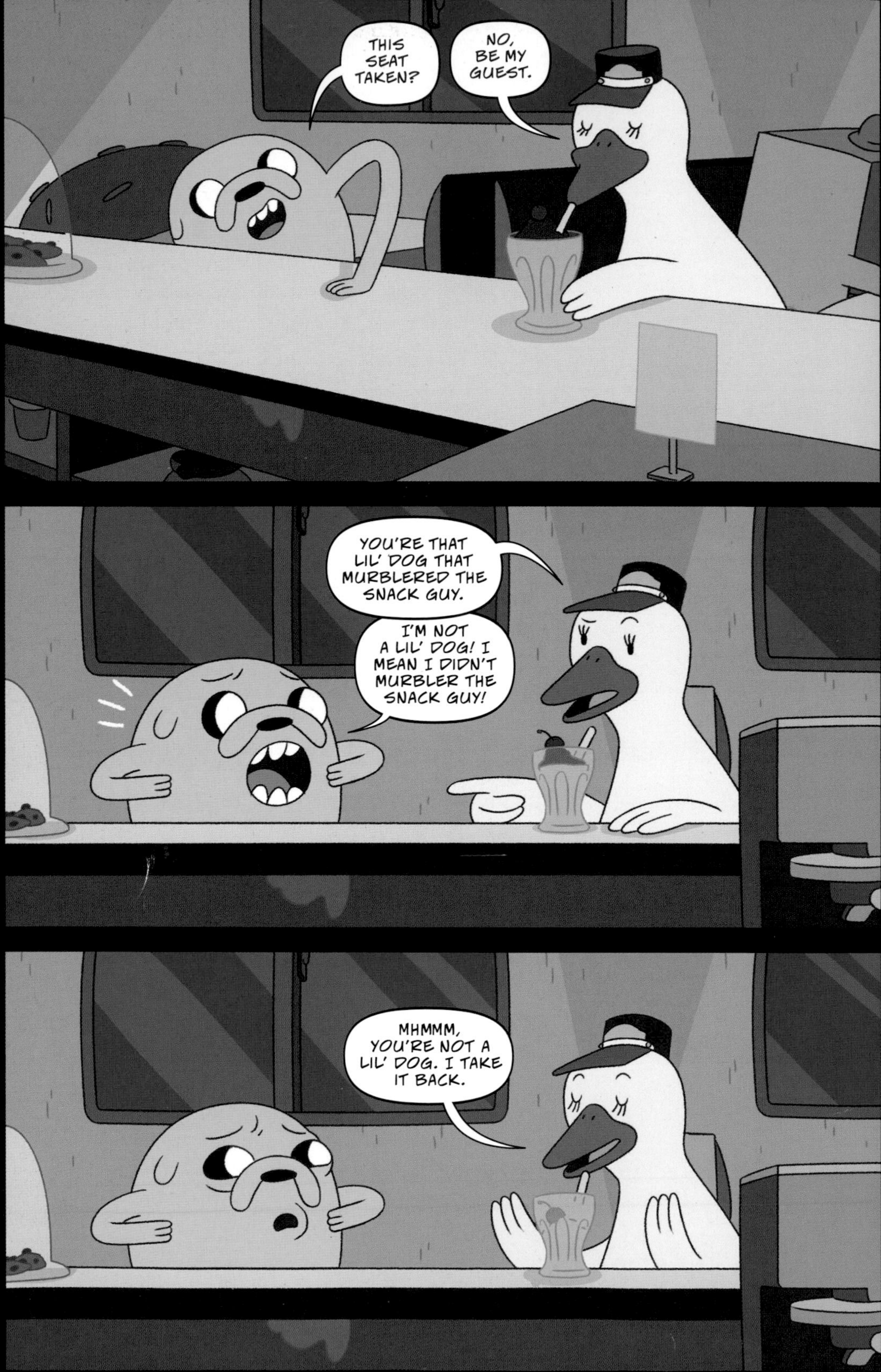
THIS SEAT TAKEN?
NO, BE MY GUEST.
YOU'RE THAT LIL' DOG THAT MURBLERED THE SNACK GUY.
I'M NOT A LIL' DOG! I MEAN I DIDN'T MURBLER THE SNACK GUY!
MHMMM, YOU'RE NOT A LIL' DOG. I TAKE IT BACK.

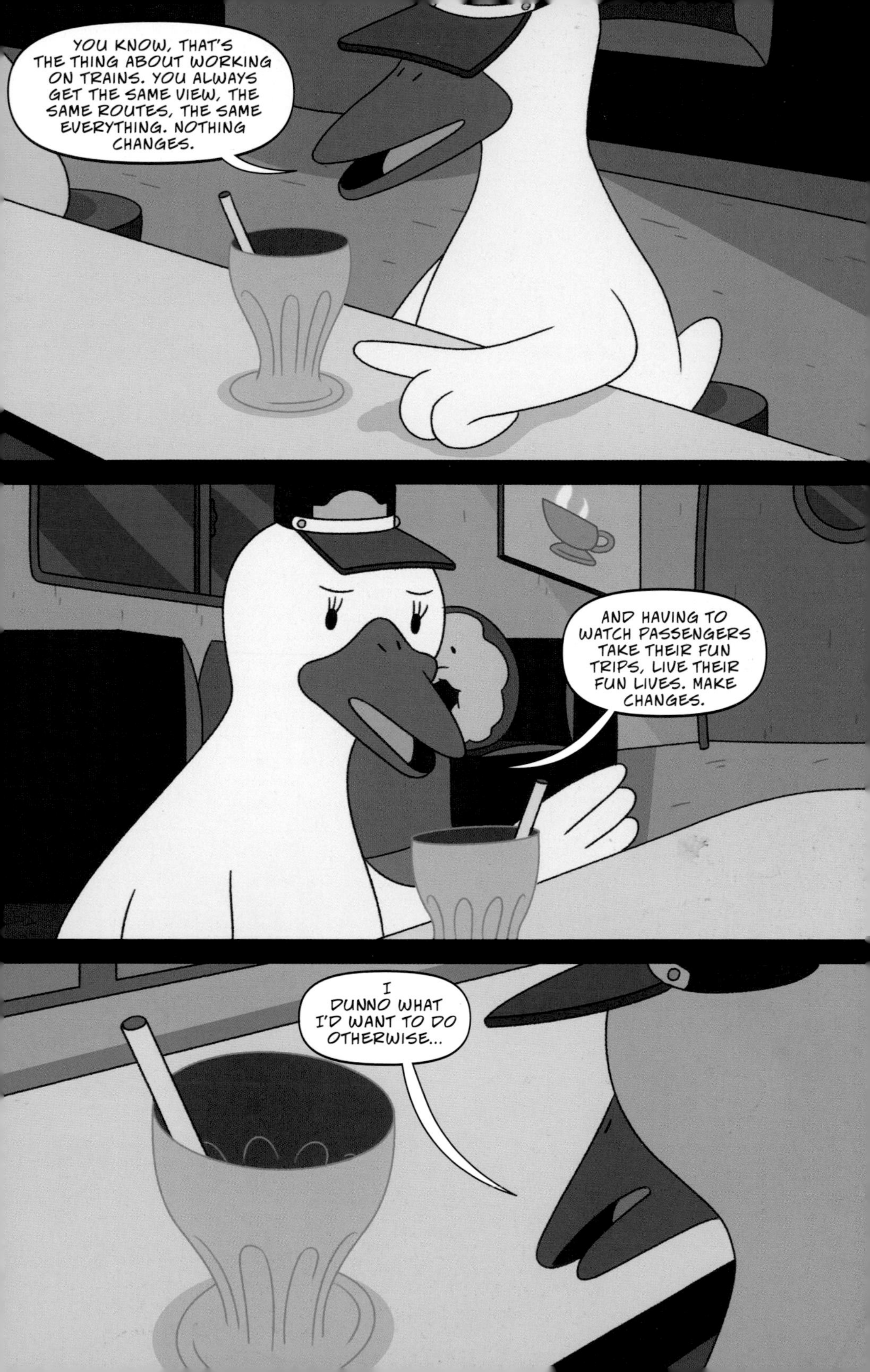
YOU KNOW, THAT'S THE THING ABOUT WORKING ON TRAINS. YOU ALWAYS GET THE SAME VIEW, THE SAME ROUTES, THE SAME EVERYTHING. NOTHING CHANGES.
AND HAVING TO WATCH PASSENGERS TAKE THEIR FUN TRIPS, LIVE THEIR FUN LIVES. MAKE CHANGES.
I DUNNO WHAT I'D WANT TO DO OTHERWISE...

...BUT SOMETIMES YOU JUST WANT SOMETHING SO BADLY BUT HAVE NO IDEA WHAT THAT EVEN LOOKS LIKE.

FOR A WHILE, THE WEIRD THINGS THAT HAPPEN ONBOARD GAVE ME SOME EXCITEMENT.

WEIRD THINGS?

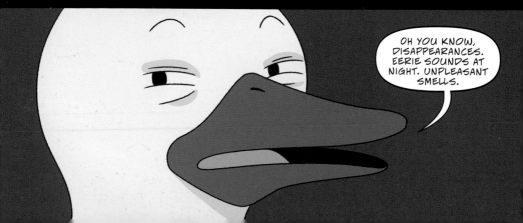

OH YOU KNOW, DISAPPEARANCES. EERIE SOUNDS AT NIGHT. UNPLEASANT SMELLS.

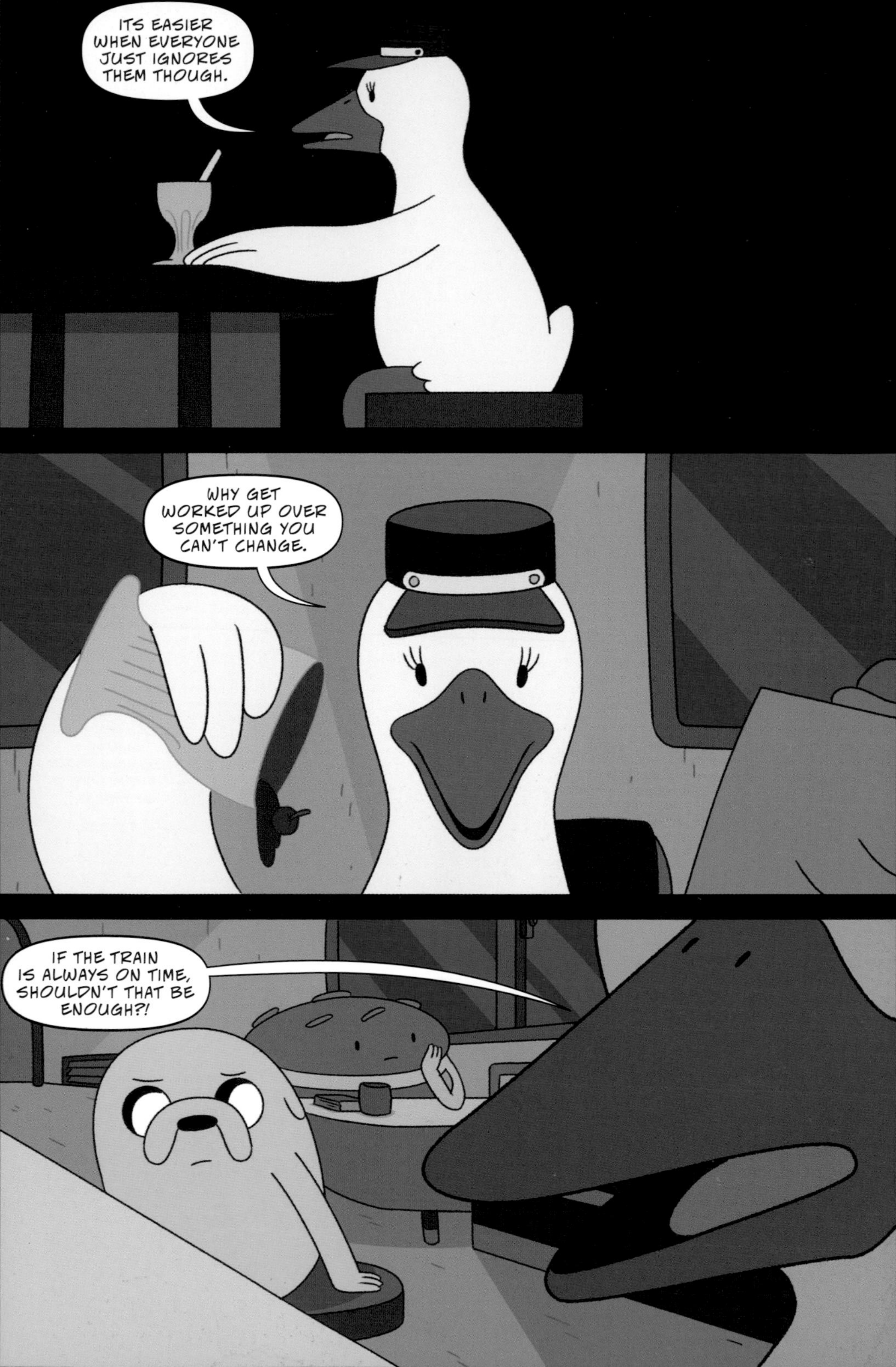
ITS EASIER WHEN EVERYONE JUST IGNORES THEM THOUGH.
WHY GET WORKED UP OVER SOMETHING YOU CAN'T CHANGE.
IF THE TRAIN IS ALWAYS ON TIME, SHOULDN'T THAT BE ENOUGH?!

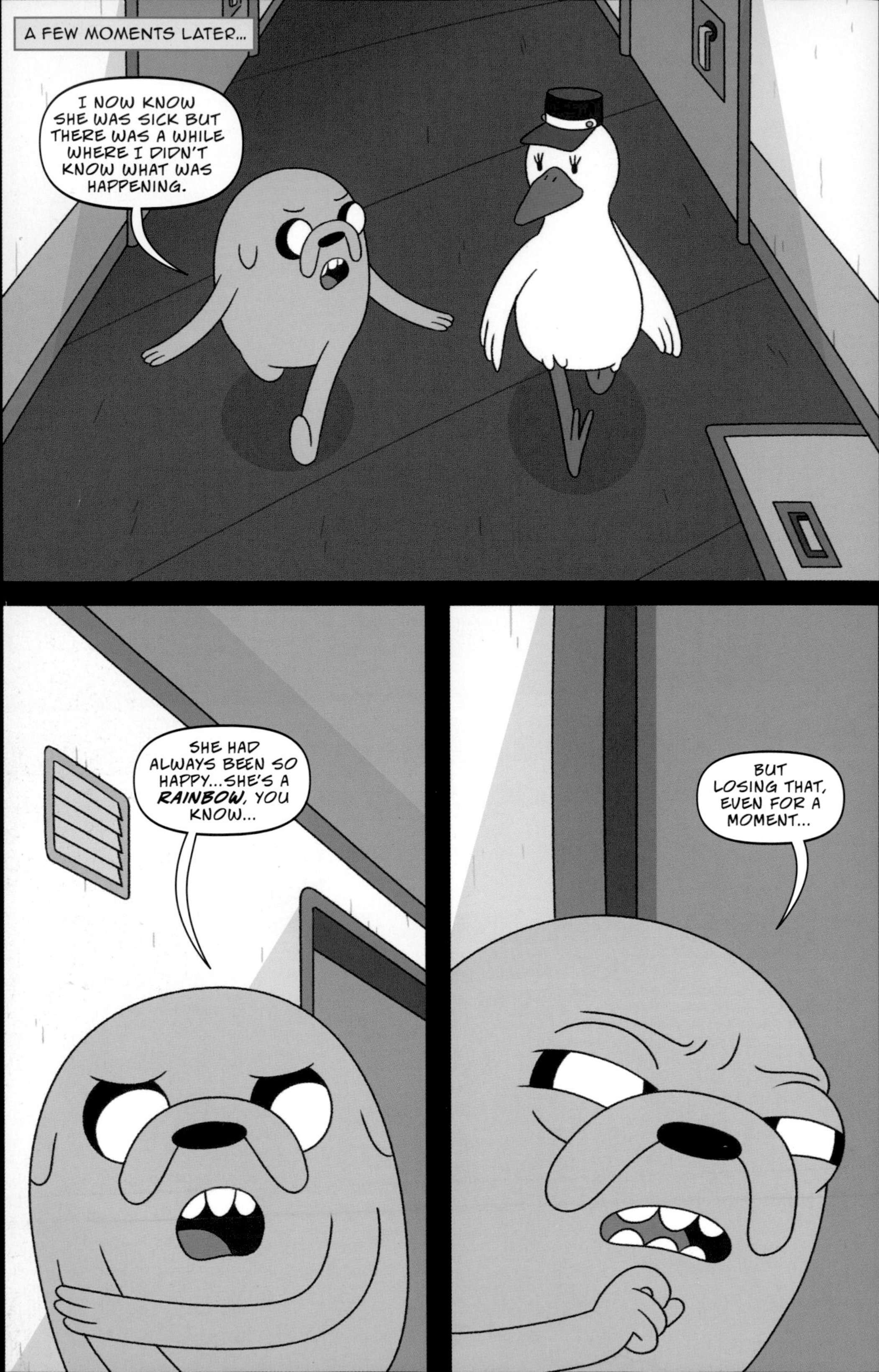
A FEW MOMENTS LATER...
I NOW KNOW SHE WAS SICK BUT THERE WAS A WHILE WHERE I DIDN'T KNOW WHAT WAS HAPPENING.
SHE HAD ALWAYS BEEN SO HAPPY...SHE'S A *RAINBOW*, YOU KNOW...
BUT LOSING THAT, EVEN FOR A MOMENT...

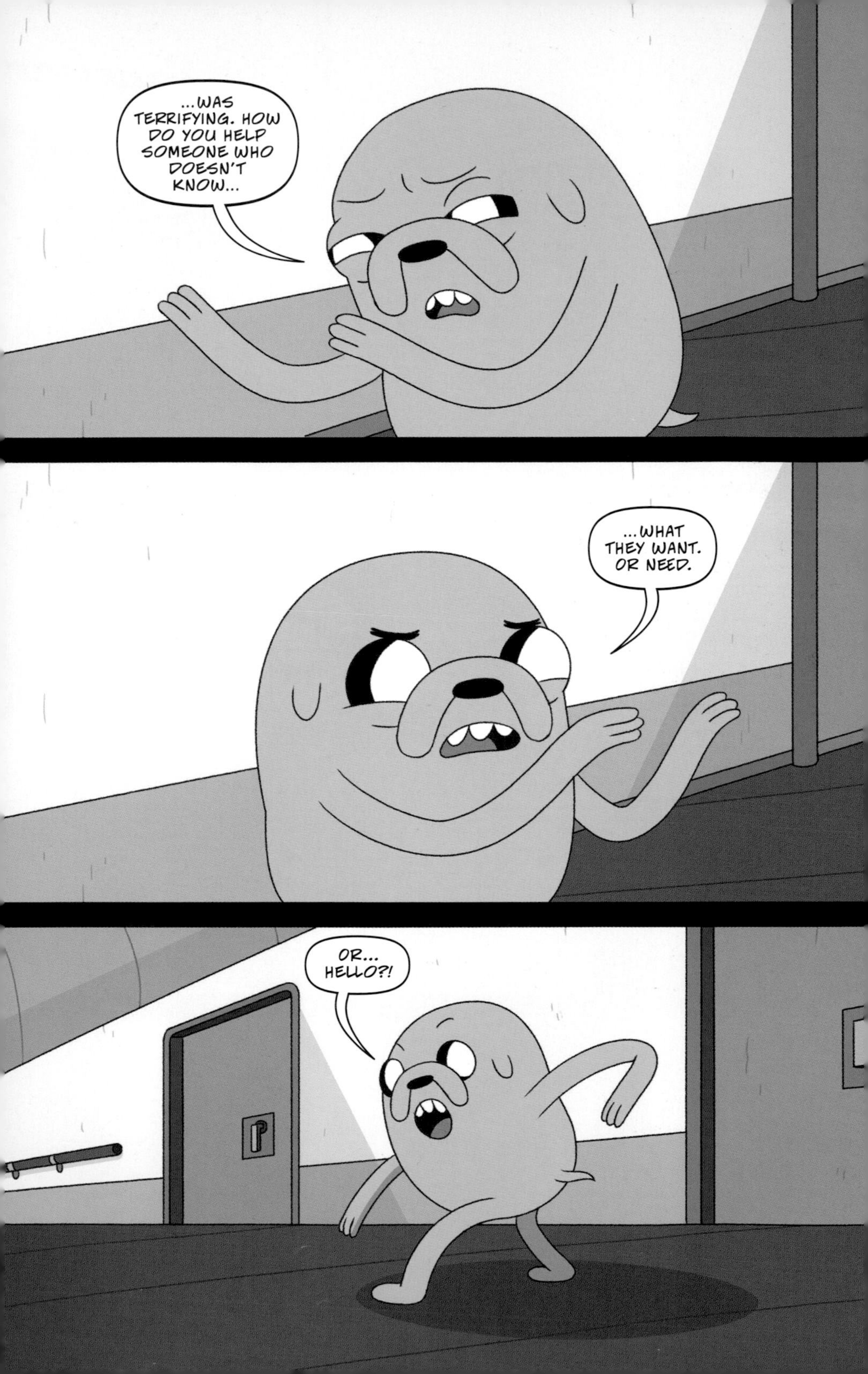
...WAS TERRIFYING. HOW DO YOU HELP SOMEONE WHO DOESN'T KNOW...
...WHAT THEY WANT. OR NEED.
OR... HELLO?!

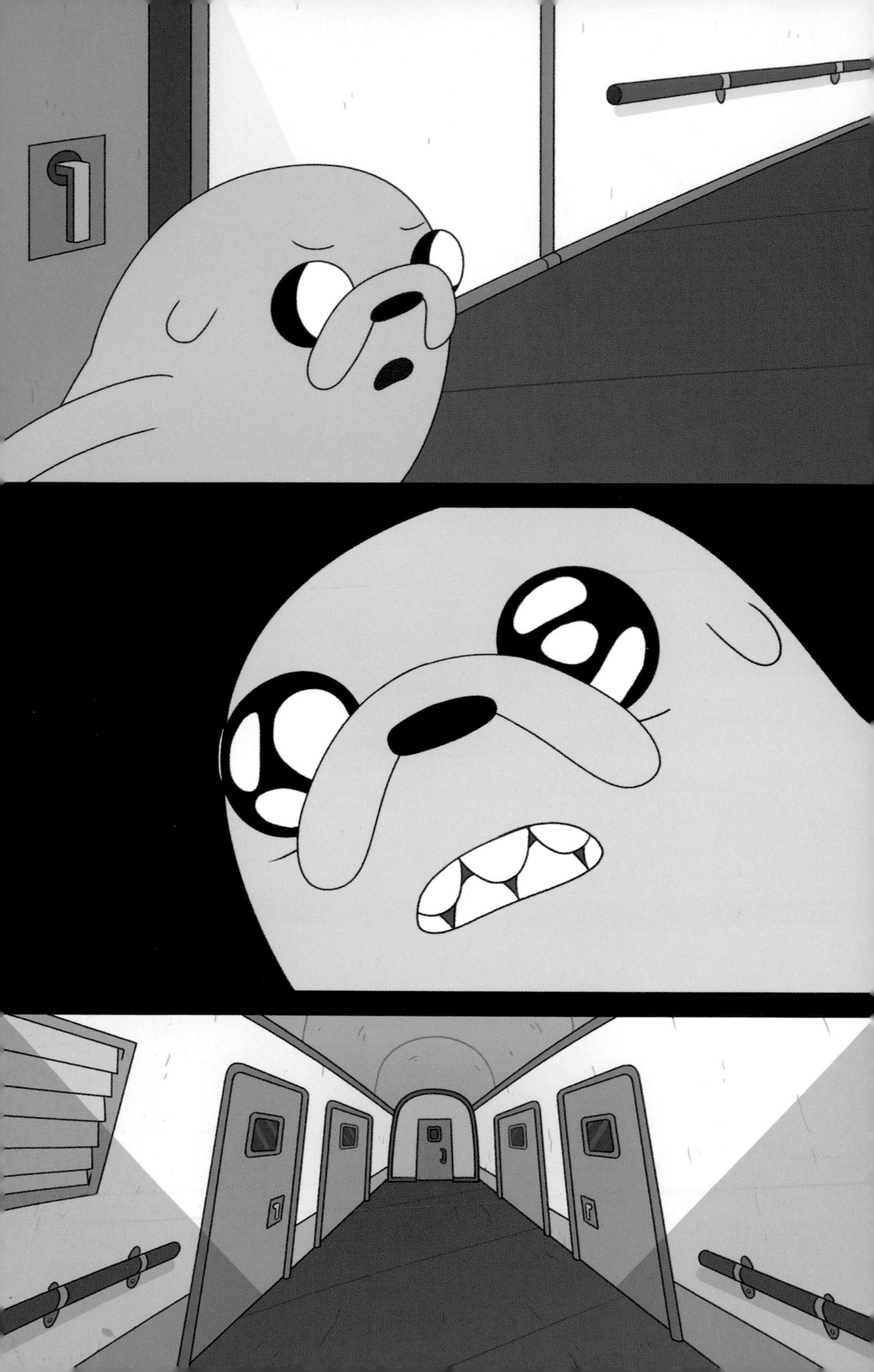

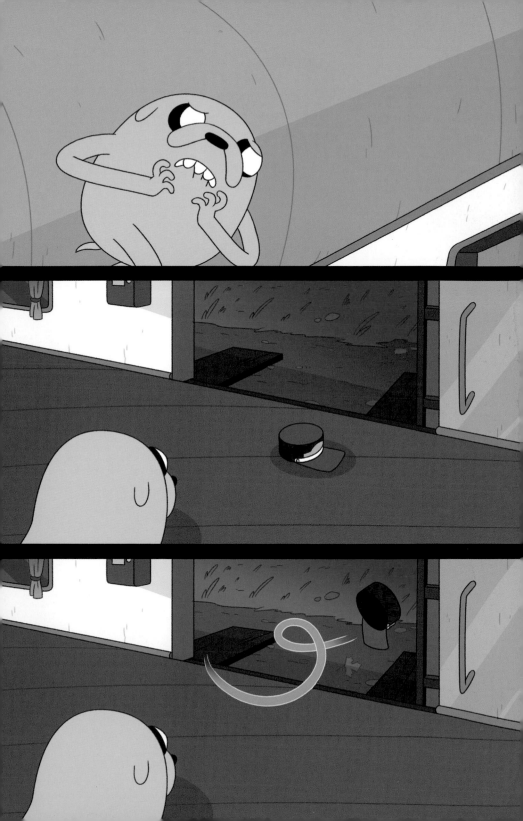

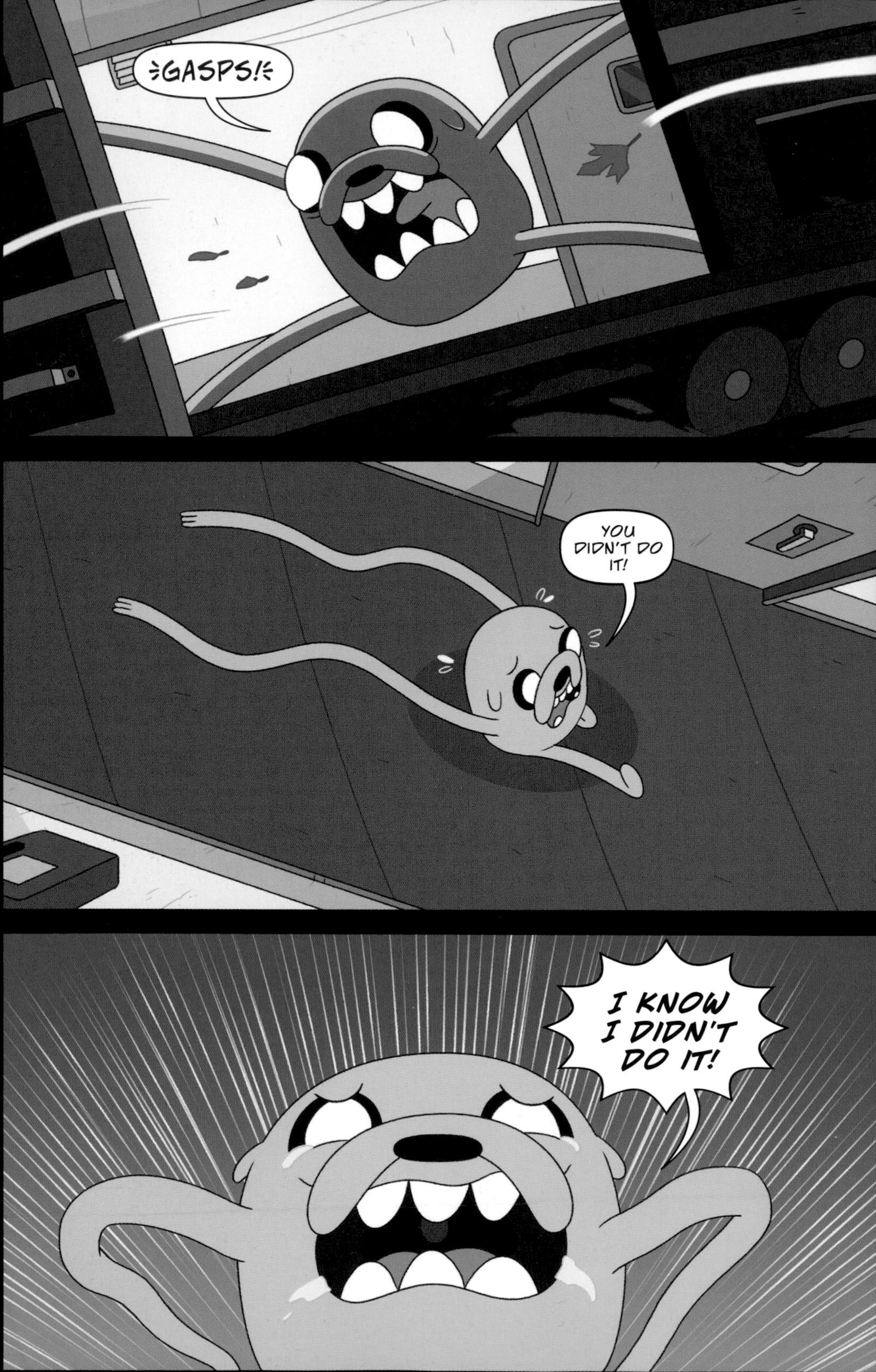
GASPS!
YOU DIDN'T DO IT!
I KNOW I DIDN'T DO IT!

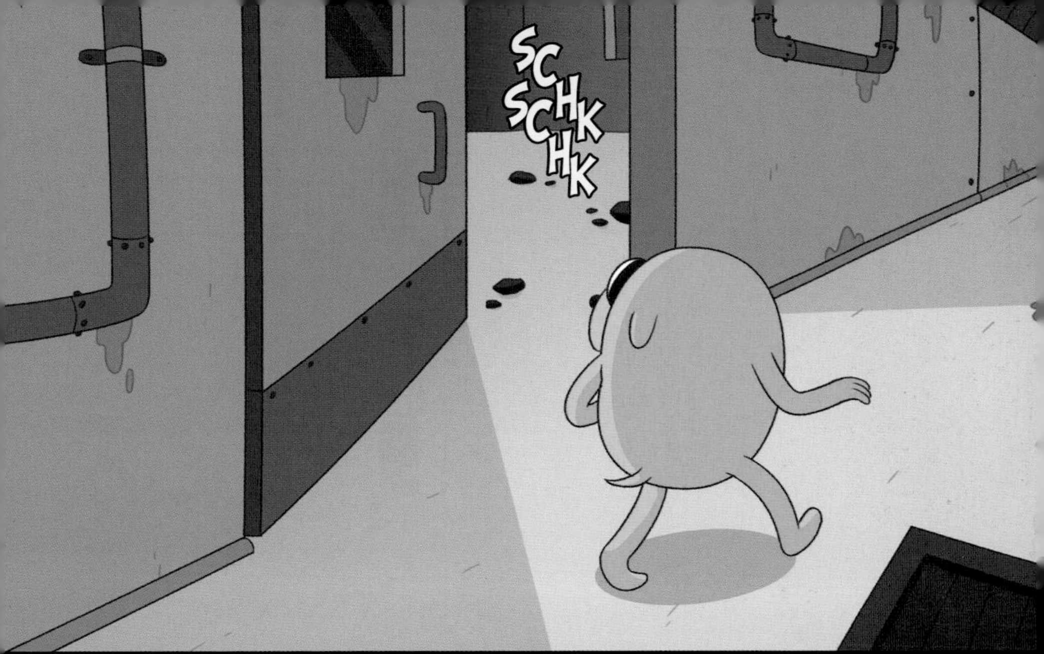
SCHK SCHK

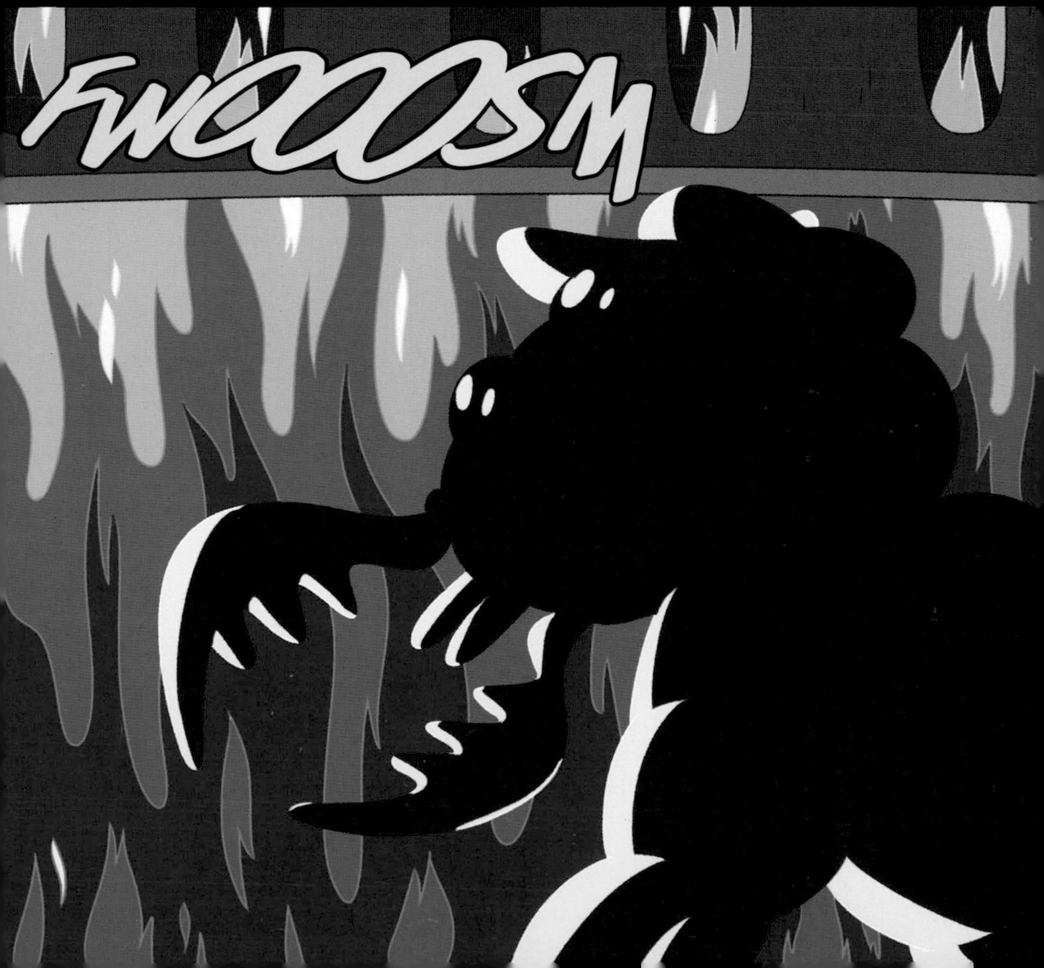
FWOOOSM

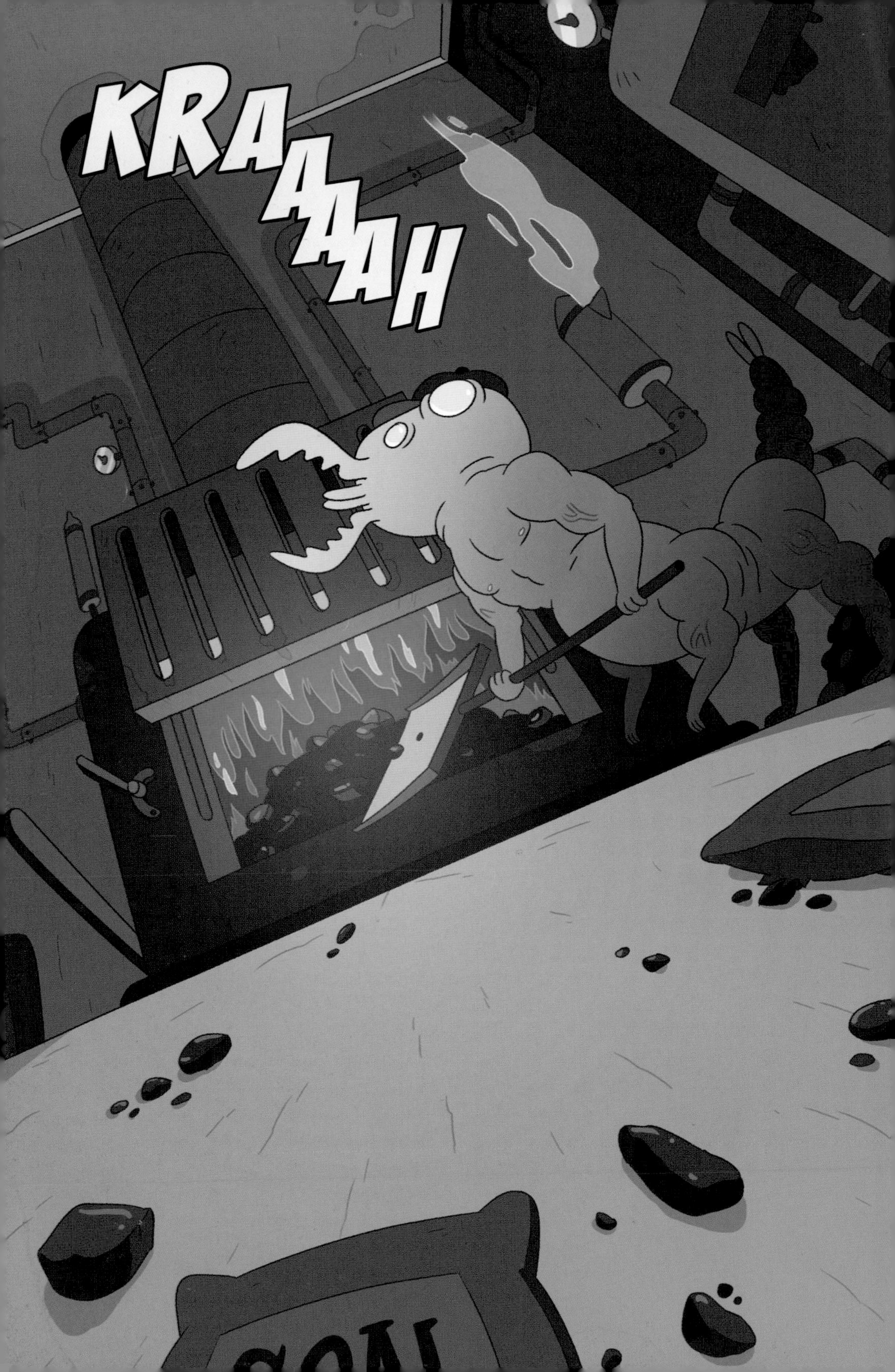
KRAAAAAH

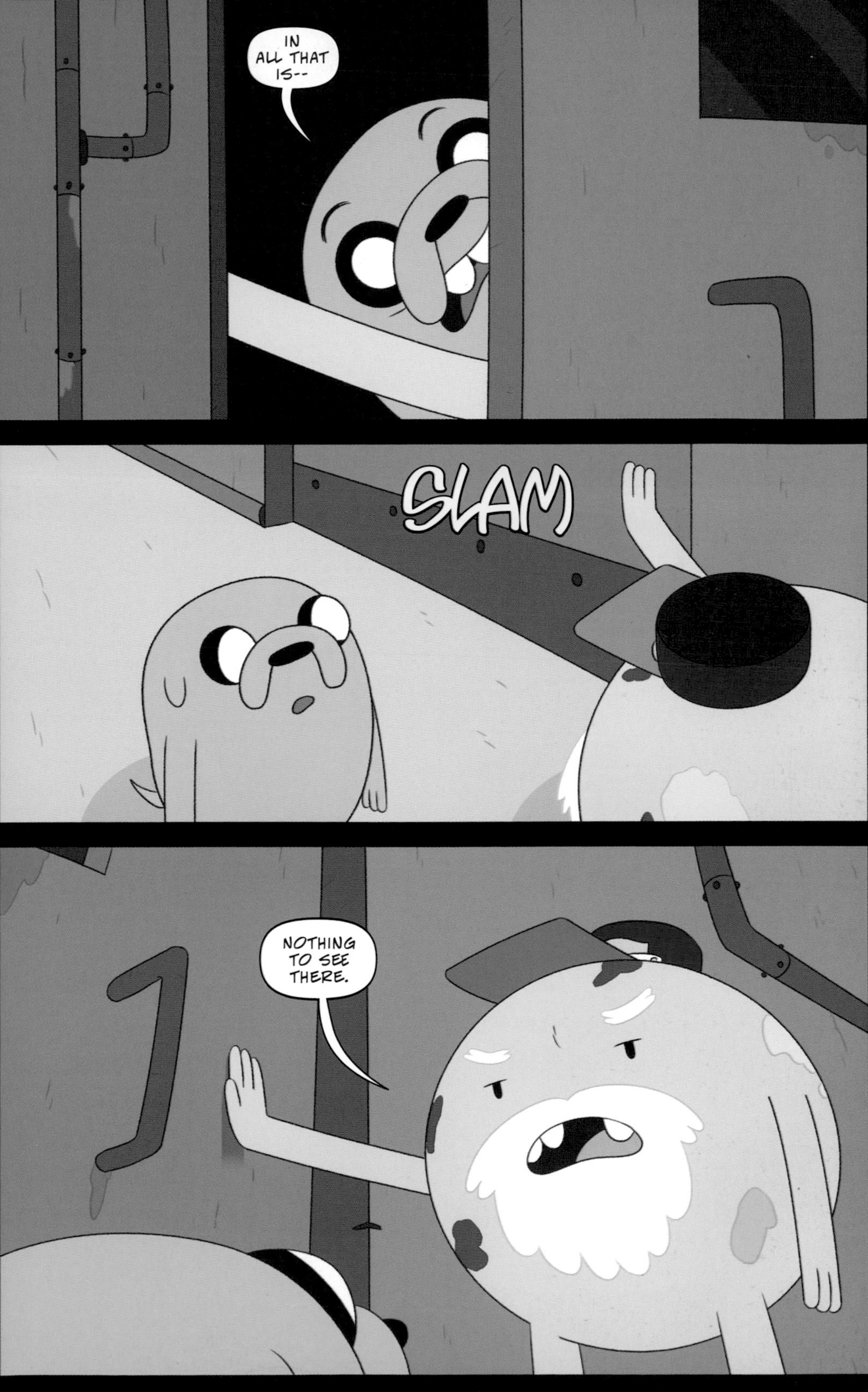
IN ALL THAT IS--
SLAM
NOTHING TO SEE THERE.

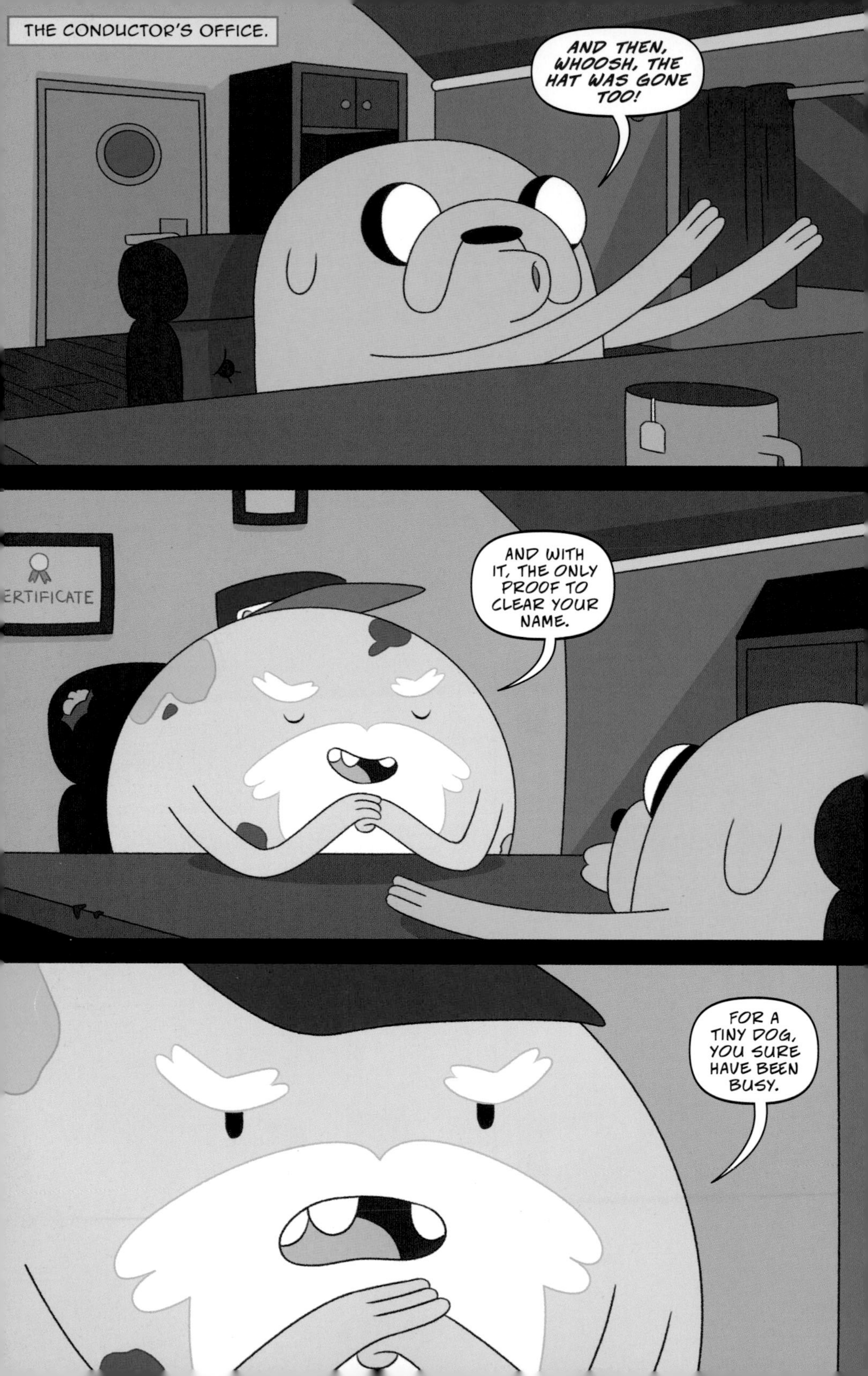
THE CONDUCTOR'S OFFICE.
AND THEN, WHOOSH, THE HAT WAS GONE TOO!
ERTIFICATE
AND WITH IT, THE ONLY PROOF TO CLEAR YOUR NAME.
FOR A TINY DOG, YOU SURE HAVE BEEN BUSY.

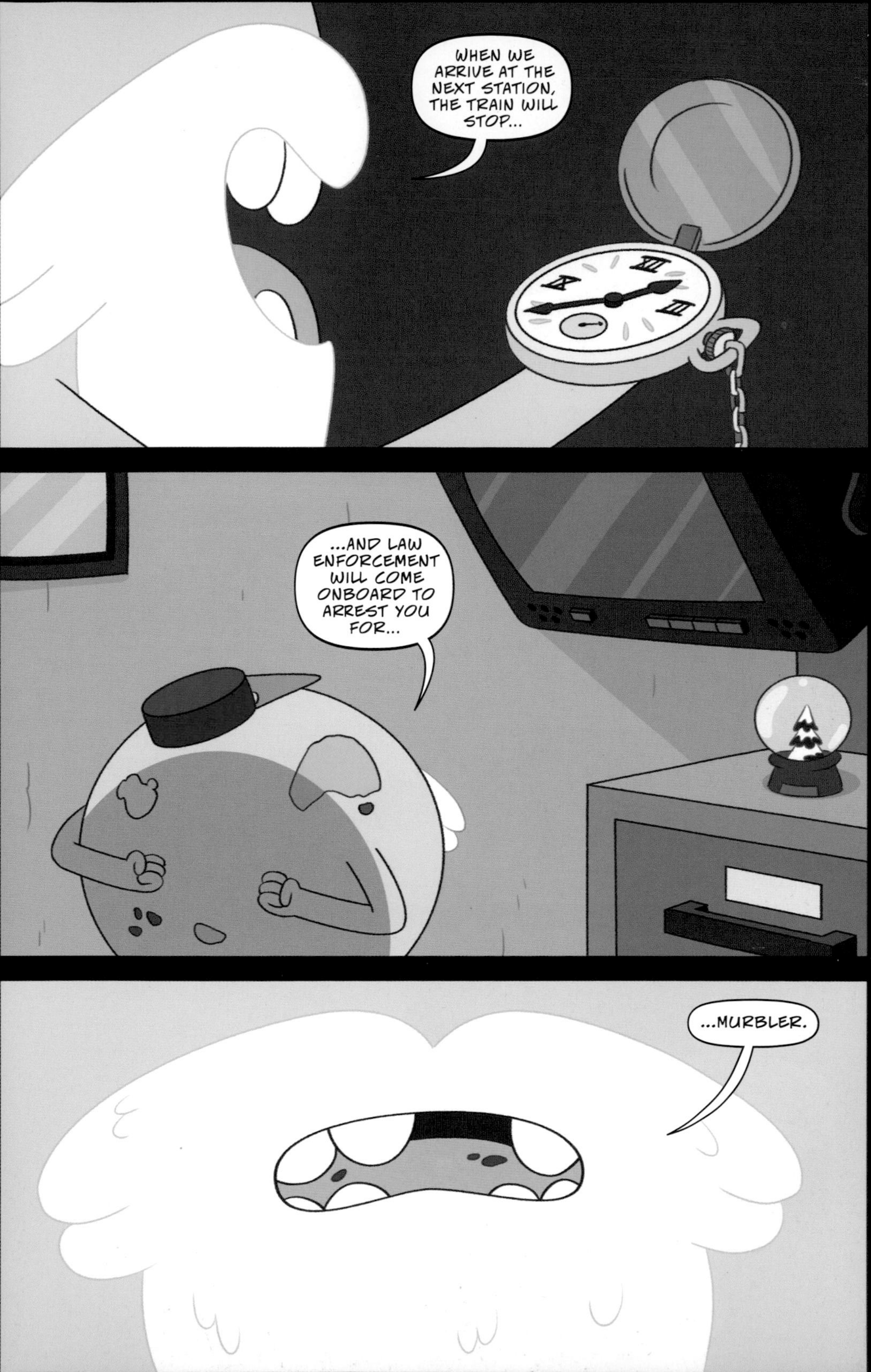
WHEN WE ARRIVE AT THE NEXT STATION, THE TRAIN WILL STOP...
...AND LAW ENFORCEMENT WILL COME ONBOARD TO ARREST YOU FOR...
...MURBLER.

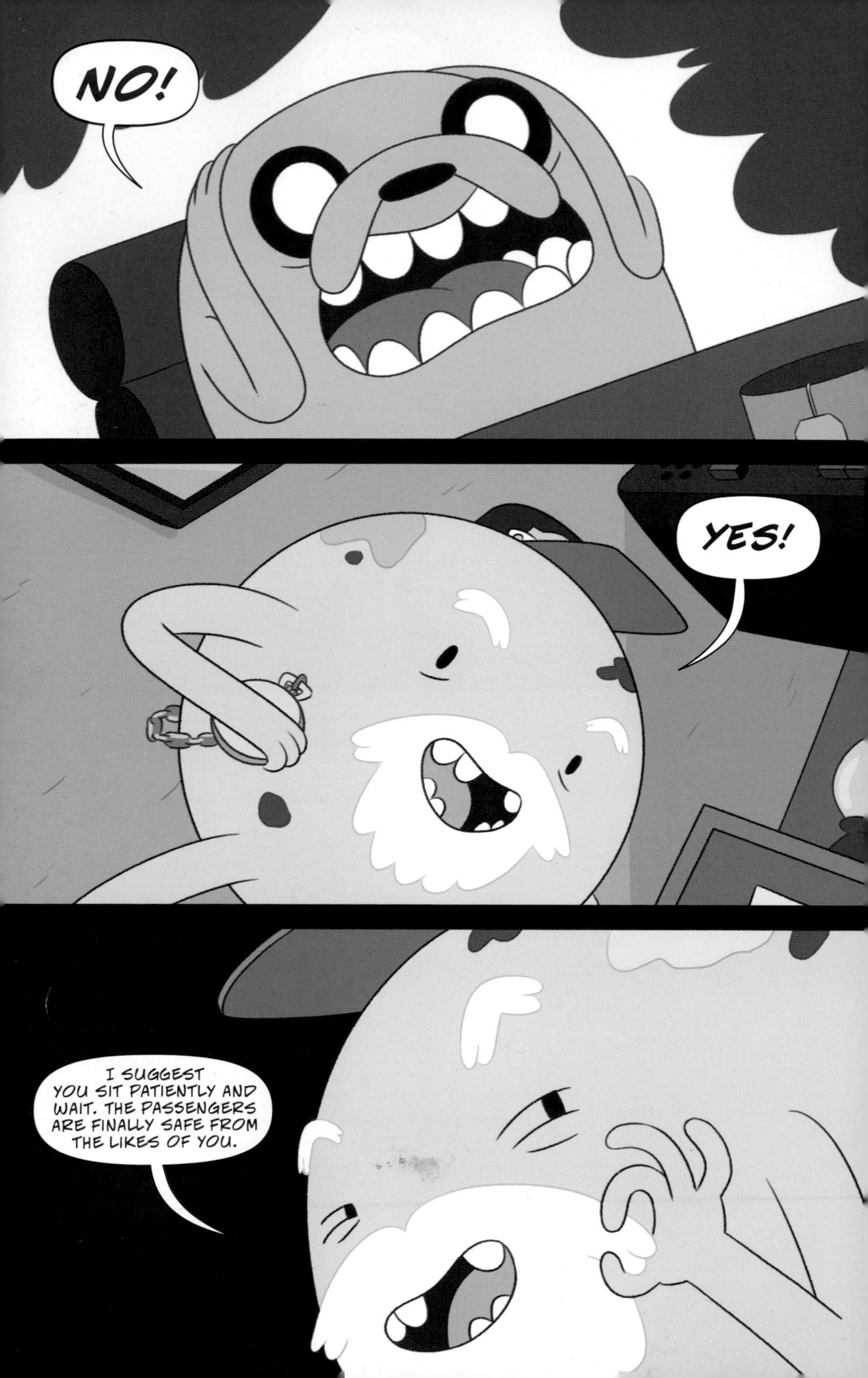
NO!
YES!
I SUGGEST YOU SIT PATIENTLY AND WAIT. THE PASSENGERS ARE FINALLY SAFE FROM THE LIKES OF YOU.

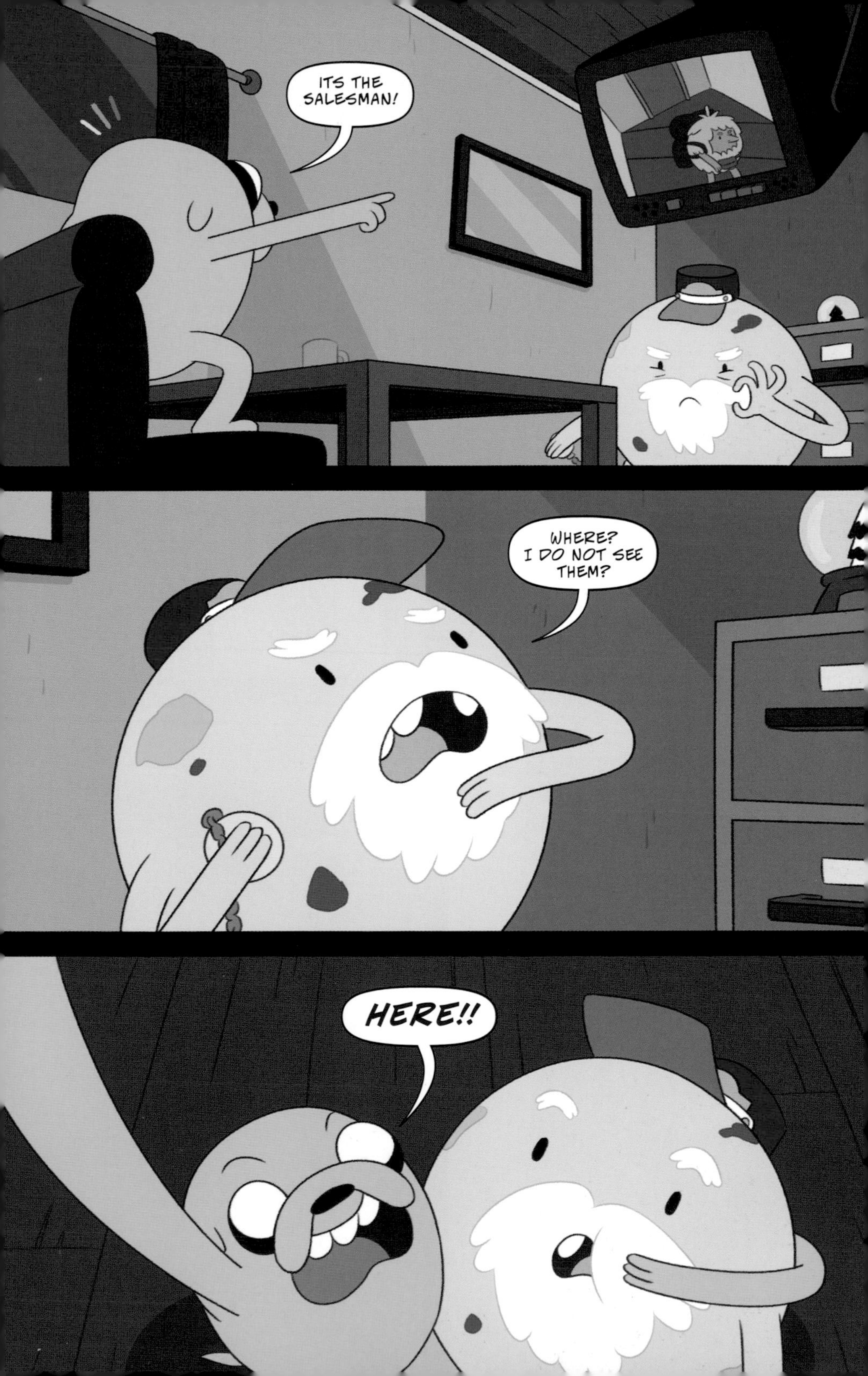
ITS THE SALESMAN!
WHERE? I DO NOT SEE THEM?
HERE!!

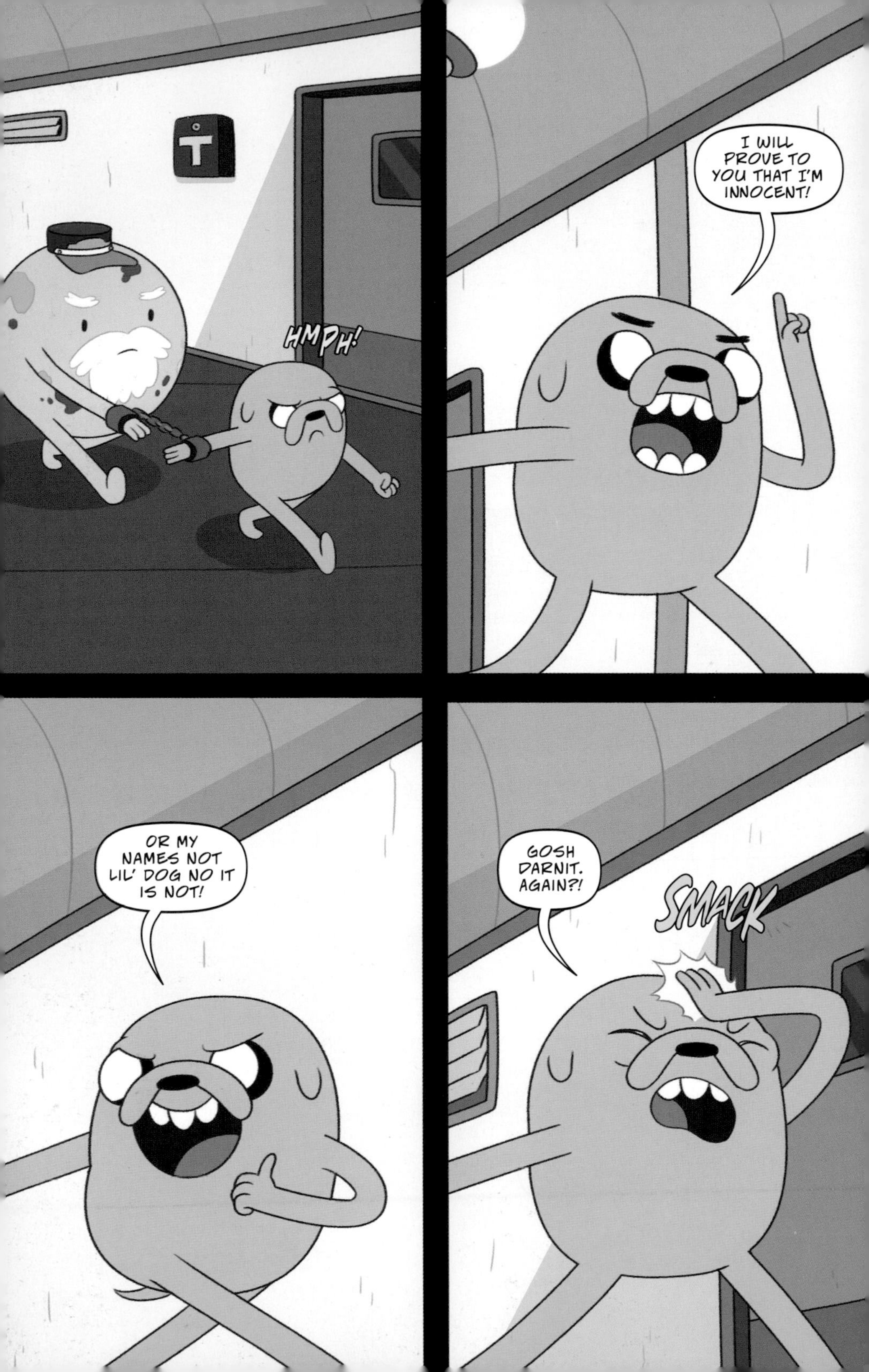
HMPH!
I WILL PROVE TO YOU THAT I'M INNOCENT!
OR MY NAMES NOT LIL' DOG NO IT IS NOT!
GOSH DARNIT. AGAIN?!
SMACK

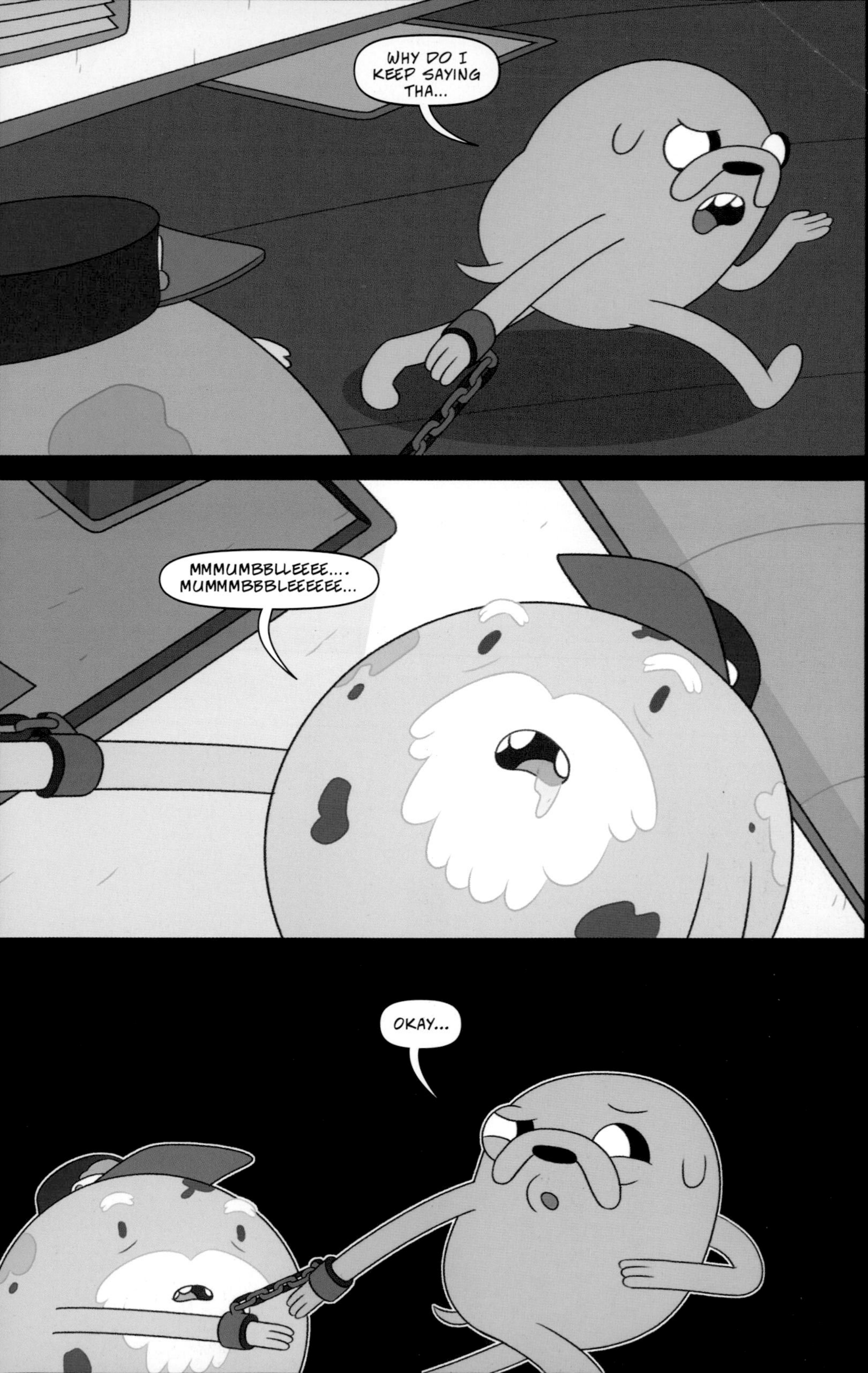
WHY DO I KEEP SAYING THA...
MMMUMBBLLEEEE.... MUMMMBBBLEEEEEE...
OKAY...

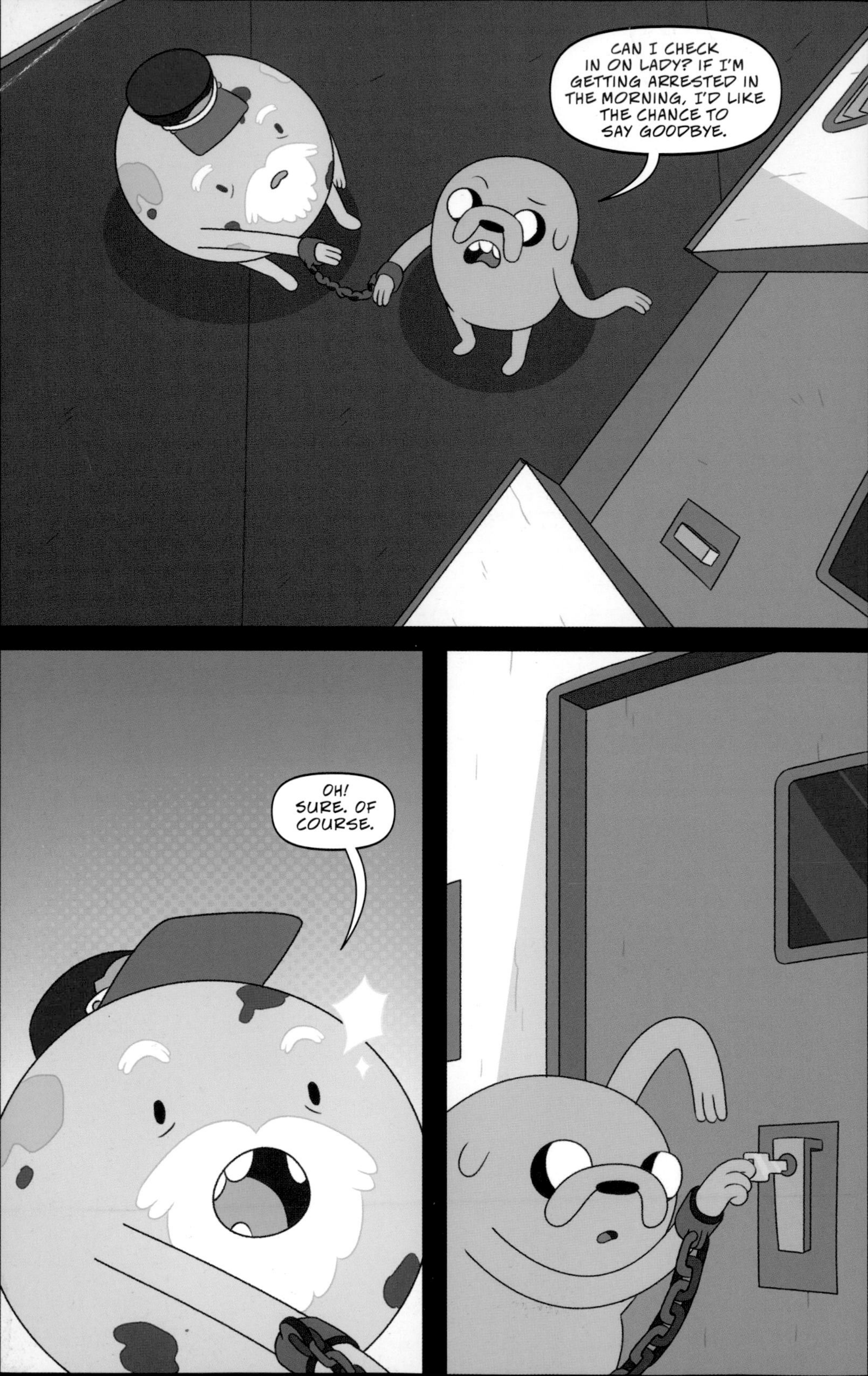
CAN I CHECK IN ON LADY? IF I'M GETTING ARRESTED IN THE MORNING, I'D LIKE THE CHANCE TO SAY GOODBYE.
OH! SURE. OF COURSE.

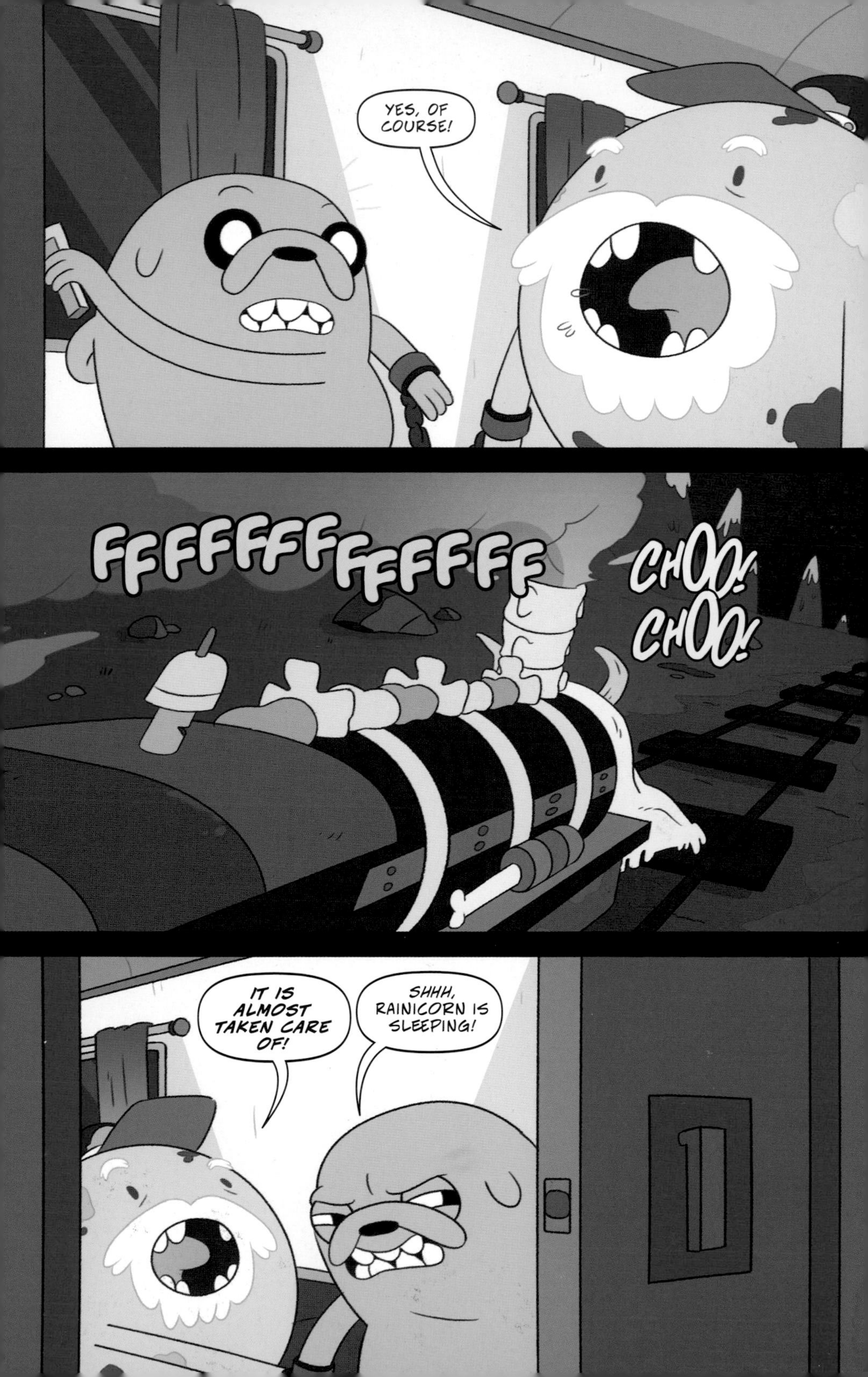
YES, OF COURSE!
FFFFFFFFFFFFF
CHOO! CHOO!
IT IS ALMOST TAKEN CARE OF!
SHHH, RAINICORN IS SLEEPING!
1

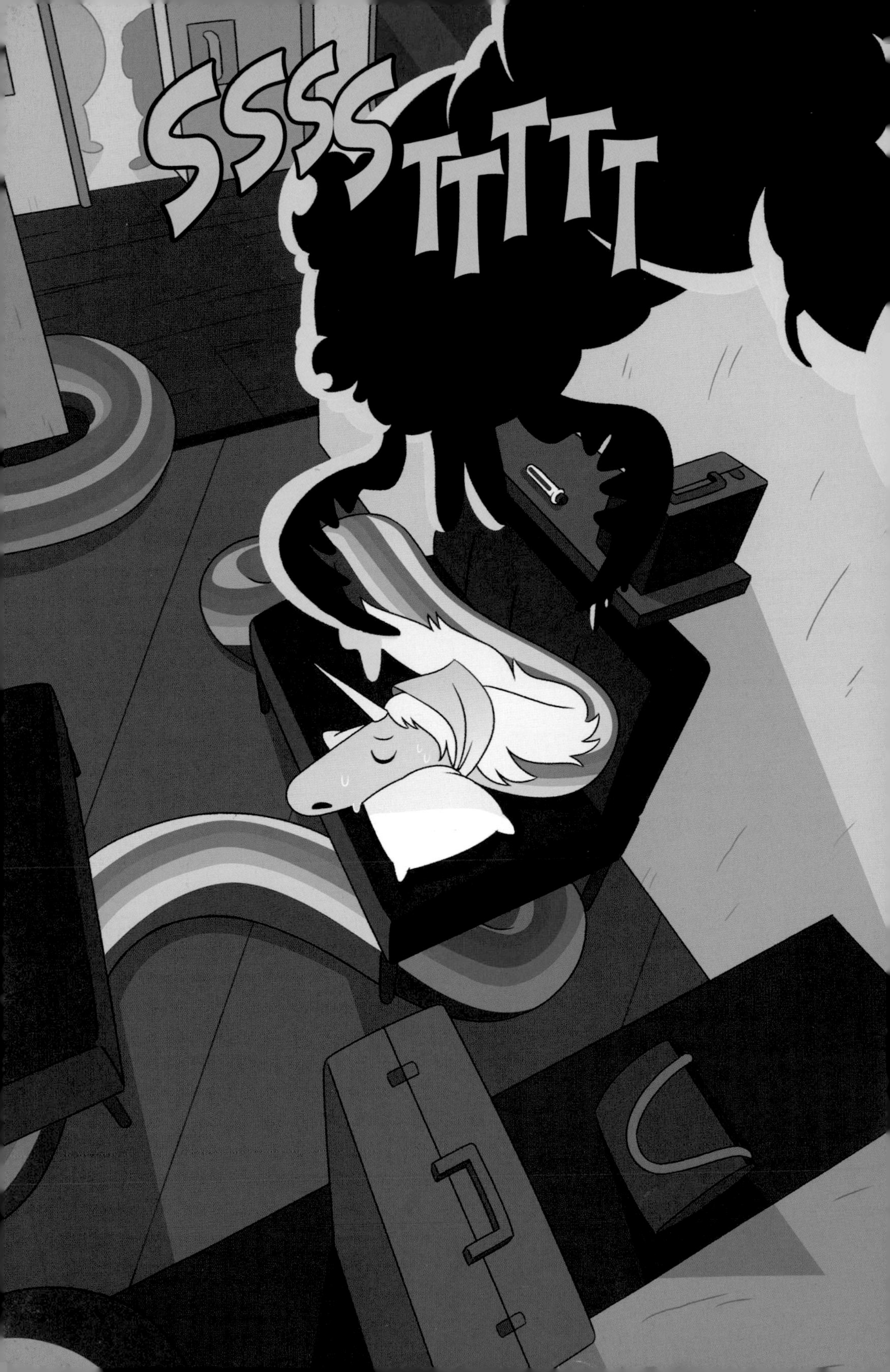
SSSSTTTTT

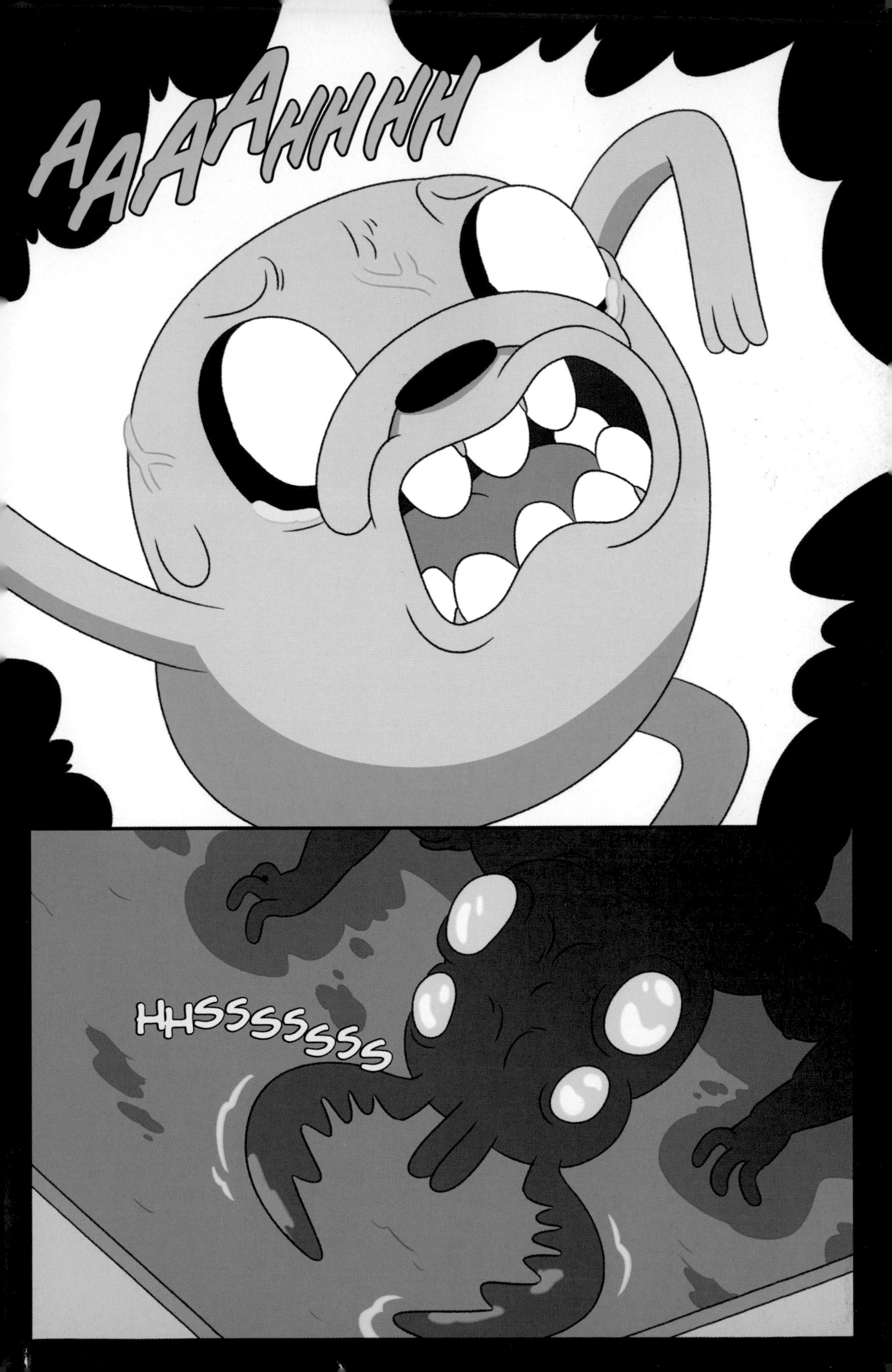
AAAAHHHHH
HHSSSSSSSSS

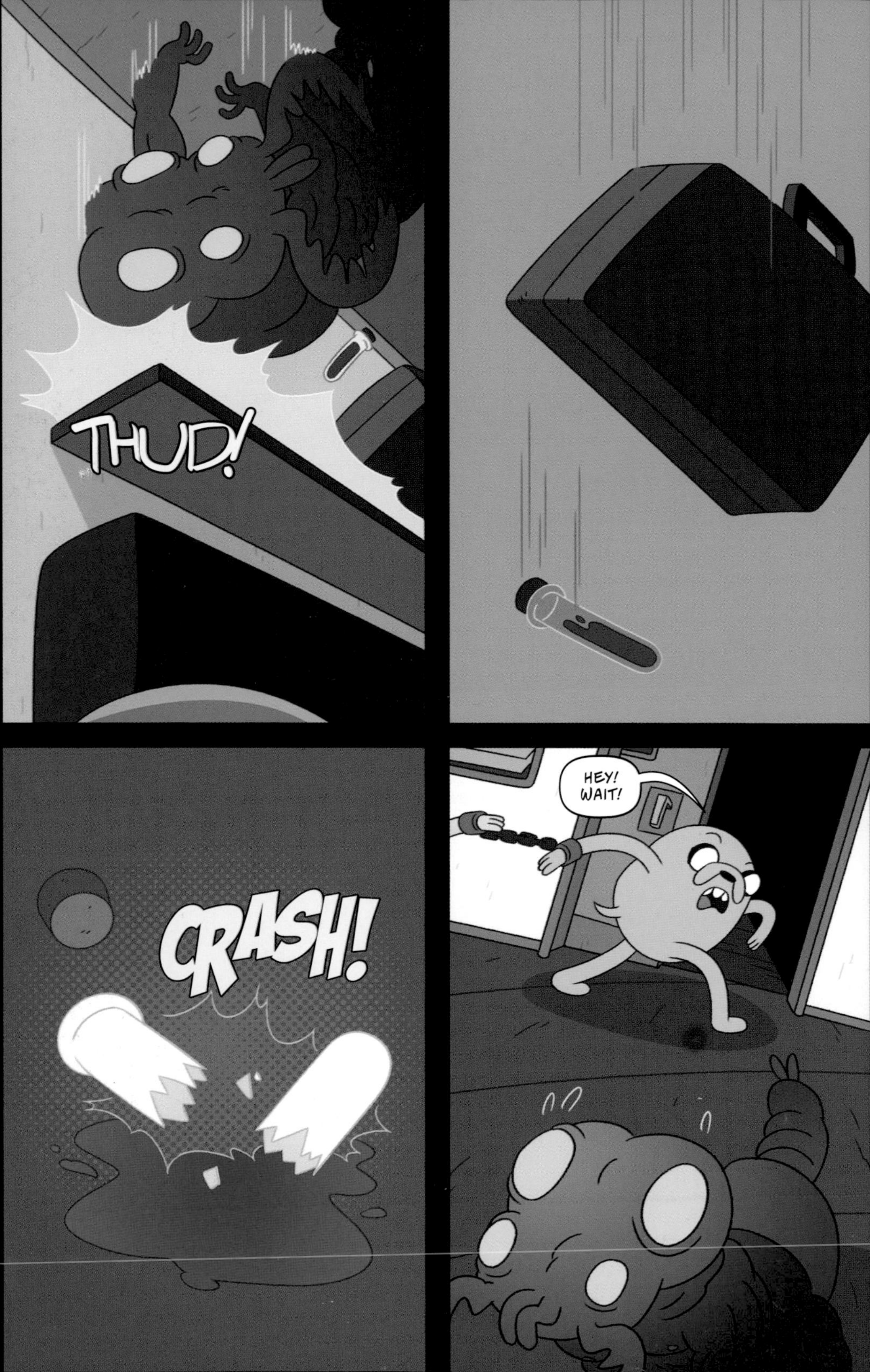
THUD!
CRASH!
HEY!
WAIT!

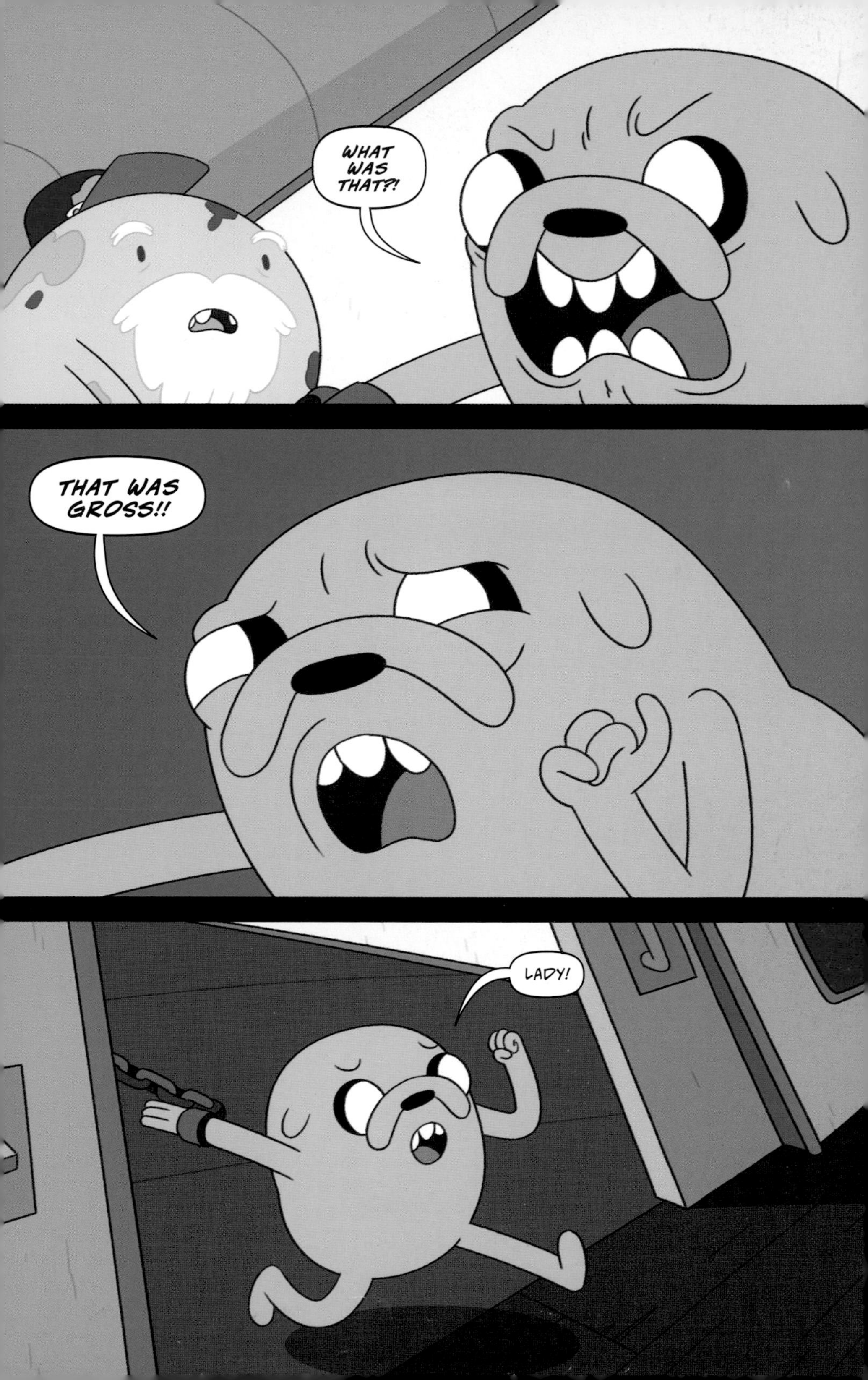
WHAT WAS THAT?!
THAT WAS GROSS!!
LADY!

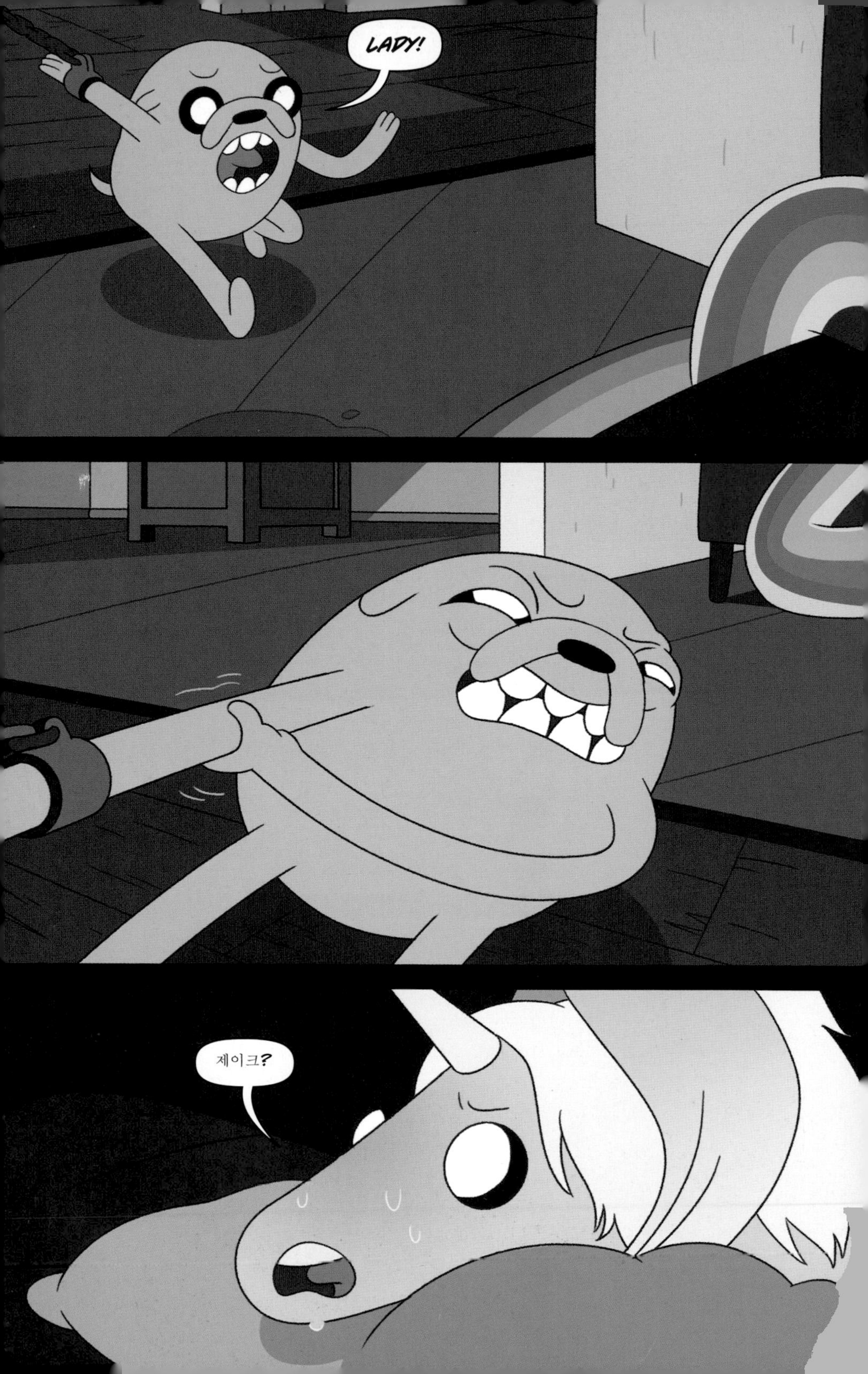
LADY!
제이크?

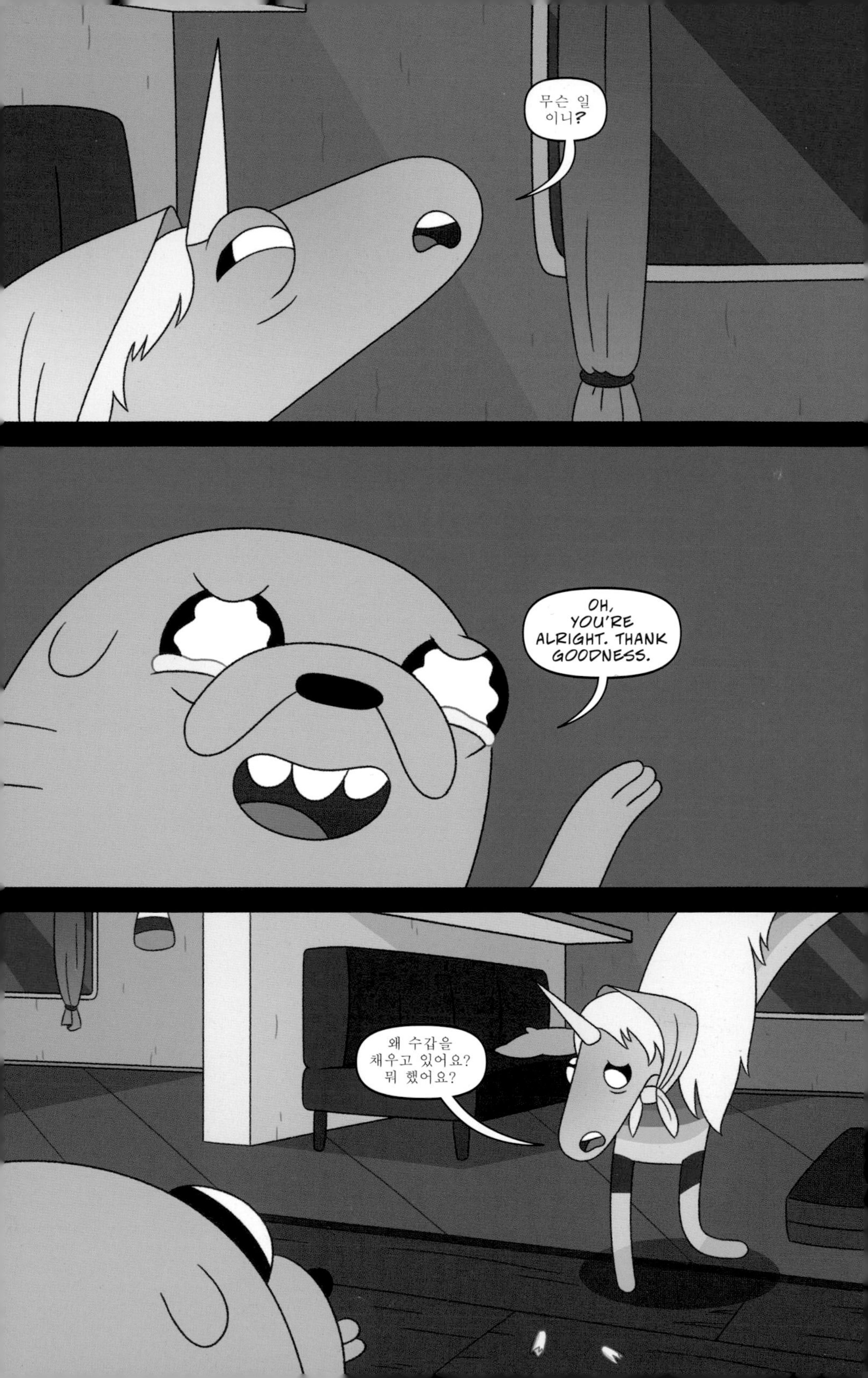
무슨 일
이니?
OH,
YOU'RE
ALRIGHT. THANK
GOODNESS.
왜 수갑을
채우고 있어요?
뭐 했어요?

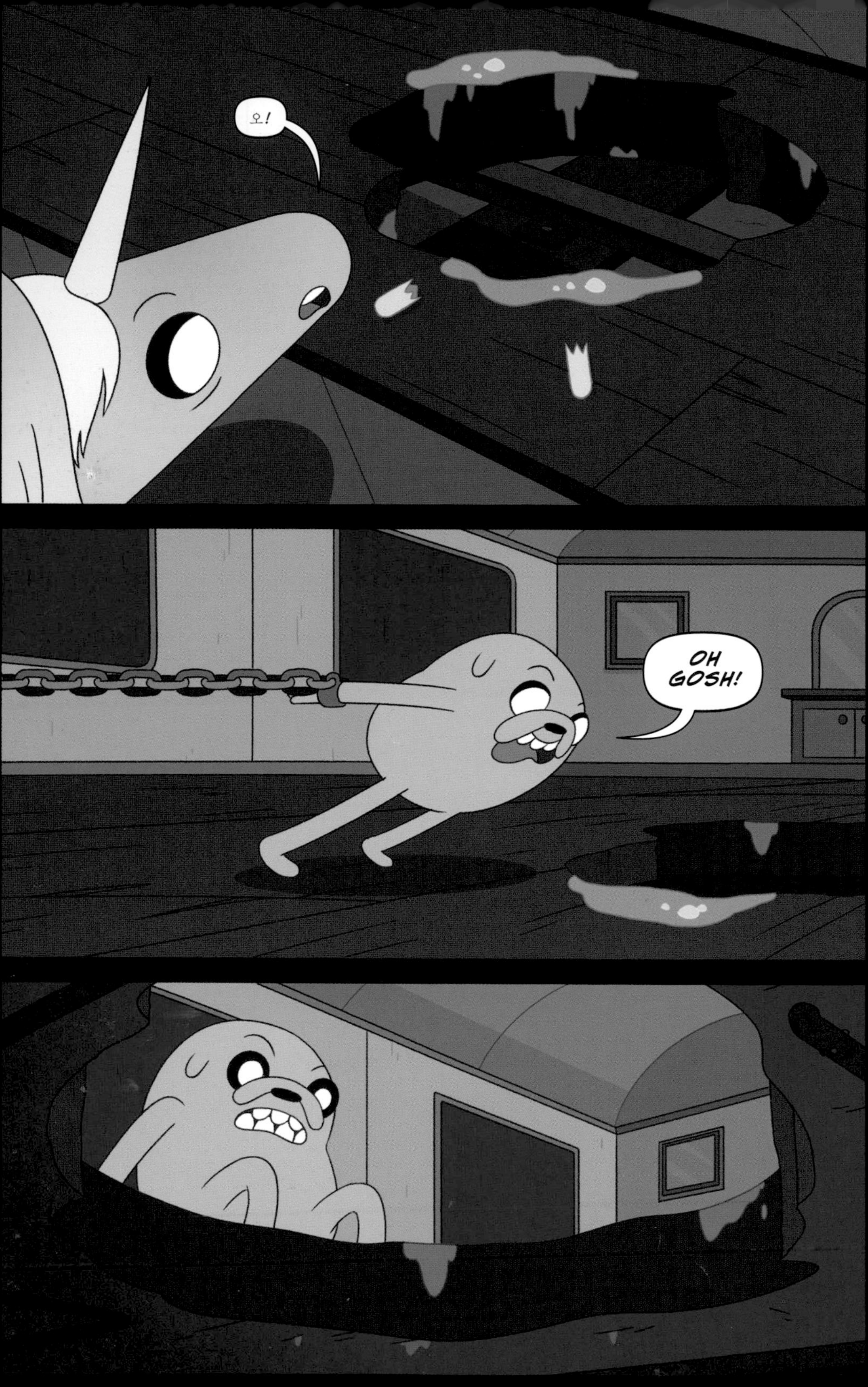
오!
OH GOSH!

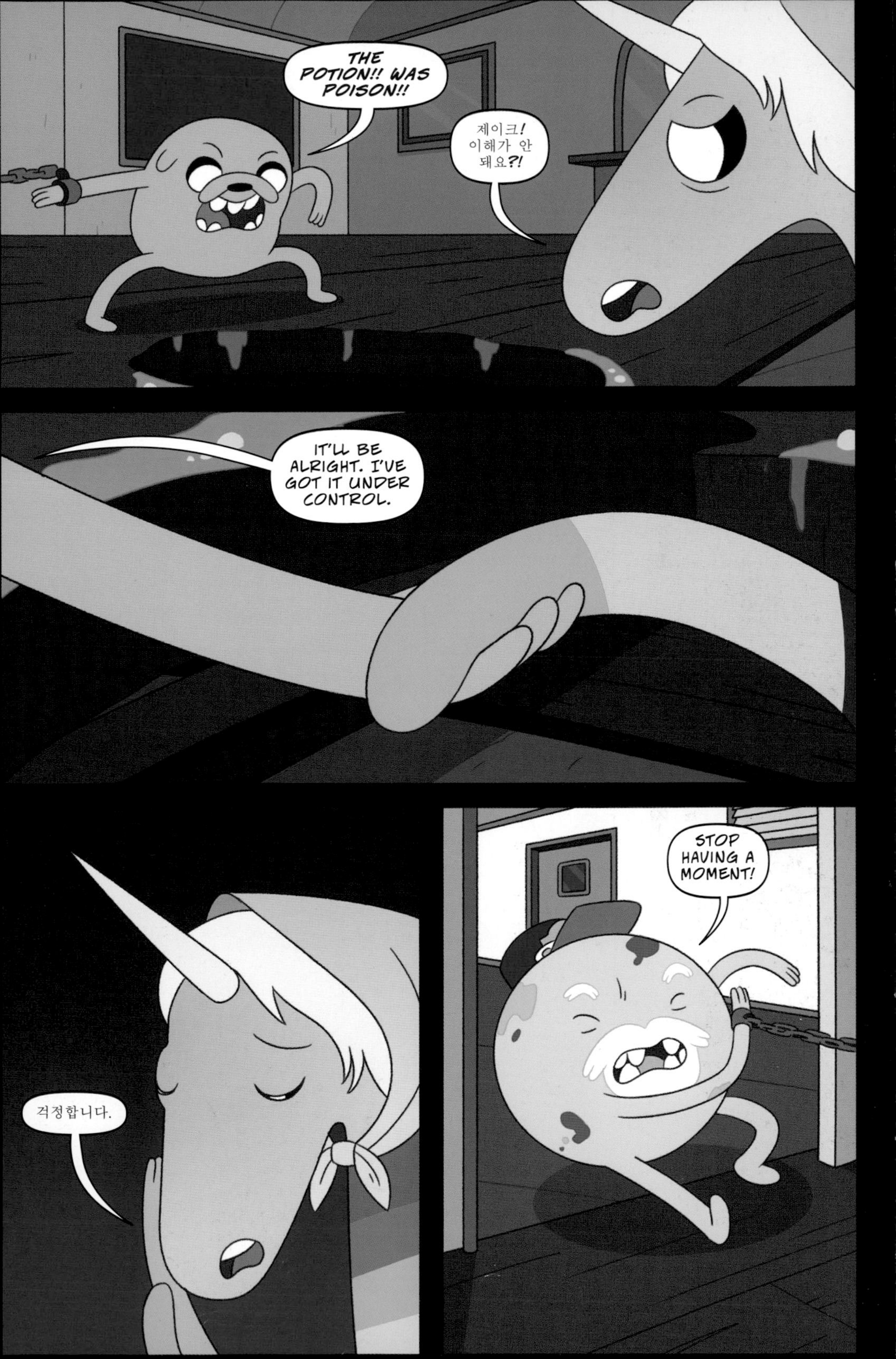
THE POTION!! WAS POISON!!
제이크! 이해가 안 돼요?!
IT'LL BE ALRIGHT. I'VE GOT IT UNDER CONTROL.
걱정합니다.
STOP HAVING A MOMENT!

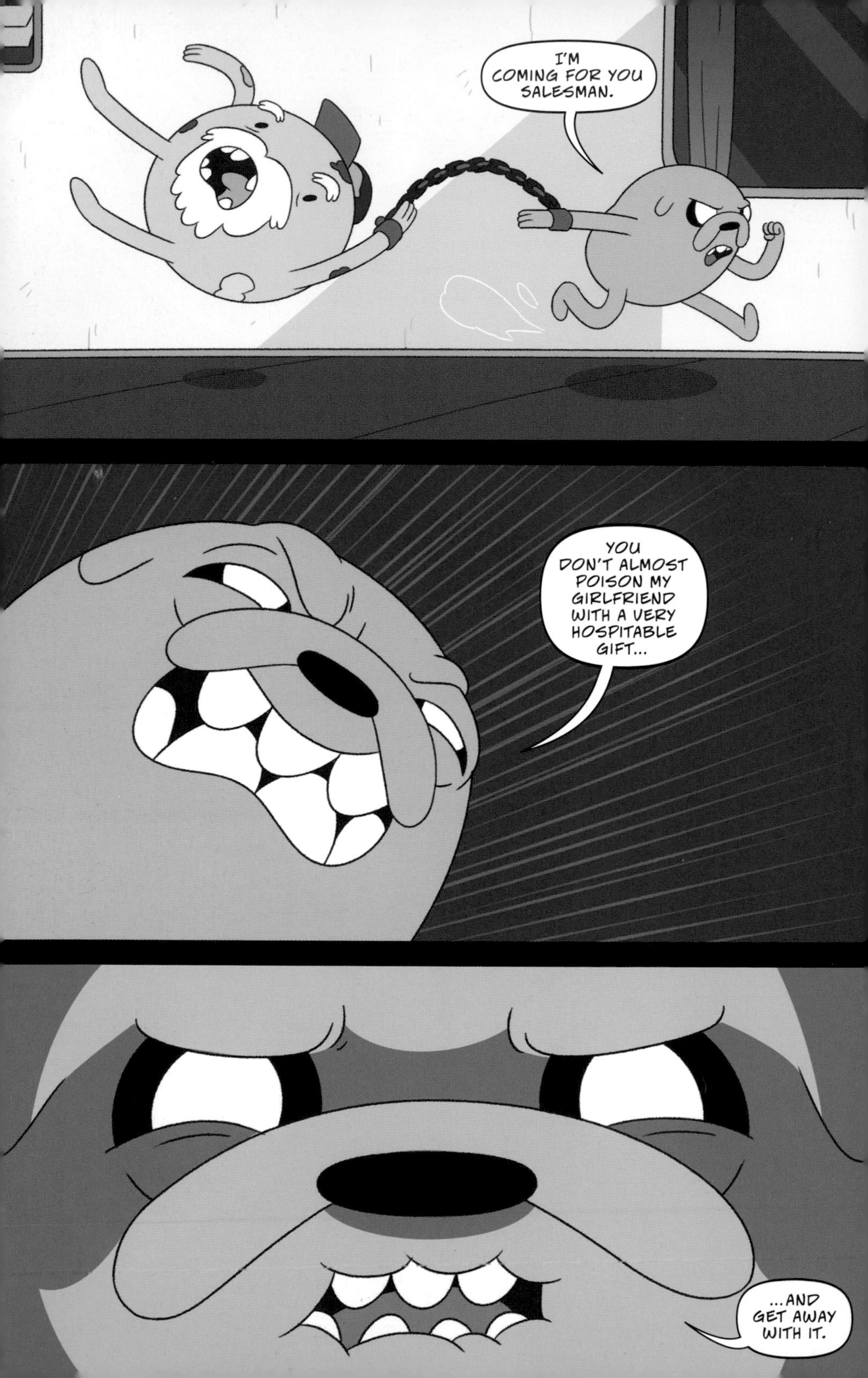
I'M COMING FOR YOU SALESMAN.
YOU DON'T ALMOST POISON MY GIRLFRIEND WITH A VERY HOSPITABLE GIFT...
...AND GET AWAY WITH IT.

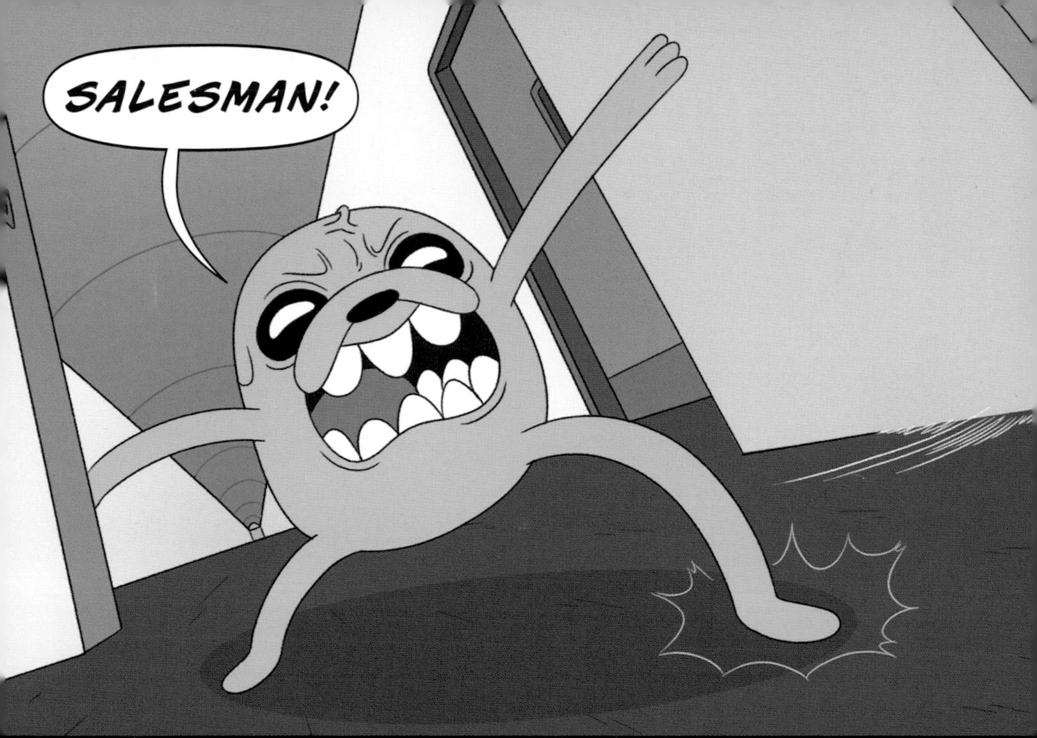
SALESMAN!

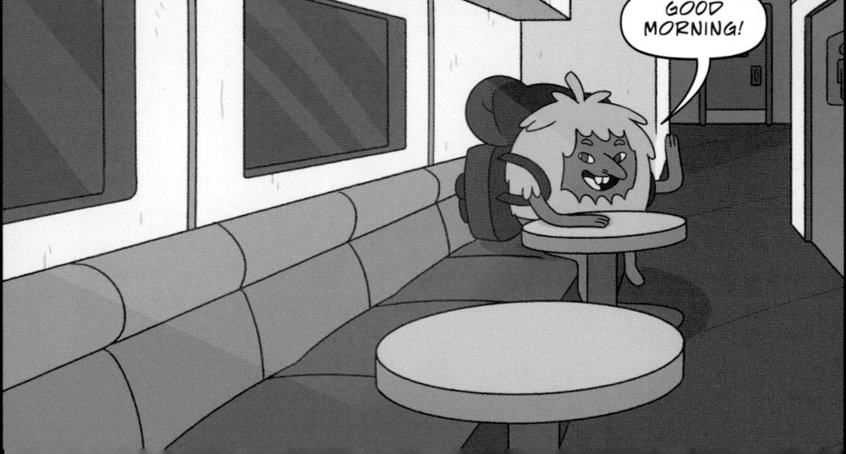
GOOD MORNING!

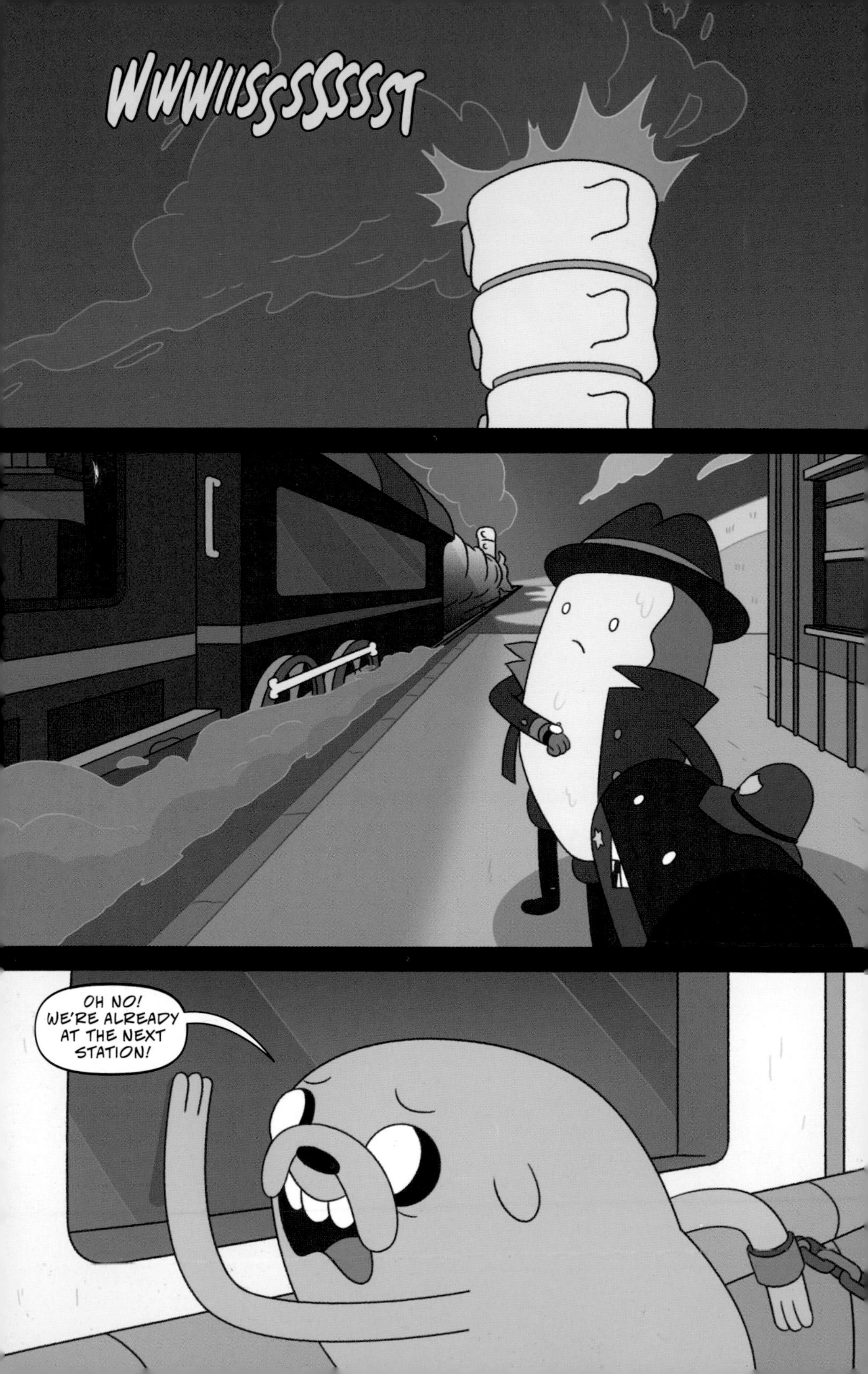
WWWIISSSSSSST
OH NO! WE'RE ALREADY AT THE NEXT STATION!

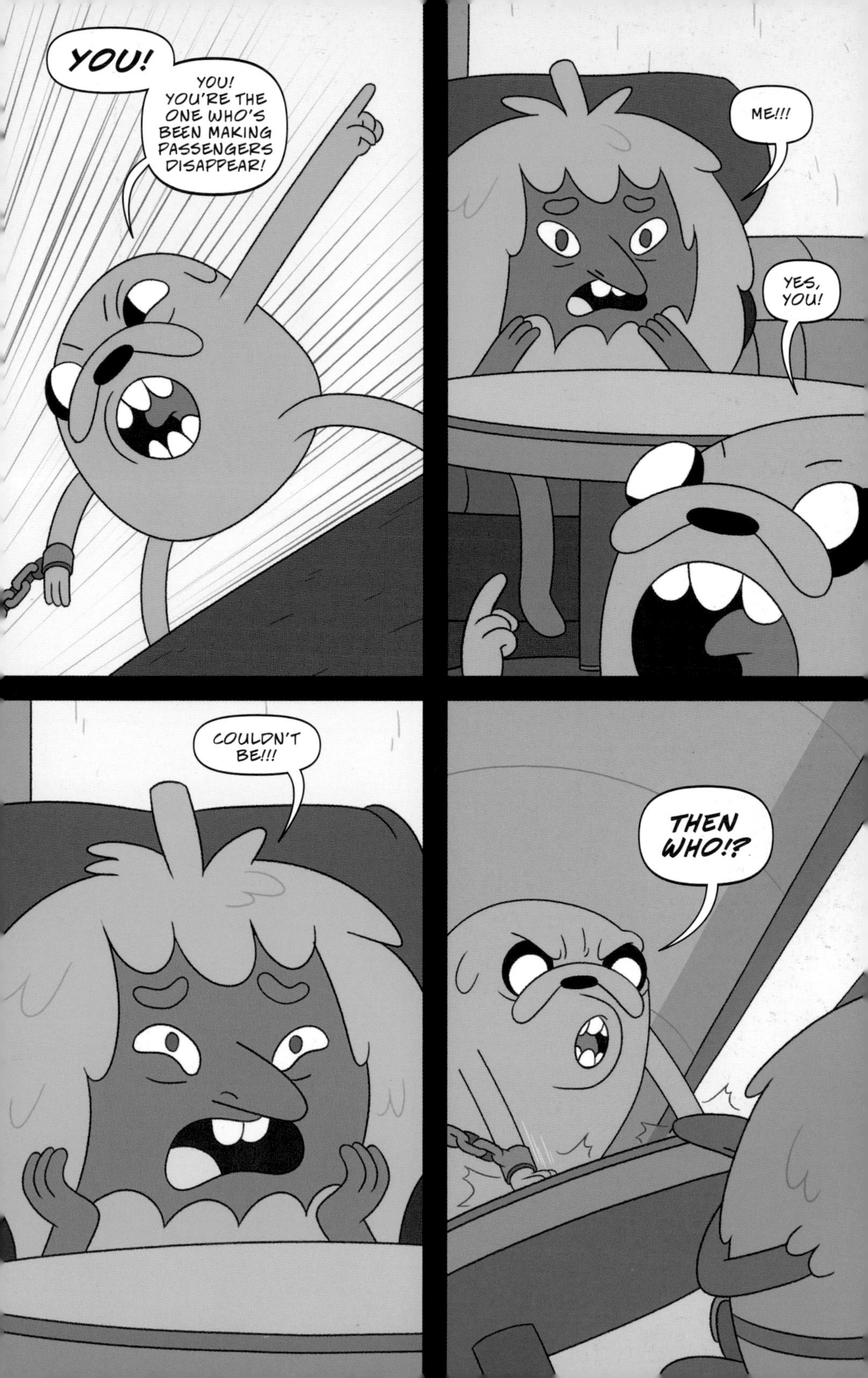
YOU!
YOU! YOU'RE THE ONE WHO'S BEEN MAKING PASSENGERS DISAPPEAR!
ME!!!
YES, YOU!
COULDN'T BE!!!
THEN WHO!?

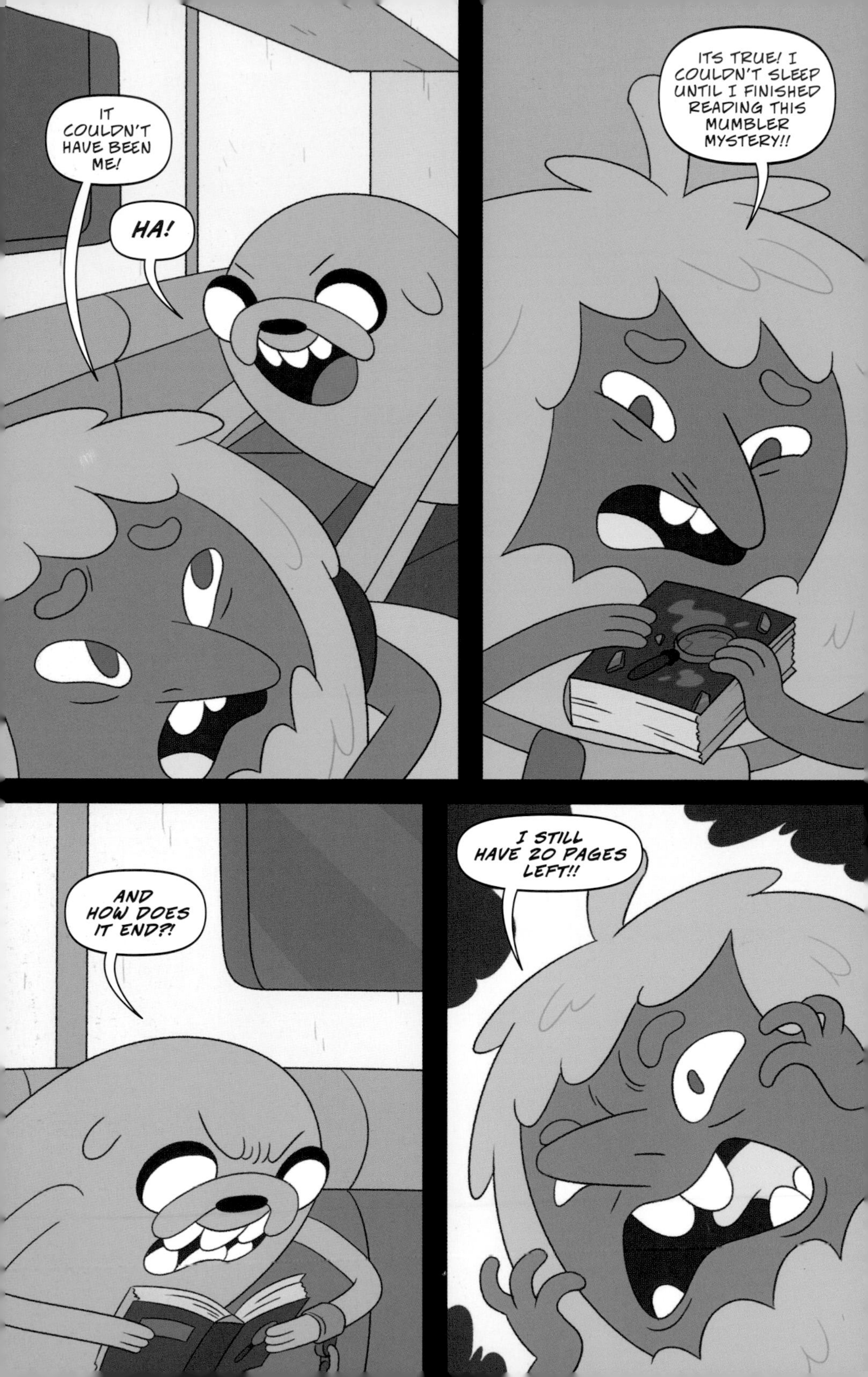
IT COULDN'T HAVE BEEN ME!
HA!
ITS TRUE! I COULDN'T SLEEP UNTIL I FINISHED READING THIS MUMBLER MYSTERY!!
AND HOW DOES IT END?!
I STILL HAVE 20 PAGES LEFT!!

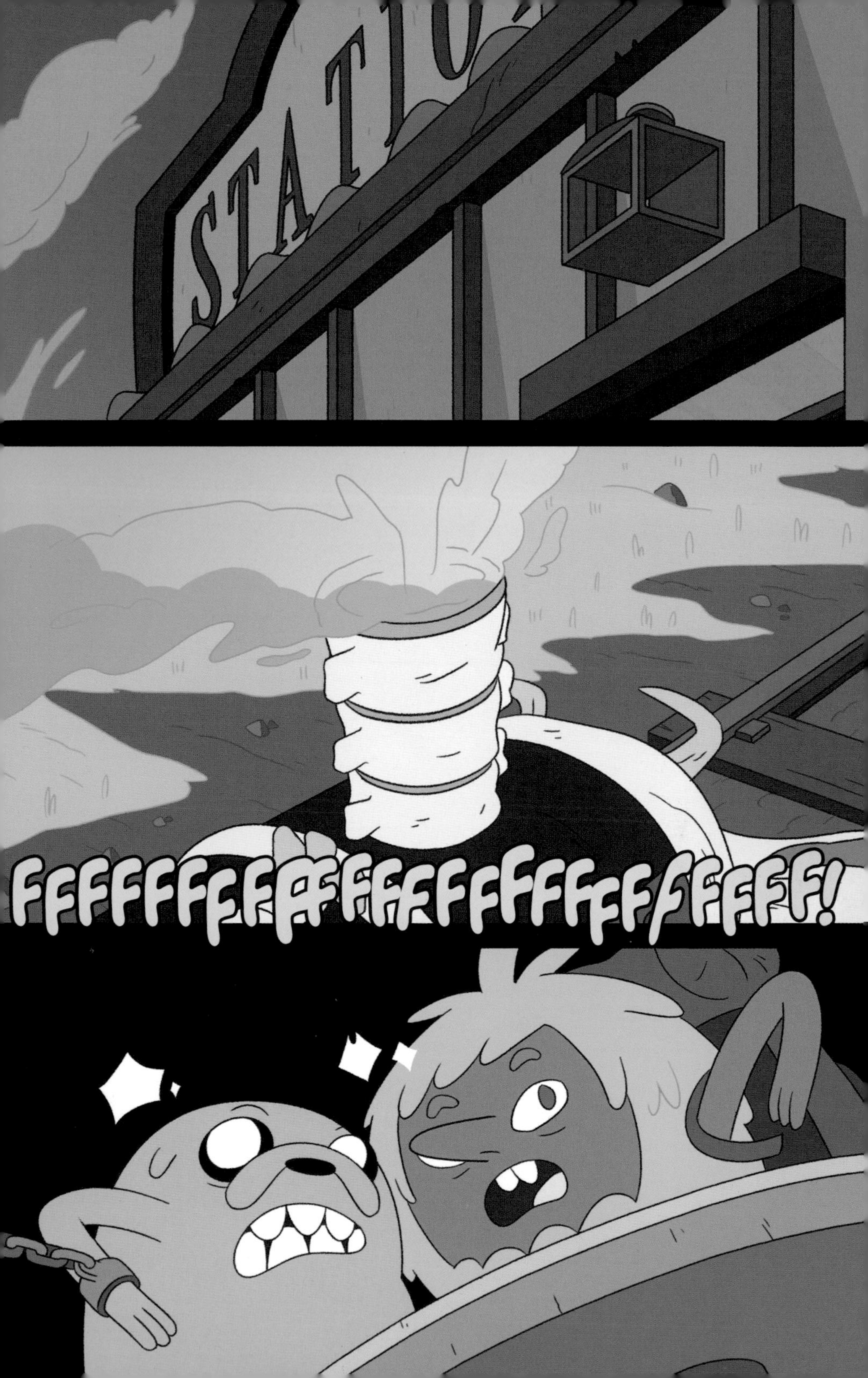
FFFFFFFFFFFFFFFFFFFFFFFFFF!

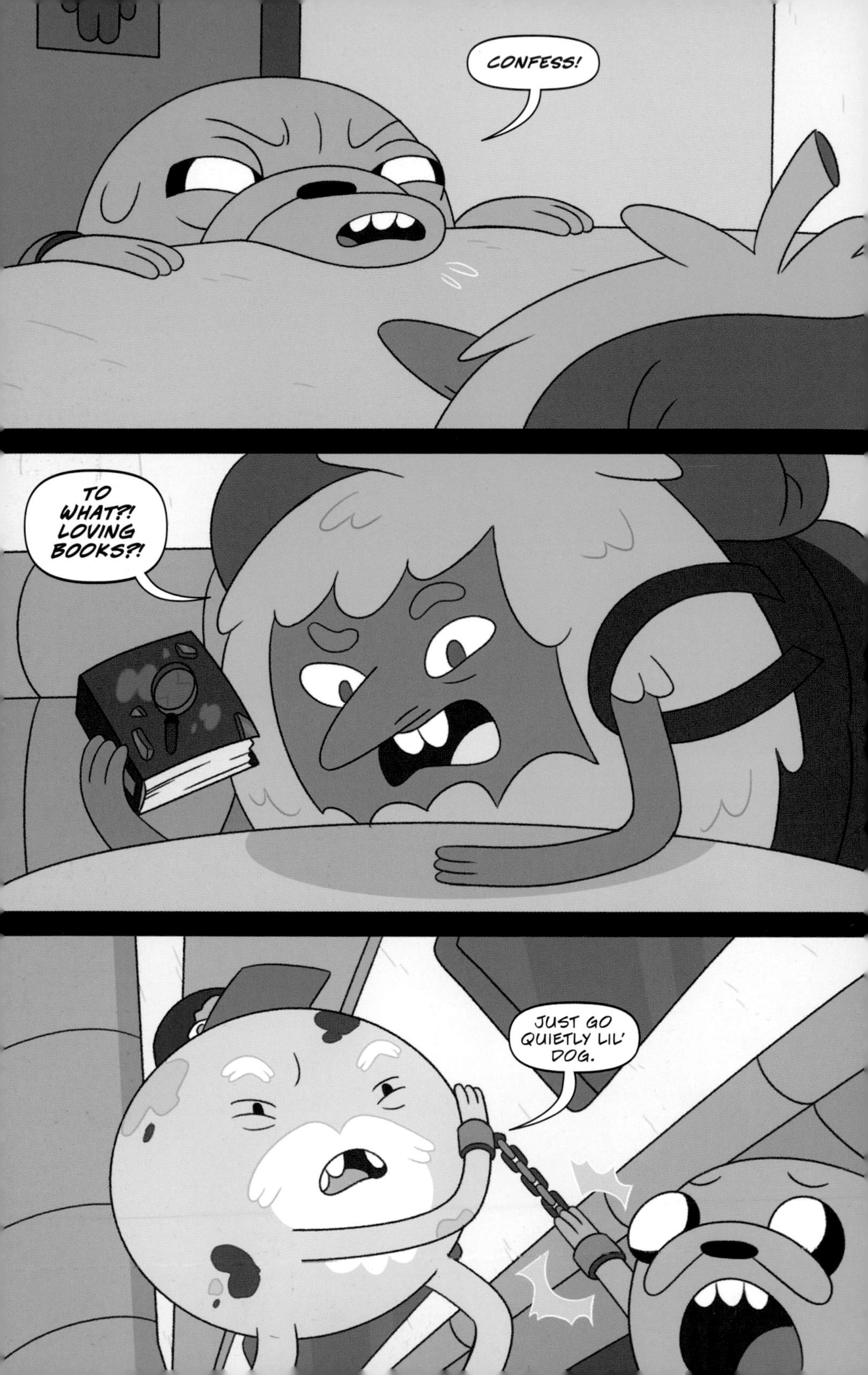
CONFESS!
TO WHAT?! LOVING BOOKS?!
JUST GO QUIETLY LIL' DOG.

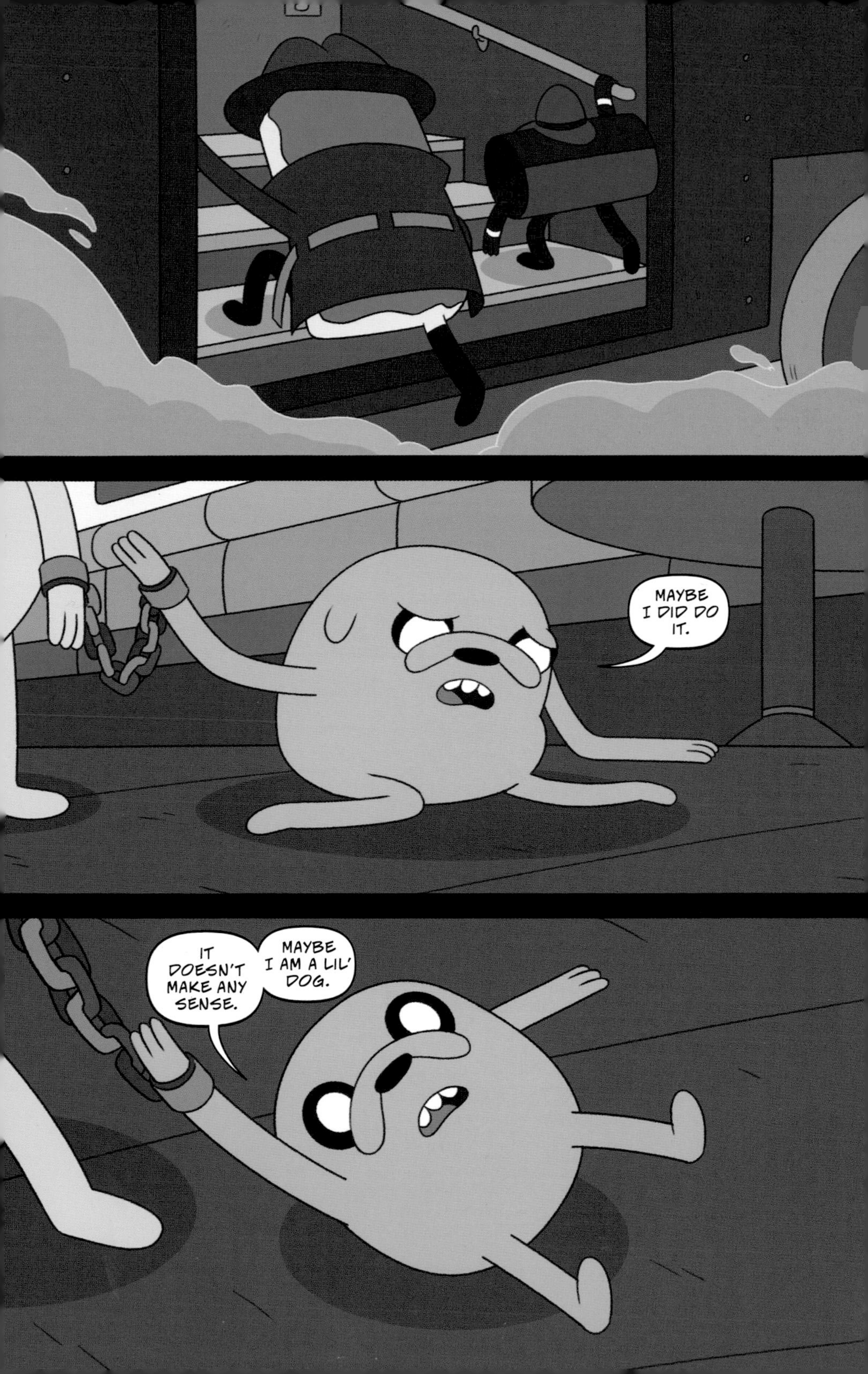
MAYBE I DID DO IT.
IT DOESN'T MAKE ANY SENSE.
MAYBE I AM A LIL' DOG.

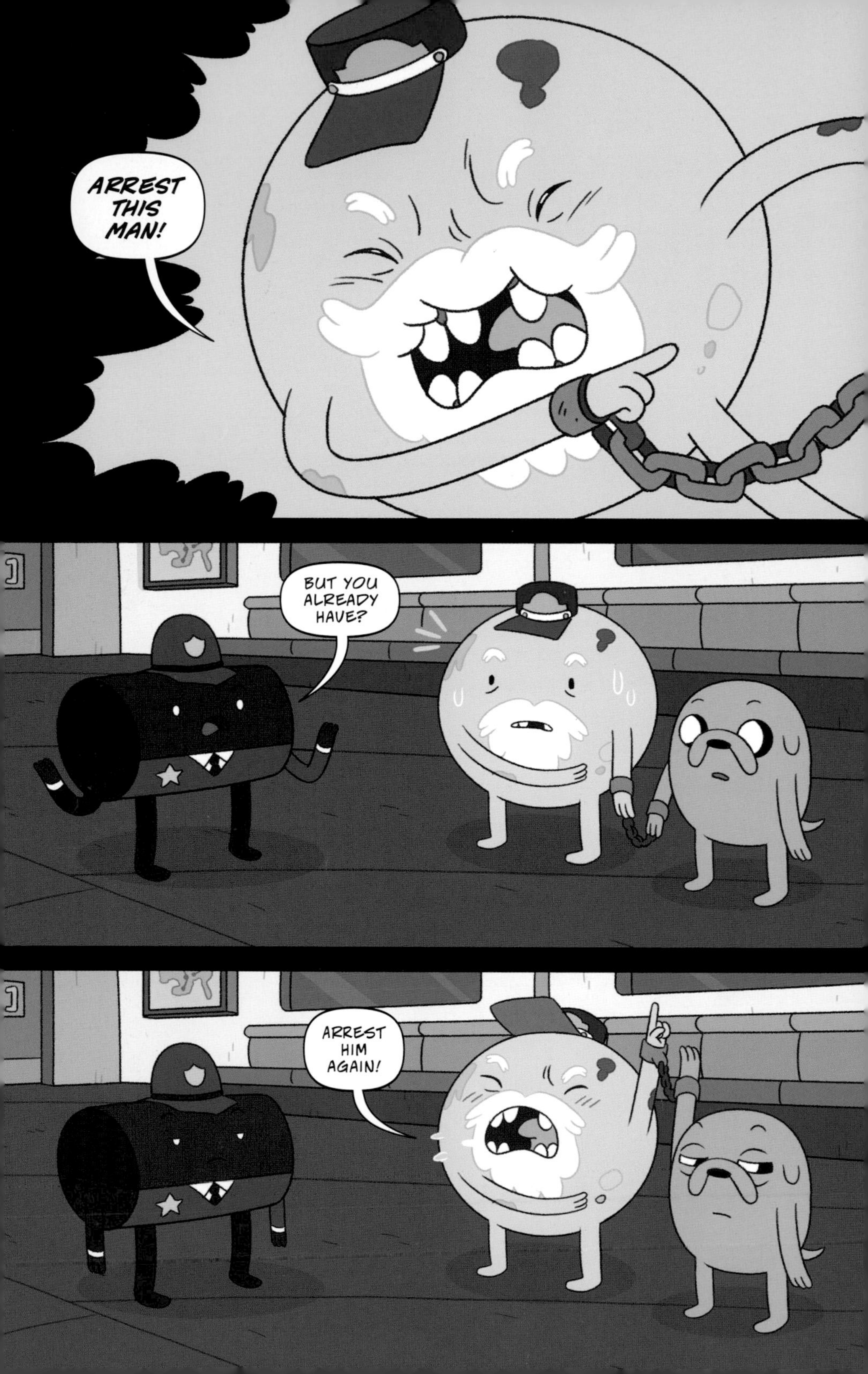
ARREST THIS MAN!
BUT YOU ALREADY HAVE?
ARREST HIM AGAIN!

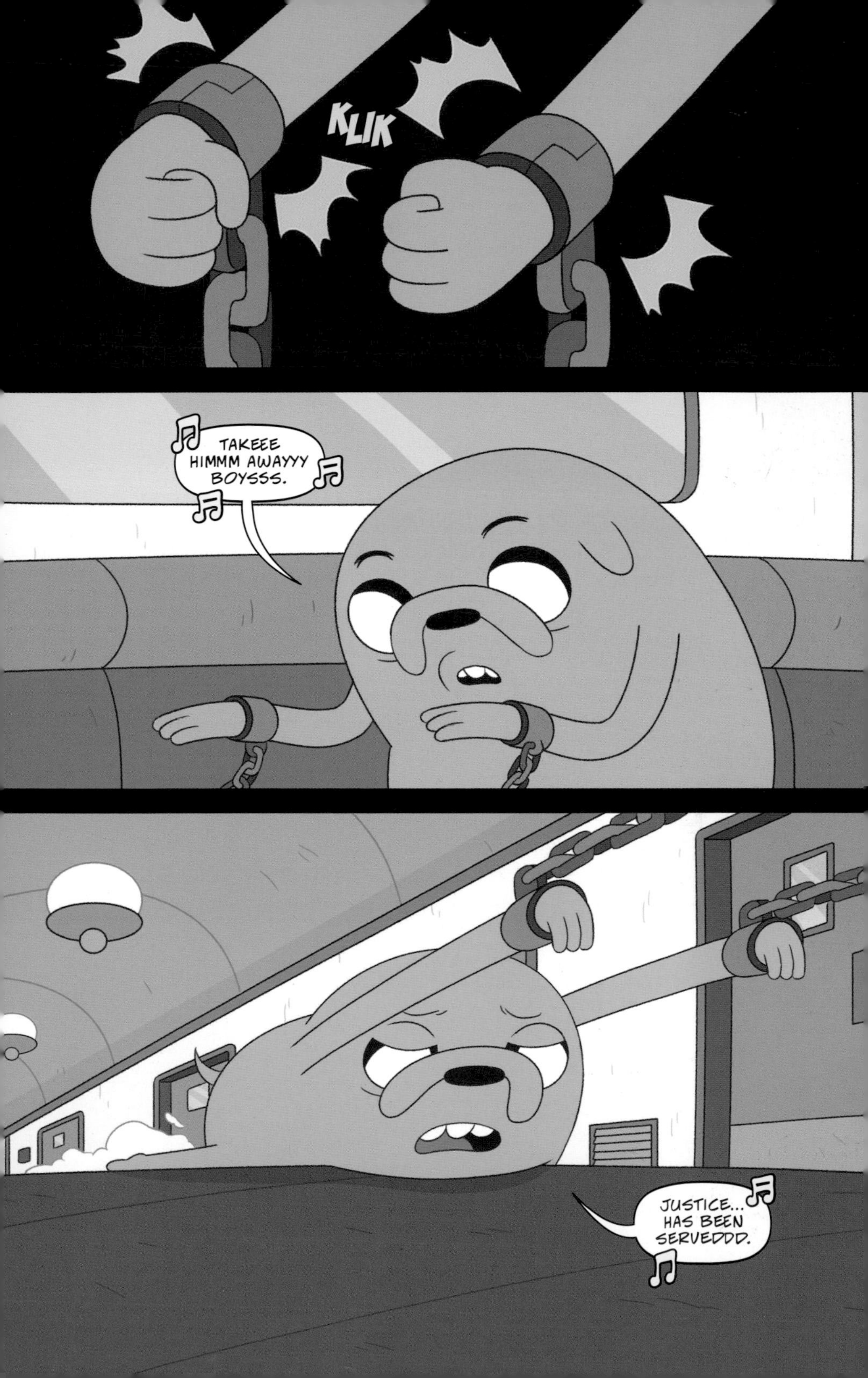
KLIK
TAKEEE HIMMM AWAYYY BOYSSS.
JUSTICE... HAS BEEN SERVEDDD.

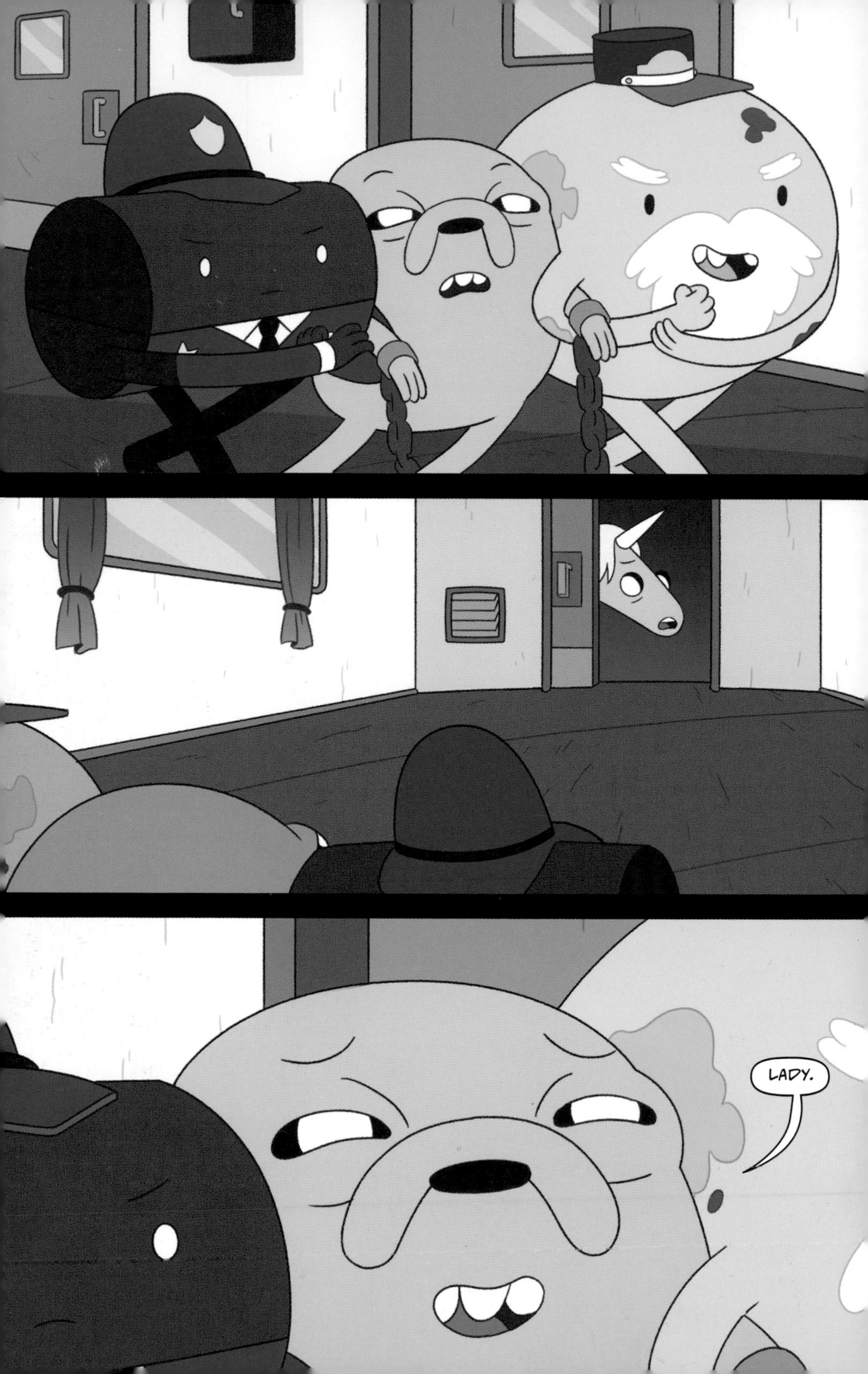
LADY.

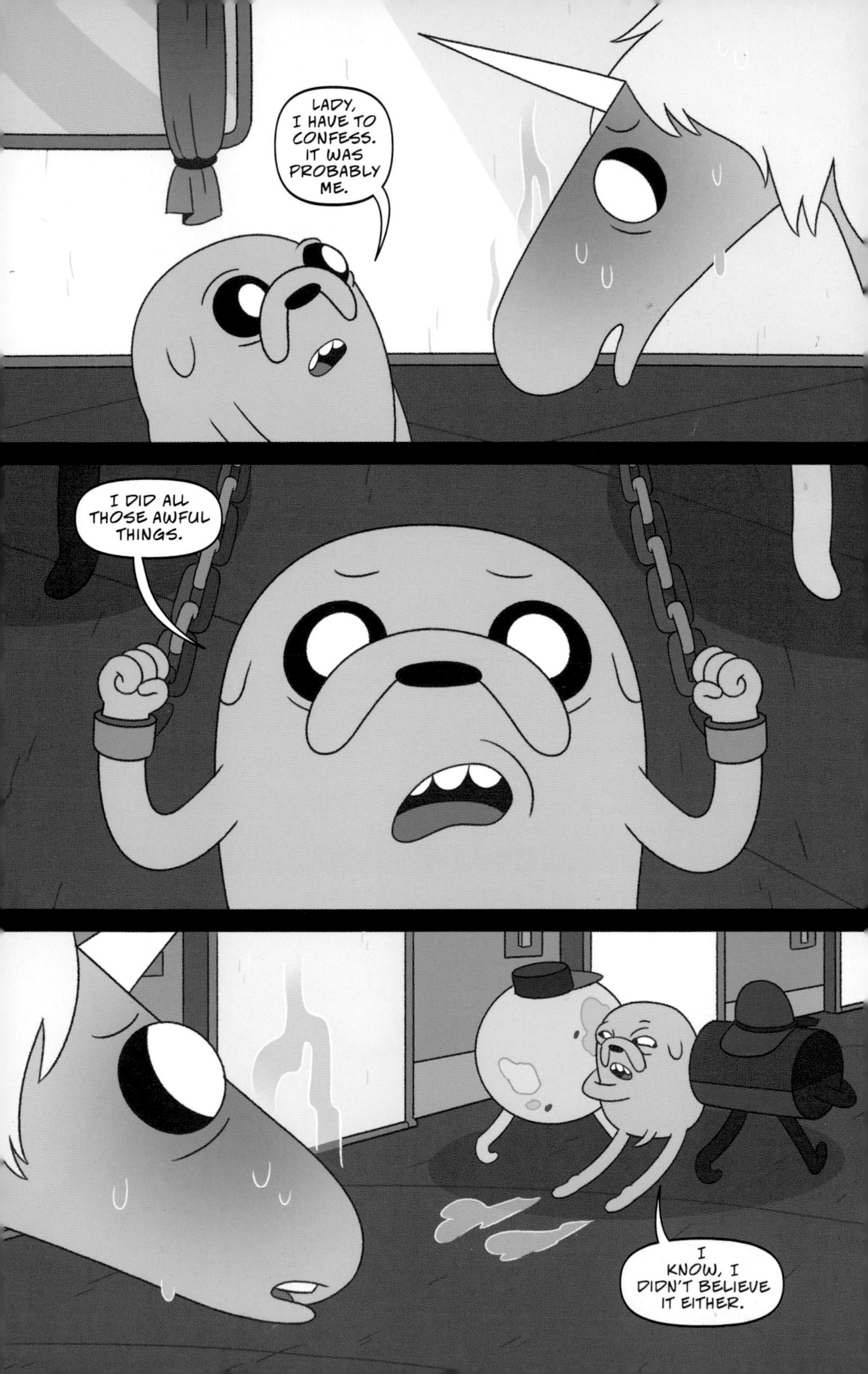
LADY, I HAVE TO CONFESS. IT WAS PROBABLY ME.
I DID ALL THOSE AWFUL THINGS.
I KNOW, I DIDN'T BELIEVE IT EITHER.

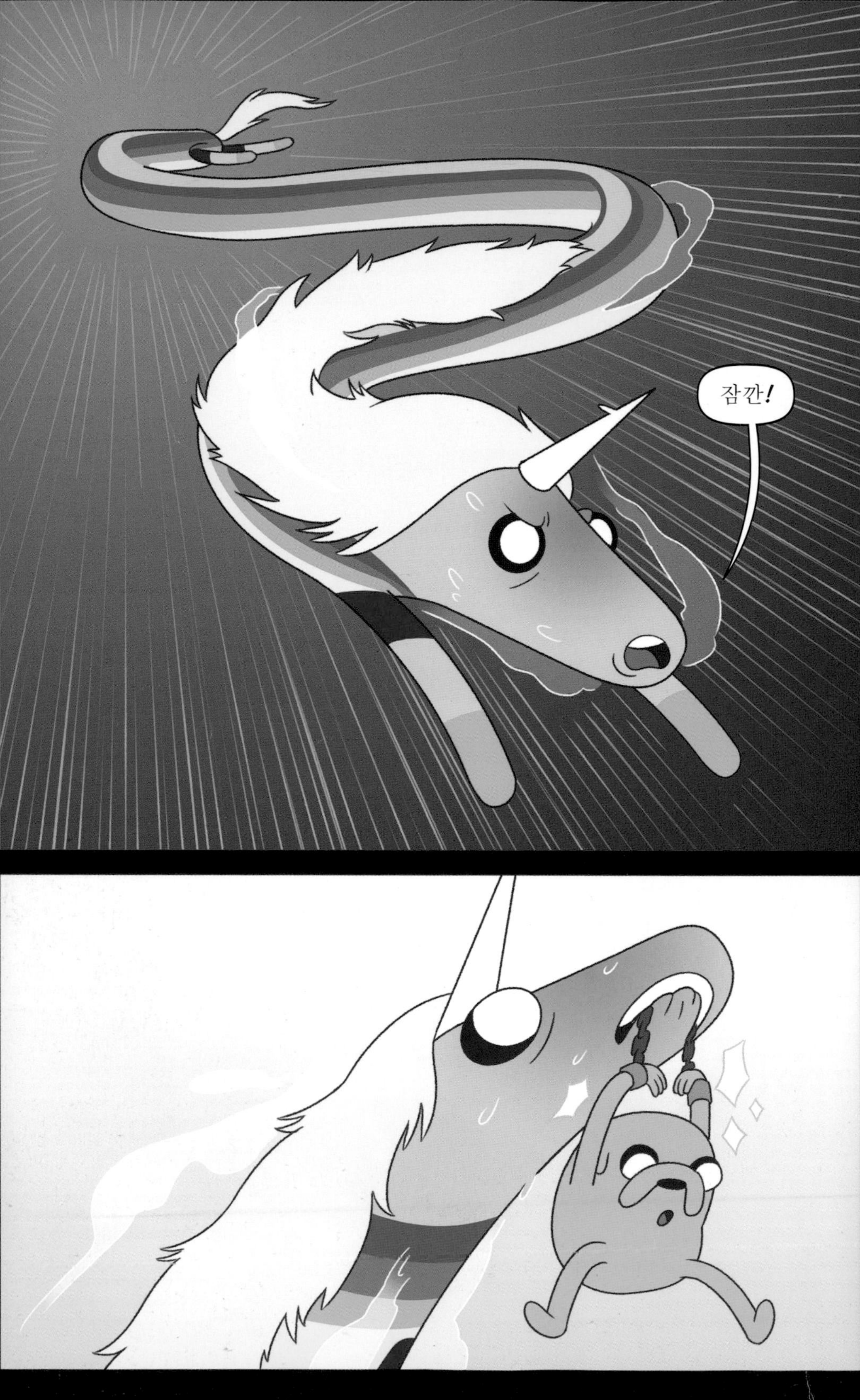
잠깐!

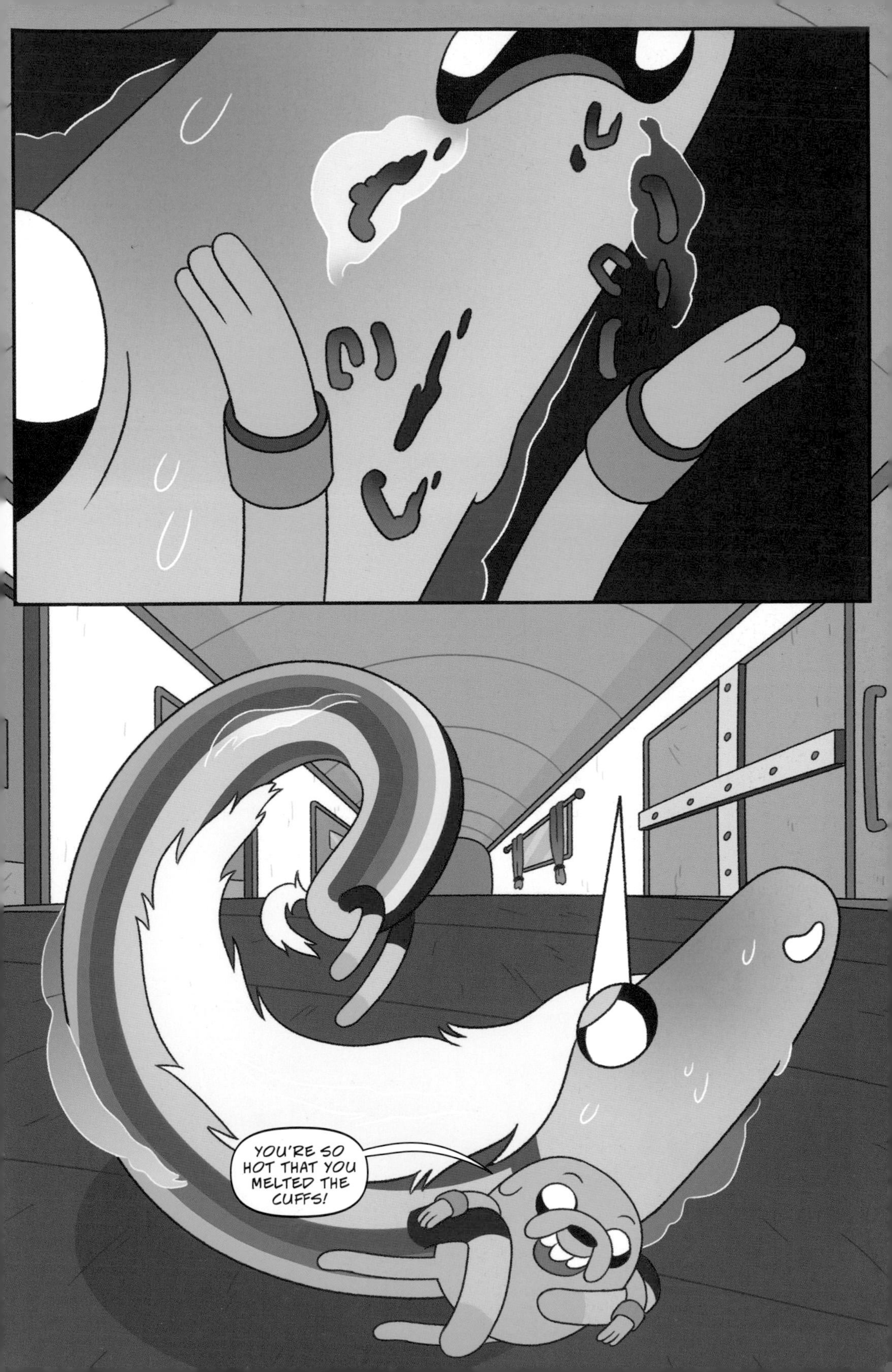
YOU'RE SO HOT THAT YOU MELTED THE CUFFS!

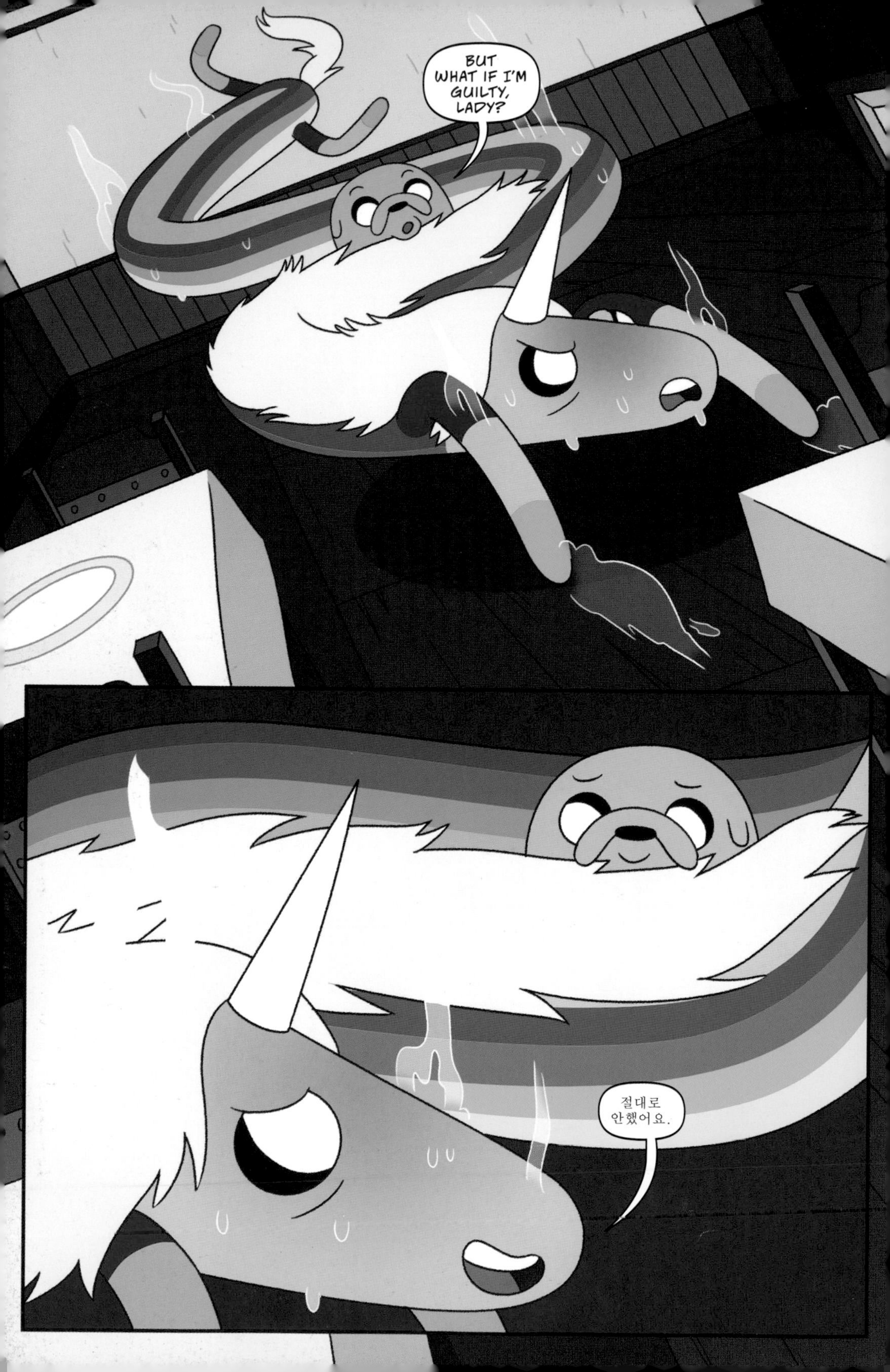
BUT WHAT IF I'M GUILTY, LADY?
절대로 안했어요.

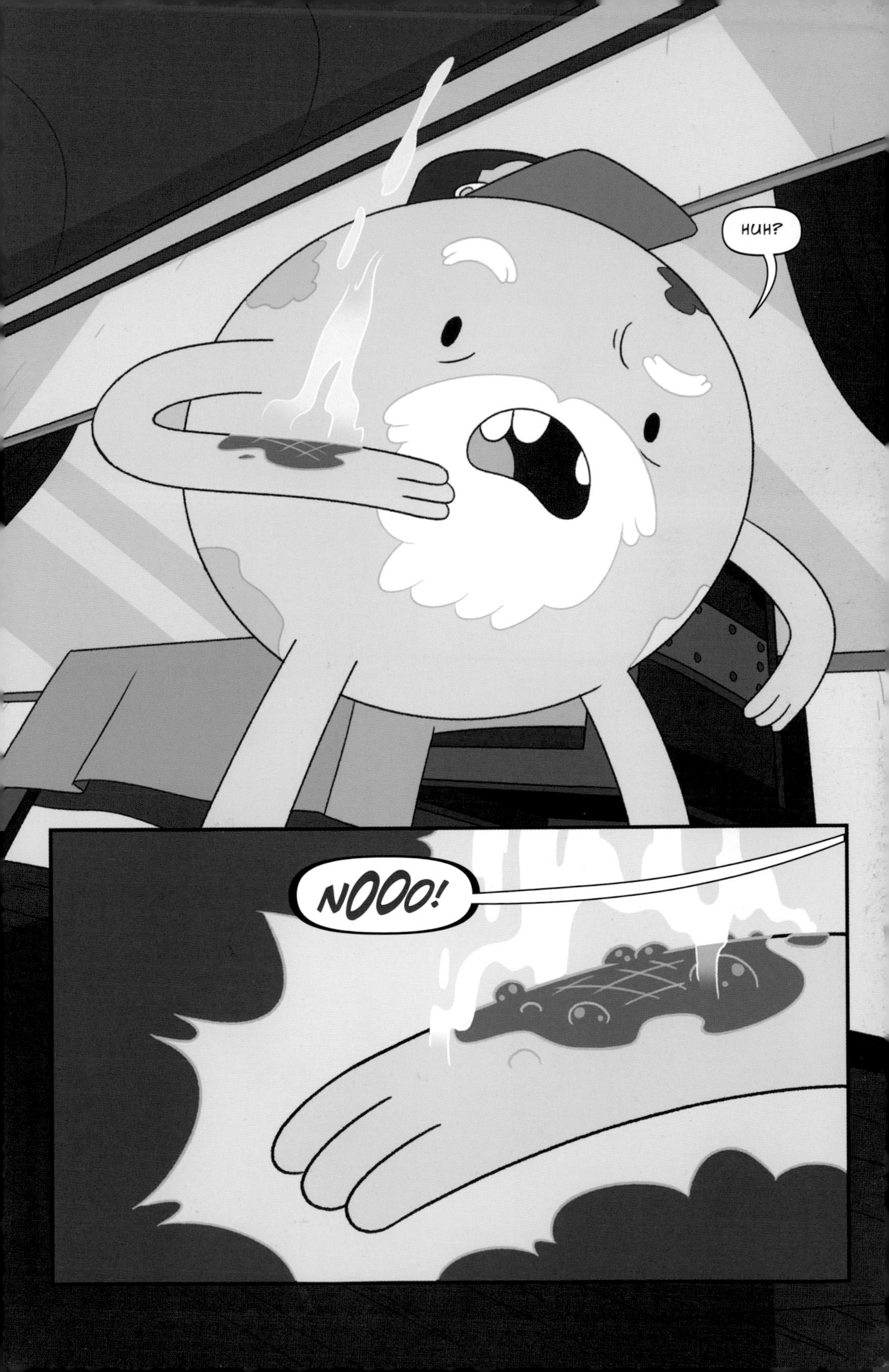
HUH?
NOOO!

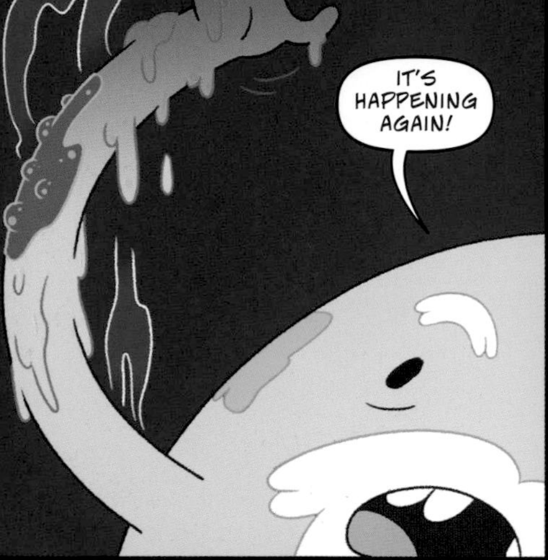
IT'S HAPPENING AGAIN!

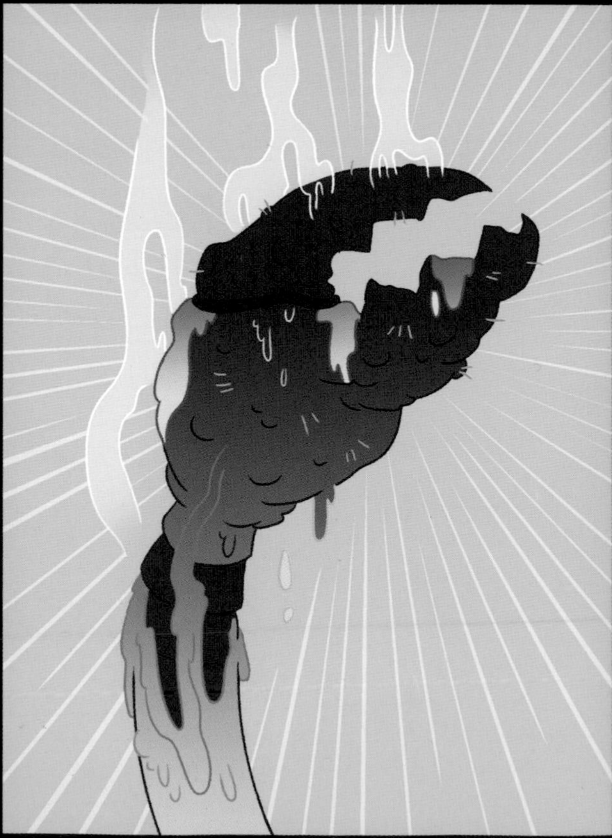

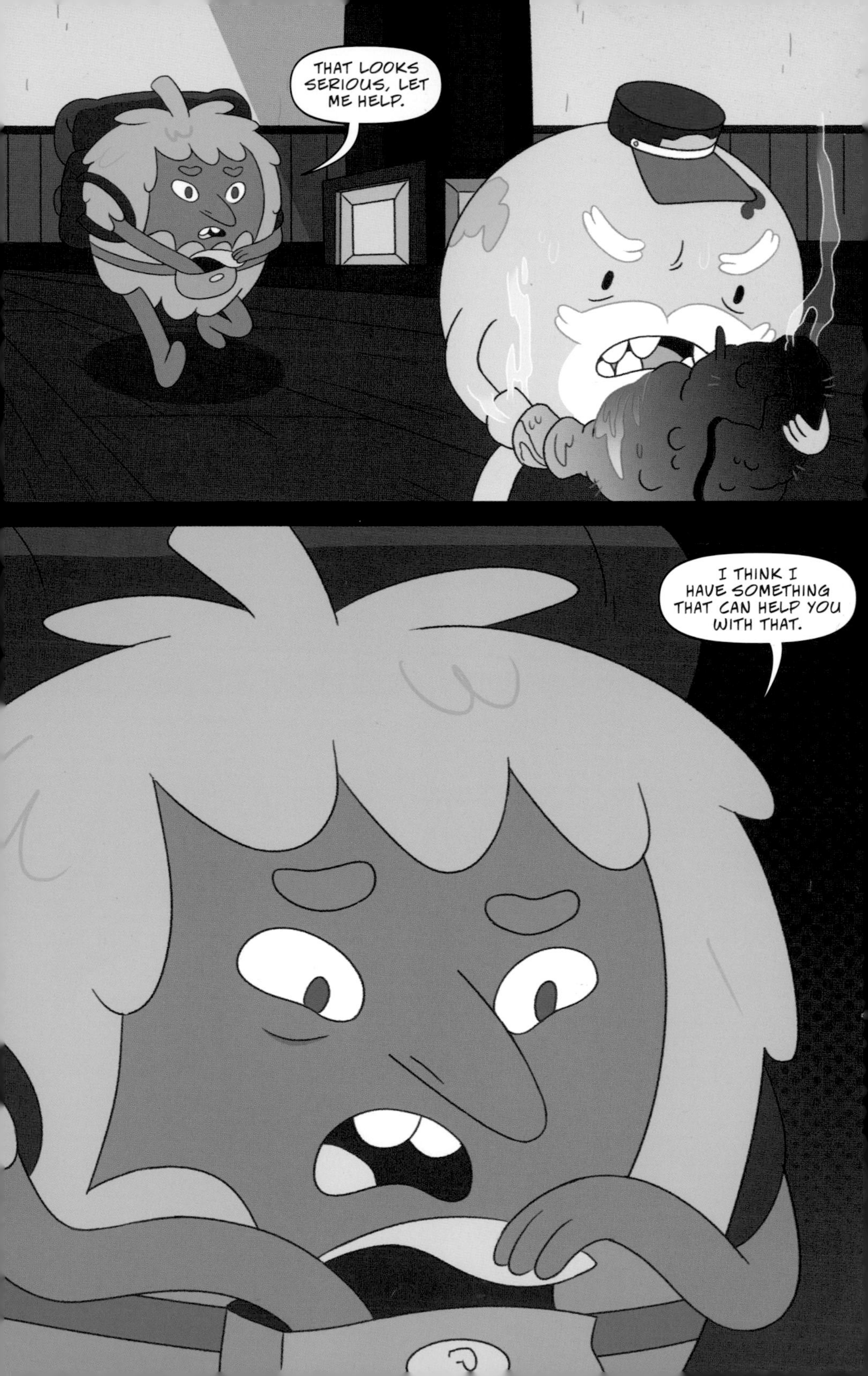
THAT LOOKS SERIOUS, LET ME HELP.
I THINK I HAVE SOMETHING THAT CAN HELP YOU WITH THAT.

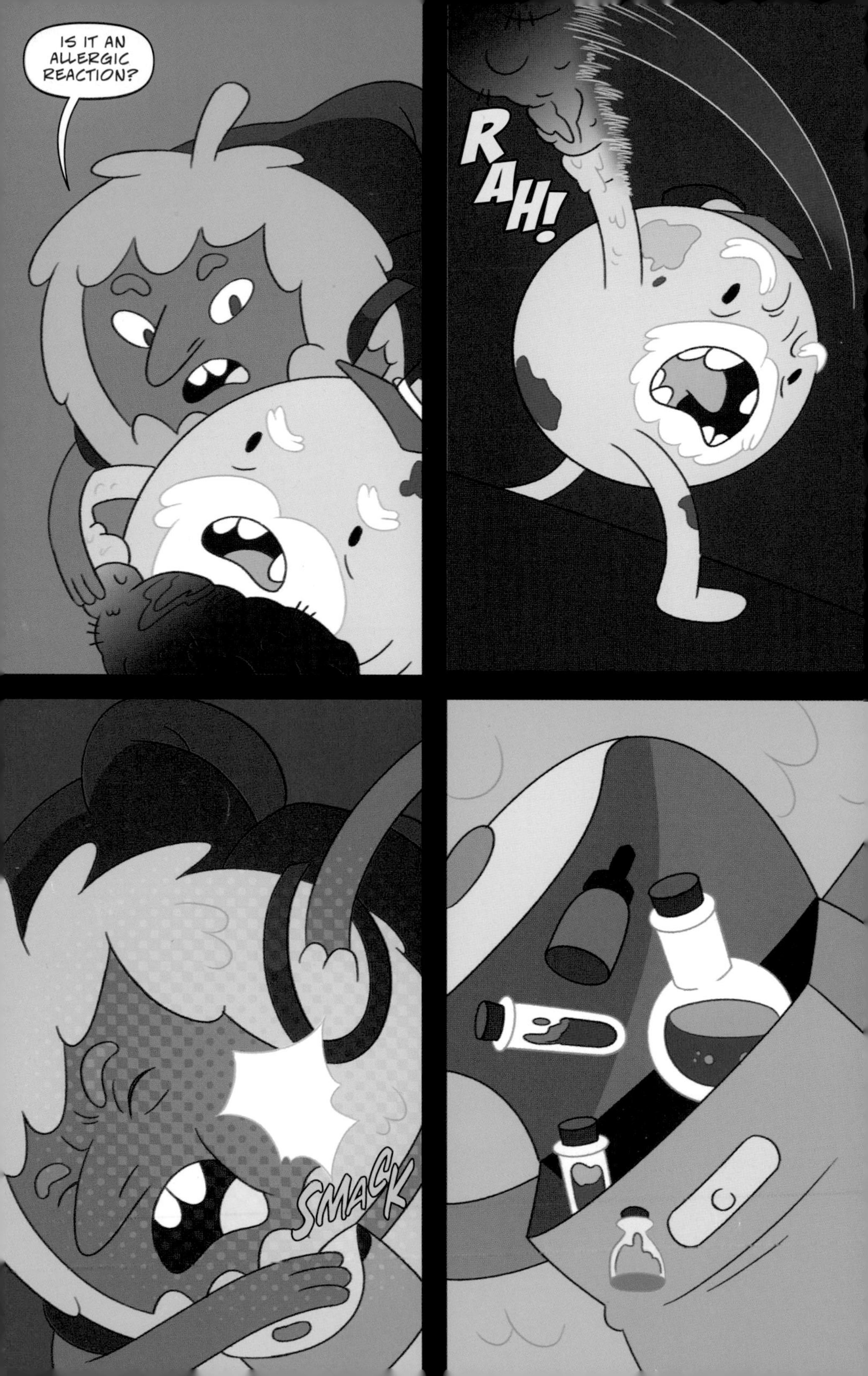
IS IT AN ALLERGIC REACTION?
RAH!
SMACK

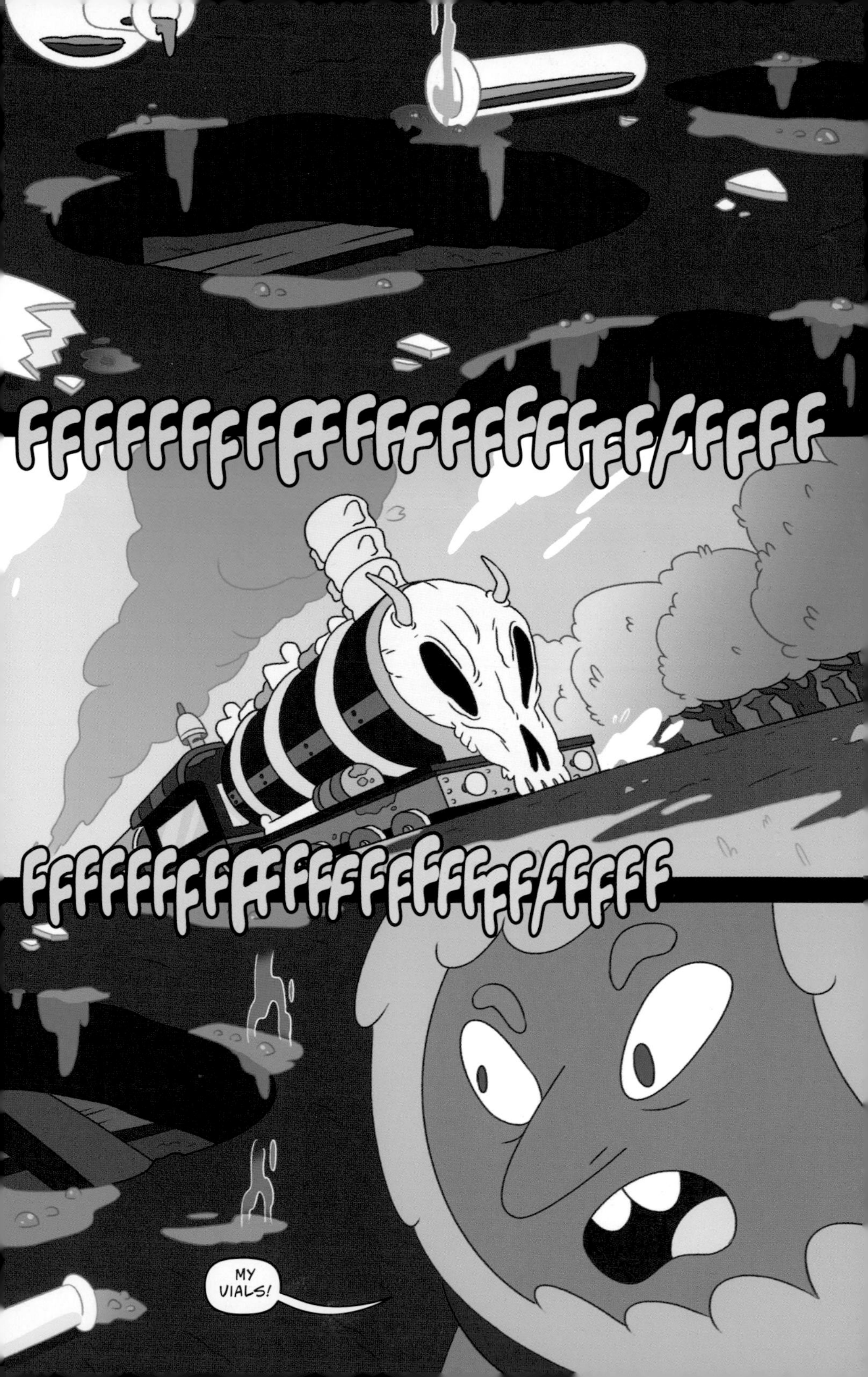
FFFFFFFFFFFFFFFFFFFFFFFFFF
FFFFFFFFFFFFFFFFFFFFFFFFF
MY VIALS!

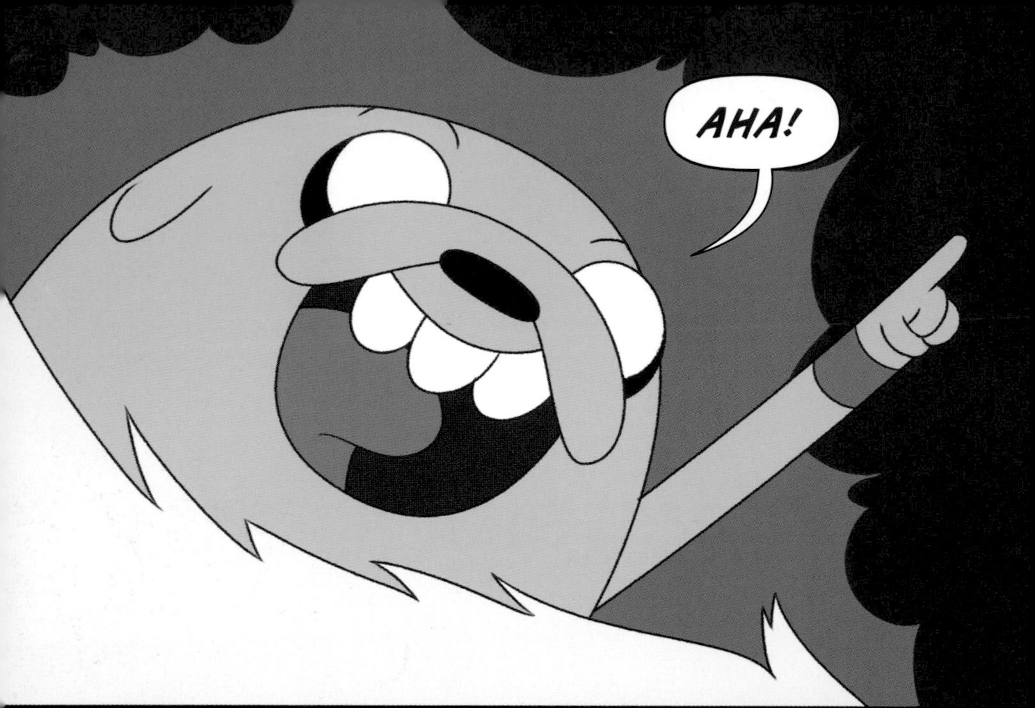
AHA!

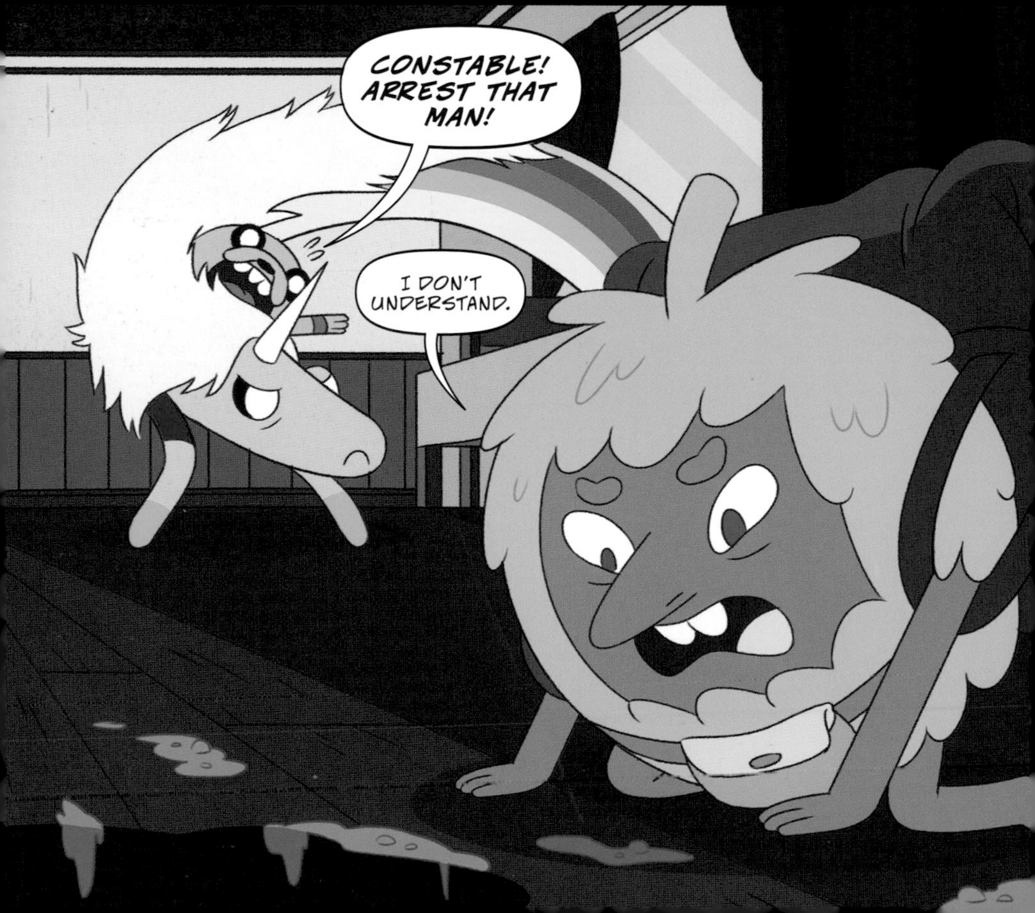
CONSTABLE! ARREST THAT MAN!
I DON'T UNDERSTAND.

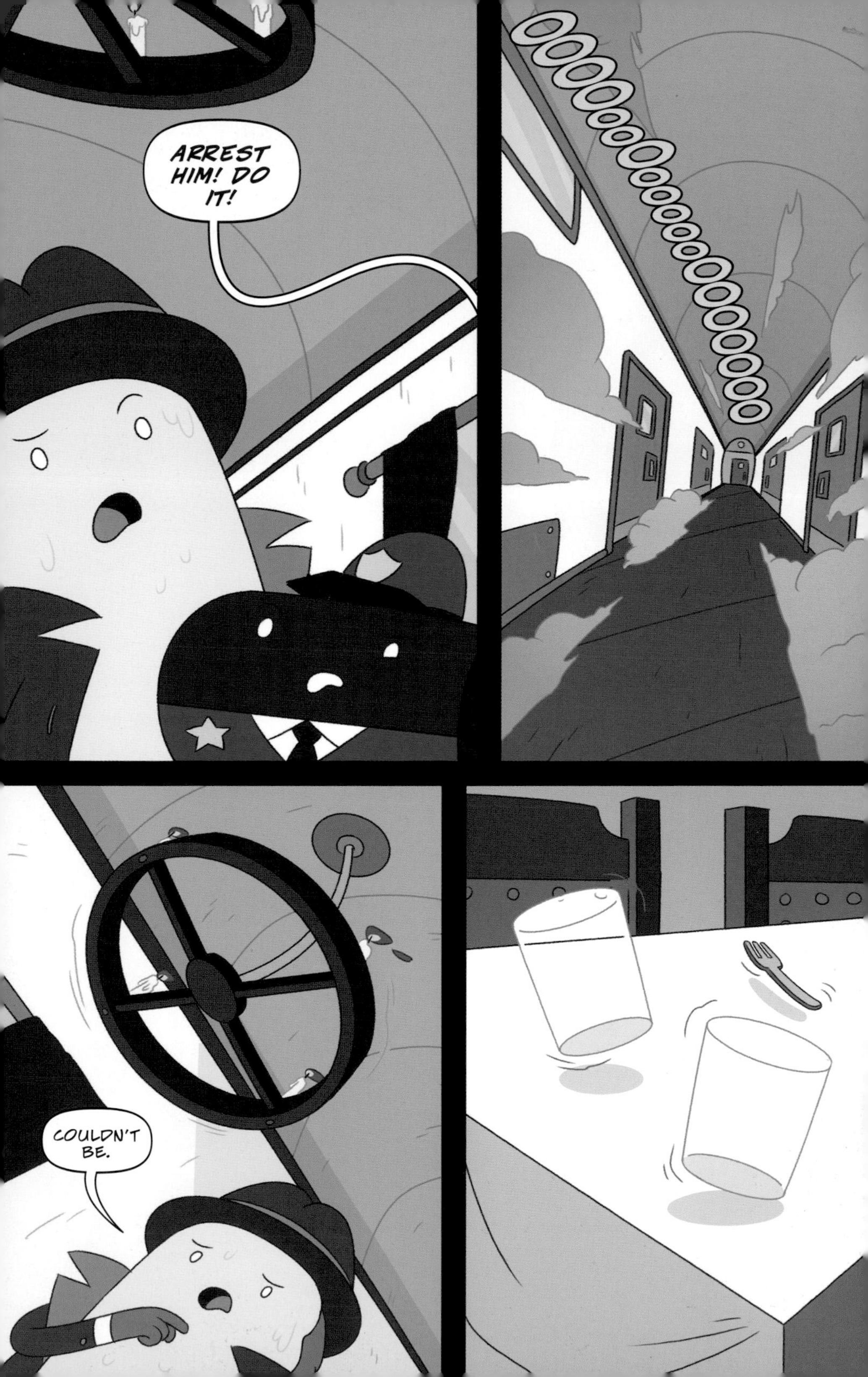
ARREST HIM! DO IT!
OOOOoooOOoooooOOOOOO
COULDN'T BE.

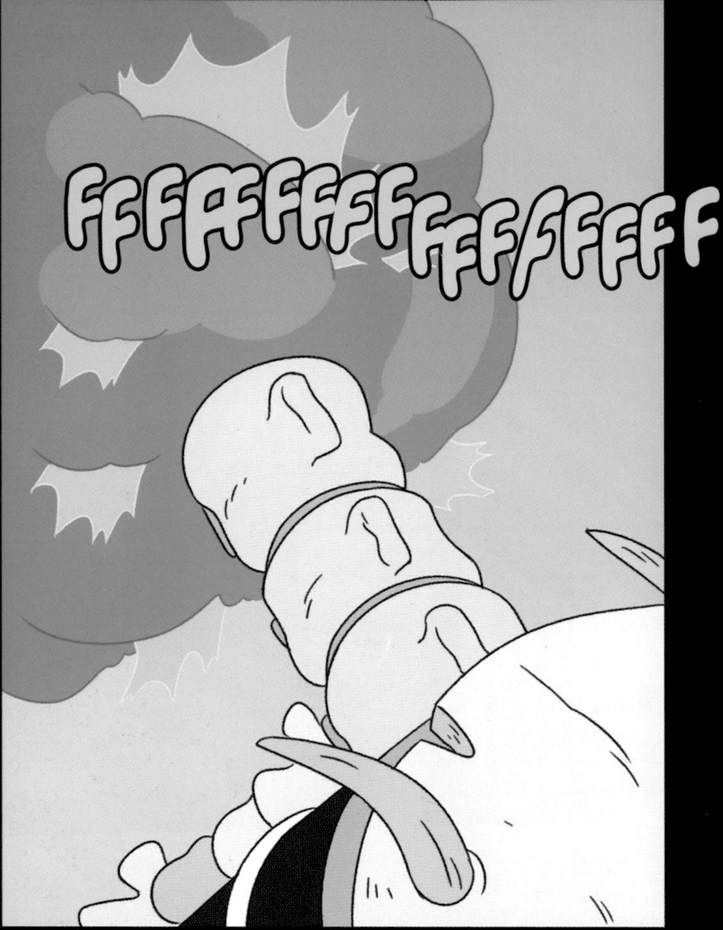
FFFFFFFFFFFFFFFFFFF

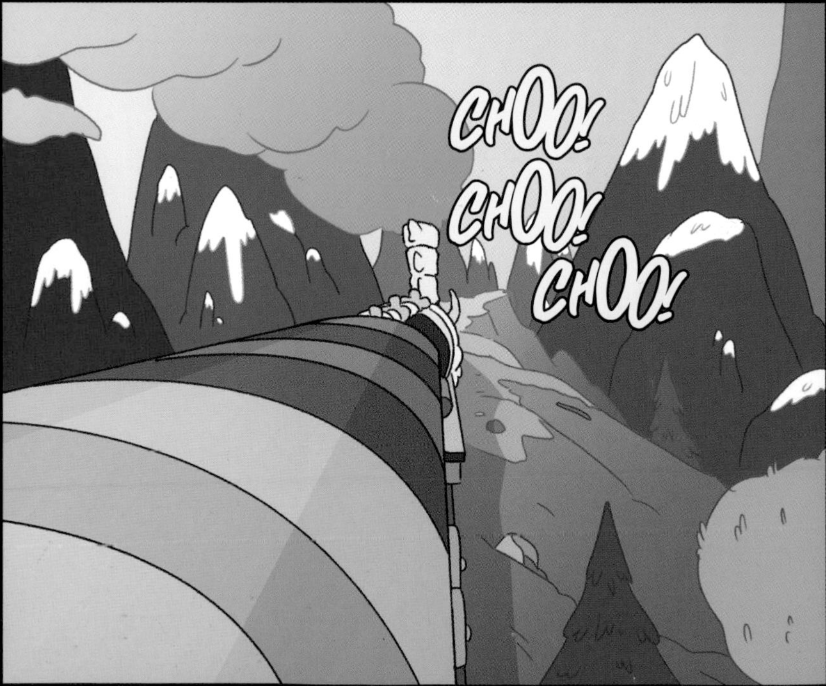
CHOO!
CHOO!
CHOO!

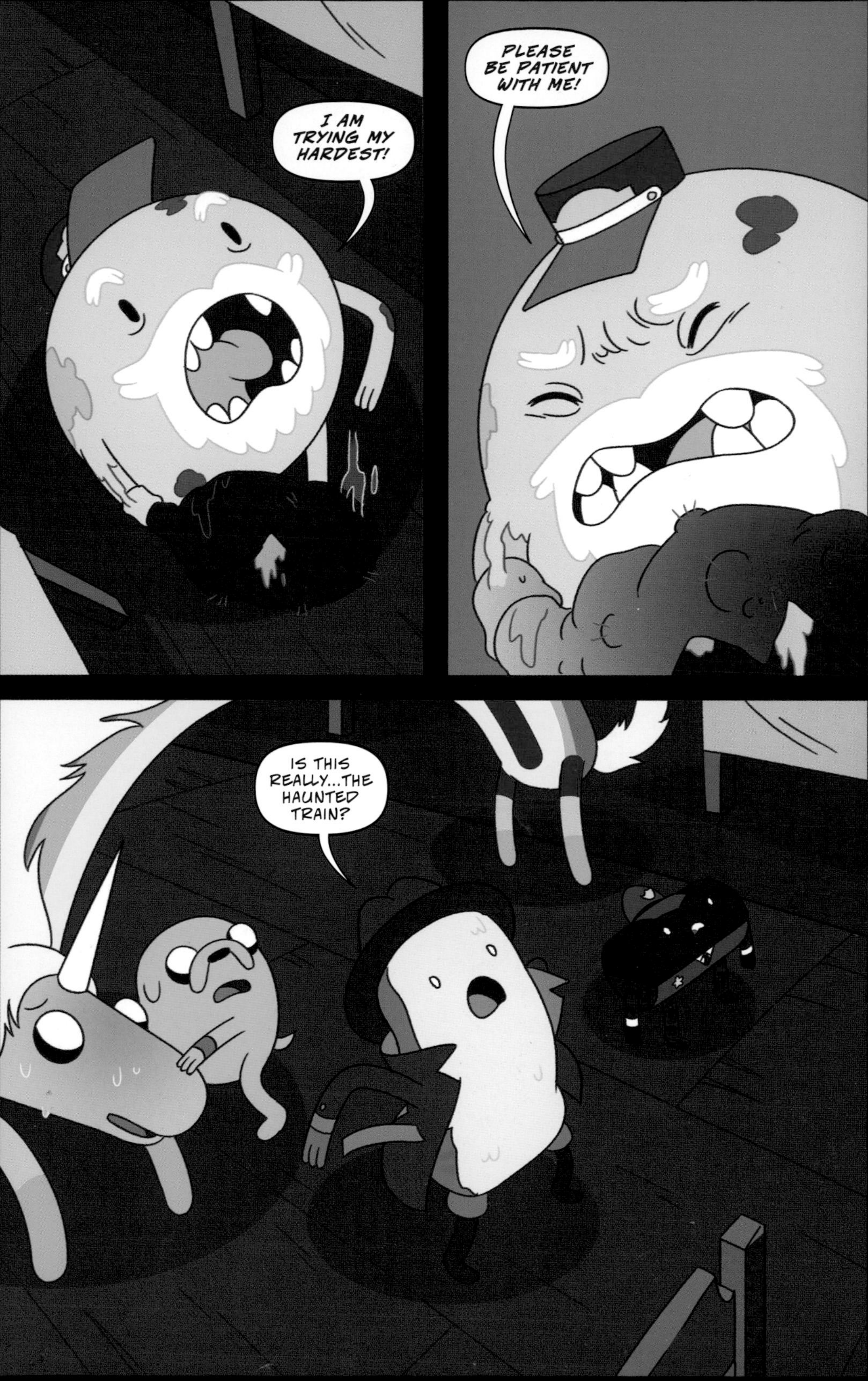
I AM TRYING MY HARDEST!
PLEASE BE PATIENT WITH ME!
IS THIS REALLY...THE HAUNTED TRAIN?

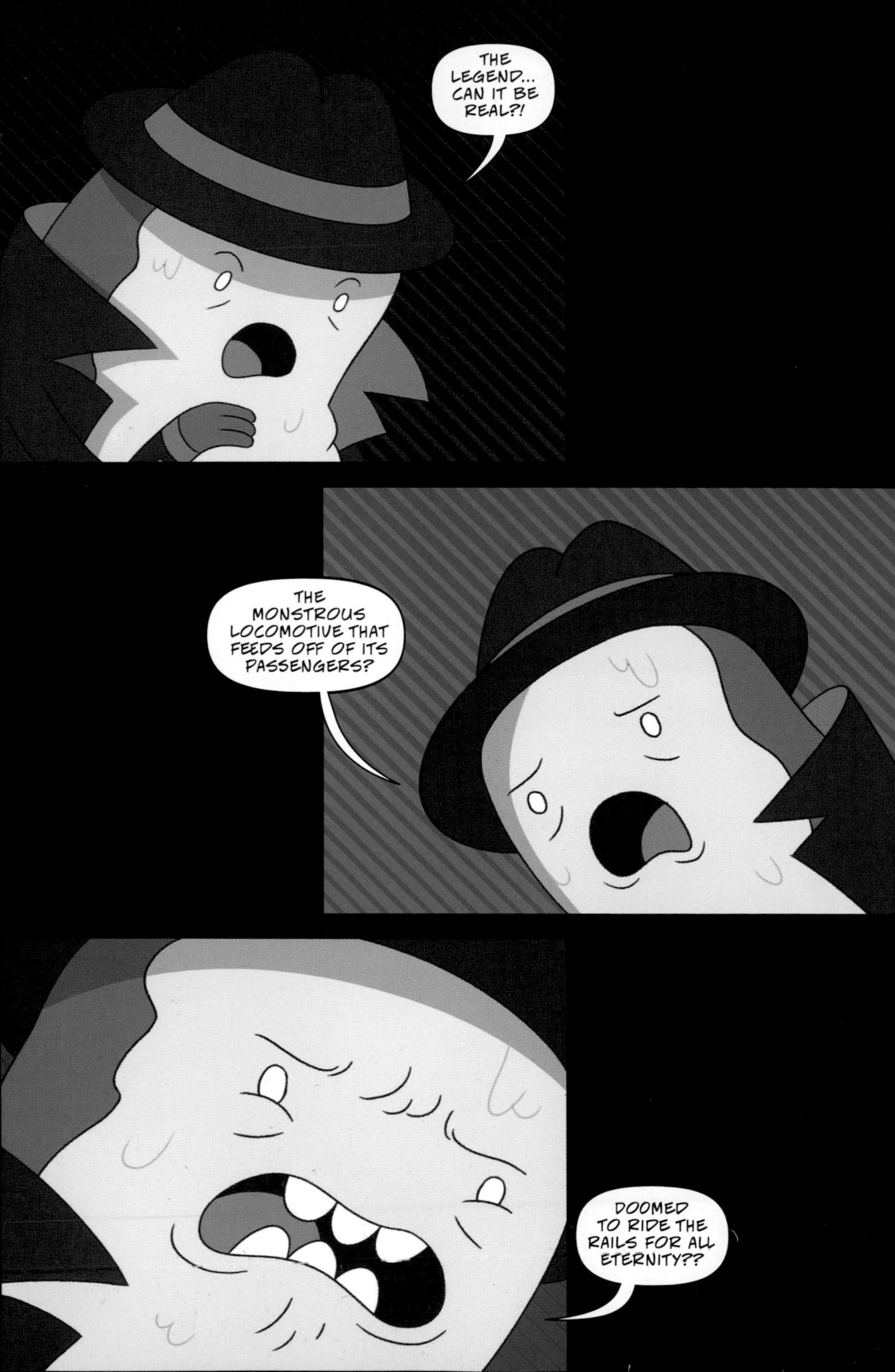
THE LEGEND... CAN IT BE REAL?!
THE MONSTROUS LOCOMOTIVE THAT FEEDS OFF OF ITS PASSENGERS?
DOOMED TO RIDE THE RAILS FOR ALL ETERNITY??

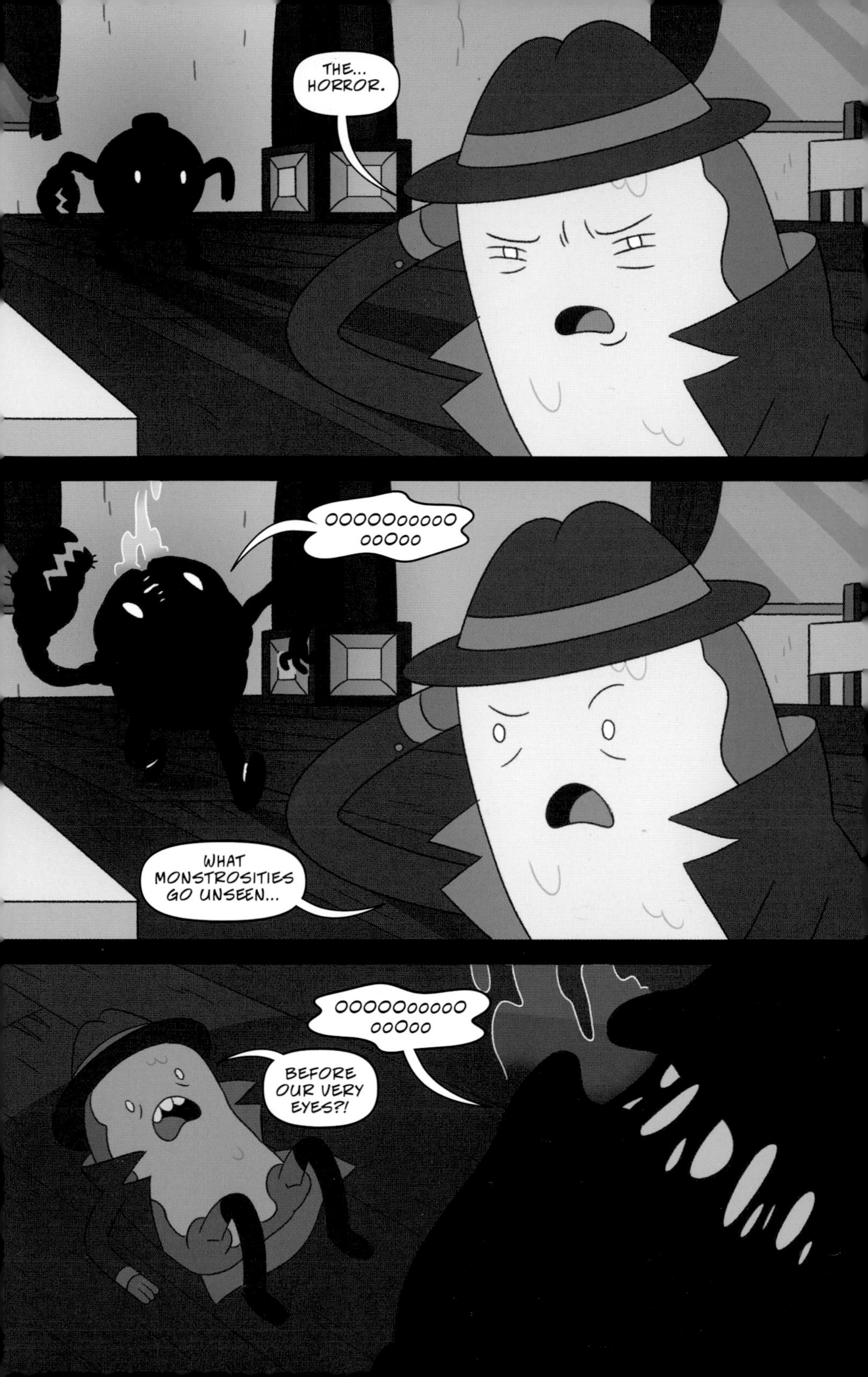
THE... HORROR.
OOOOOooooO ooOoo
WHAT MONSTROSITIES GO UNSEEN...
OOOOOooooO ooOoo
BEFORE OUR VERY EYES?!

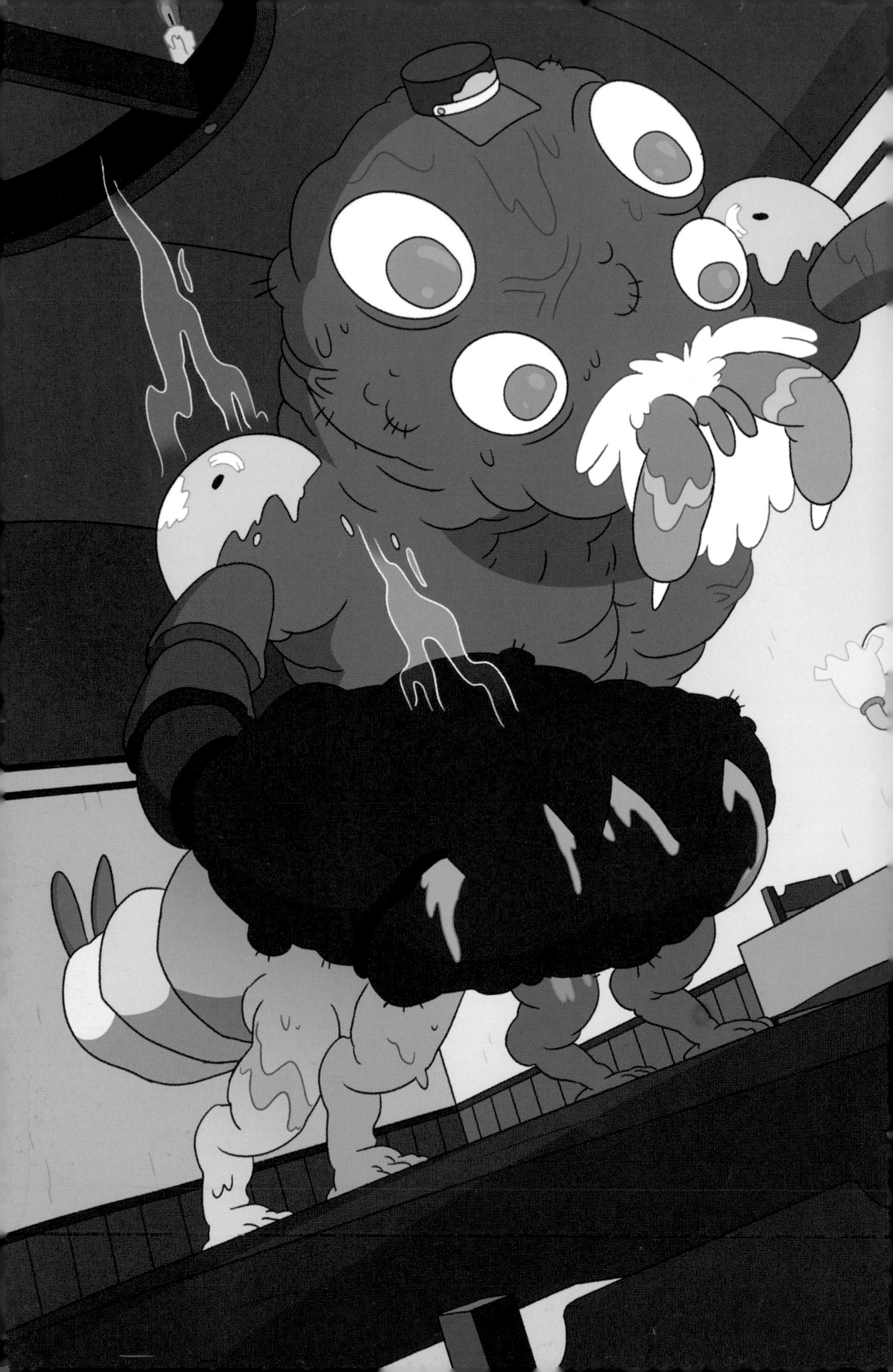

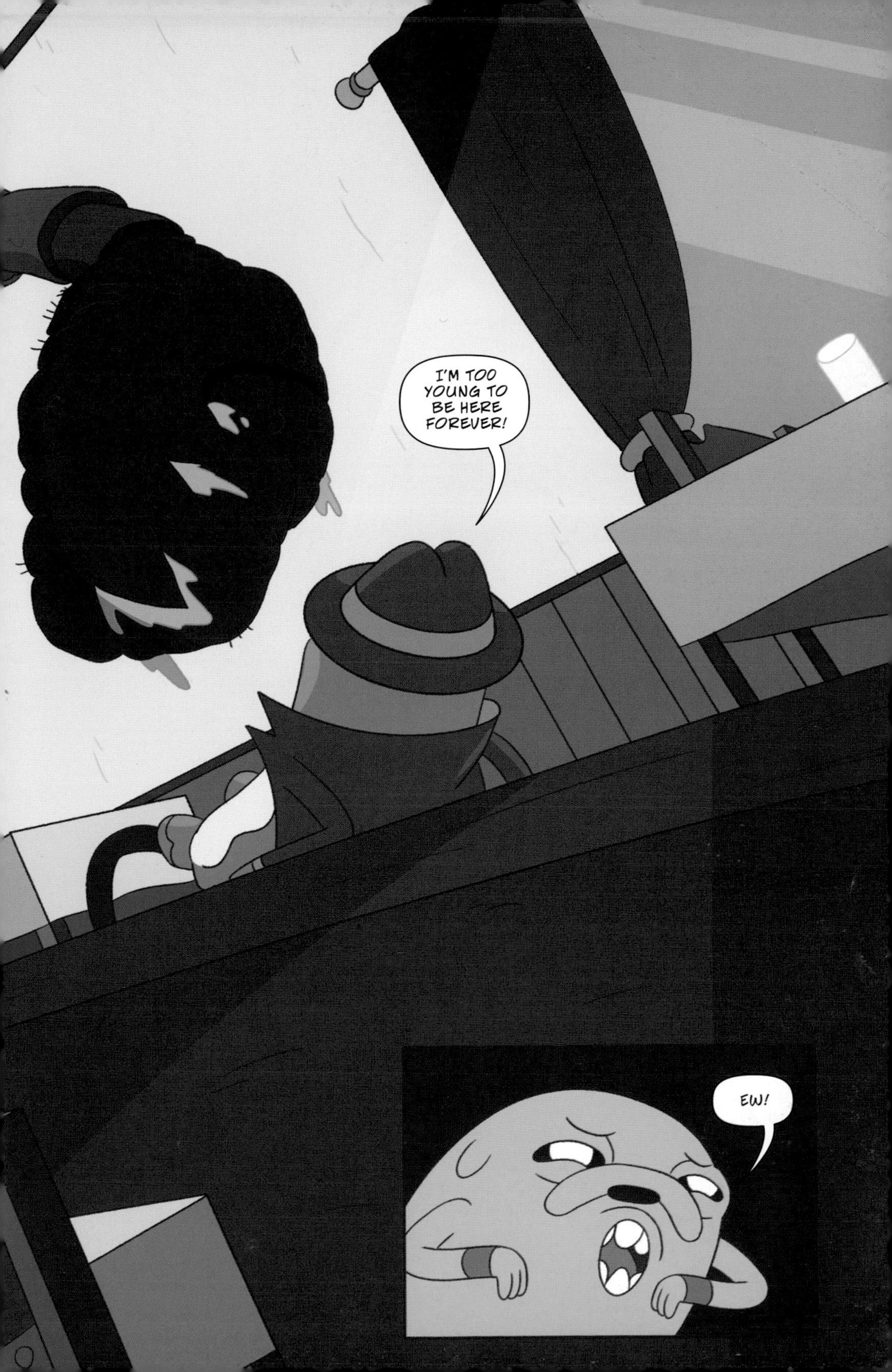
I'M TOO YOUNG TO BE HERE FOREVER!
EW!

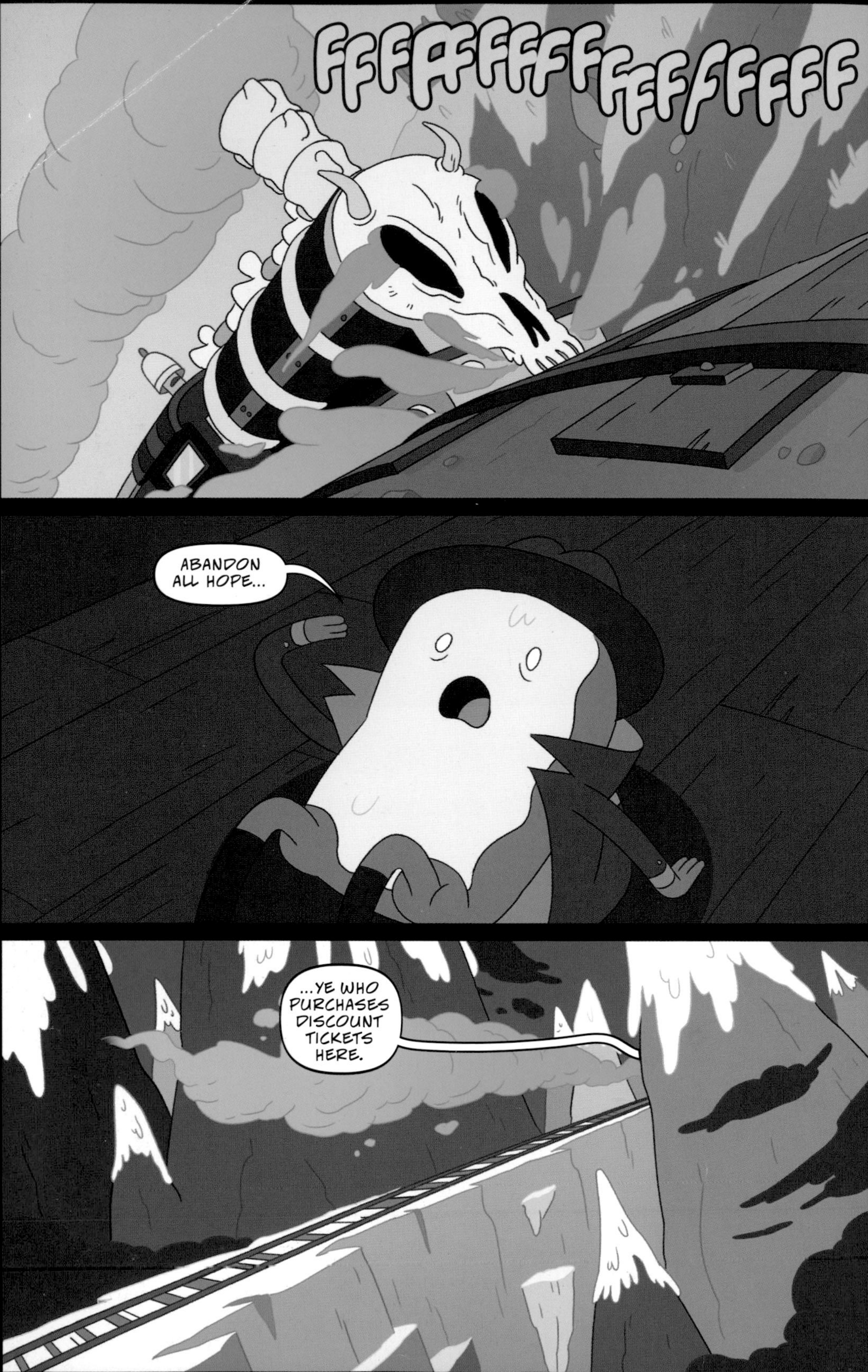
FFFFFFFFFFFFFFFF
ABANDON ALL HOPE...
...YE WHO PURCHASES DISCOUNT TICKETS HERE.

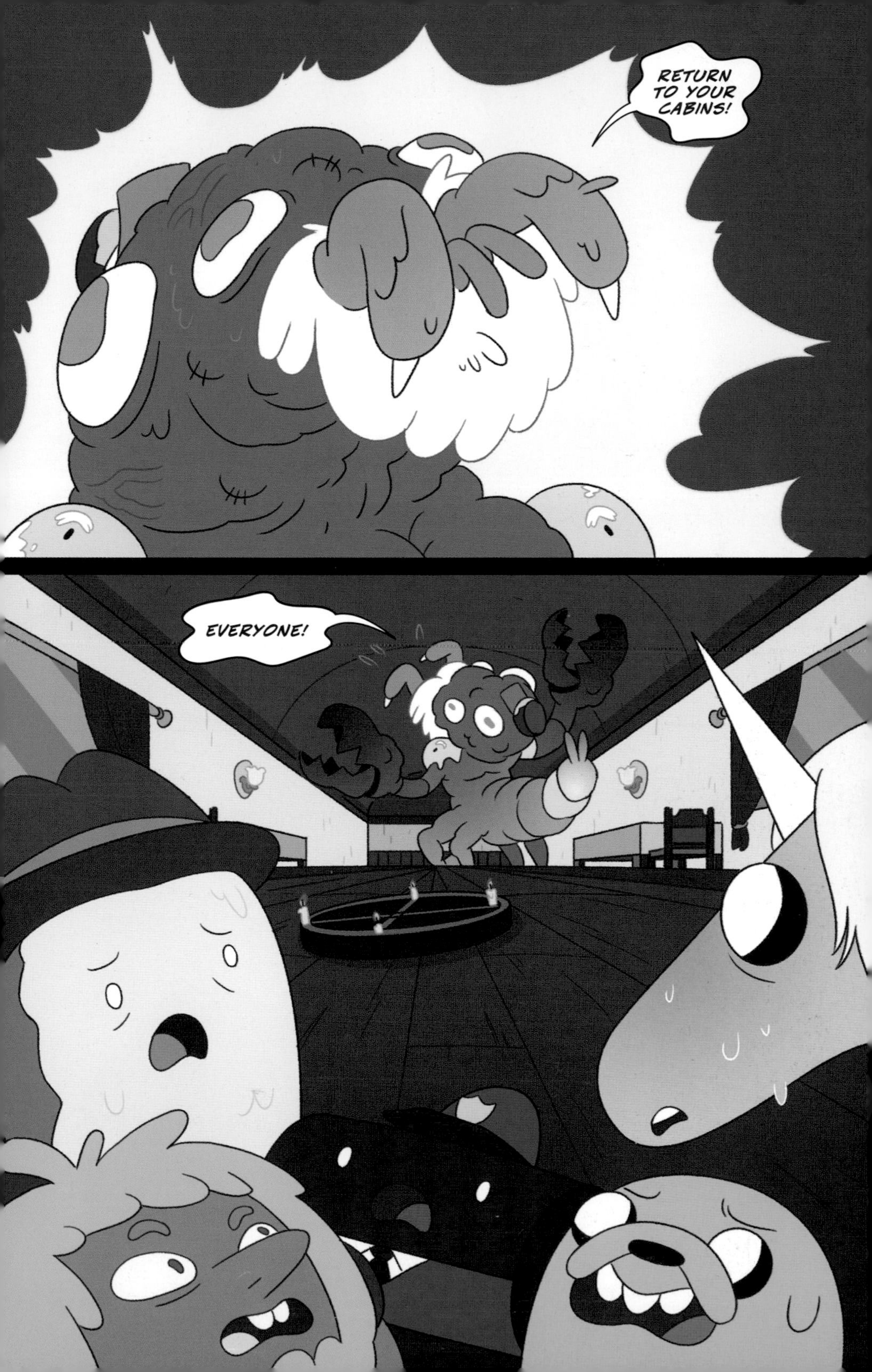
RETURN TO YOUR CABINS!
EVERYONE!

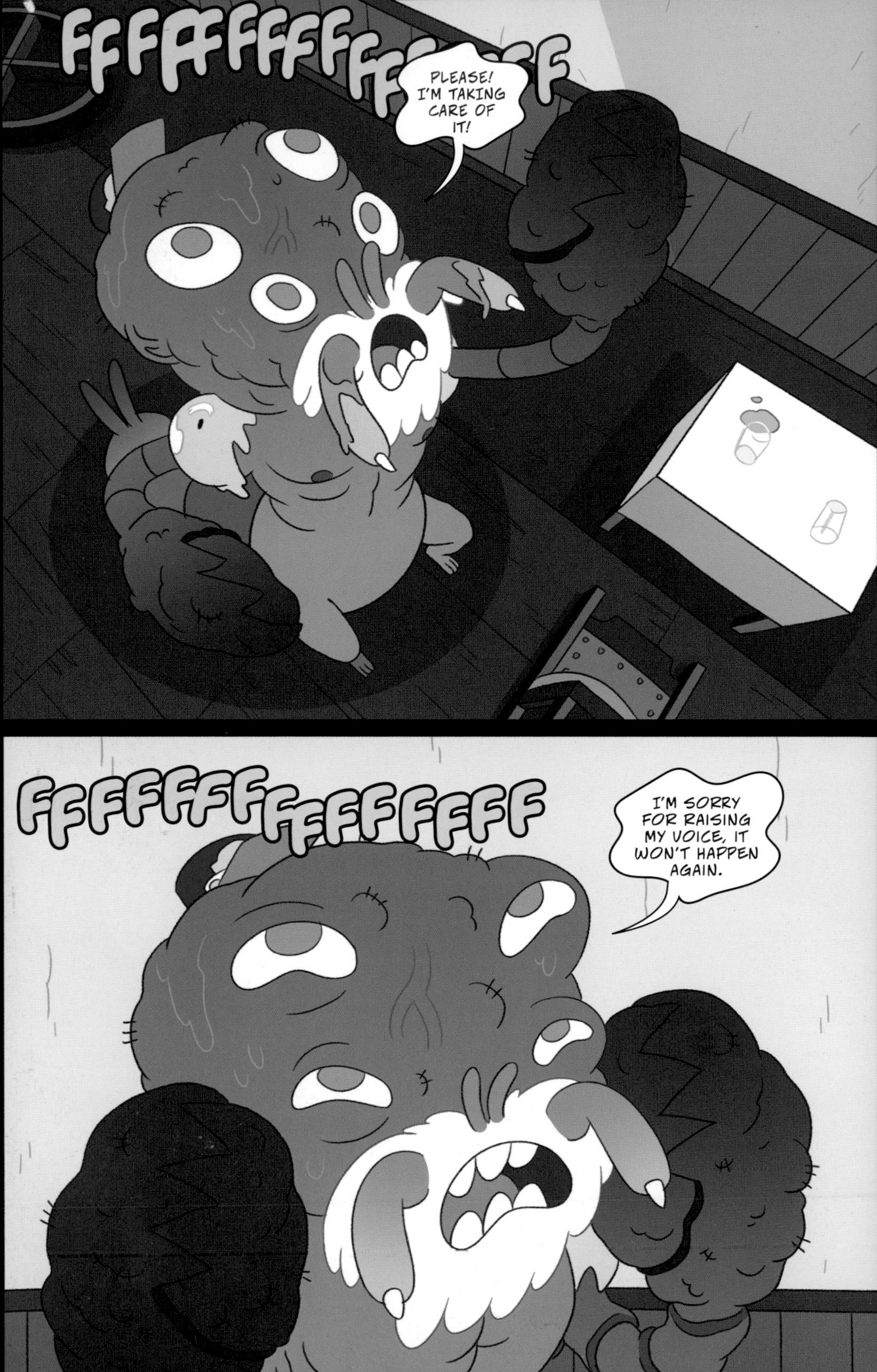
FFFFFFFFFFFFF
PLEASE! I'M TAKING CARE OF IT!
FFFFFFFFFFFFFF
I'M SORRY FOR RAISING MY VOICE, IT WON'T HAPPEN AGAIN.

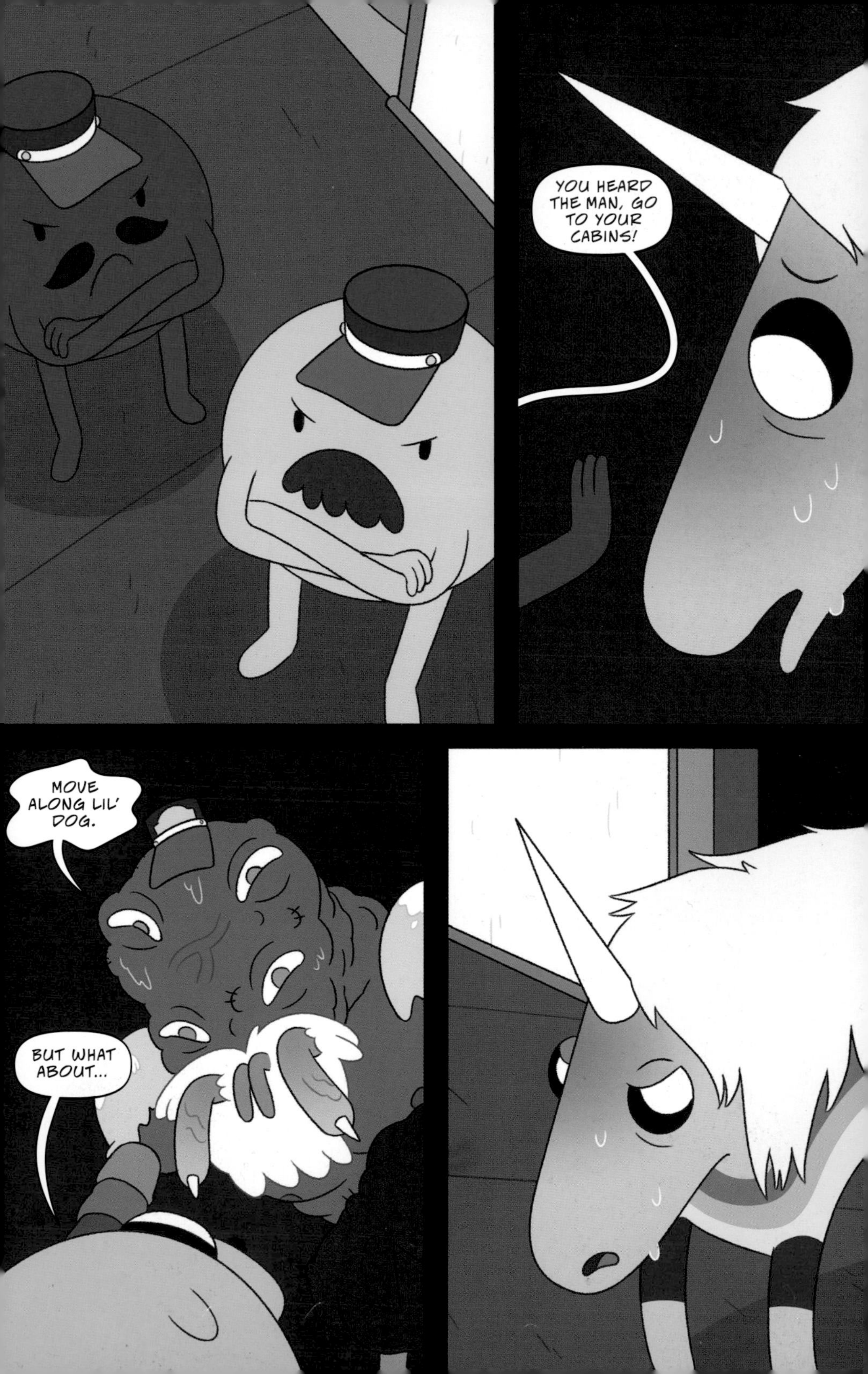
YOU HEARD THE MAN, GO TO YOUR CABINS!
MOVE ALONG LIL' DOG.
BUT WHAT ABOUT...

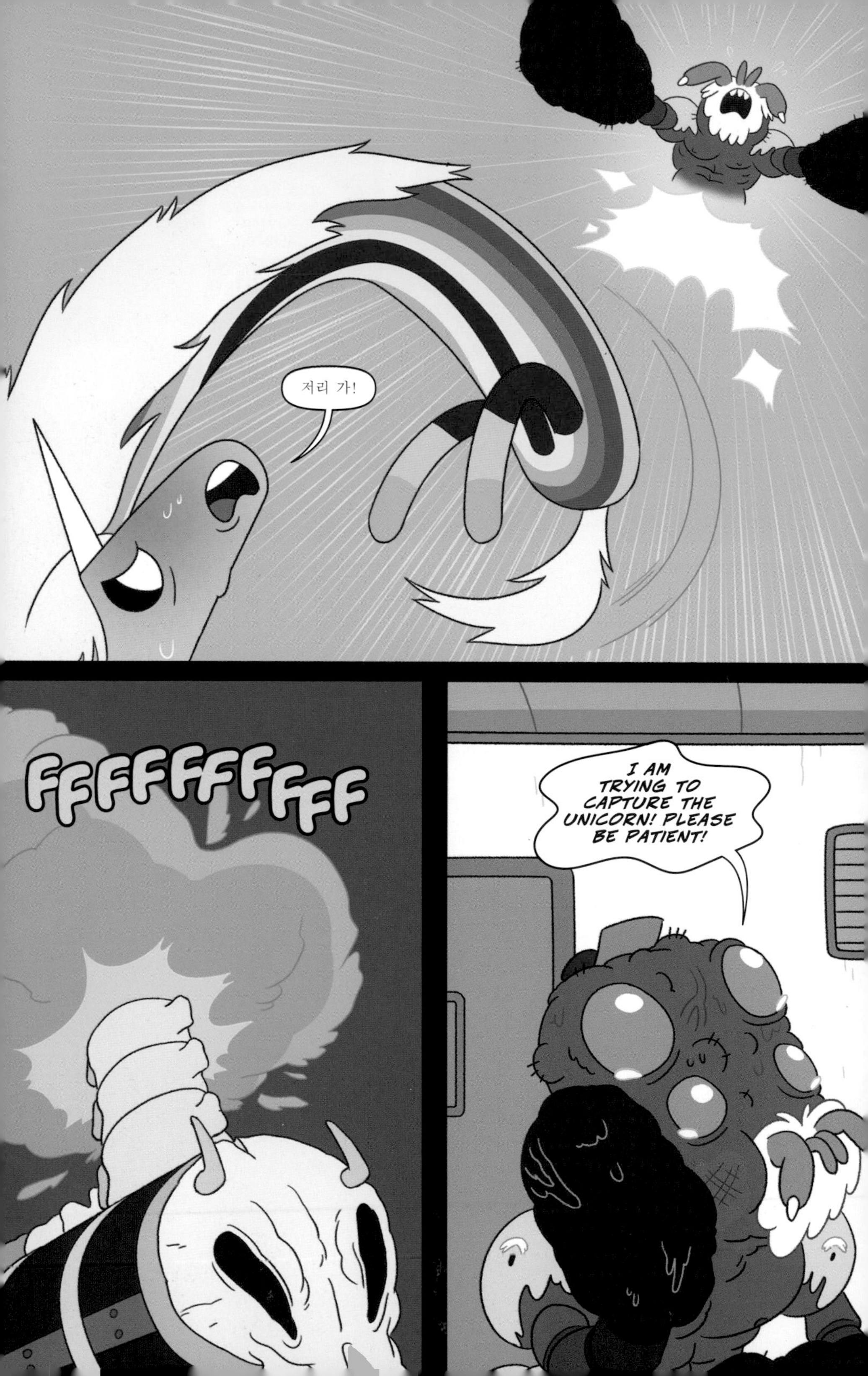
저리 가!
FFFFFFFFFFF
I AM TRYING TO CAPTURE THE UNICORN! PLEASE BE PATIENT!

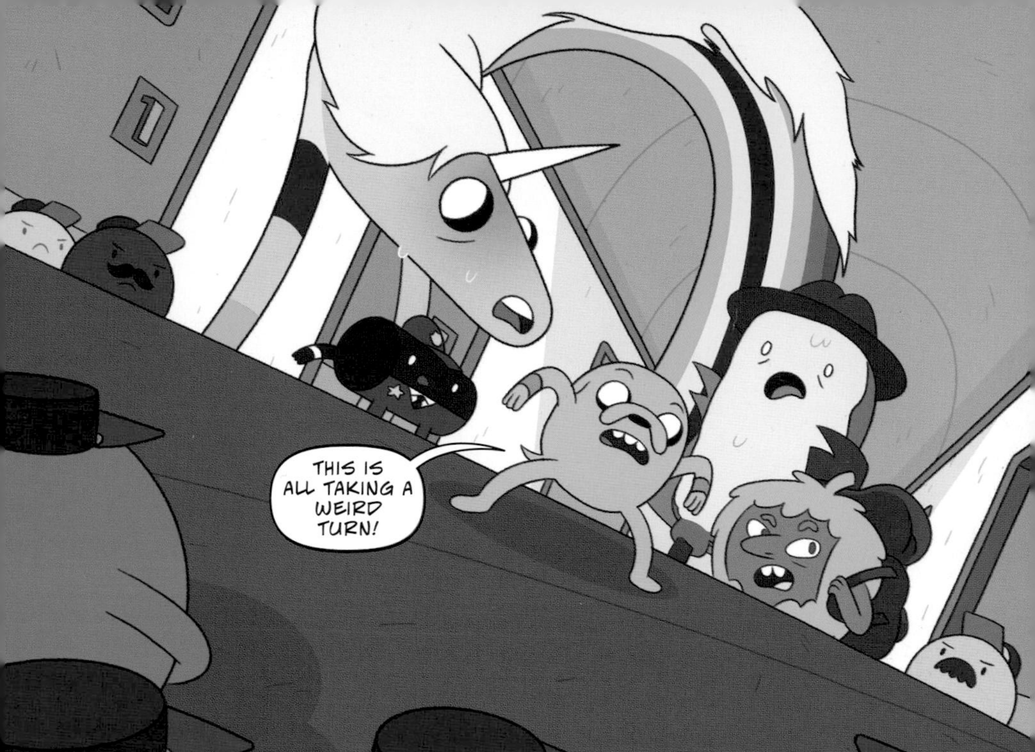
THIS IS ALL TAKING A WEIRD TURN!

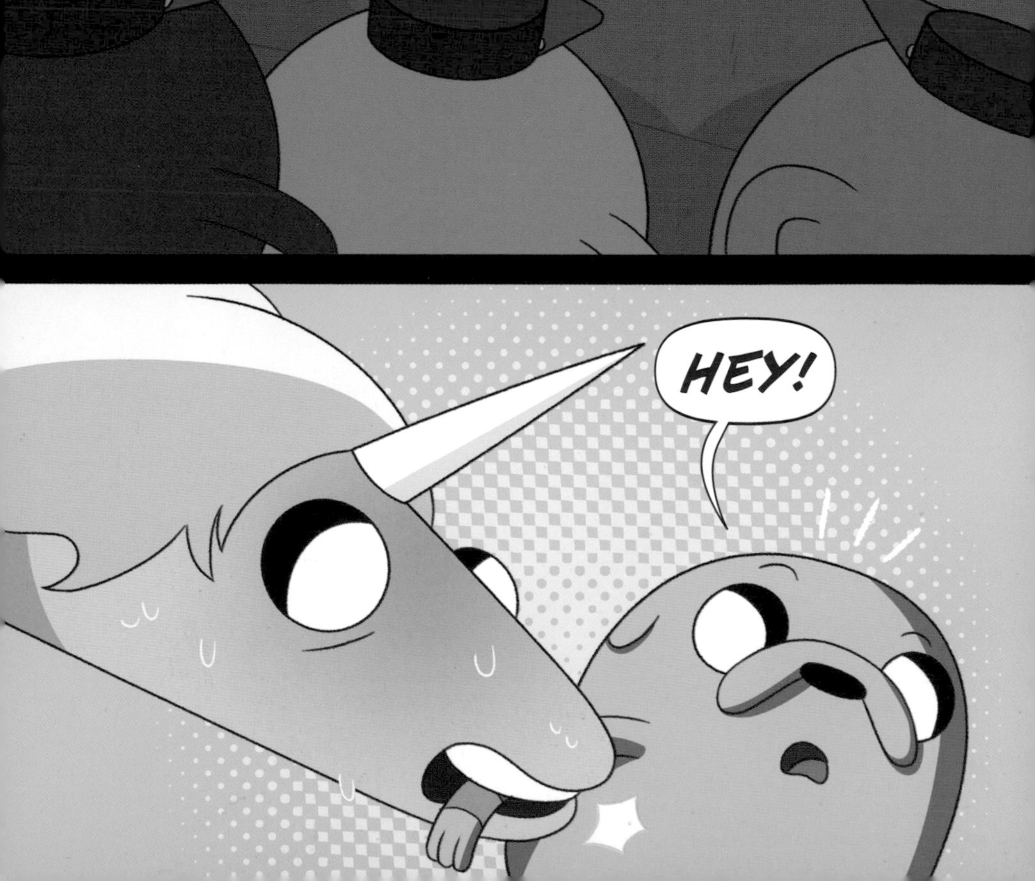
HEY!

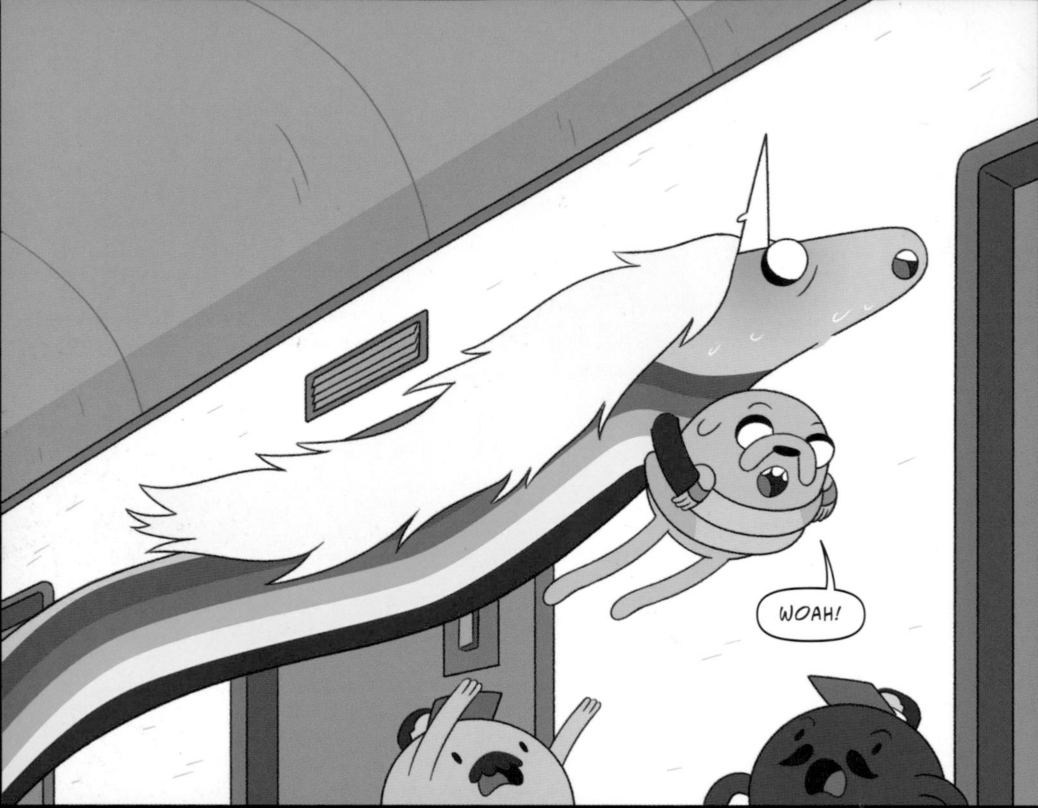
WOAH!

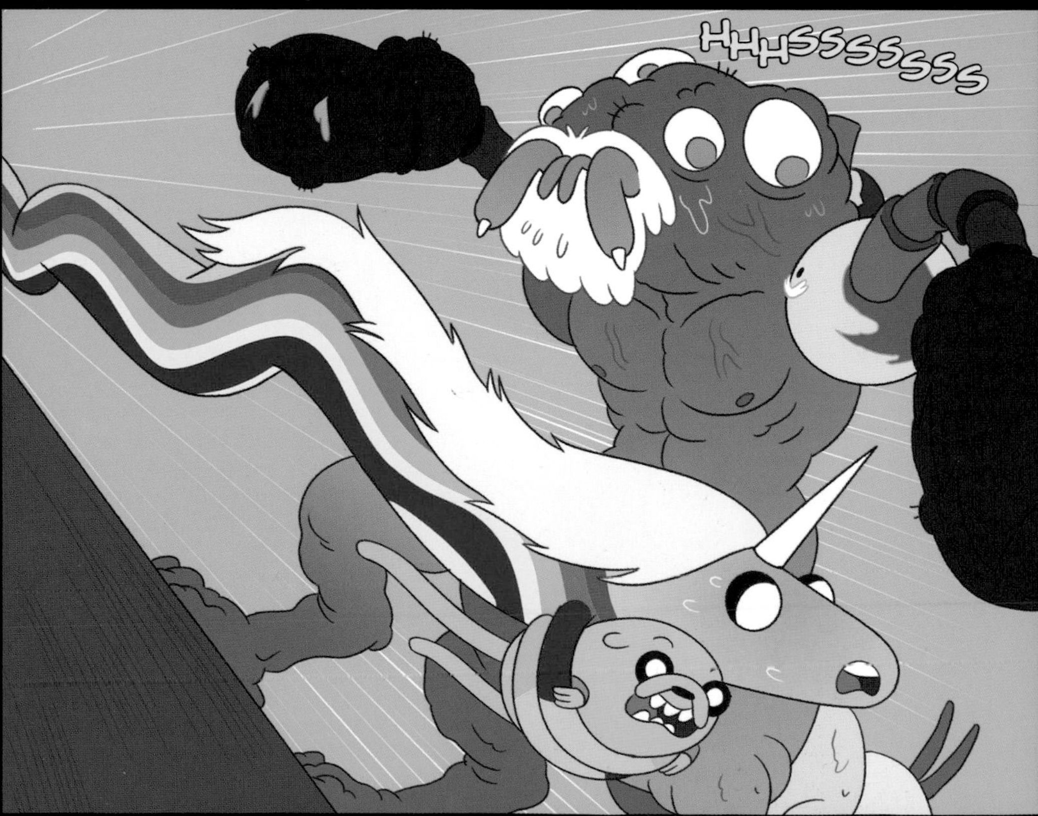
HHHSSSSSSSS

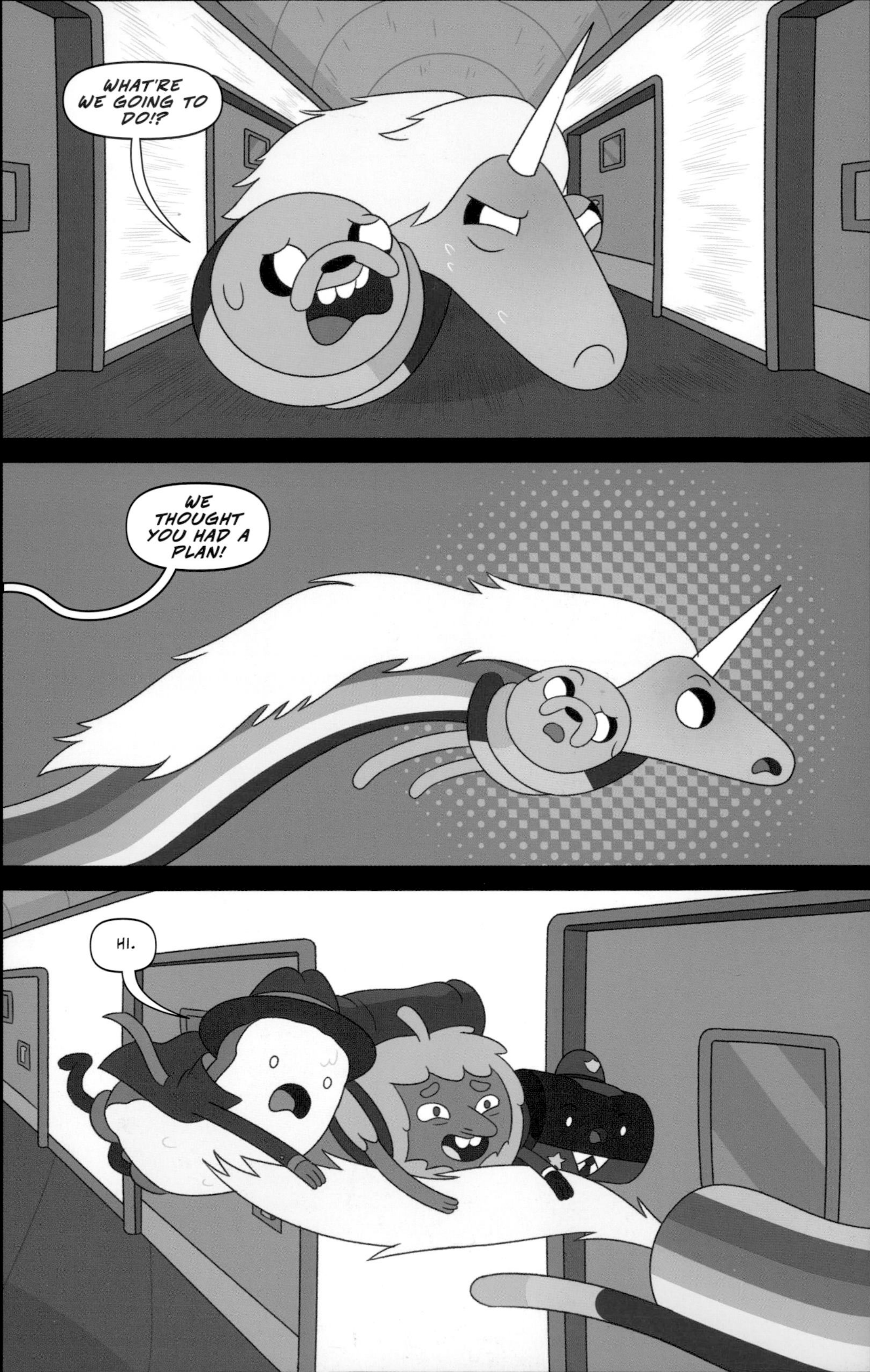
WHAT'RE WE GOING TO DO!?
WE THOUGHT YOU HAD A PLAN!
HI.

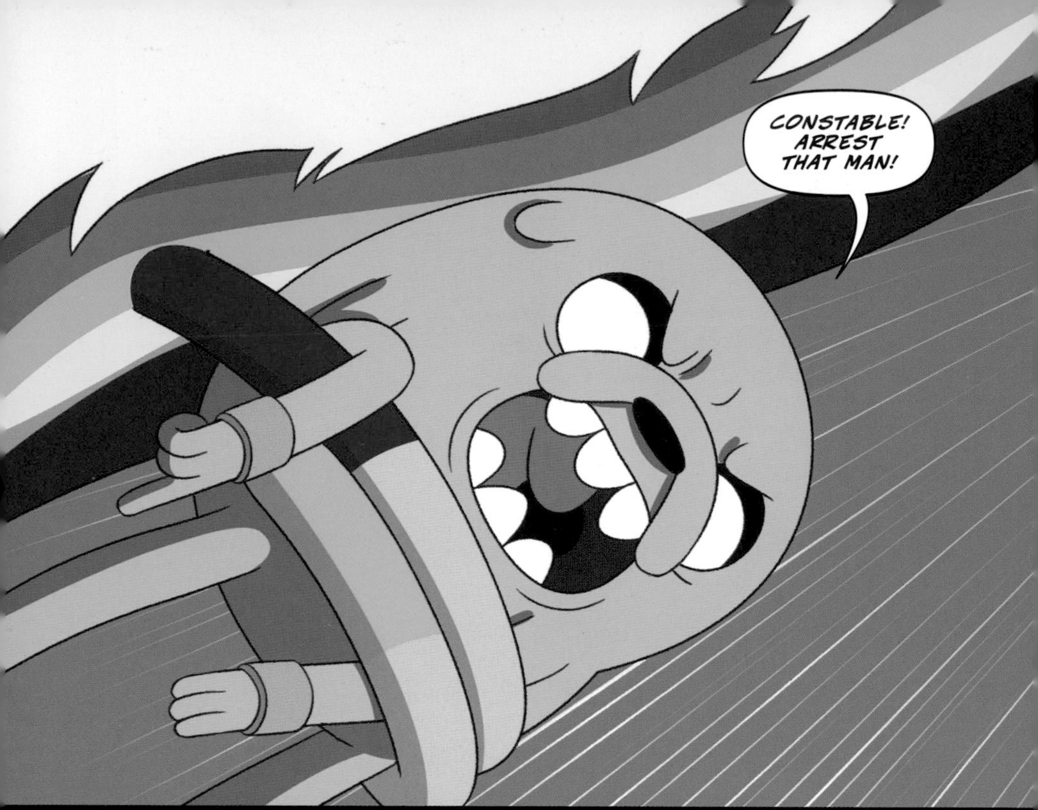
CONSTABLE! ARREST THAT MAN!
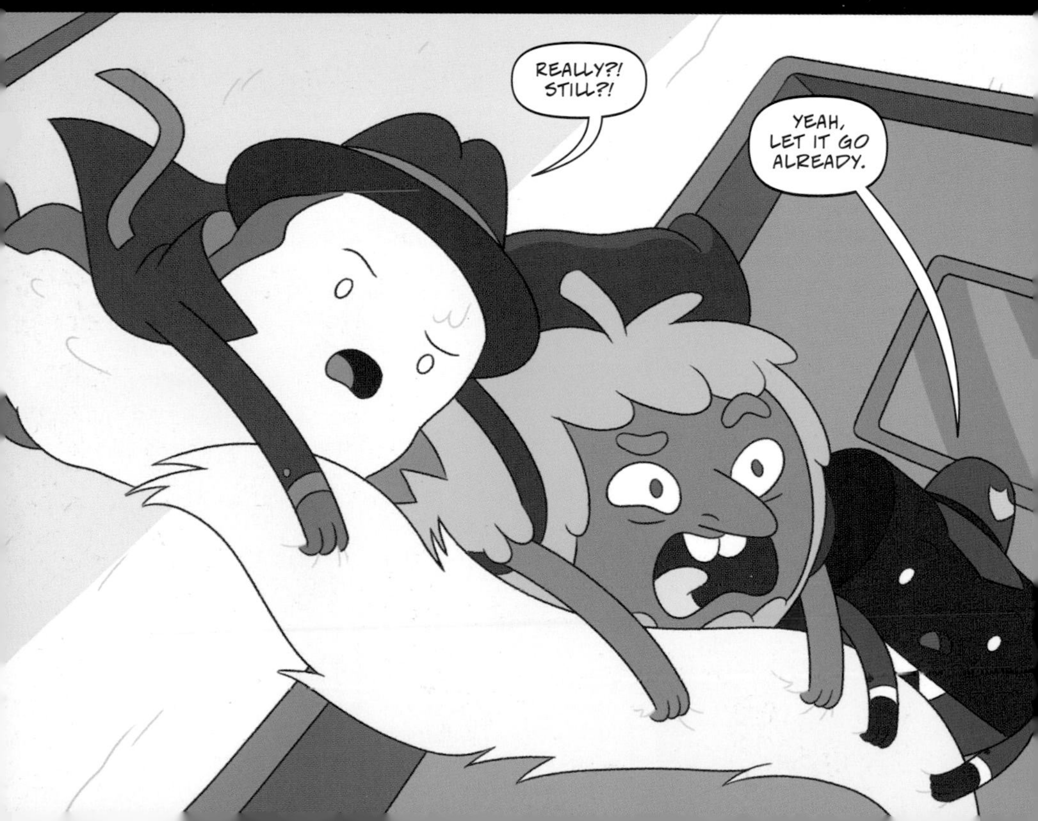
REALLY?! STILL?!
YEAH, LET IT GO ALREADY.

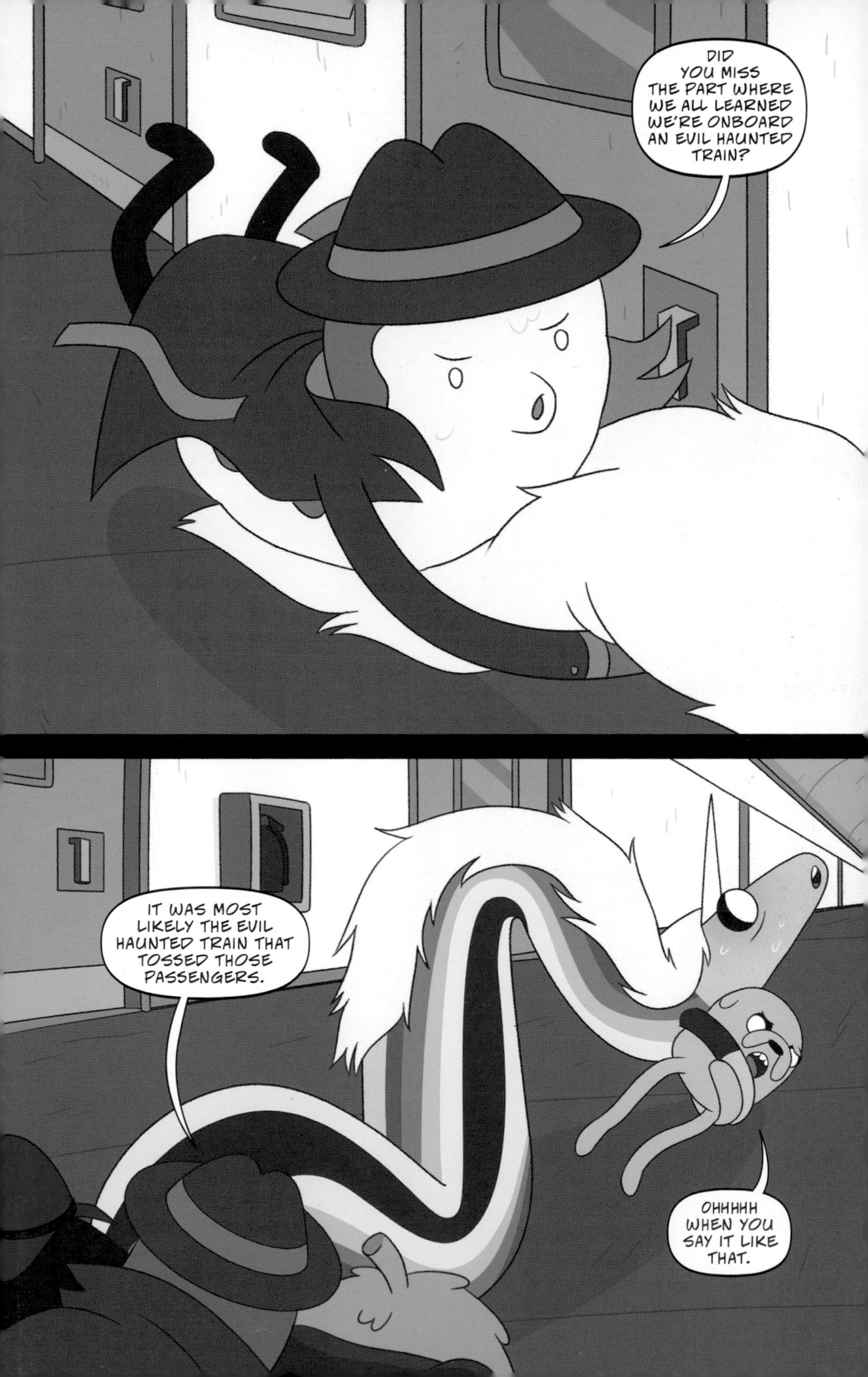
DID YOU MISS THE PART WHERE WE ALL LEARNED WE'RE ONBOARD AN EVIL HAUNTED TRAIN?
IT WAS MOST LIKELY THE EVIL HAUNTED TRAIN THAT TOSSED THOSE PASSENGERS.
OHHHHH WHEN YOU SAY IT LIKE THAT.

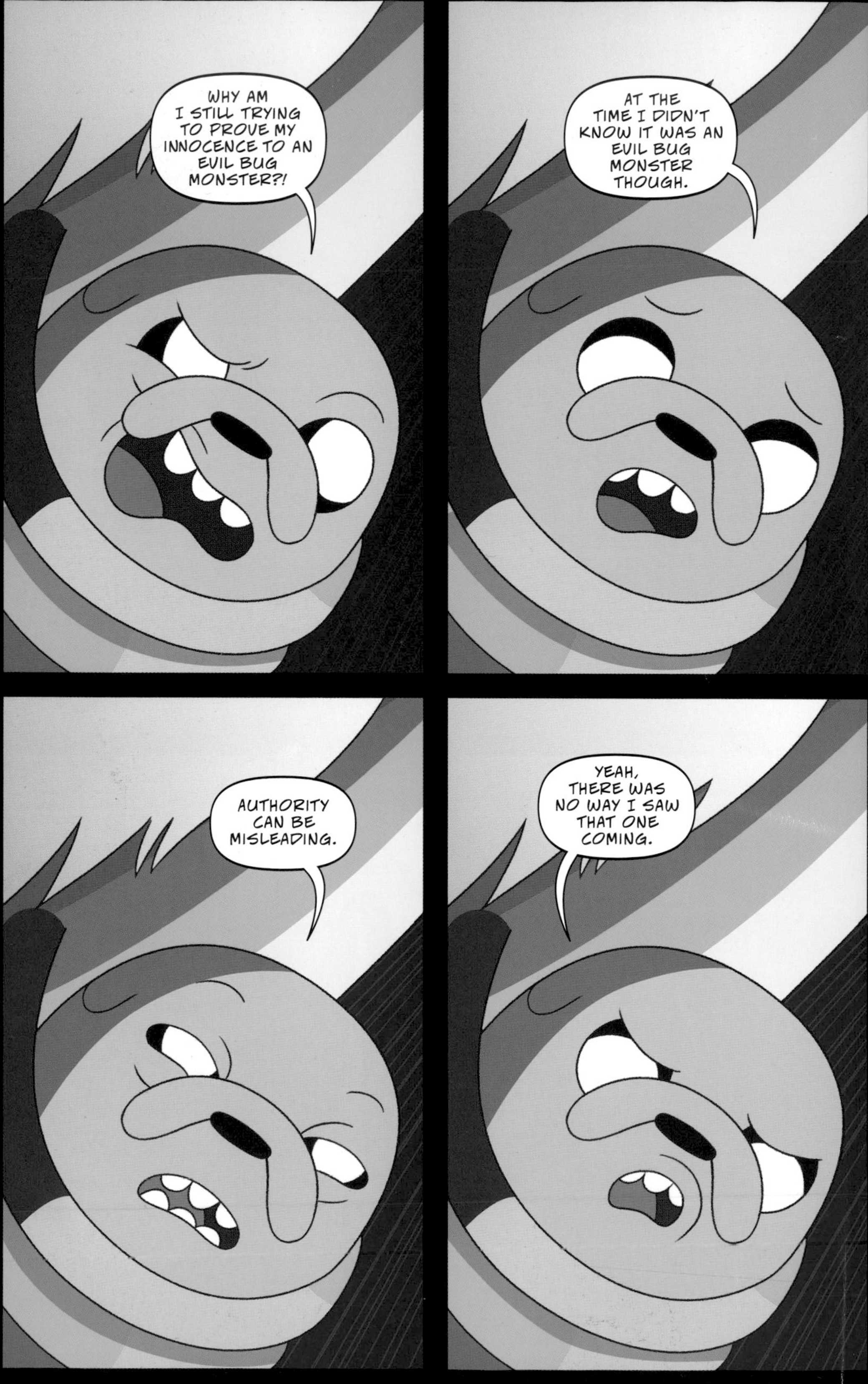
WHY AM I STILL TRYING TO PROVE MY INNOCENCE TO AN EVIL BUG MONSTER?!
AT THE TIME I DIDN'T KNOW IT WAS AN EVIL BUG MONSTER THOUGH.
AUTHORITY CAN BE MISLEADING.
YEAH, THERE WAS NO WAY I SAW THAT ONE COMING.

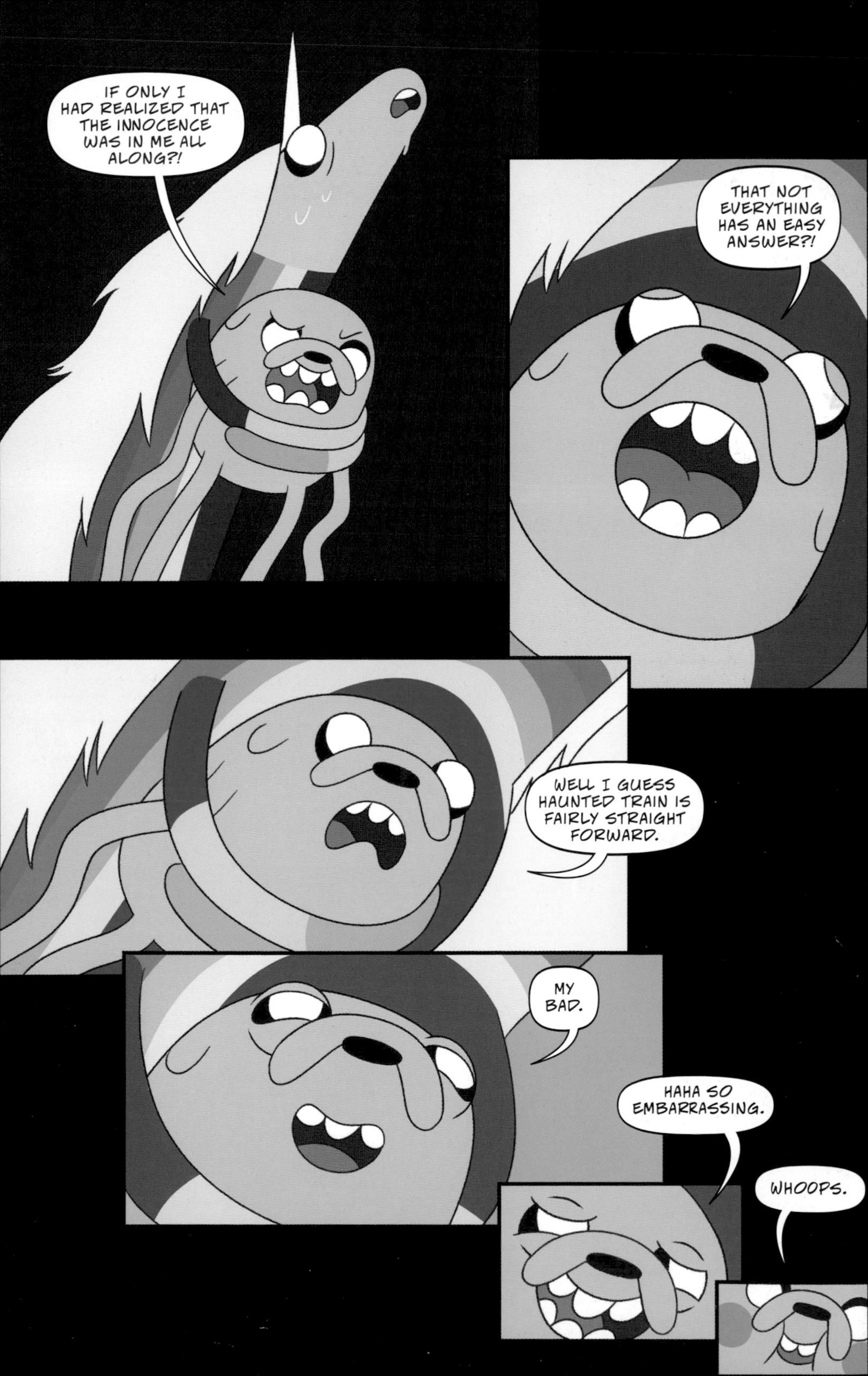
IF ONLY I HAD REALIZED THAT THE INNOCENCE WAS IN ME ALL ALONG?!
THAT NOT EVERYTHING HAS AN EASY ANSWER?!
WELL I GUESS HAUNTED TRAIN IS FAIRLY STRAIGHT FORWARD.
MY BAD.
HAHA SO EMBARRASSING.
WHOOPS.

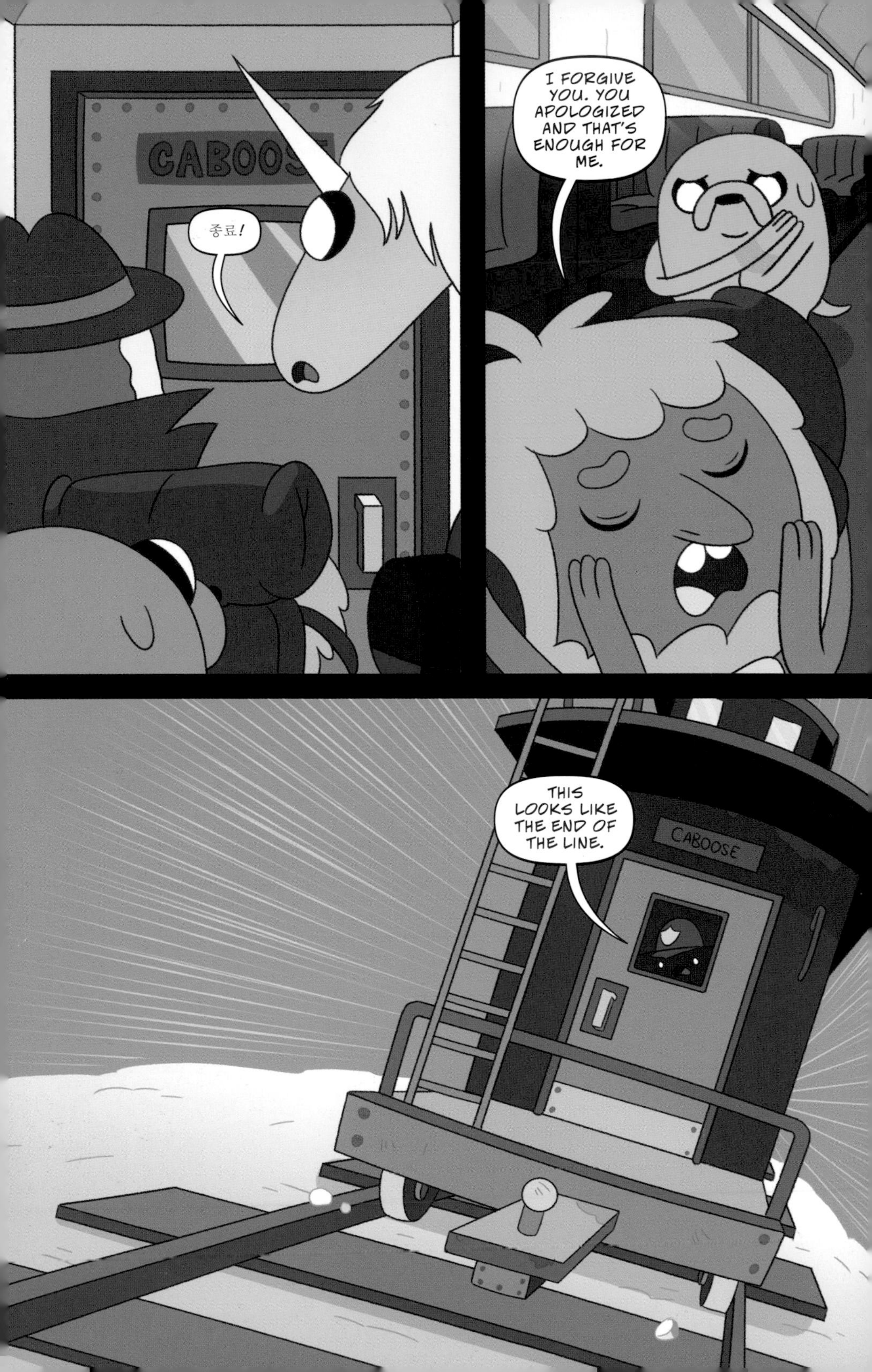
CABOOSE
종료!
I FORGIVE YOU. YOU APOLOGIZED AND THAT'S ENOUGH FOR ME.
THIS LOOKS LIKE THE END OF THE LINE.
CABOOSE

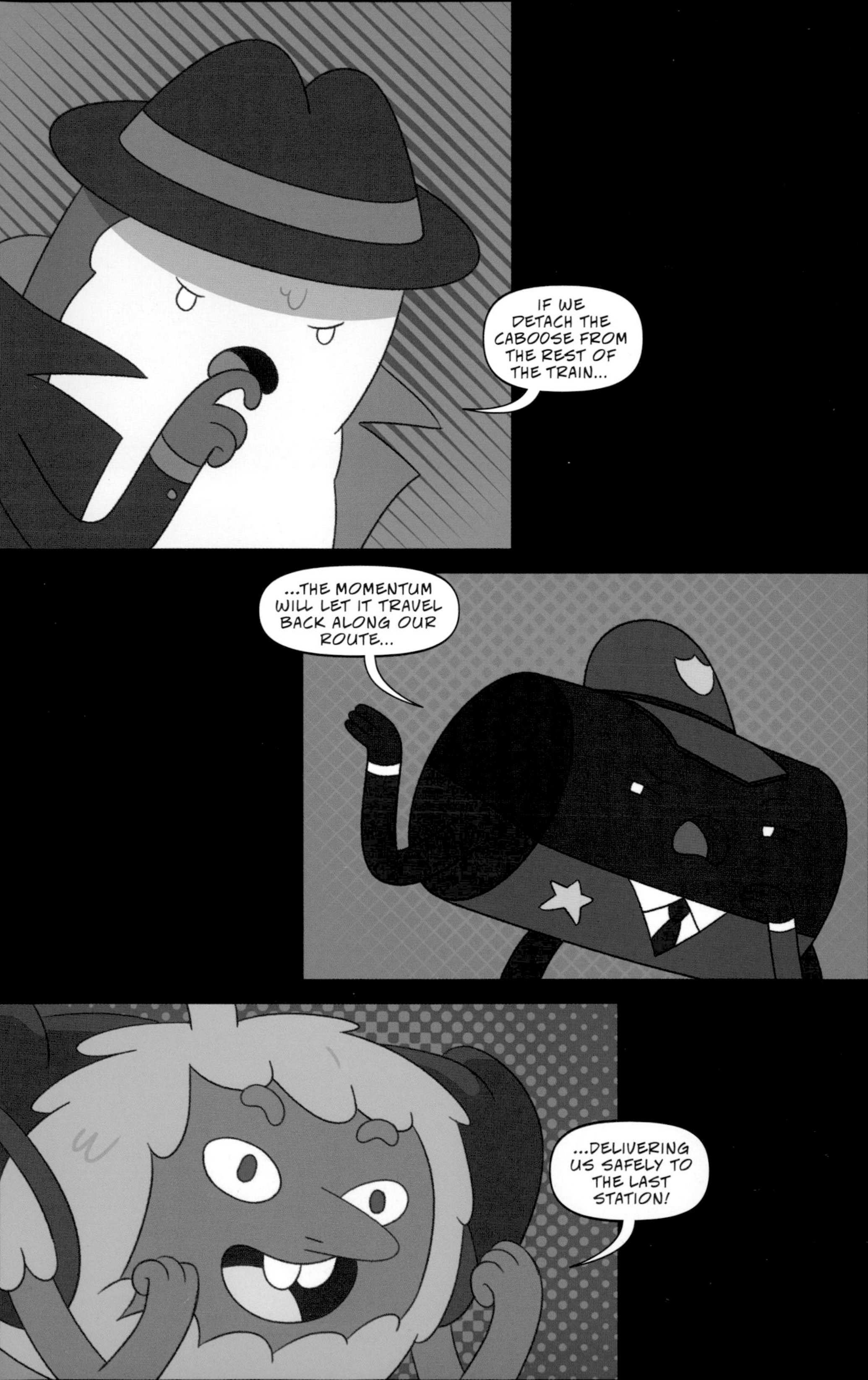
IF WE DETACH THE CABOOSE FROM THE REST OF THE TRAIN...
...THE MOMENTUM WILL LET IT TRAVEL BACK ALONG OUR ROUTE...
...DELIVERING US SAFELY TO THE LAST STATION!

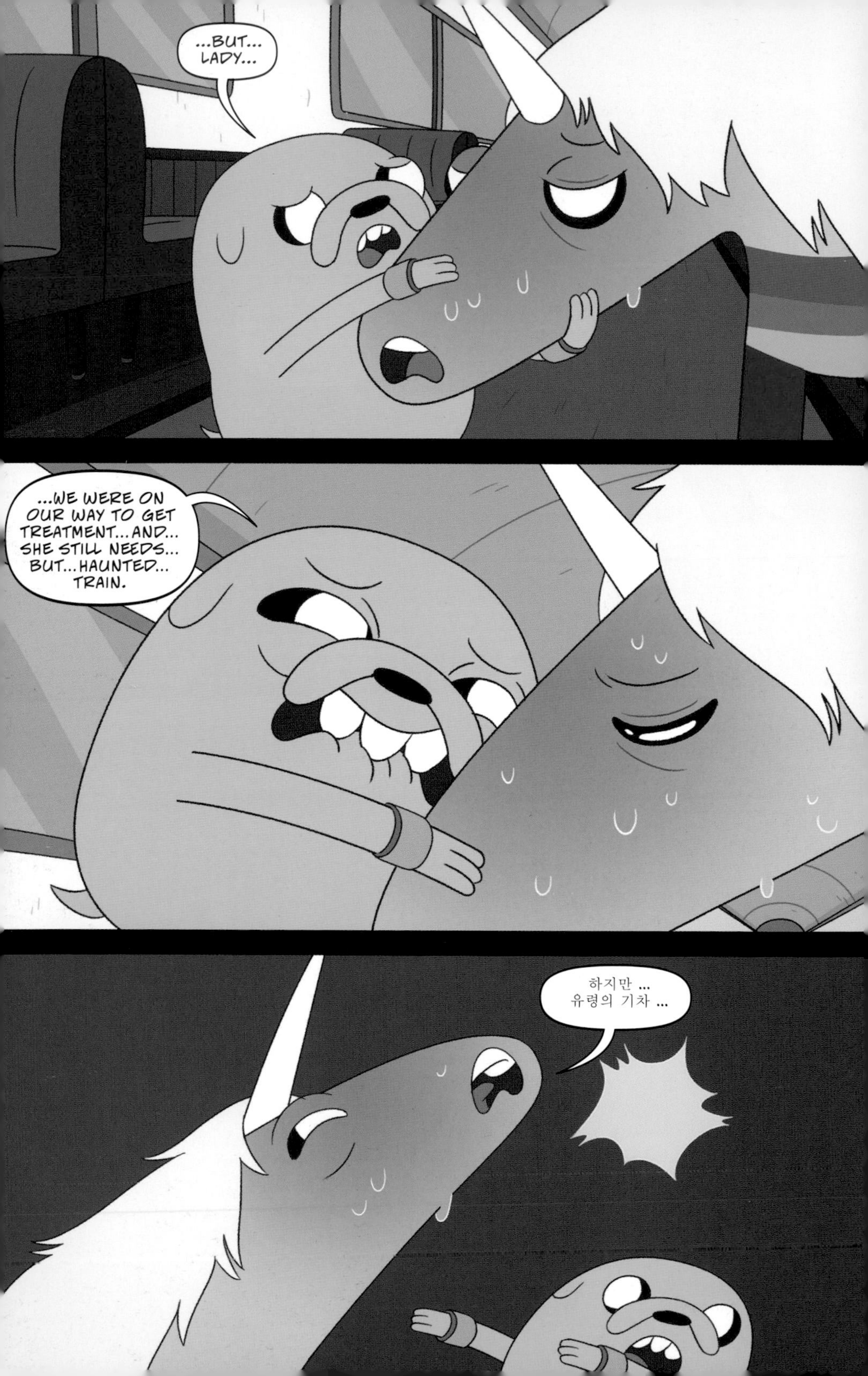
...BUT... LADY...
...WE WERE ON OUR WAY TO GET TREATMENT...AND... SHE STILL NEEDS... BUT...HAUNTED... TRAIN.
하지만 ... 유령의 기차 ...

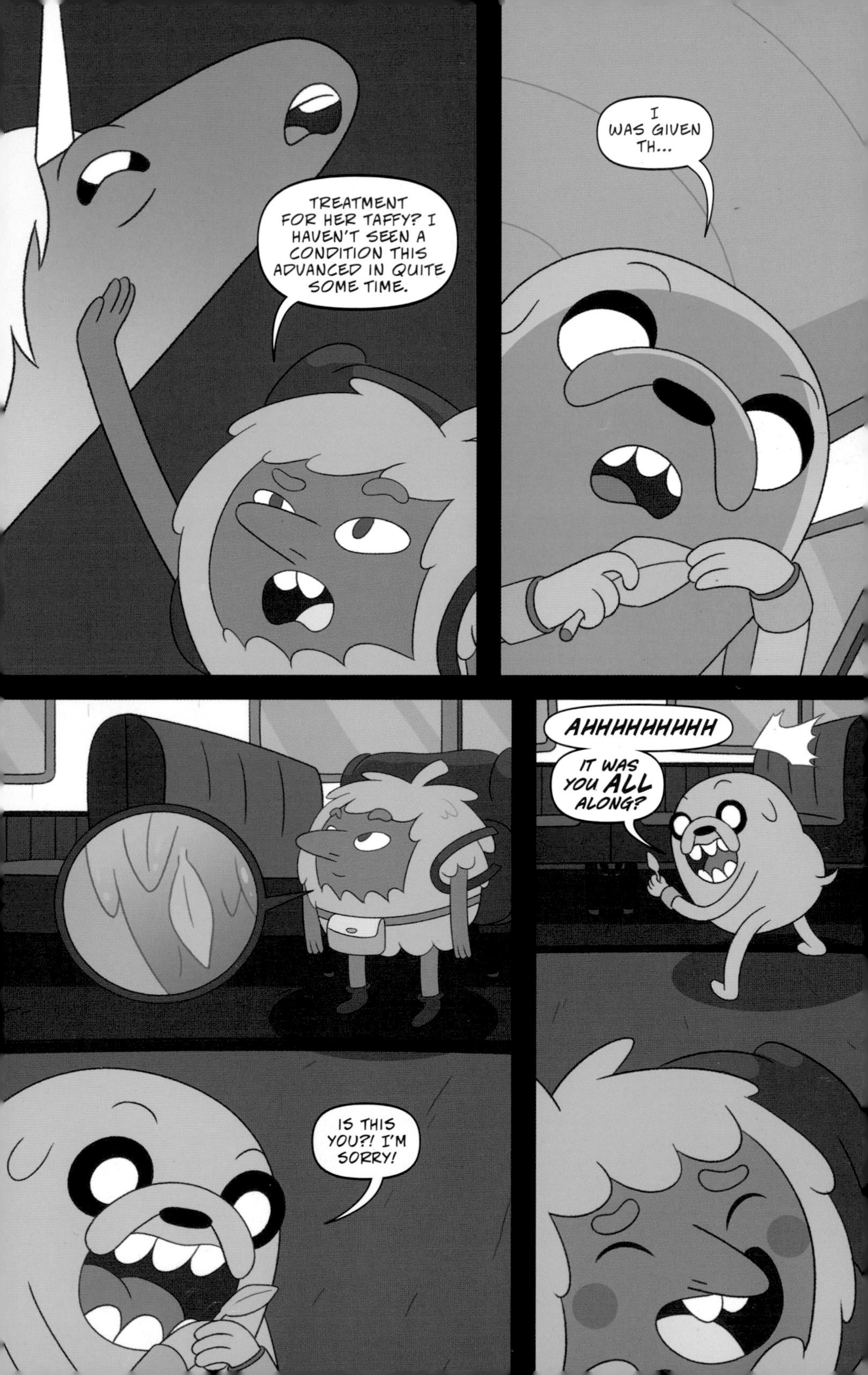
TREATMENT FOR HER TAFFY? I HAVEN'T SEEN A CONDITION THIS ADVANCED IN QUITE SOME TIME.
I WAS GIVEN TH...
AHHHHHHHHH
IT WAS YOU ALL ALONG?
IS THIS YOU?! I'M SORRY!

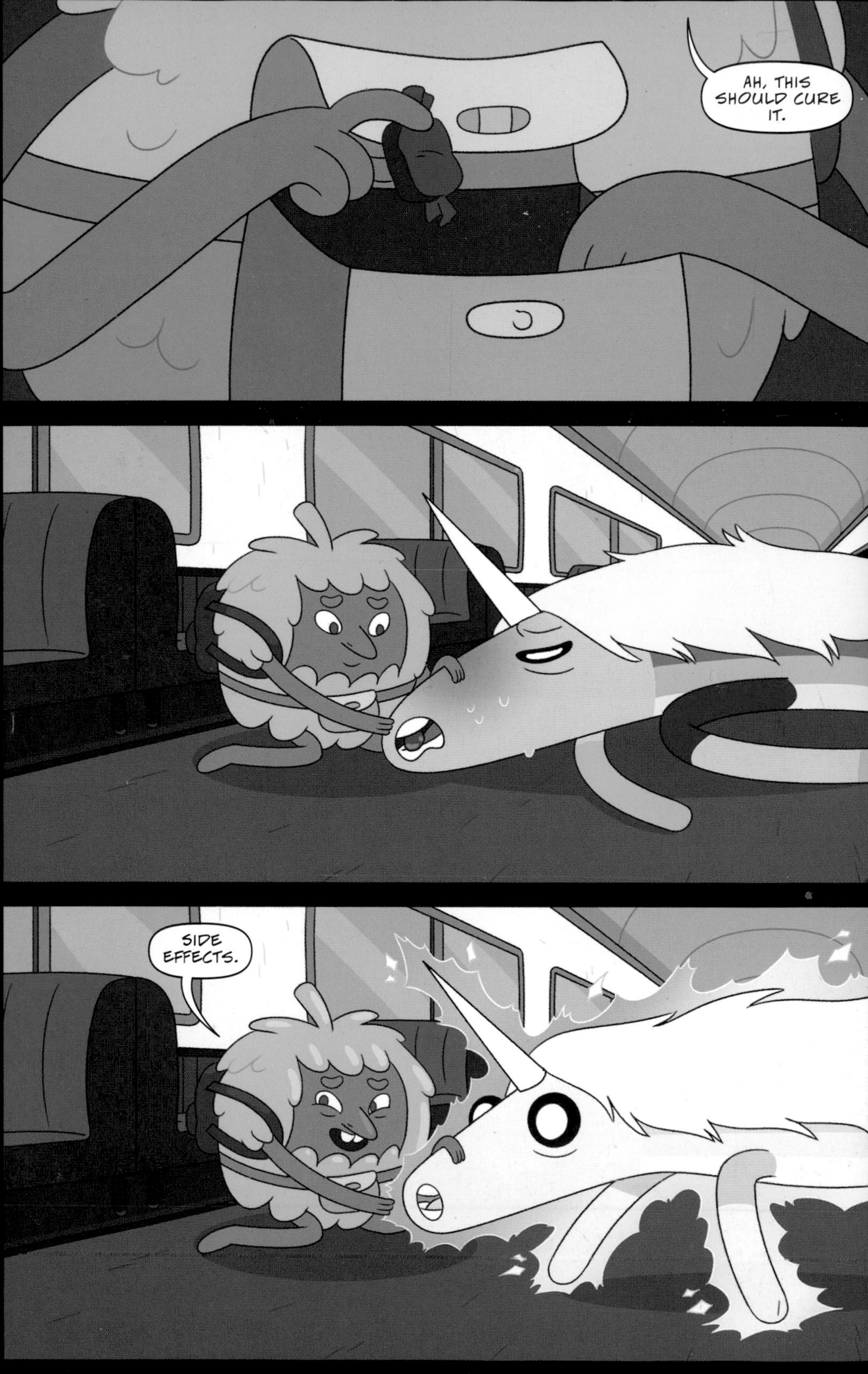
AH, THIS SHOULD CURE IT.
SIDE EFFECTS.

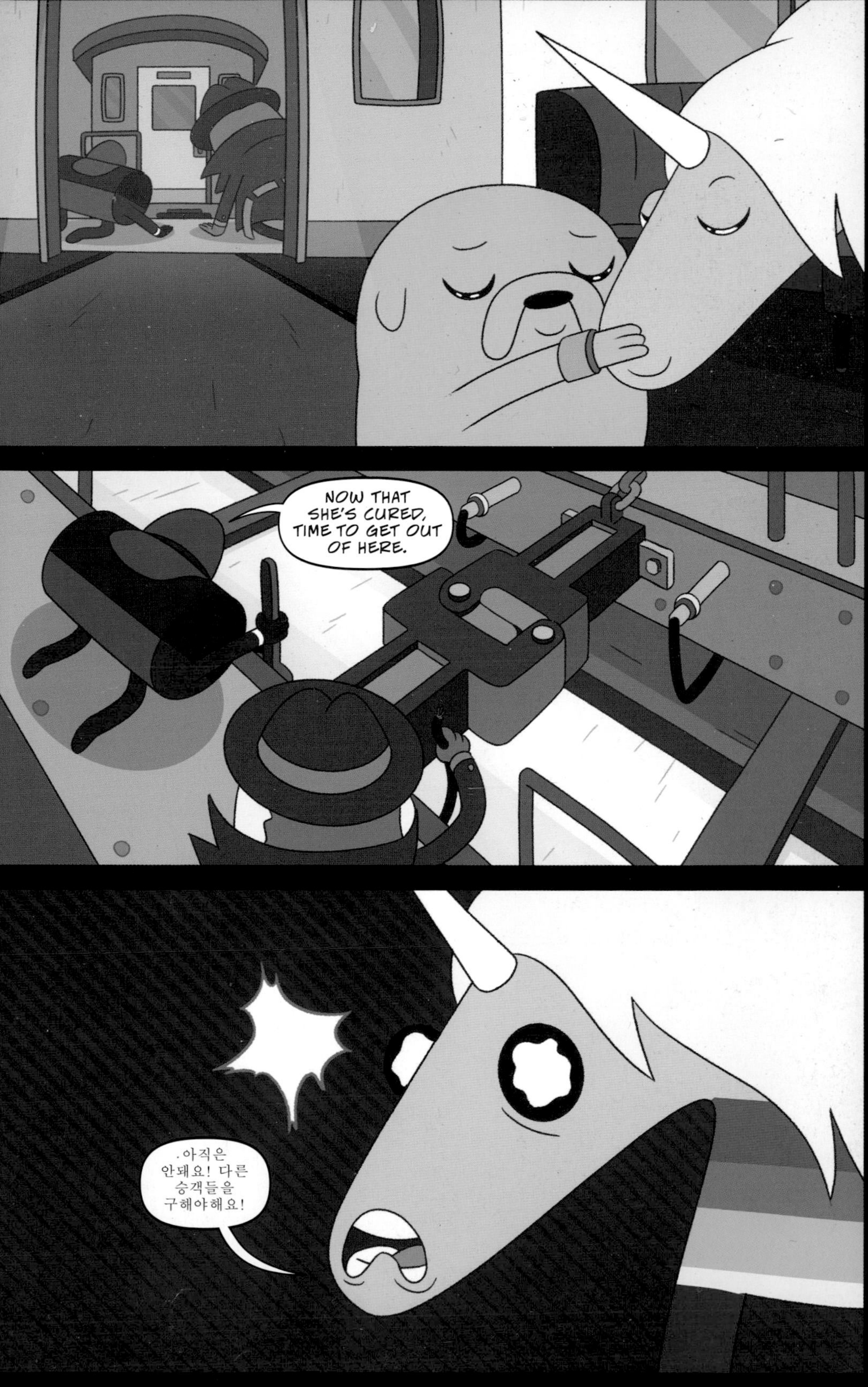
NOW THAT SHE'S CURED, TIME TO GET OUT OF HERE.
.아직은 안돼요! 다른 승객들을 구해야해요!

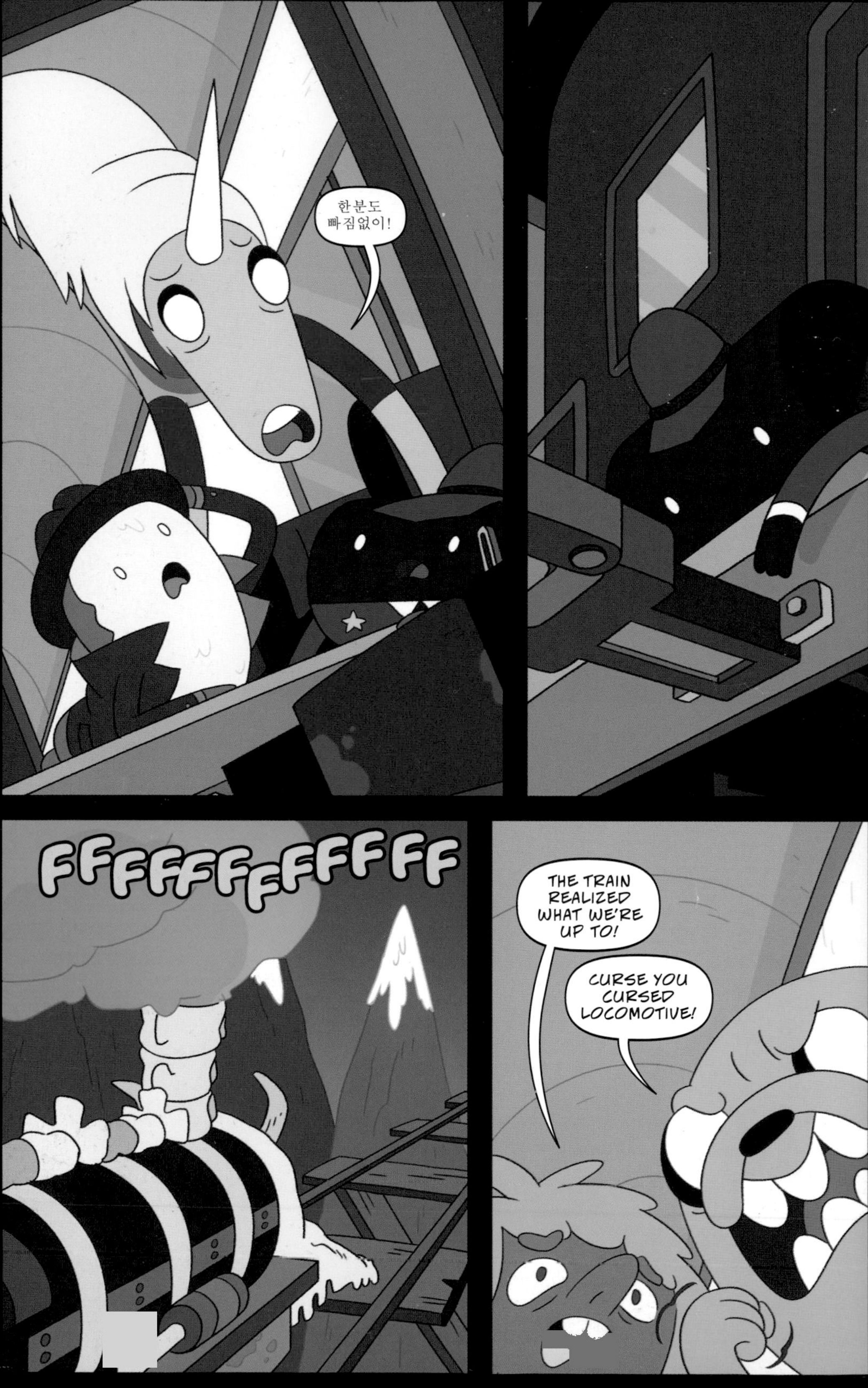

한분도
빠짐없이!
FFFFFFFFFFFFFF
THE TRAIN REALIZED WHAT WE'RE UP TO!
CURSE YOU CURSED LOCOMOTIVE!

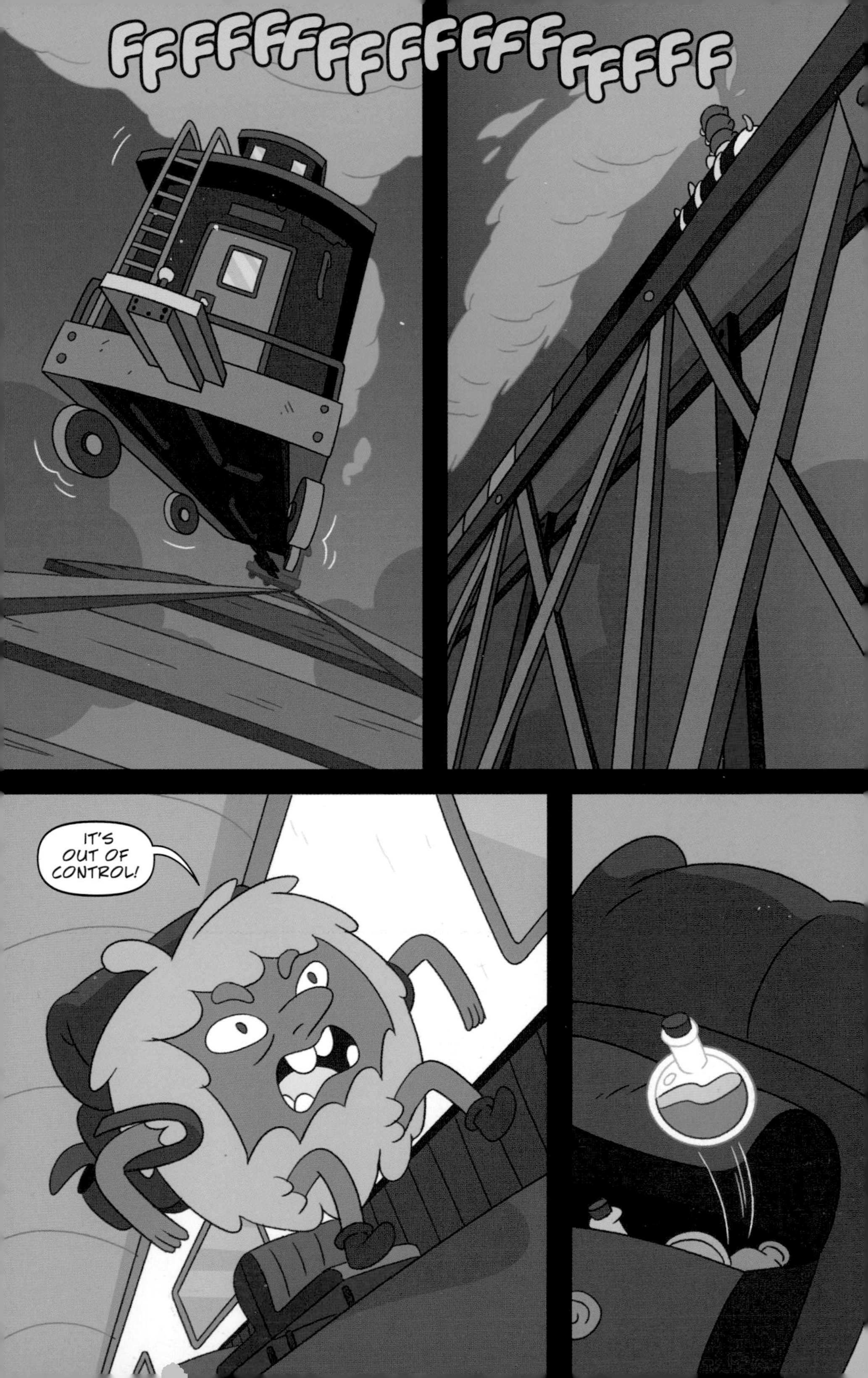
FFFFFFFFFFFFFFFFFF
IT'S OUT OF CONTROL!

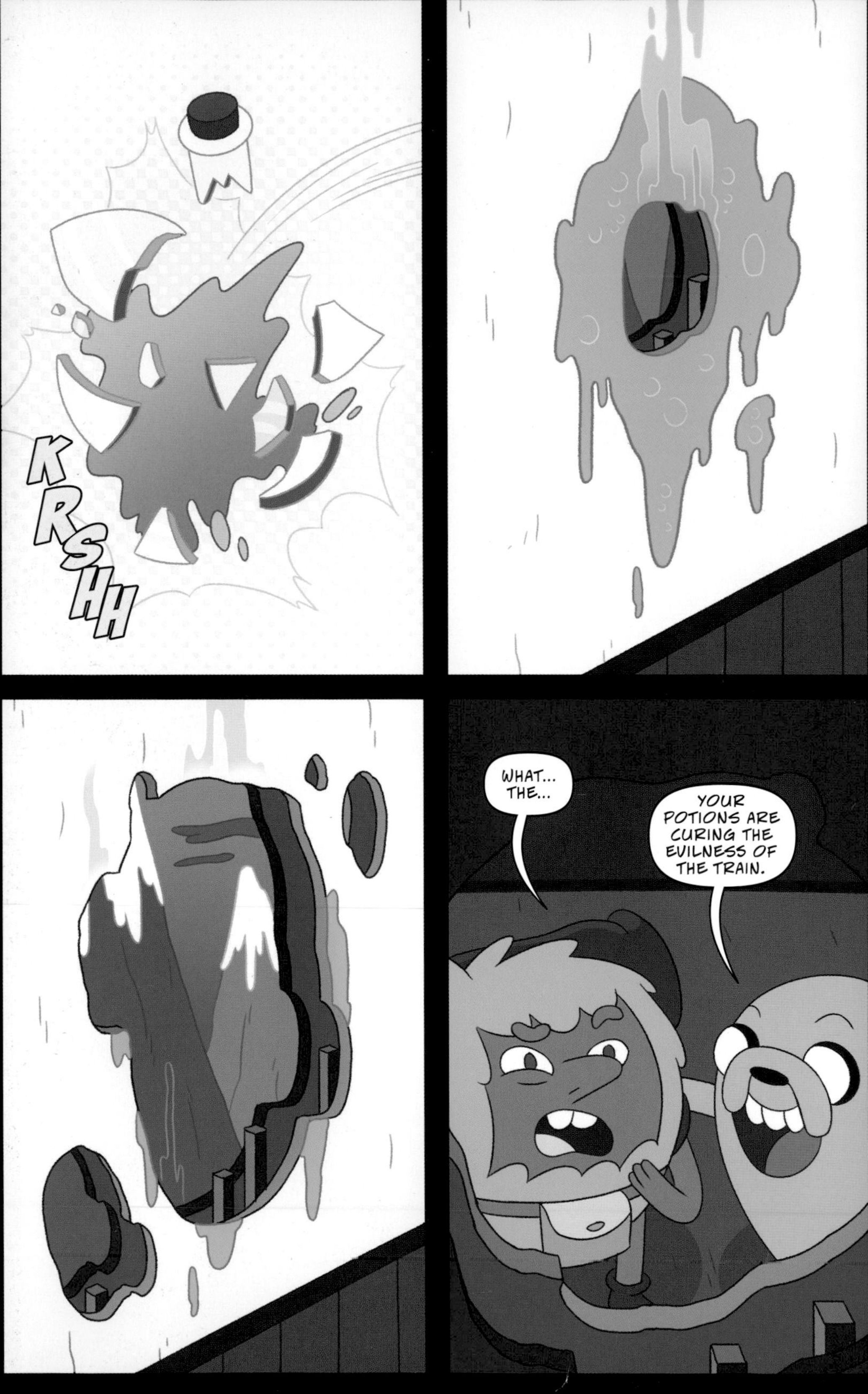
KRSHH
WHAT... THE...
YOUR POTIONS ARE CURING THE EVILNESS OF THE TRAIN.

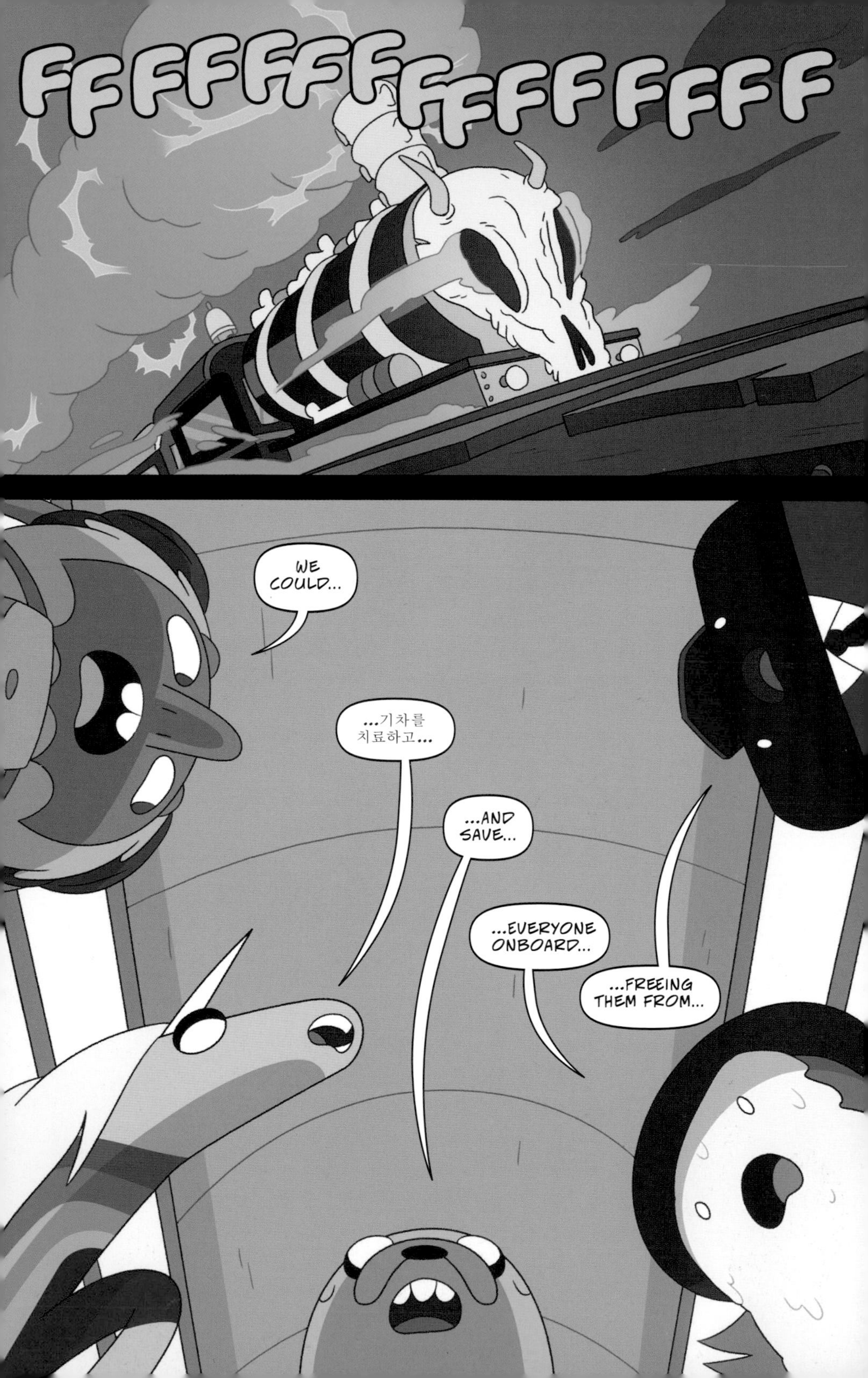
FFFFFFFFFFFFF
WE COULD...
...기차를 치료하고...
...AND SAVE...
...EVERYONE ONBOARD...
...FREEING THEM FROM...

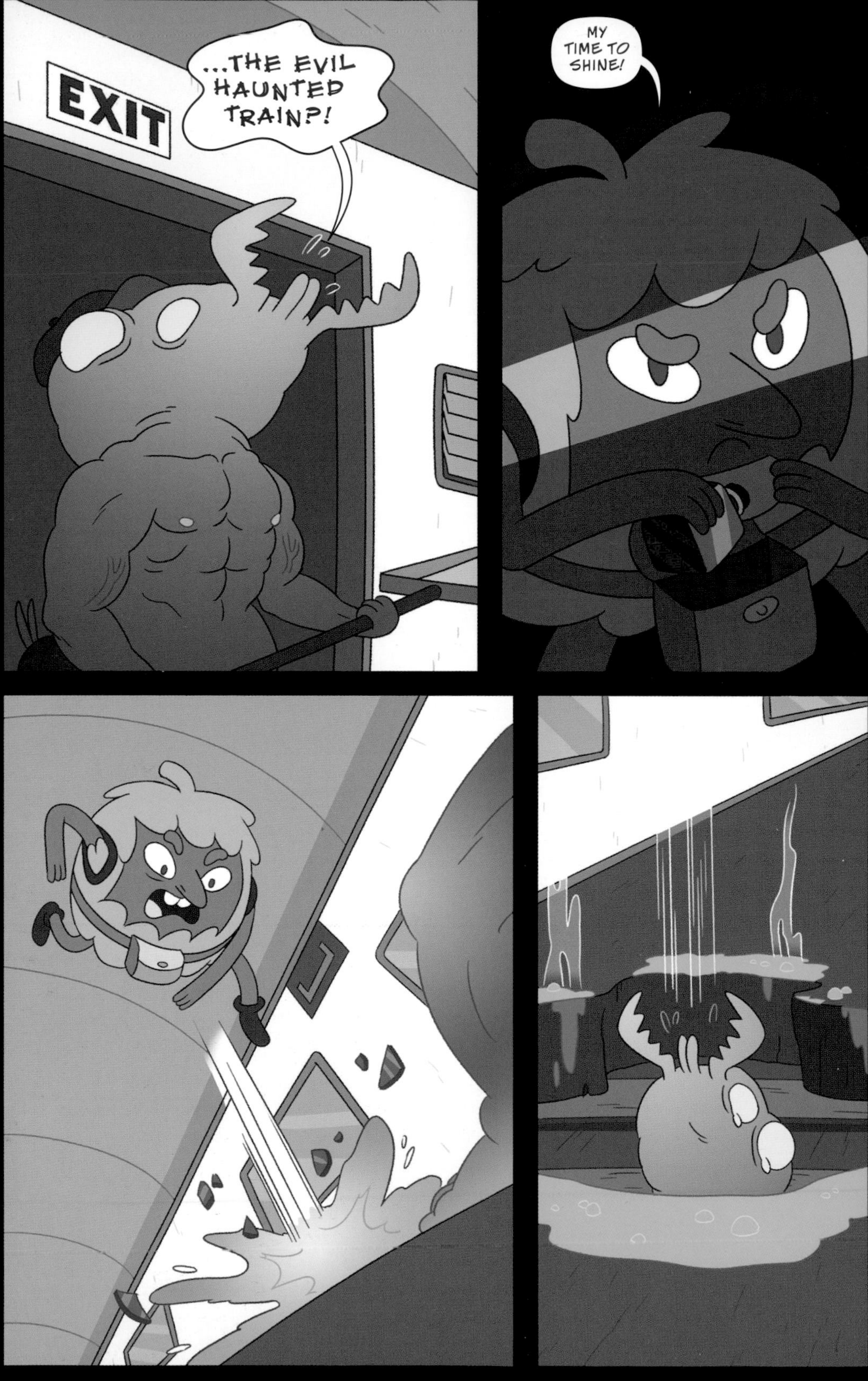
...THE EVIL HAUNTED TRAIN?!
EXIT
MY TIME TO SHINE!

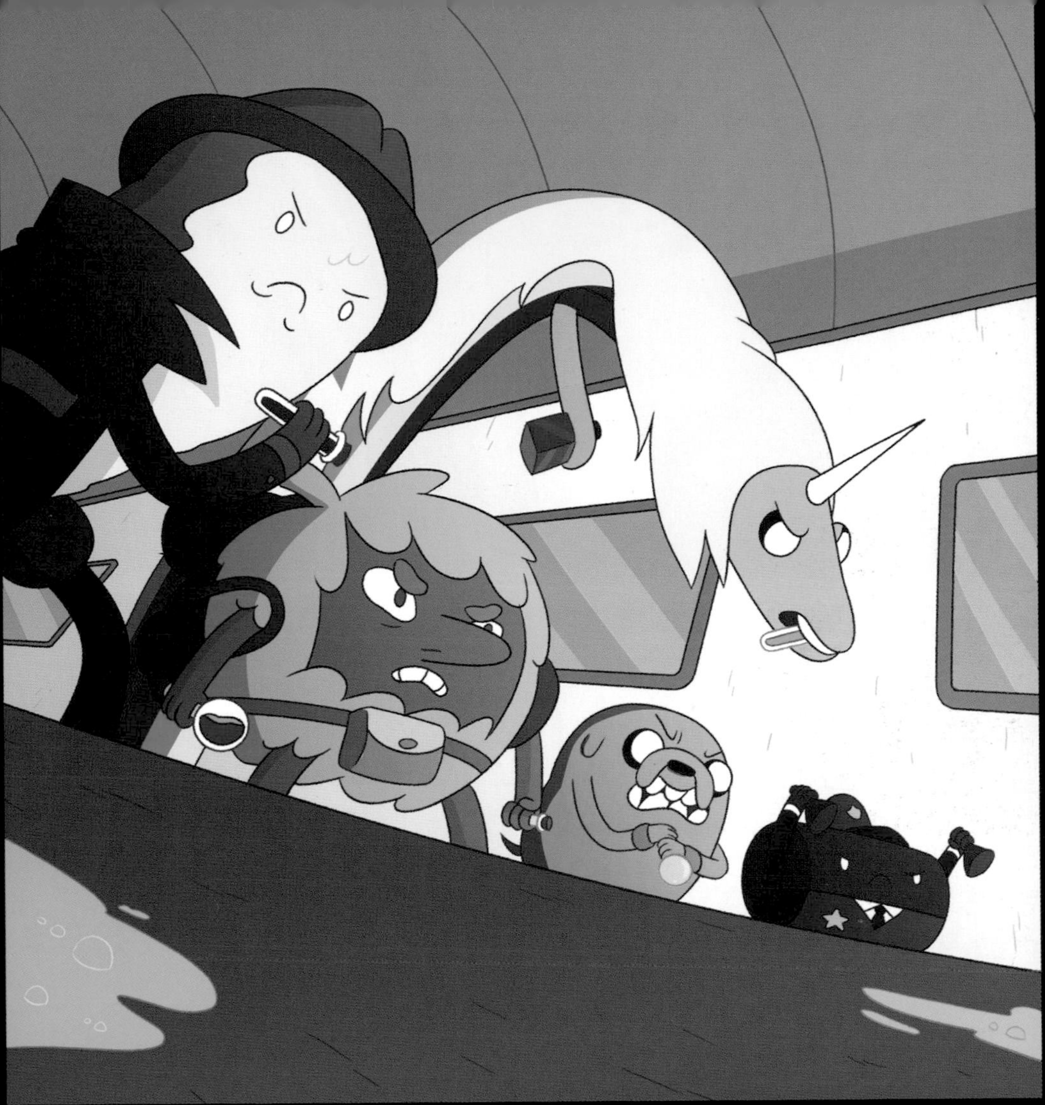
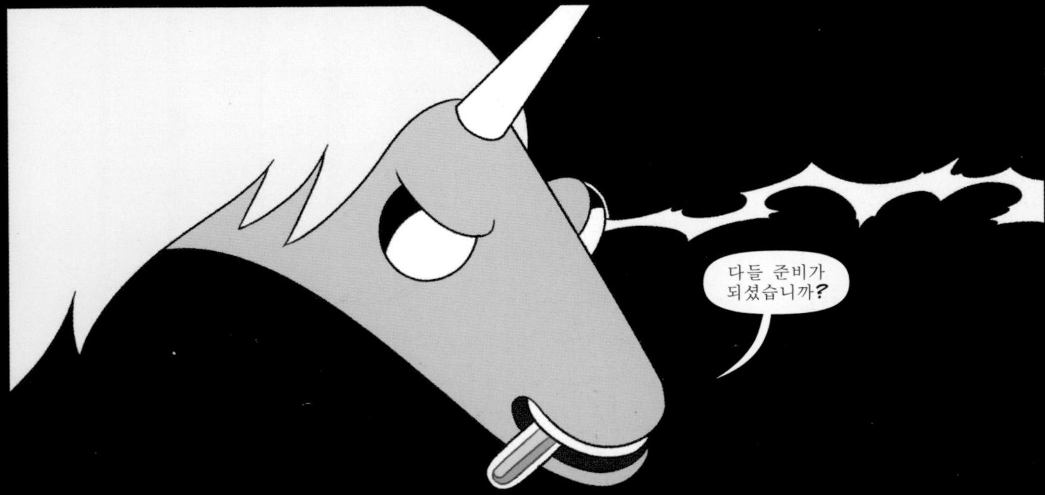
다들 준비가 되셨습니까?

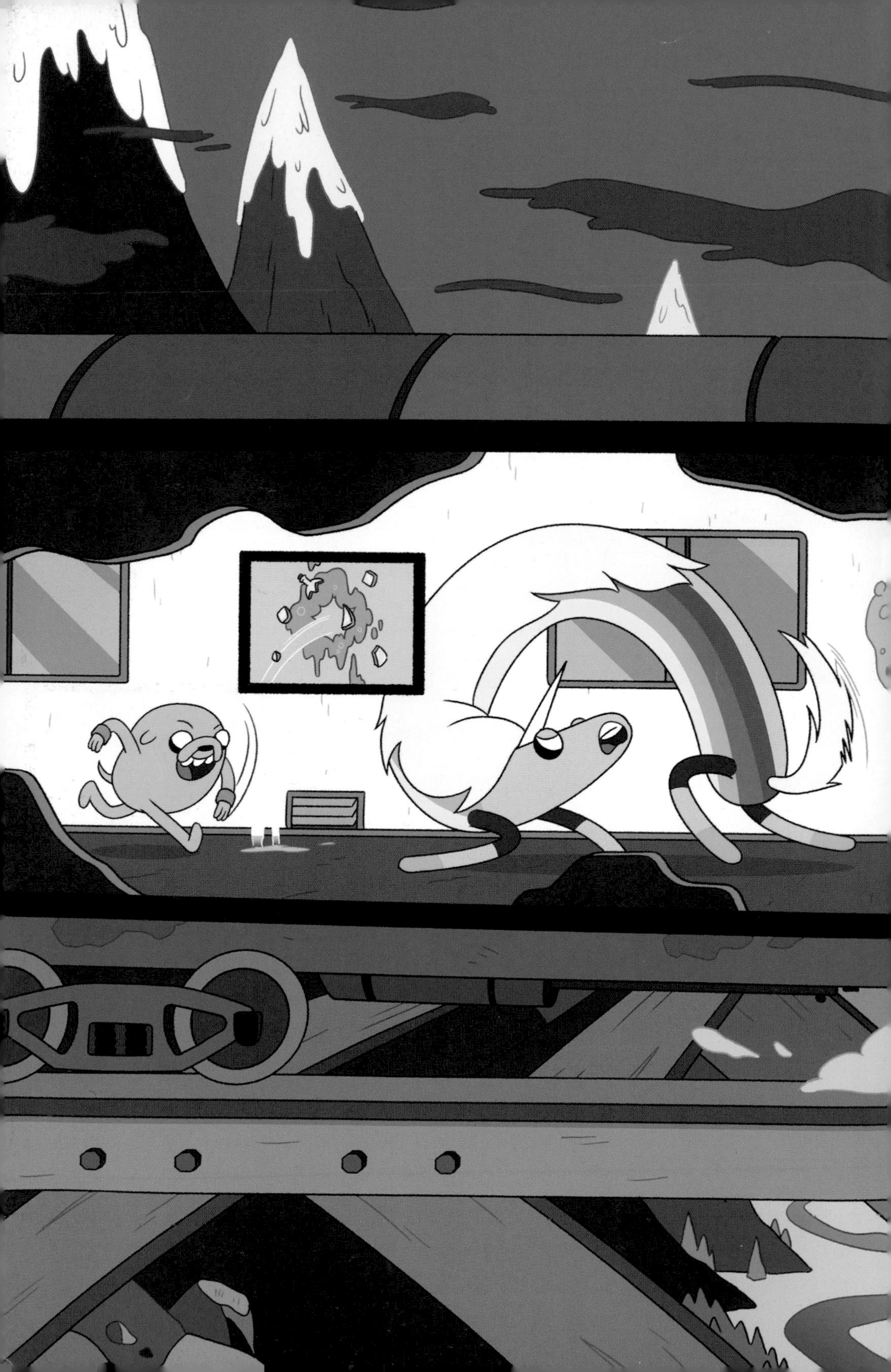

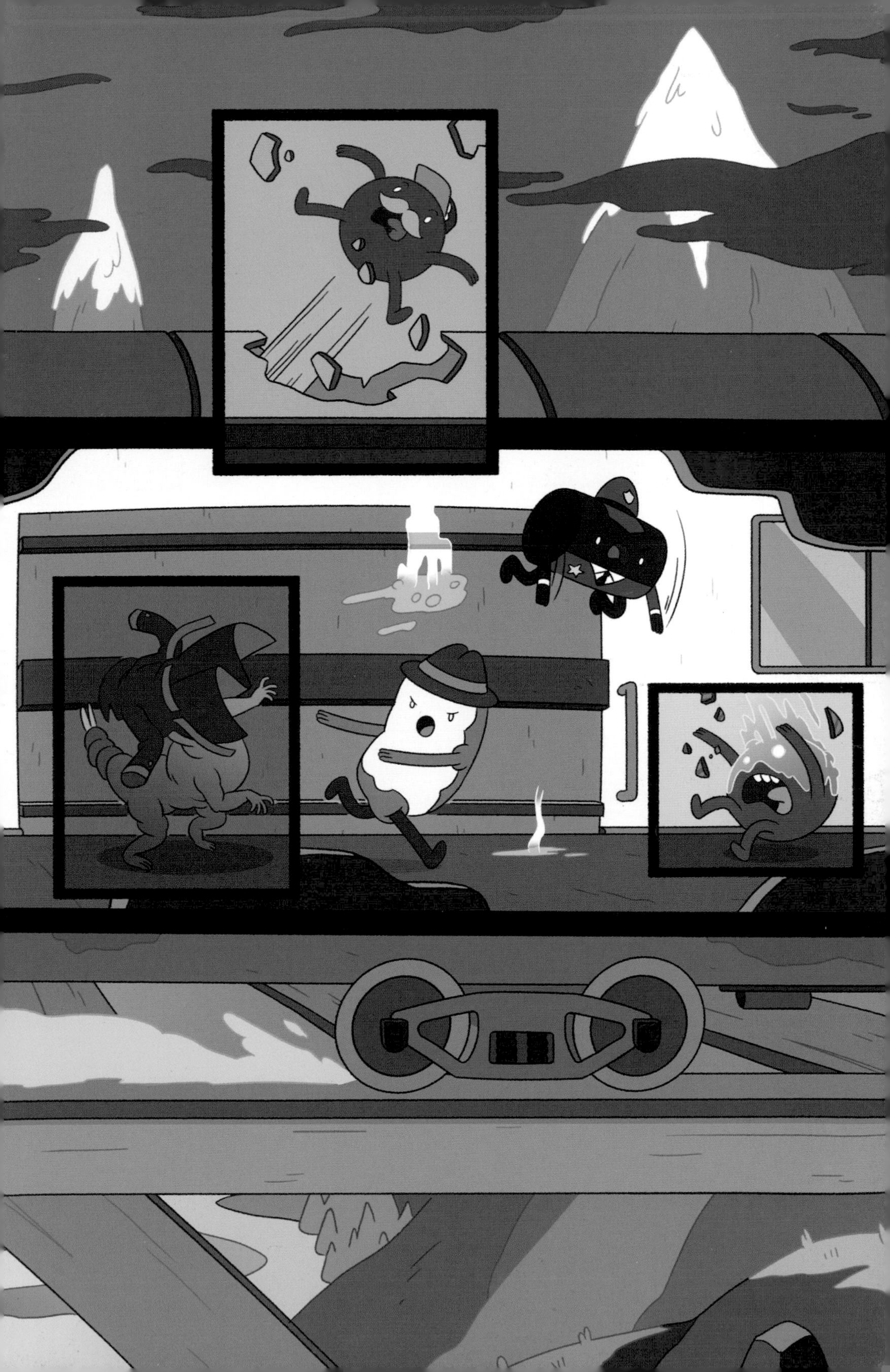

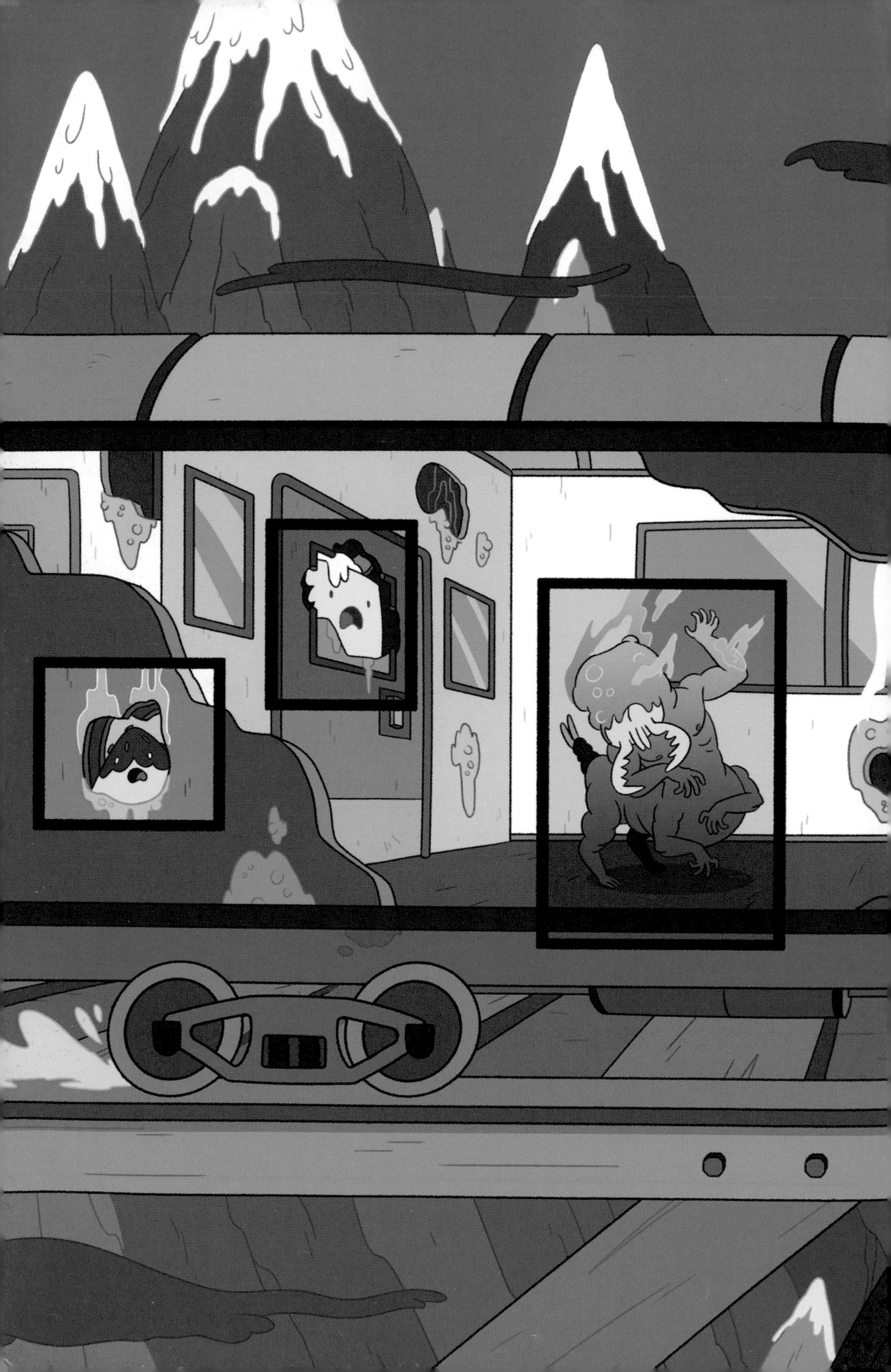

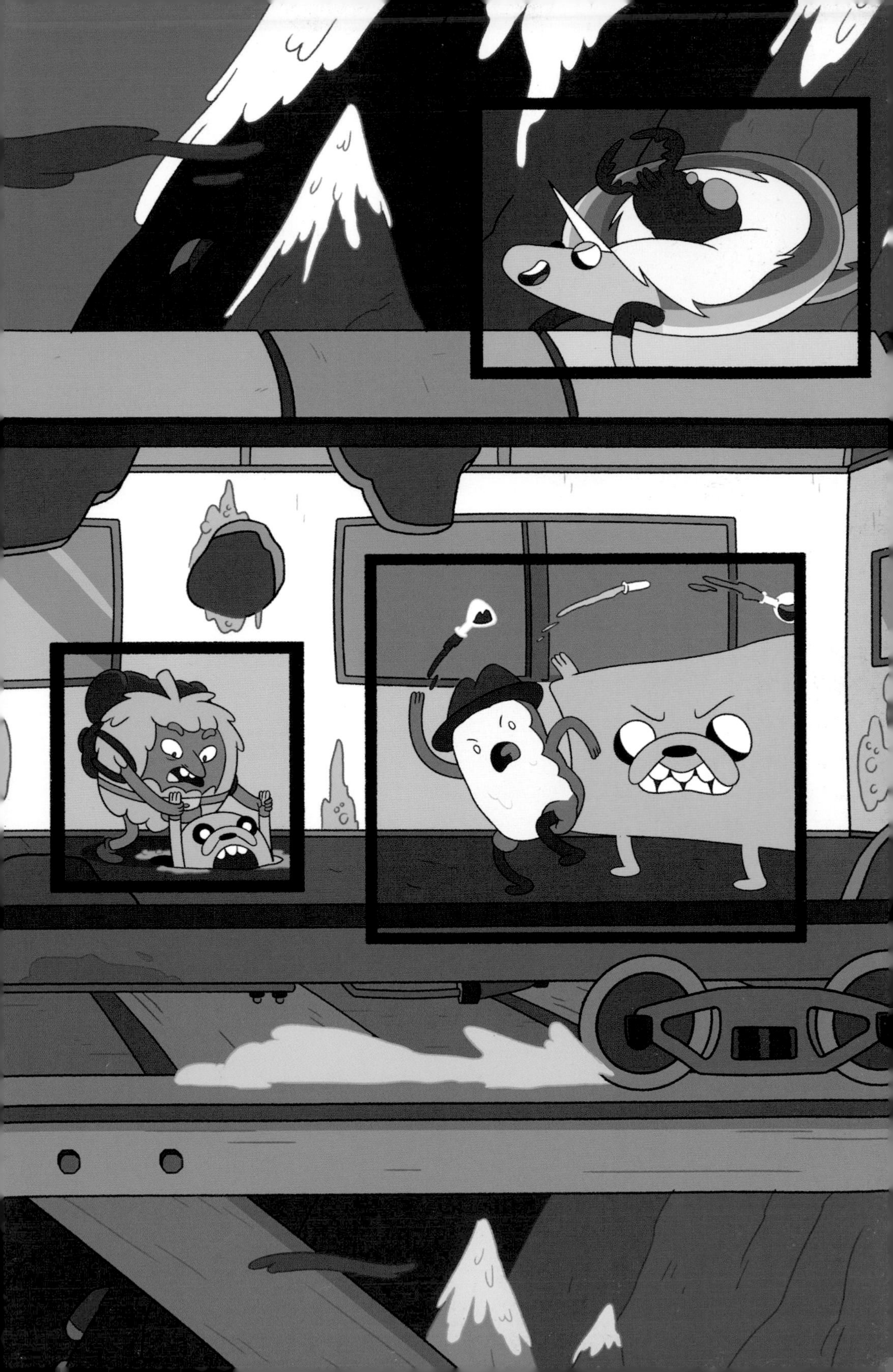

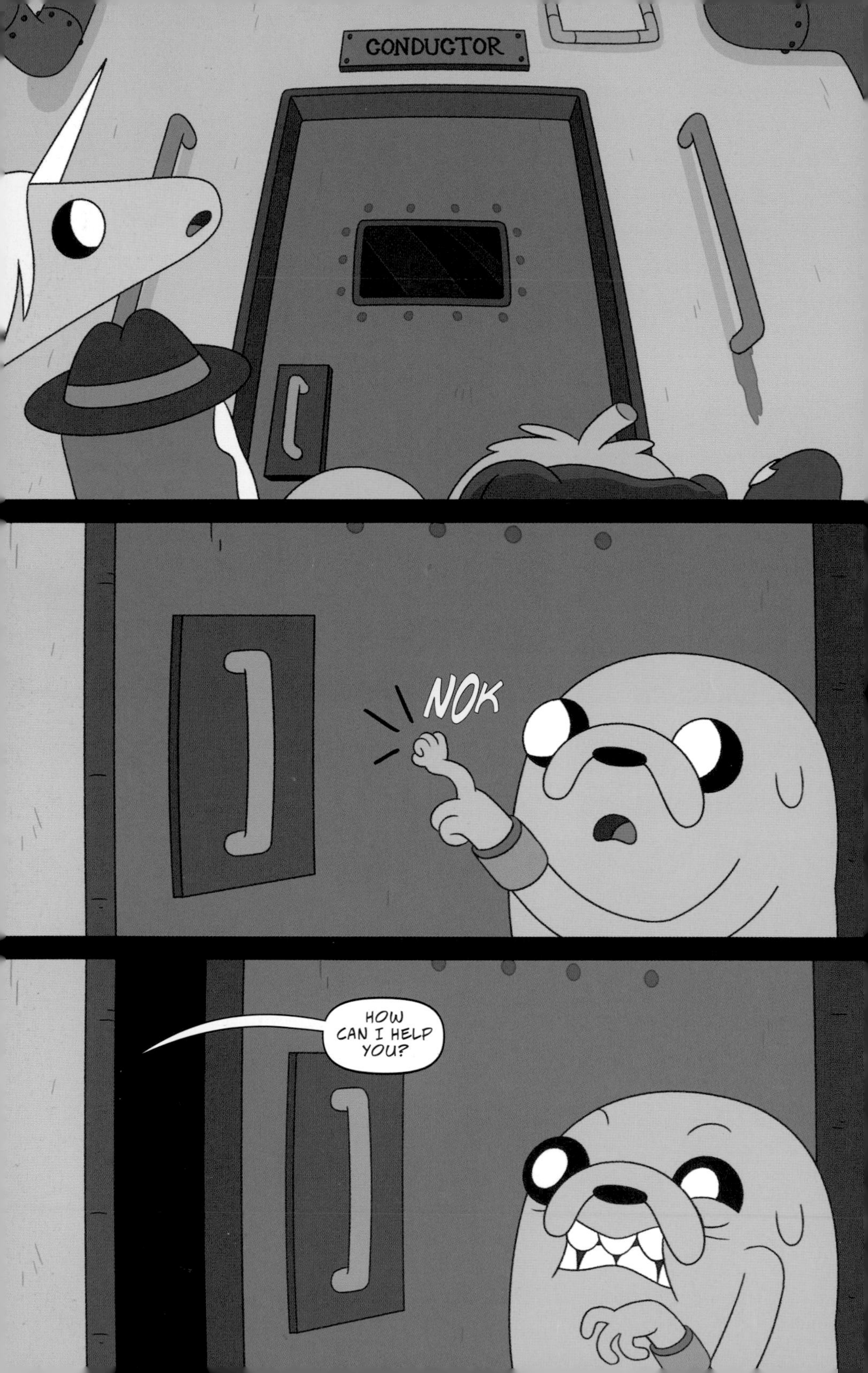
CONDUCTOR
NOK
HOW CAN I HELP YOU?

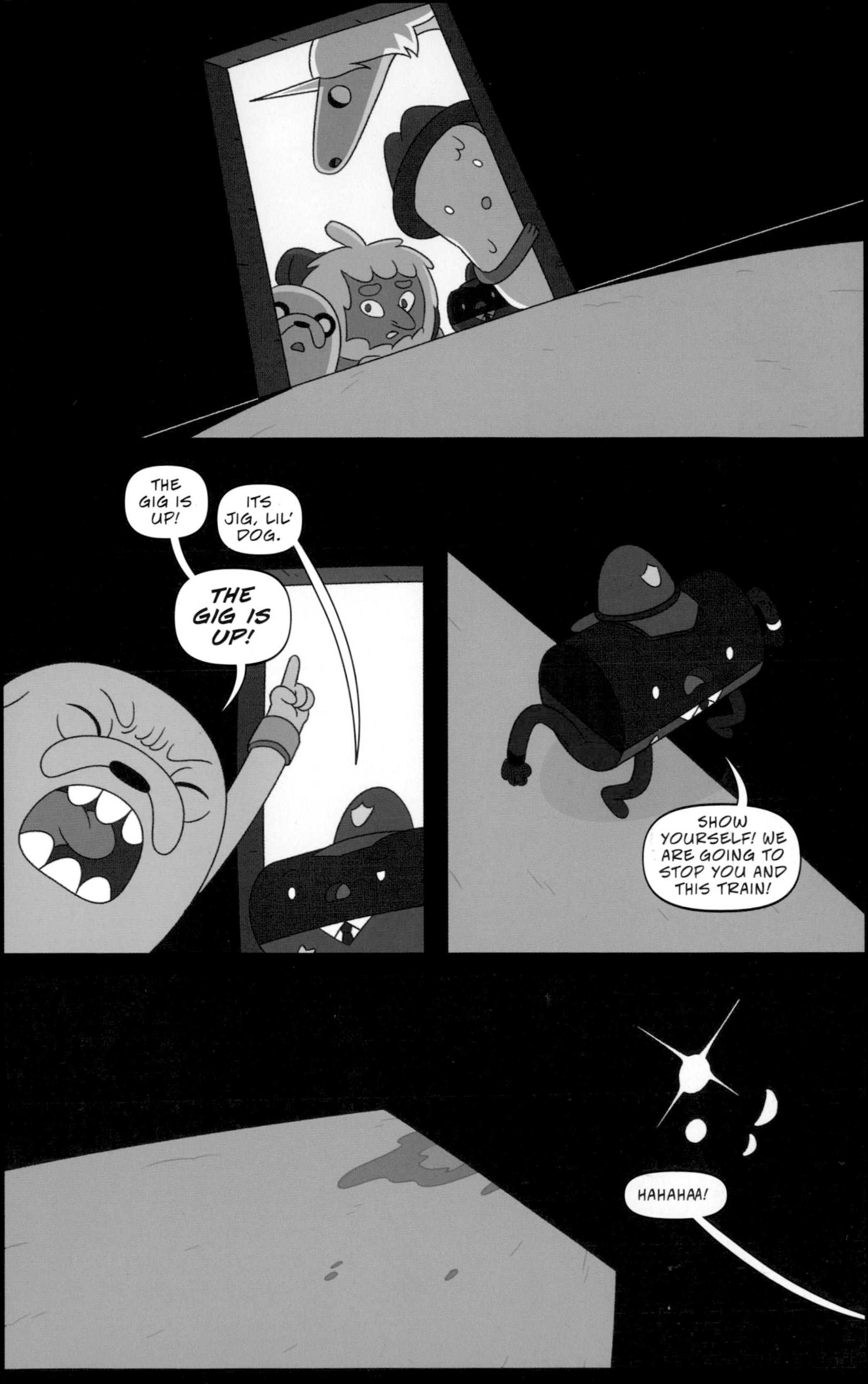

THE GIG IS UP!
ITS JIG, LIL' DOG.
THE GIG IS UP!
SHOW YOURSELF! WE ARE GOING TO STOP YOU AND THIS TRAIN!
HAHAHAA!

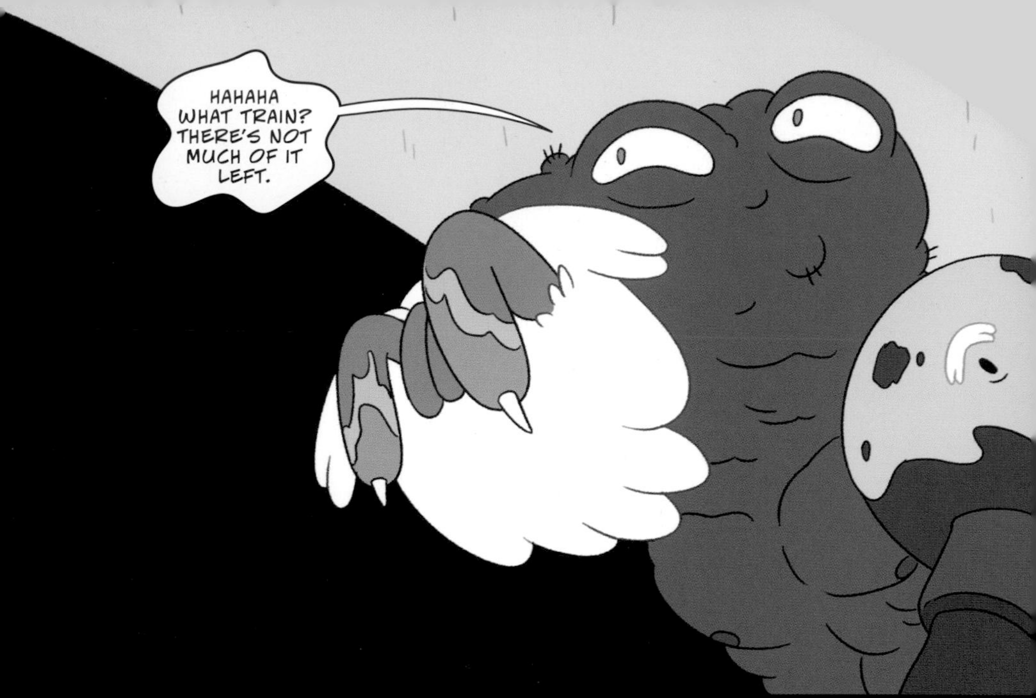
HAHAHA WHAT TRAIN? THERE'S NOT MUCH OF IT LEFT.
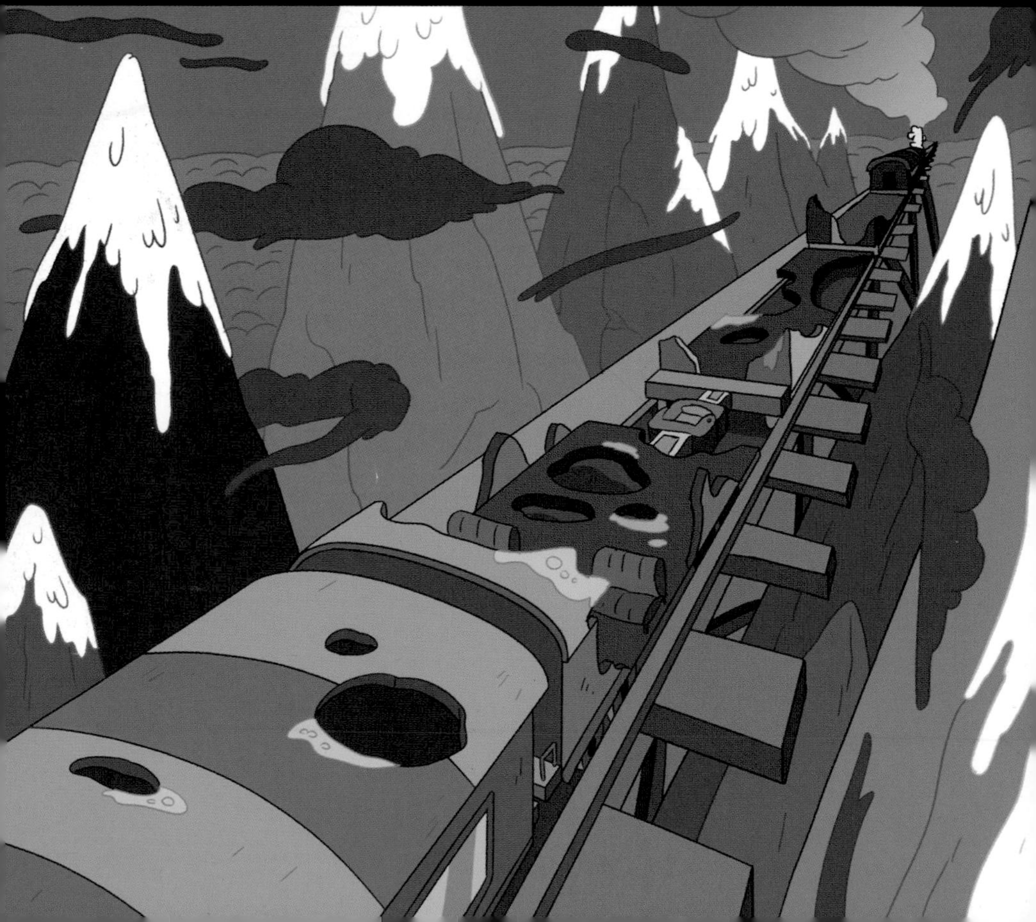

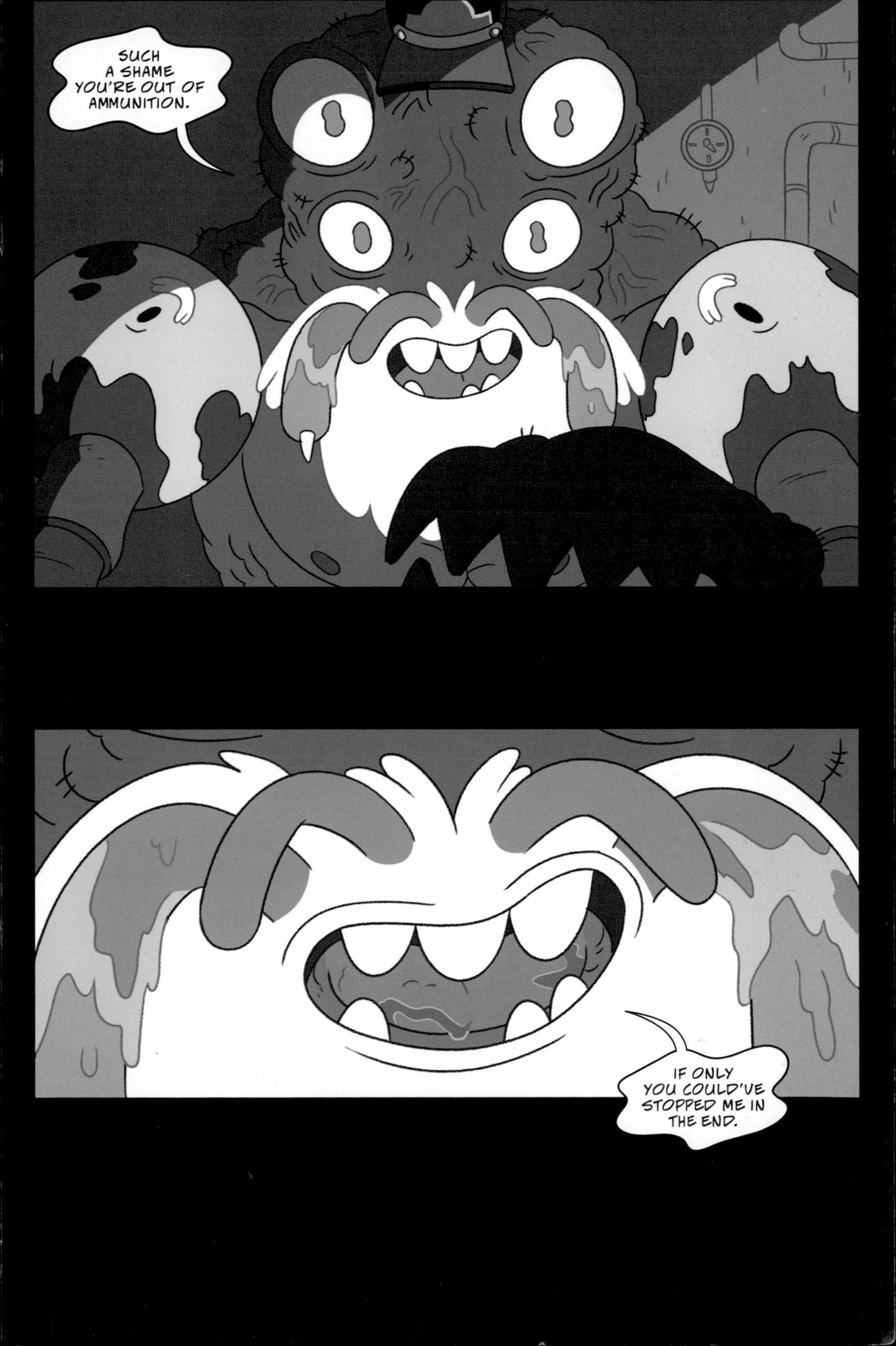
SUCH A SHAME YOU'RE OUT OF AMMUNITION.
IF ONLY YOU COULD'VE STOPPED ME IN THE END.

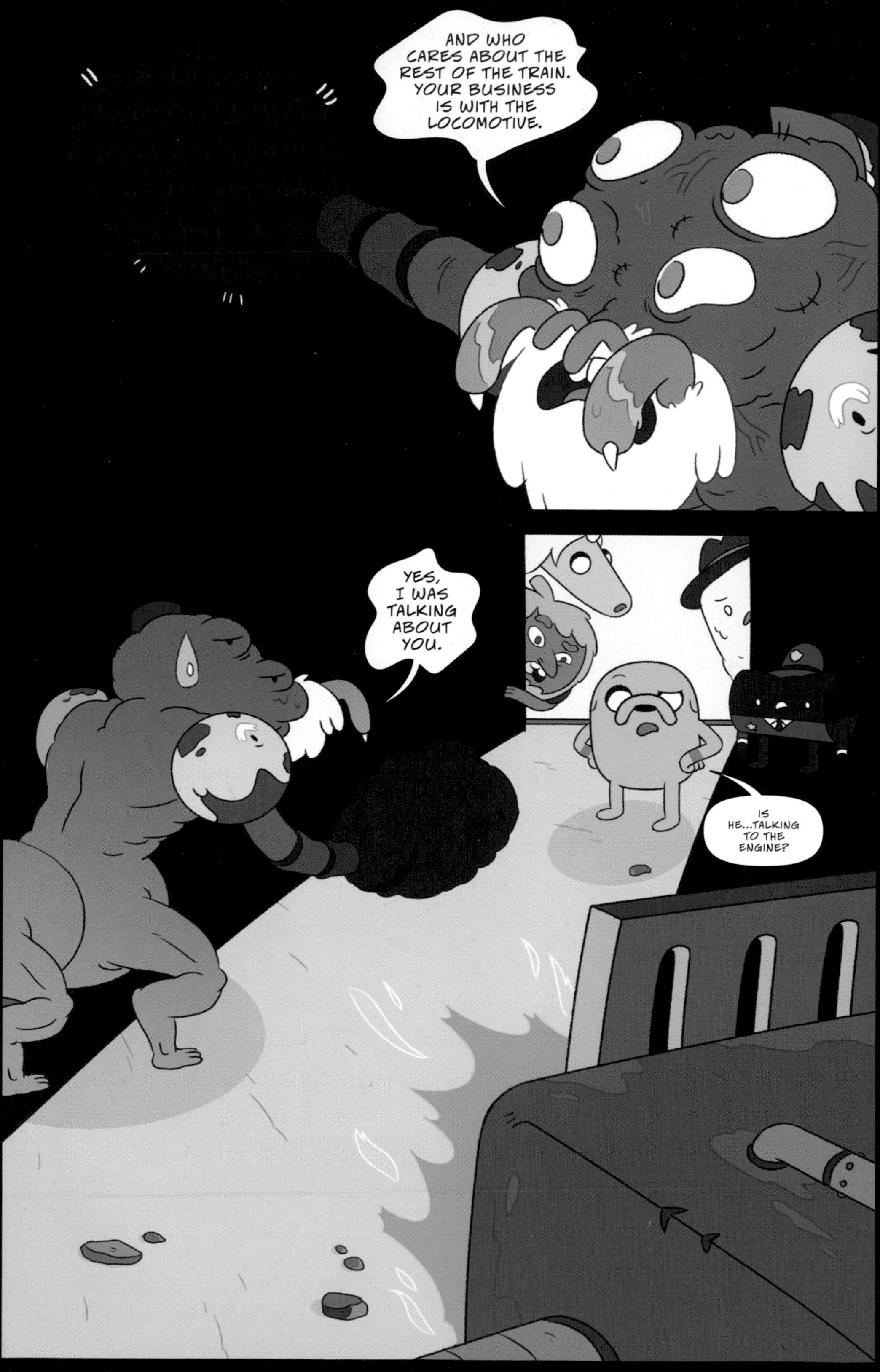
AND WHO CARES ABOUT THE REST OF THE TRAIN. YOUR BUSINESS IS WITH THE LOCOMOTIVE.
YES, I WAS TALKING ABOUT YOU.
IS HE...TALKING TO THE ENGINE?

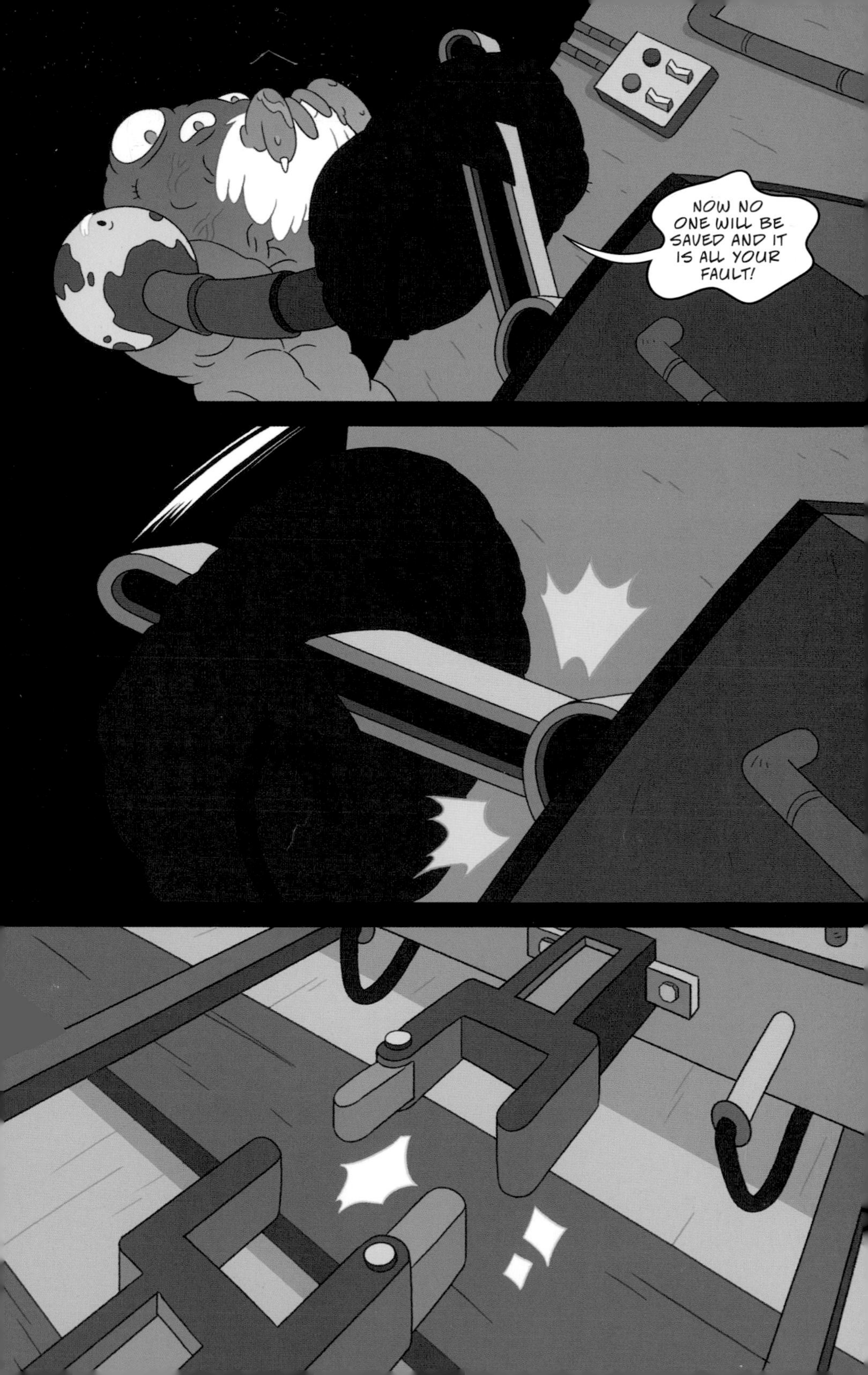
NOW NO ONE WILL BE SAVED AND IT IS ALL YOUR FAULT!

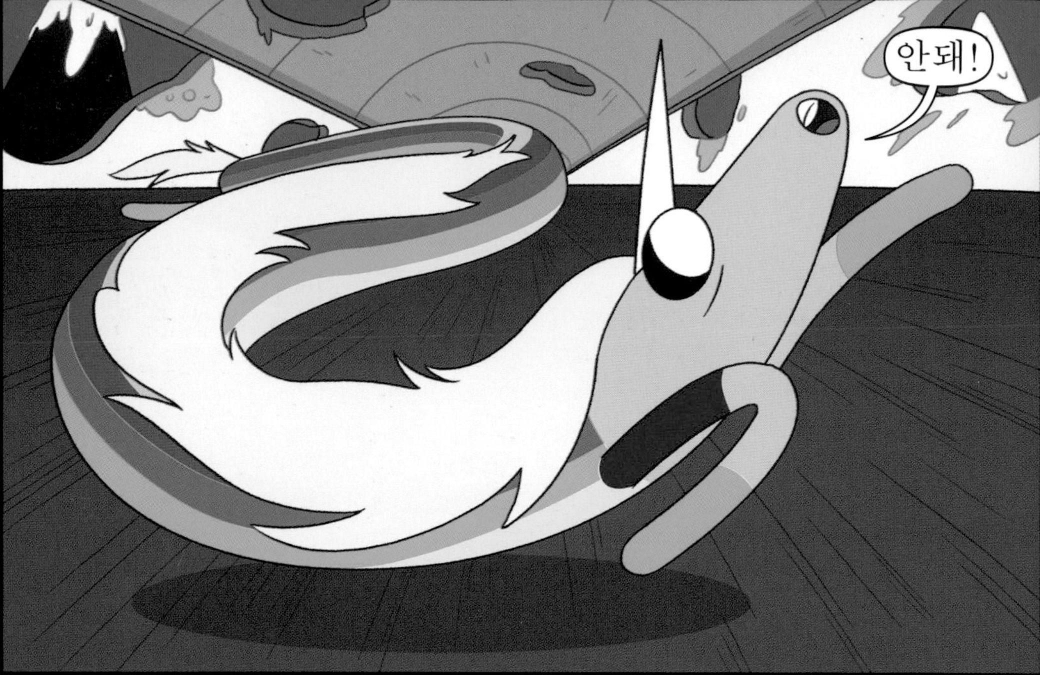
안돼!

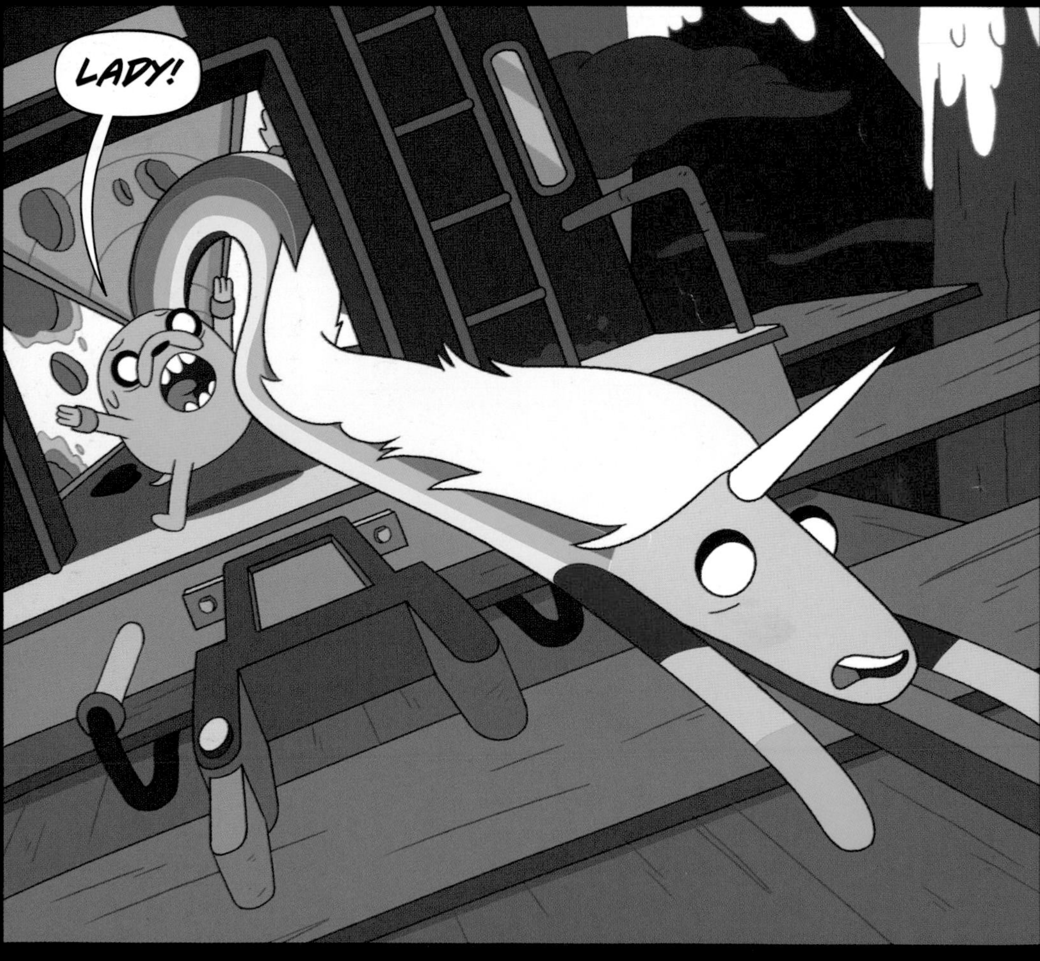
LADY!

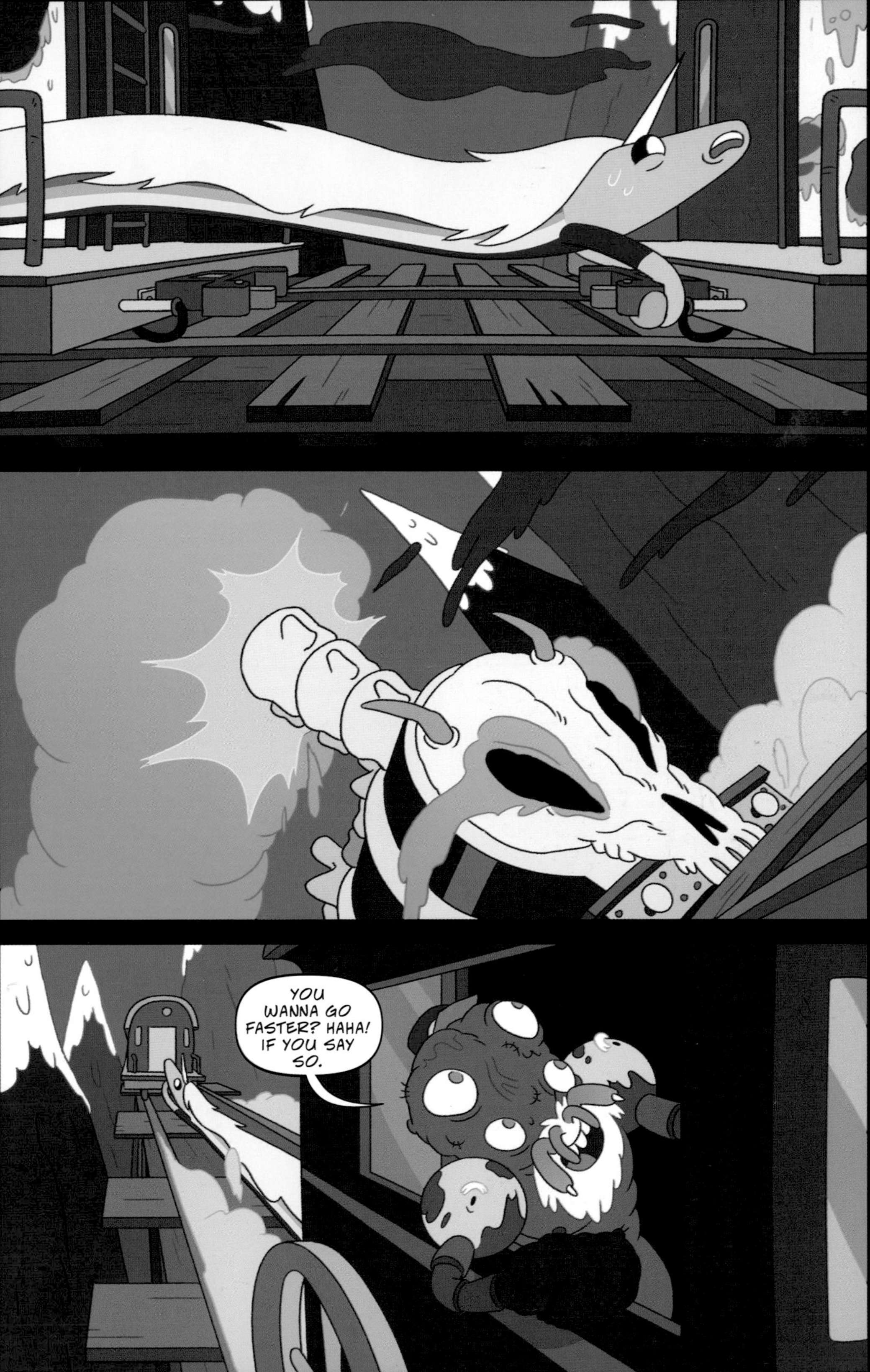
YOU WANNA GO FASTER? HAHA! IF YOU SAY SO.

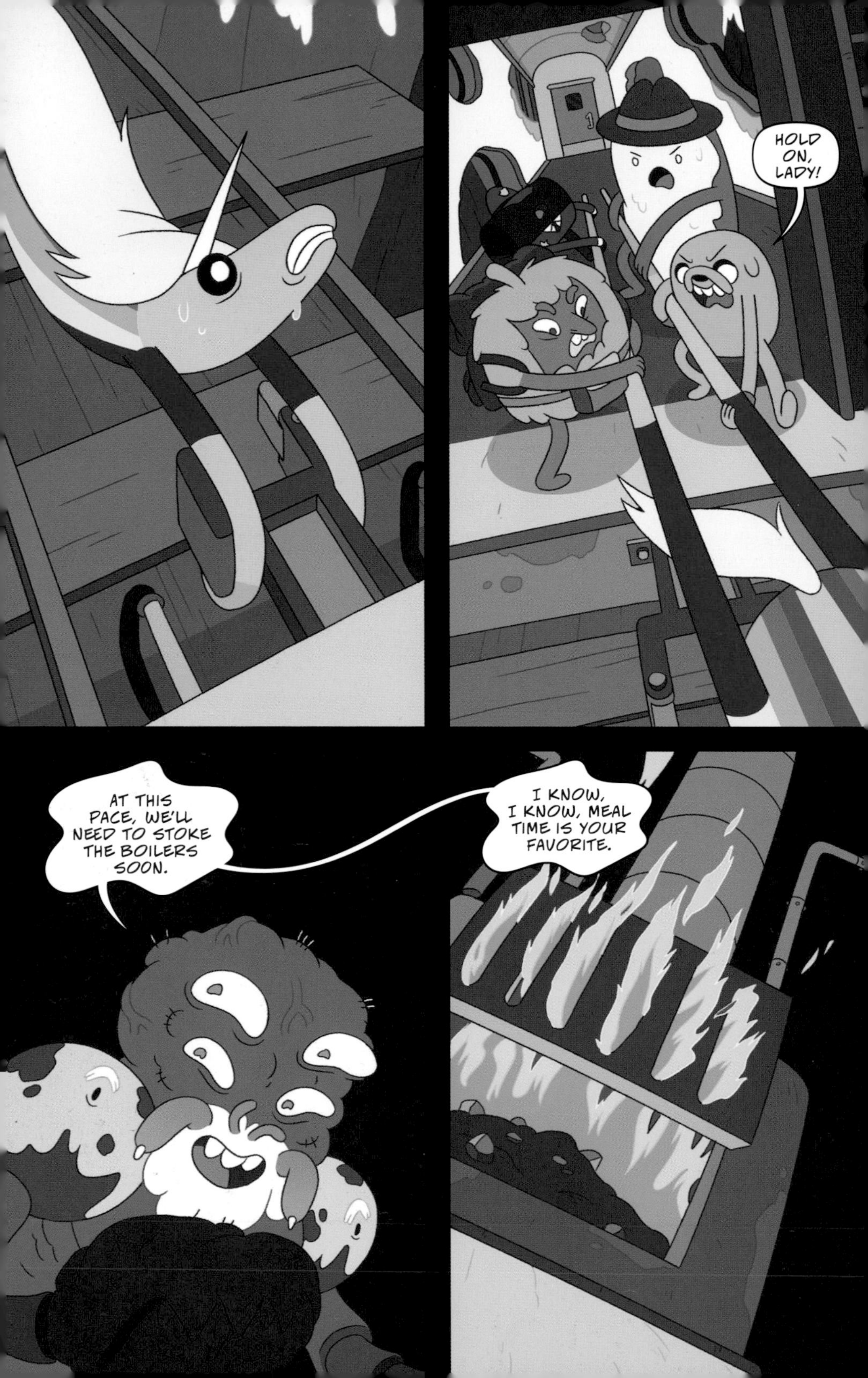
HOLD ON, LADY!
AT THIS PACE, WE'LL NEED TO STOKE THE BOILERS SOON.
I KNOW, I KNOW, MEAL TIME IS YOUR FAVORITE.

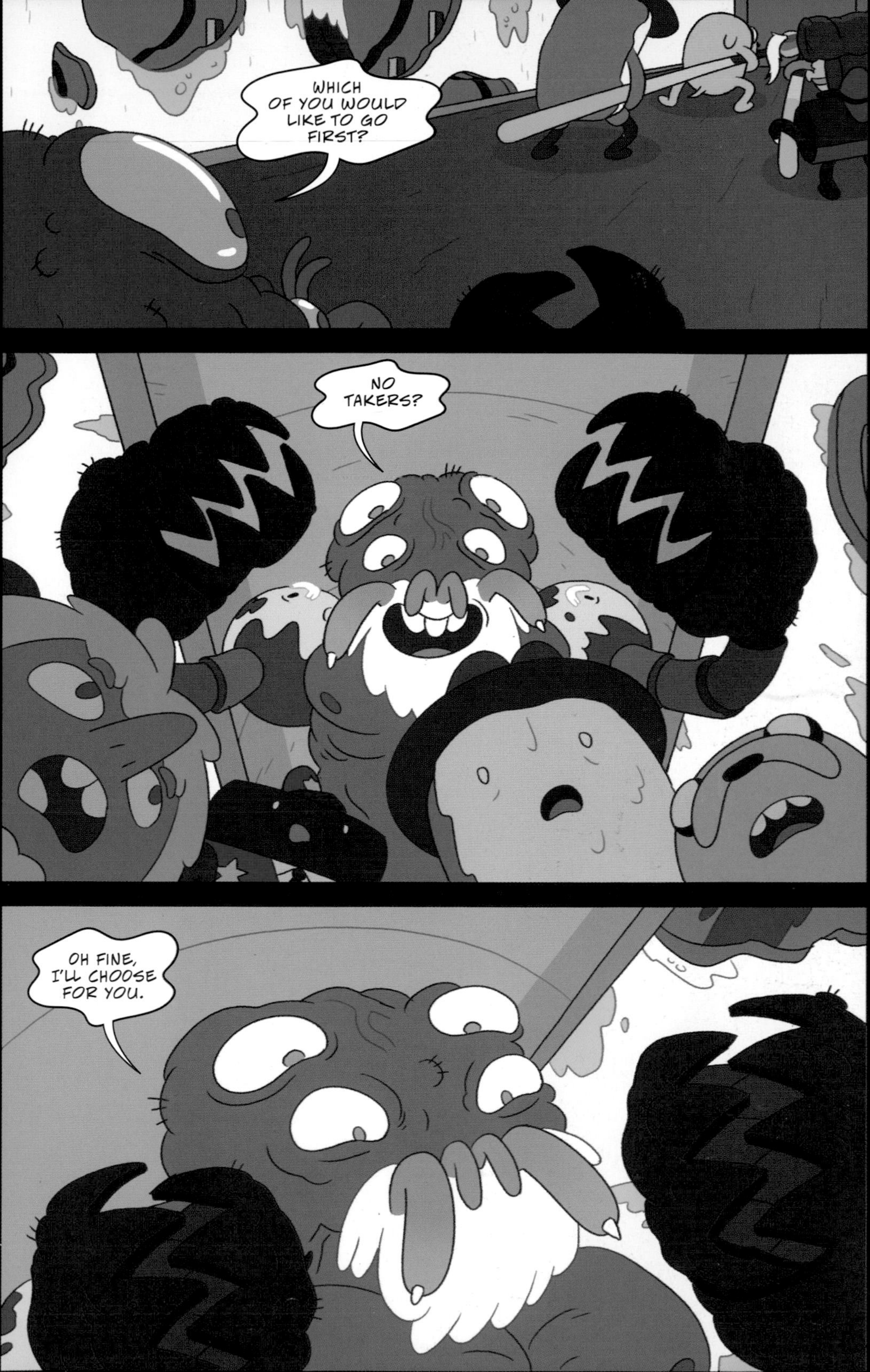
WHICH OF YOU WOULD LIKE TO GO FIRST?
NO TAKERS?
OH FINE, I'LL CHOOSE FOR YOU.

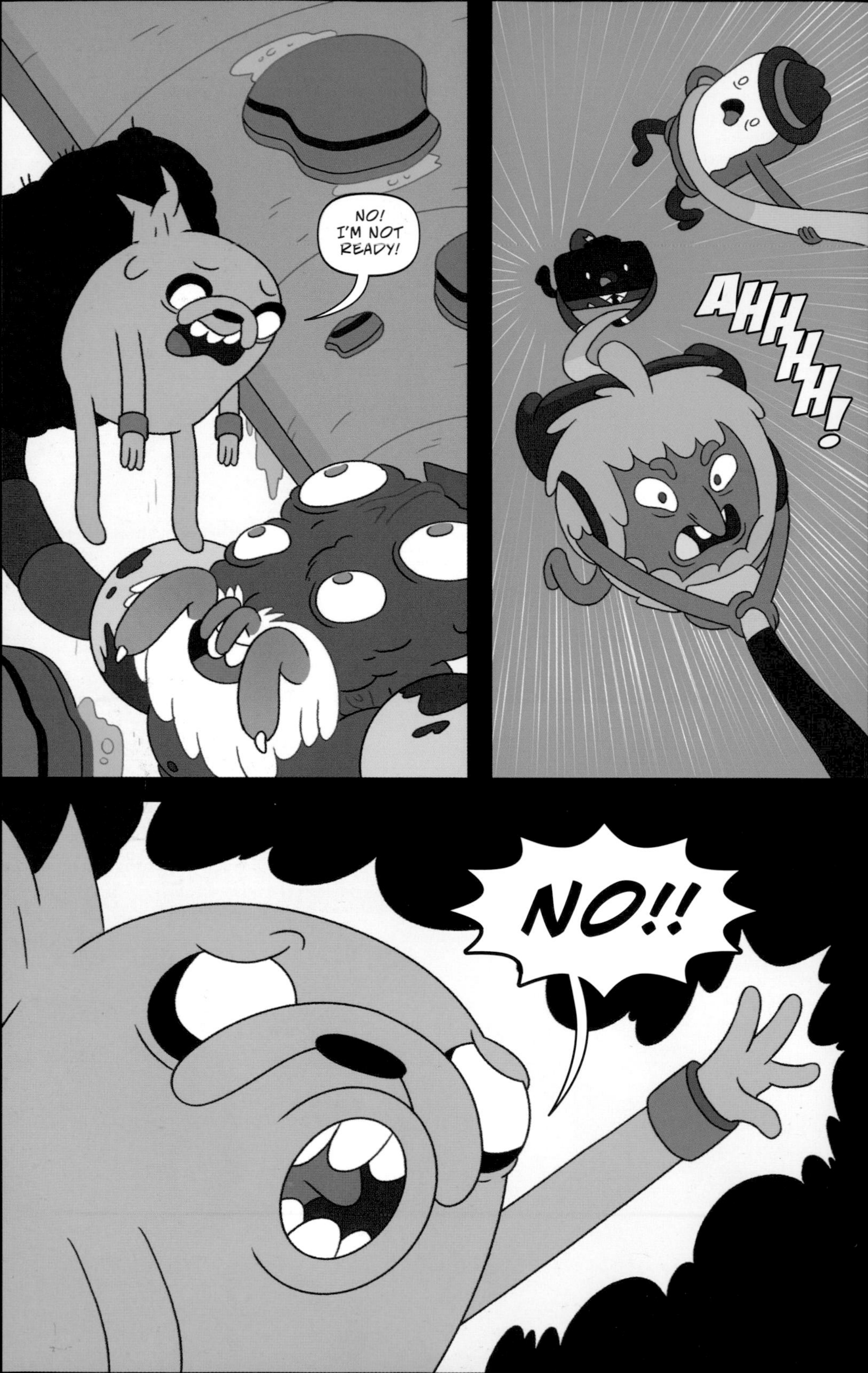
NO! I'M NOT READY!
AHHHHH!
NO!!

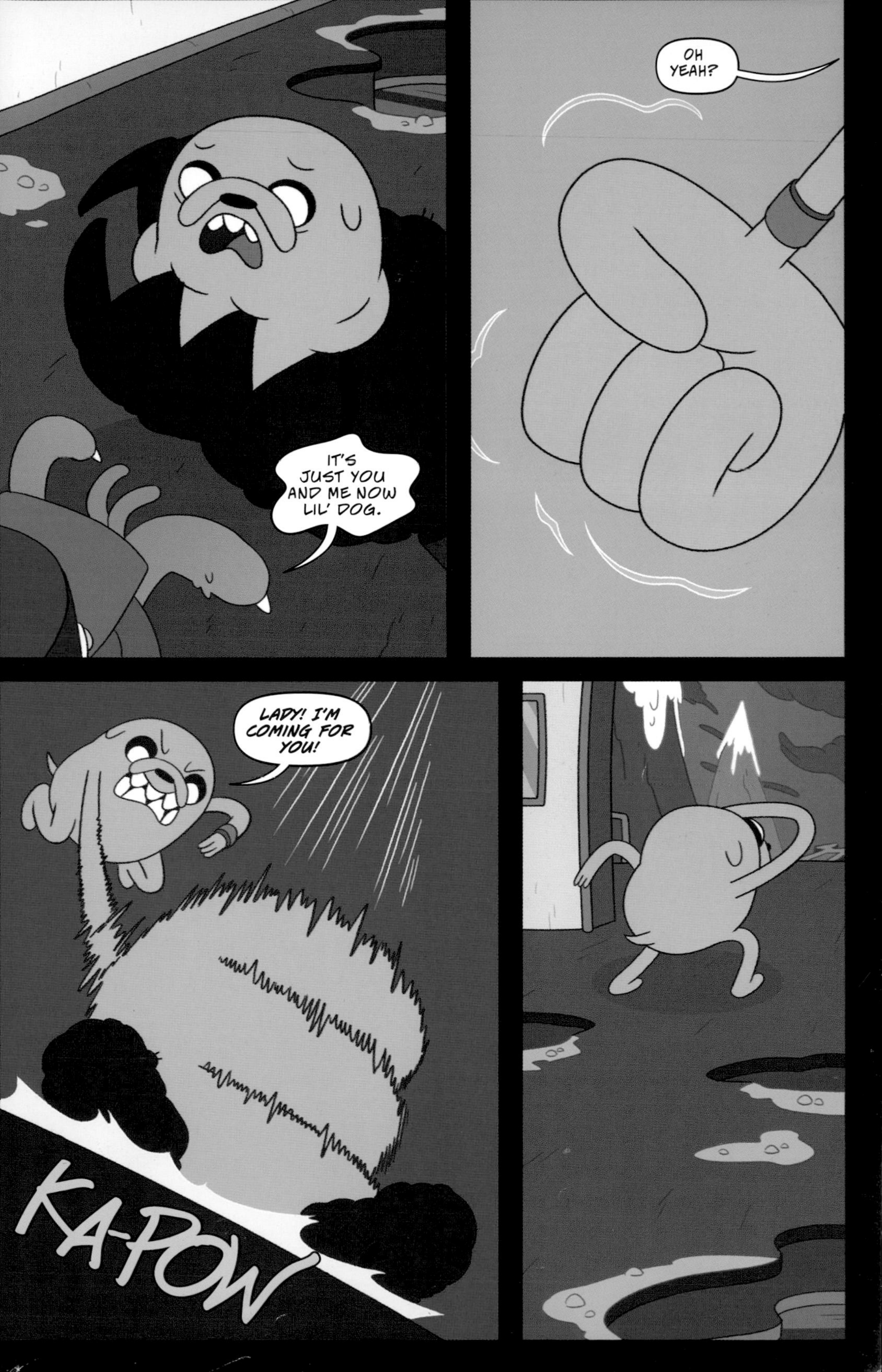

IT'S JUST YOU AND ME NOW LIL' DOG.
OH YEAH?
LADY! I'M COMING FOR YOU!
KA-POW

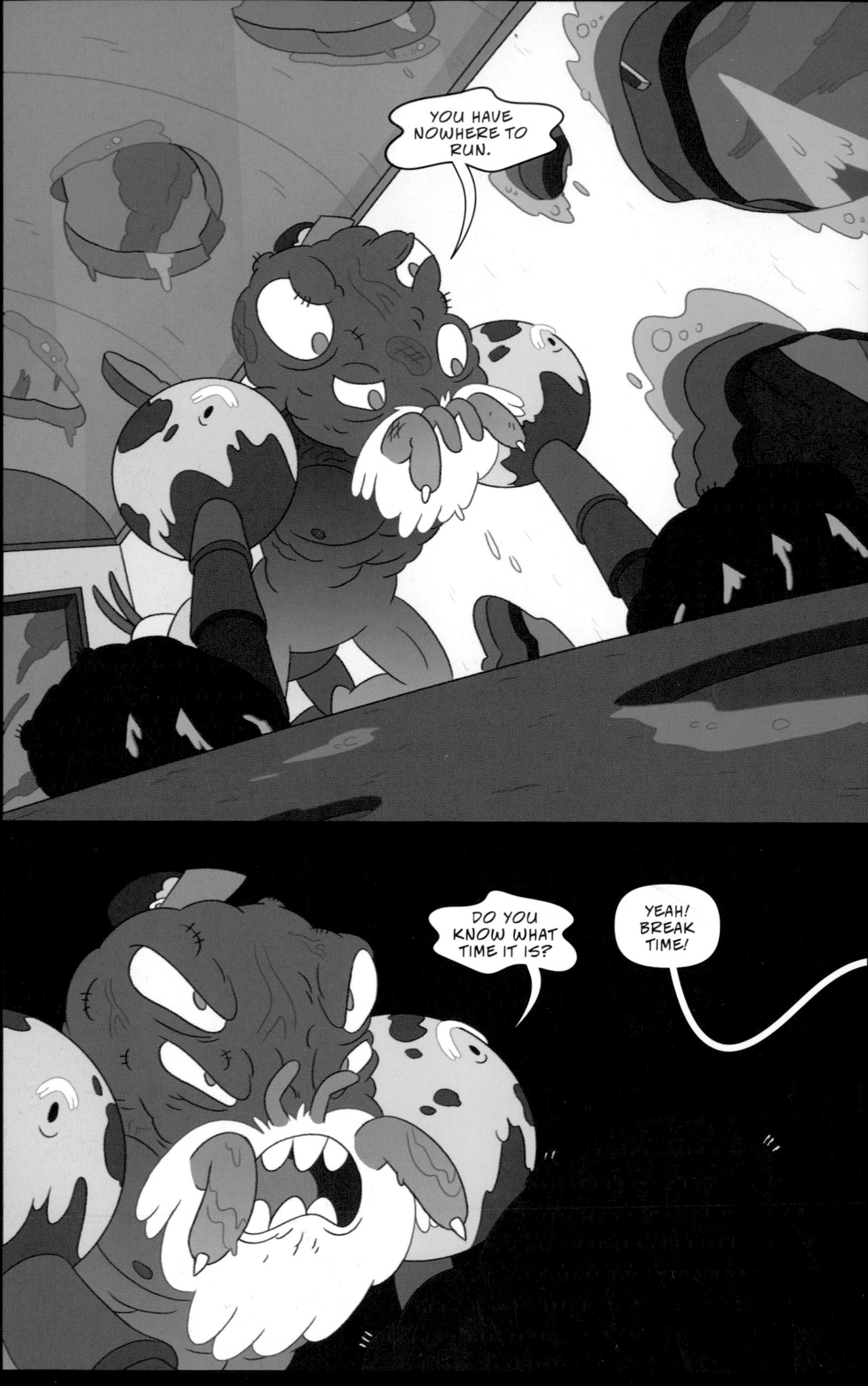
YOU HAVE NOWHERE TO RUN.
DO YOU KNOW WHAT TIME IT IS?
YEAH! BREAK TIME!

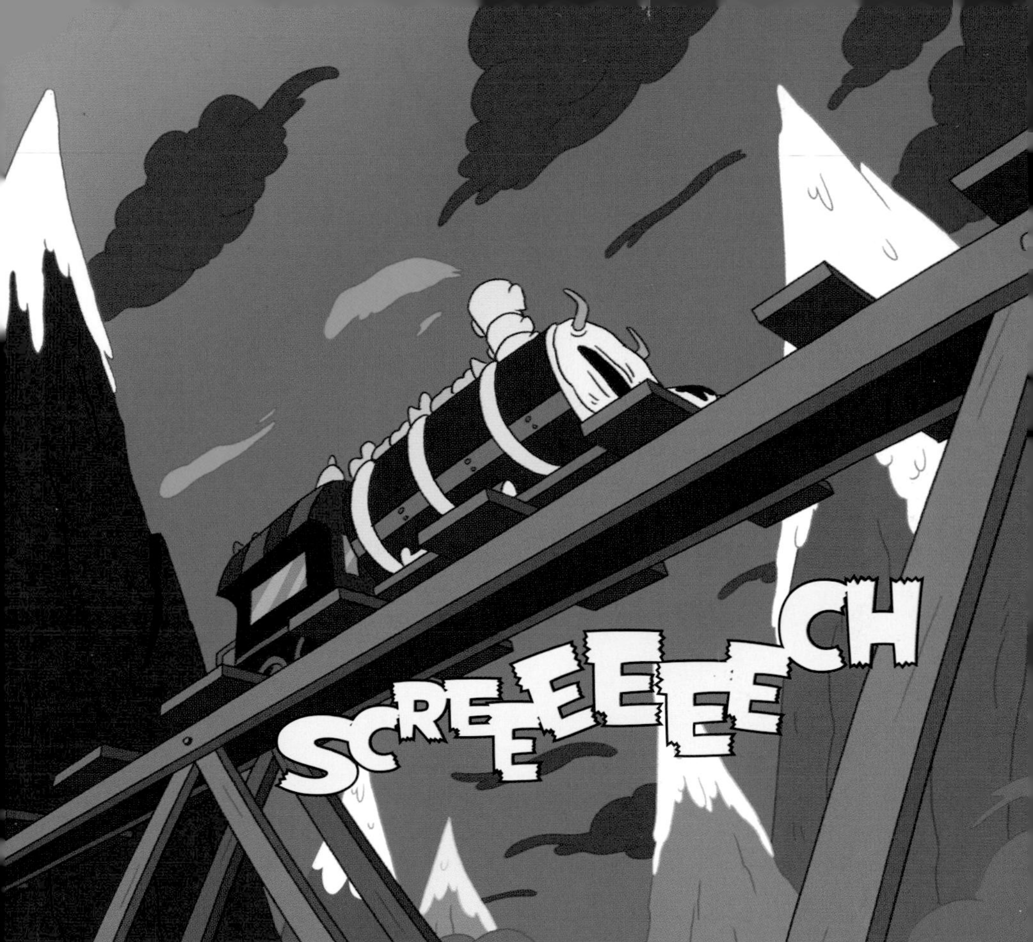
SCREEEEEEECH

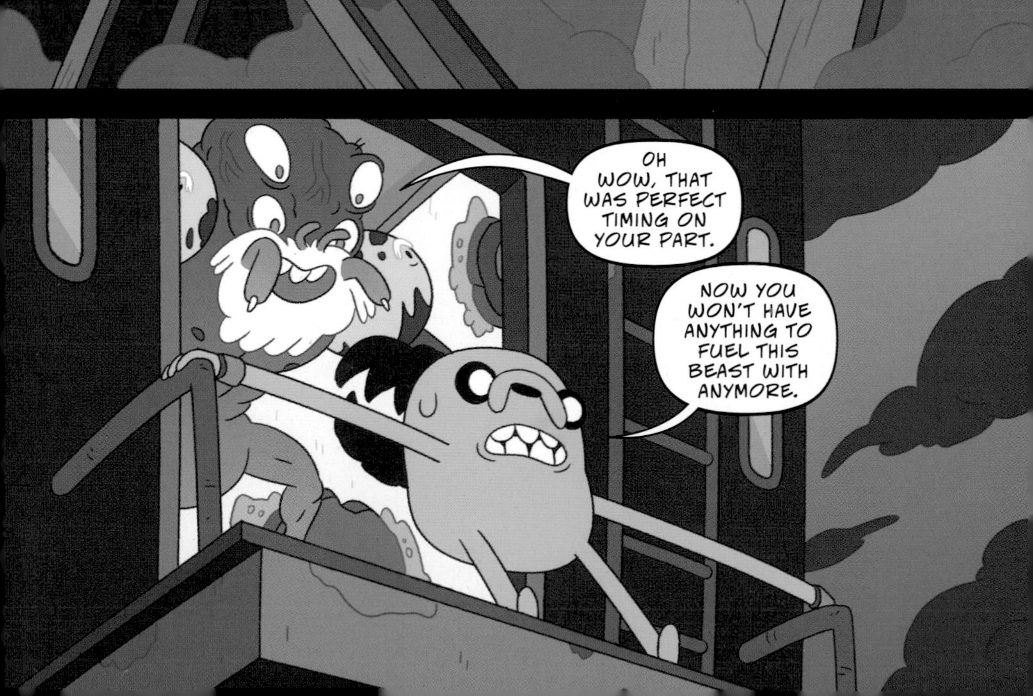
OH WOW, THAT WAS PERFECT TIMING ON YOUR PART.
NOW YOU WON'T HAVE ANYTHING TO FUEL THIS BEAST WITH ANYMORE.

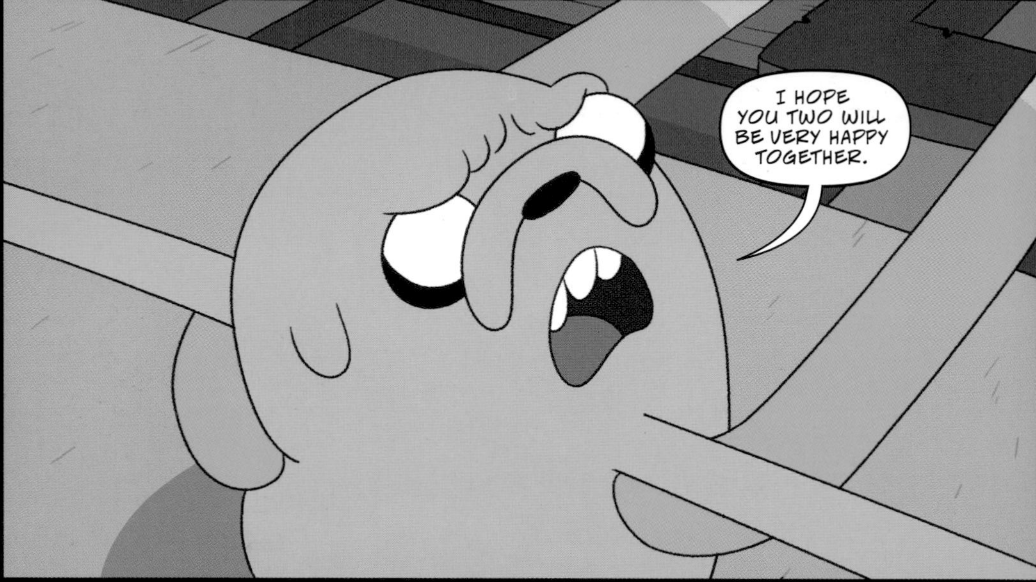
I HOPE YOU TWO WILL BE VERY HAPPY TOGETHER.

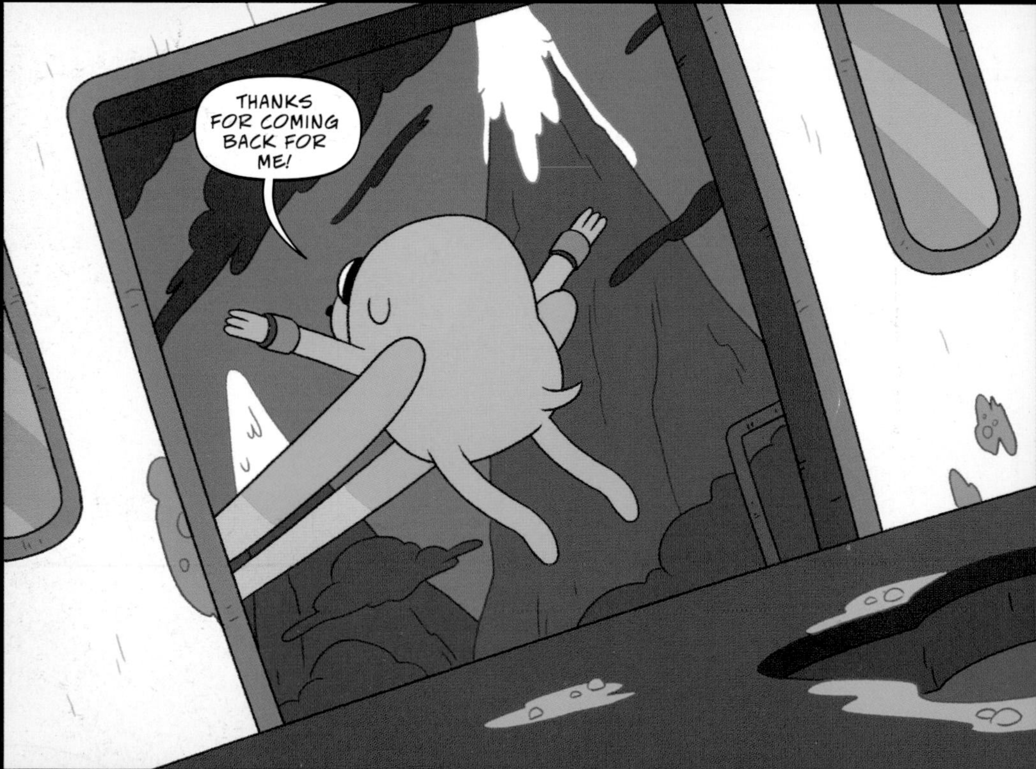
THANKS FOR COMING BACK FOR ME!

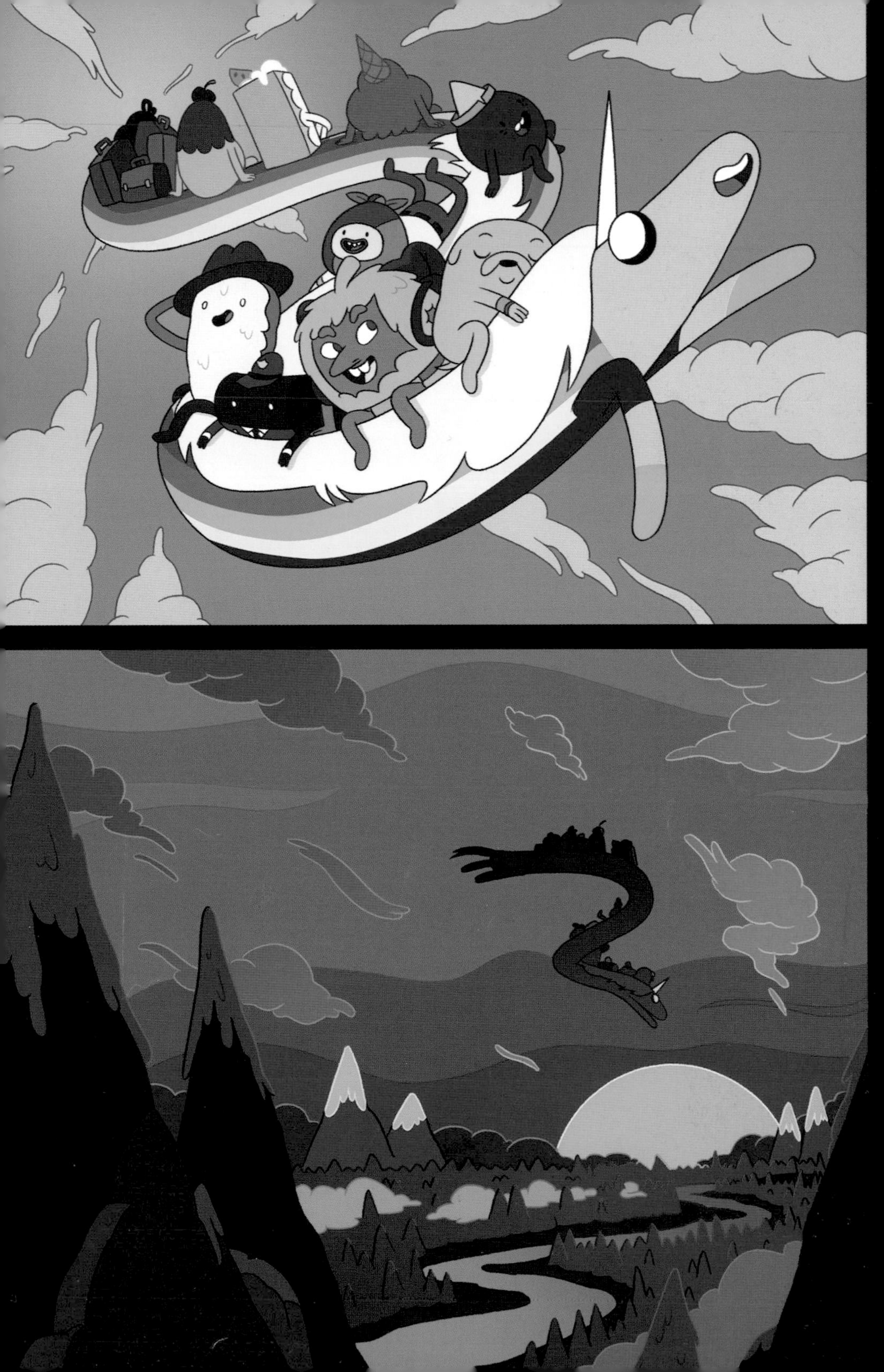

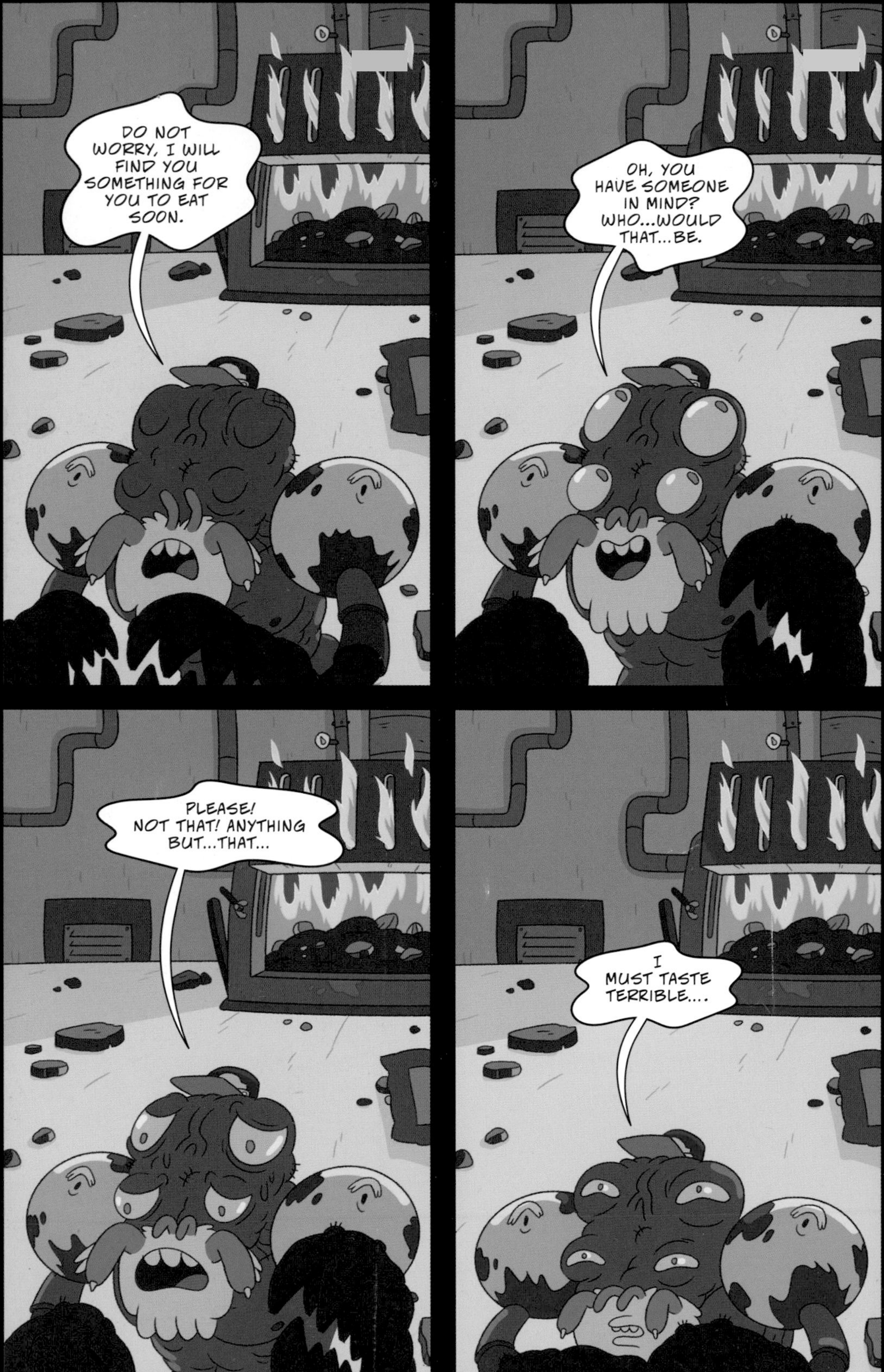
DO NOT WORRY, I WILL FIND YOU SOMETHING FOR YOU TO EAT SOON.
OH, YOU HAVE SOMEONE IN MIND? WHO...WOULD THAT...BE.
PLEASE! NOT THAT! ANYTHING BUT...THAT...
I MUST TASTE TERRIBLE....

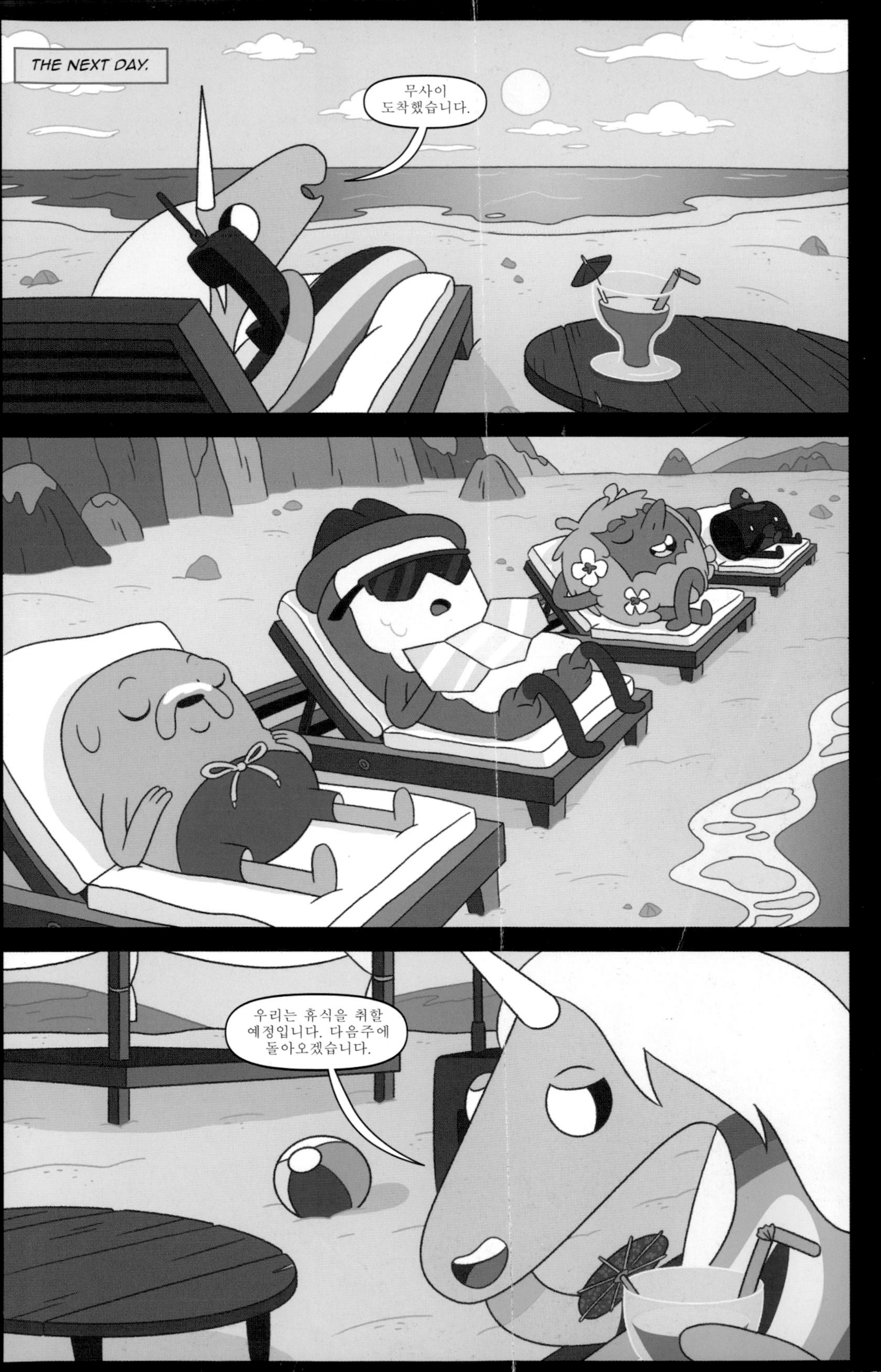
THE NEXT DAY.
무사이 도착했습니다.
우리는 휴식을 취할 예정입니다. 다음주에 돌아오겠습니다.

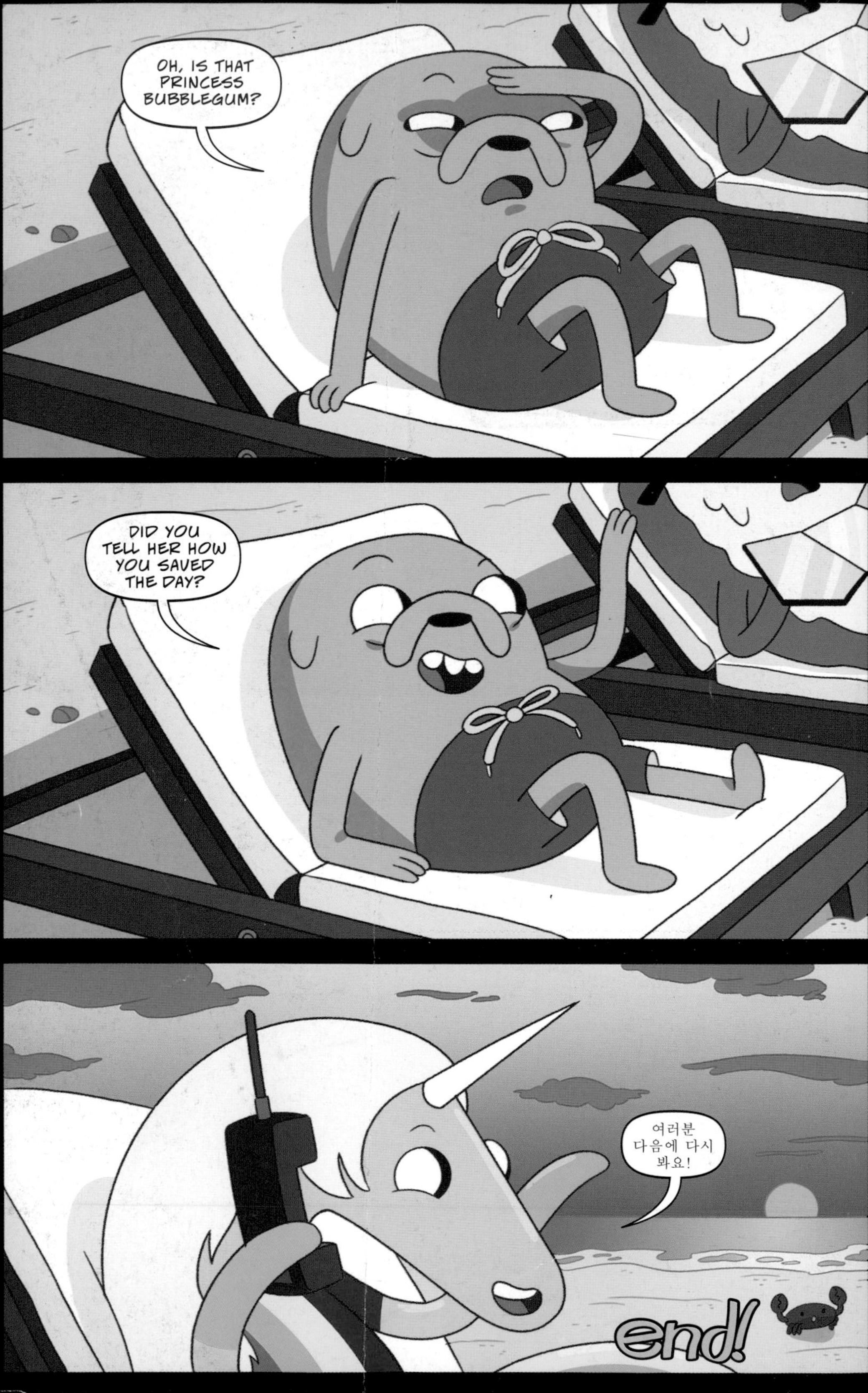
OH, IS THAT PRINCESS BUBBLEGUM?
DID YOU TELL HER HOW YOU SAVED THE DAY?
여러분
다음에 다시
봐요!
end!

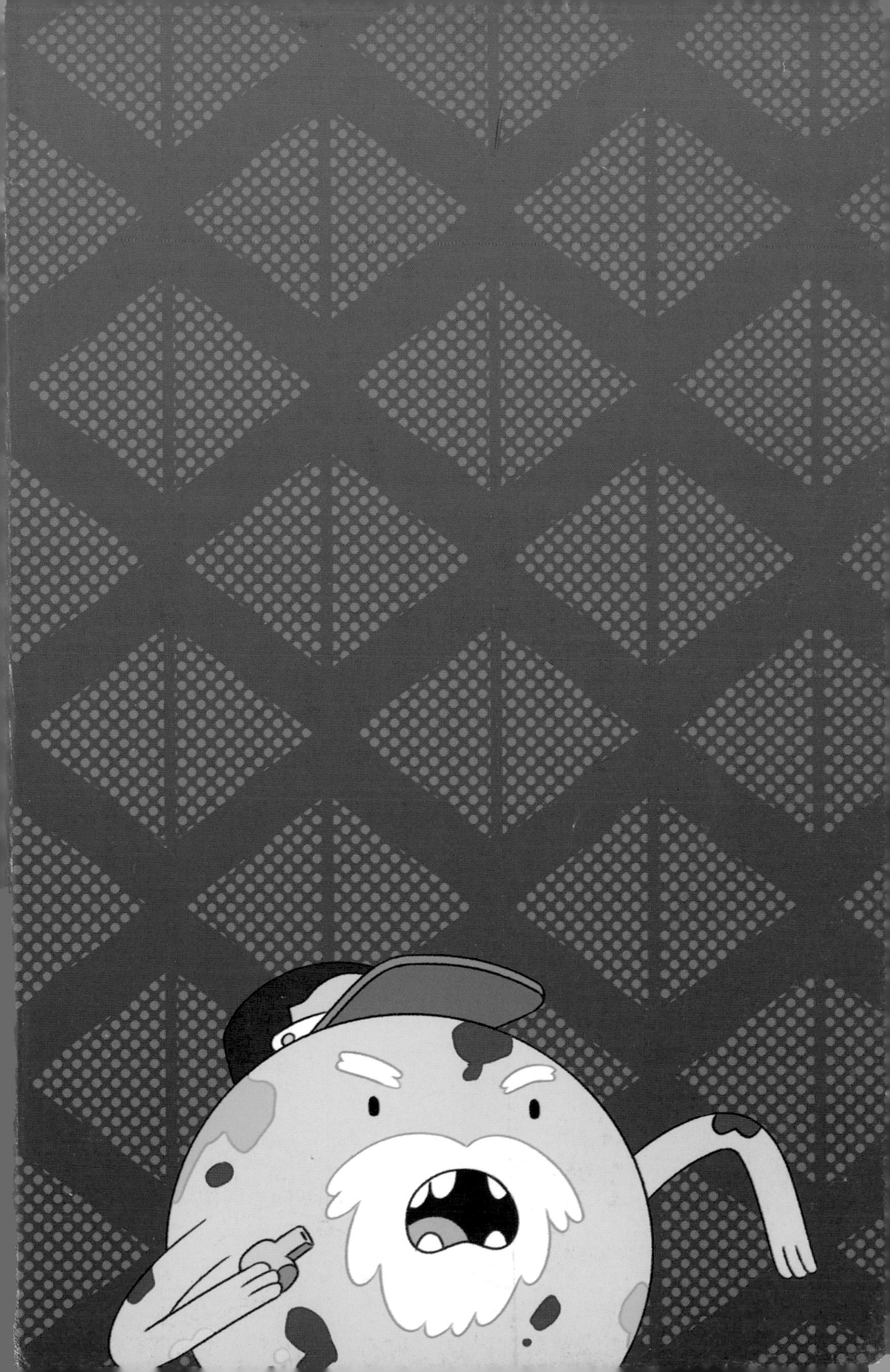

DISCOVER
EXPLOSIVE NEW WORLDS

Adventure Time
Pendleton Ward and Others
Volume 1
ISBN: 978-1-60886-280-1 | $9.99
Volume 2
ISBN: 978-1-60886-323-5 | $14.99 US
Adventure Time: Islands
ISBN: 978-1-60886-972-5 | $9.99

Regular Show
J.G. Quintel and Others
Volume 1
ISBN: 978-1-60886-362-4 | $14.99
Volume 2
ISBN: 978-1-60886-426-3 | $14.99

Regular Show: Hydration
ISBN: 978-1-60886-339-6 | $12.99

The Amazing World of Gumball
Ben Bocquelet and Others
Volume 1
ISBN: 978-1-60886-488-1 | $14.99
Volume 2
ISBN: 978-1-60886-793-6 | $14.99

Over the Garden Wall
Patrick McHale, Jim Campbell and Others
Volume 1
ISBN: 978-1-60886-940-4 | $14.99
Volume 2
ISBN: 978-1-68415-006-9 | $14.99

Steven Universe
Rebecca Sugar and Others
Volume 1
ISBN: 978-1-60886-706-6 | $14.99
Volume 2
ISBN: 978-1-60886-796-7 | $14.99

Steven Universe &
The Crystal Gems
ISBN: 978-1-60886-921-3 | $14.99

Steven Universe:
Too Cool for School
ISBN: 978-1-60886-771-4 | $14.99

Peanuts
Charles Schultz and Others
Volume 1
ISBN: 978-1-60886-260-3 | $13.99

Garfield
Jim Davis and Others
Volume 1
ISBN: 978-1-60886-287-0 | $13.99

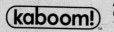

AVAILABLE AT YOUR LOCAL
COMICS SHOP AND BOOKSTORE
To find a comics shop in your area, call 1-888-266-4226
WWW.**BOOM-STUDIOS**.COM